THE LONESOME ISLE

THE LONESOME ISLE

Lisa Groszek

First paperback edition: January 2010
Updated edition: July 2022

Groszek, Lisa 1976-
The Lonesome Isle: A novel by Lisa Groszek - Updated edition

ISBN   9781449919795

EAN-13 is 9781449919795
Copyright Office Registration: TXu 1-617-970

Printed in the United States of America

Acknowledgments

Years ago I wrote this novel as I was nursing my first child through his infancy. It was published and promoted to the best of my ability during that time. I wrote the second novel, "Above and Below" while my second child was in her infancy. Again, I published and promoted it to the best of my ability during that time. In the years since, I have learned much and have felt the call to write the third and final novel in the series. In addition to that call, I felt a call to update the two first novels in the series and here we are.

It is quite an incredible thing when the draft is complete to sit back and think that the story has been told and the novel is finished. However, at that point, the novel is hardly finished. The story has been told, that much is true, but the novel is not ready for publication. Without the help of many that I will acknowledge here, it simply remains a story on the page.

Many thanks and much love goes out to the following individuals for their various roles in making the updated version of this novel into a reality. My mother, Kathy, has always believed in my creative talents, even when I have not. My husband Sebastian, and children, Sal and Izzy, for continuing to inspire me. My sisters-in-law Jennifer and Melissa: Jennifer for always looking for the best way to spread the word. Melissa for creating amazing book cover art. Finally, I'd like to thank my beta readers Christa and Allison for taking the time and effort to read through the first draft and helping me find the best way to present this story to the world.

I'd also like to thank my readers for giving this story a chance to come alive as you turn the pages and ride along for the journey presented within these pages.

Chapter 1

The night sky on the island was always the same. Stars sprinkled the black night and there was a full moon that shone down on the sandy beach. The warm air seemed oddly calm though the treetops would sway periodically as if there was a wind that wasn't making it to the surface. Two figures outlined in the distance were having a heated discussion regarding what I may or may not do at some future point.

"She won't do it. I know it's been a long time, but I know my daughter. She is not about to come over here of her own free will just because you want her to. She has too much to live for. She's young and just starting out in life. I don't care how convincing you can be. She will not want to come," my mother said to the man with the bright green eyes.

"Oh, I think I can take care of her desires," he smiled.

"You're ridiculous. Dominic, she's full of life. She will want to go back to her friends and family."

"Well then, we'll just have to bring her friends and family here, my pet. Don't worry, I know what I'm doing. Clarissa is just about ready and so is Elizabeth. We'll all be together soon."

"And why do we want the Renzen family here?" she asked.

"Oh, it's all part of the plan, my dear. You'll see."

There was that bothersome confidence again. My dream is coming to an end now. I'd been having the same dream so often lately that it was more like a rerun playing on a loop. Dominic was about to kiss my mother on the lips, then turn and look directly at me and wink. Then I'd wake up wondering, again, who the Renzen family was, who Clarissa was, who Dominic was, and why my mother, dead for the last sixteen years, was arguing with him about me.

I woke up to the sound of the bus driver telling us about the next stop on the tour. The word "stop" is a little misleading. The bus would stop moving, that was true, but we'd simply sit on the bus and be told a little bit of rehearsed background of what we could see. I tuned that out and took in the site for myself. It was odd to see a piece of land floating on water when you were on a piece of land floating on water. The island itself wasn't big, maybe two or three miles wide at most. From my view on Seaview Avenue, looking across the mile or so of water in between, I could see that a large portion of the small island was beachy, but that there was also a small forest where the beach became more solid ground. There were many trees clumped together and that was about all there was to see. I found myself surprised that this would even be a stop on the tour until I remembered that there had been some strange stories about storms and disappearances associated with this island. I tuned back in as the tour guide completed his spiel.

"It's out that way," growled a grumpy tour guide, Roger, "only the 'island within an island' has been deserted for nearly twenty years. Hateful place it is."

That last sentence was not meant for the tour, but I was paying attention as there was an odd familiarity about him. He must know something more. This is what I've been waiting for. How lucky to find a clue so early on in my trip. He must have noticed the spark because he gave a quick start as his pale blue eyes met my doe-brown ones. Suddenly he was extra-attentive to the road ahead. My dream was forgotten as I realized I'd found someone that could help me. He became the object of my focus.

He looked to be in his sixties. He had short, neatly cut brown hair with just a hint of graying around the temples. The pale blue in his eyes held an intensity that I could only guess meant that that blue had cooled over time. He dressed comfortably, jeans and a T-shirt, but added a light jacket to combat the air conditioning on the bus. This man looked tired both physically and emotionally. It looked as though life had done a number on him.

"Roger," I spoke up, "I'm Elizabeth Milton, a reporter with the East Coast News. Is there a reason that the island has stayed deserted for so long? Any type of strange activity?" I was getting excited at the prospect of wrapping up my first story assignment so quickly. I could just see the headline, "Writer Reveals Mysterious Island's Secrets". Well, something like that anyway. My editor would be amazed.

I was firmly grounded by the surly, sarcastic reply, "No, Elizabeth from the East Coast News. Just a bunch of stories told by conspiracy theorists about mysterious storms popping up over the island. Nothing true though, nothing that a reporter that had vetted the topic would even make the trip for. Plenty of people have been interviewed and nothing definitive has ever been found. While there are plenty of sensationalists out there looking to make headlines, this is not the topic to do that with."

Several of the passengers tried to stifle a laugh at Roger's words and I immediately broke eye contact. I knew that my anger at his sarcasm would show plainly on my face, though it would come in the form of glassy, tearful eyes. I didn't want to give him that satisfaction. My hope had been slashed and I felt a bit foolish for a moment, but I rallied. I wouldn't be sent away that easily. My pride had been wounded though and I felt the need to defend my profession.

"Well, I guess us sensationalists were wrong for blowing the lid off of important political events like Watergate or the truth of events like the terrorist attack in New York on the Twin Towers. It's interesting how easily you'll dismiss a reporter as nothing more than someone to be annoyed by, yet you'll greatly appreciate us when you are eagerly anticipating information about certain world events. So sorry to have interrupted your enthralling tour."

Roger looked back at my stone, cold face, not giving away any emotion now, and I thought I saw a moment of apology in his eyes. Or maybe it was a fleeting wish as I noticed the scowl return before he returned his eyes to the road and his mind to the tour. He rambled on some more about this area and that. I was actively tuning him out now. I could tell that he was holding something back, but he clearly didn't like reporters so I had to figure something else out. I noticed the angered tears were back so I did my best to stifle them and took in the scenery while allowing my mind to drift.

I imagined that Roger had been much more forthcoming with a smile instead of a scowl. I imagined that he and I happily talked over coffee or lunch, me taking feverish notes while he did the talking. Later that night, in my hotel room, I'd sit in front of my computer, transcribe all the notes that I'd taken, and begin outlining the article that I'd write.

"The bus has stopped, will you be getting off or would you like to continue the war of the scowling faces?"

I felt a nudge at my shoulder and heard the words, belatedly, as I came back to myself. I realized I'd been dosing and this relatively attractive man was trying to hide his annoyance by politely recommending I get off the bus. I smiled apologetically as he passed by, gathered my things, and exited the bus without looking in Roger's direction. I figured that if I tried to run into Roger another day, now that I knew his daily routine, or at least part of it, I could see if I could catch him in a better mood and maybe he'd be more willing to talk. He was, afterall, my only lead at this point. I was going to hang onto it even if I would have to swallow my pride once again. As it happened, the opportunity presented itself in the form of the kind, attractive stranger who'd woken me.

"There is more to that island than he told you, but he doesn't like to talk about it much." I took him in as he finished his ominous statement.

He was tall and looked to be thirty-something. His skin was tanned from many days in the sun; it reflected a warm, golden color. He had strong arms emphasized by the black T-shirt he was wearing. I felt a glimmer of hope as I looked back at him with what I hoped was humbled curiosity. "Sorry, I ride along sometimes to keep an eye on him. He's getting older and his moods have become worse and worse. Hard to believe, but often I like to throw a joke or two in, especially around that island. I didn't get the opportunity today. Hi Elizabeth, my name is Thomas, Thomas Renzen. It's nice to meet you."

The name shook my entire being. Did he really just say Renzen? I needed to conceal…no, too late, he'd noticed my shock. I wasn't ready to reveal this particular coincidence to a complete stranger. Dang, I need to get better at this part of the job. My father always said I wore my emotions on my sleeve and this was not helping right now. I tried to compose myself and took a closer look at him. One could do that, right, look at someone closely as if they may know them. That could explain my shock. His short, dark hair was a wonderful compliment to those electric gray-blue eyes; the same color eyes I could imagine Roger having back when he was a younger man. The resemblance between the two left little doubt that I was talking to Roger's son.

"It's nice to hear some kindness. So, there is more to that island? Your dad knows more than he's telling?" I smiled confident in my assumption.

"I didn't say he was…Oh, I guess I don't have to; we do look a lot alike. Yes, there is more to that island, but I'm not here to tell you about it. I'm here to warn you away from it. My father was not very kind in the way that he spoke to you, but his heart is in the right place. That island is dangerous and he's just trying to steer you away from the danger. Just let it go, okay? Isn't there something else that you can write about? Some local tourism piece?"

"The story was assigned to me; I didn't come up with it on my own," I hated to admit how new I was to all of this, "If I ever want to grow as a writer and find my own stories, I have to take what I'm handed for the time being. I do appreciate your candor, and the fact that you recognize poor treatment when you see it, but if you seriously believe that there is a danger to that island, shouldn't those that are around it or those that come to see it be aware of that danger so that they know how to avoid it? Don't others have a right to be able to recognize danger? Thanks for the suggestion, but if you're not going to be helpful, I don't really see what else we have to talk about," I was pushing to see if he'd open up.

The expression in his eyes told me that my hopes were in vain. He looked angry and I was trying to figure out why he would be, he barely knew me, after all.

"I can't do either; it's too dangerous. Other reporters have been out this direction and have not come back. I'm not going to lead you into harm so that you can get yourself hurt or killed chasing after a story. I won't have that on my conscience. It's too risky," he argued.

"If I didn't want to do anything risky, I wouldn't make much of a reporter, would I? I am willing to assume the risk and the responsibility. If you were that worried about your conscience I'm guessing you wouldn't have said anything in the first place. You've already confirmed for me that there's something going on on that island. If that's all that I can get from you, I'll move on and find someone else that knows. Thank you for what you've given me. It's been nice meeting you." I replied.

He looked at me for a moment longer, probably trying to figure out if there was any point to arguing further, and must have seen my resolve. He shook his head and turned away. As he was turning, I heard him mutter quietly, "He was always after the danger too."

"Who, Thomas? Who was always after the danger? Was it Roger, your father, is that why he doesn't want to talk? I think I'm understanding now. He was a writer and was assigned to this island as well and something happened that he doesn't want to talk about. Is that it?"

"Well, yeah, you…," he began, but my mind was working overtime.

"Whatever happened was bad which is why he's still here and also why you're here warning me away. Did you warn these others that you spoke of? Did they turn tail and go back to wherever they came from? Did they get hurt? What happened?"

"If you'd let me…," he tried again, but the questions, comments, and accusations just kept coming as if I'd been saving them all up.

"Clearly, it sounds like the danger is very real and keeping it to yourself only expands the reach of that danger. Are you now saying that you want to be complicit in the dangers and find yourselves responsible for any consequences that come out of that?" I could see the anger grow in his face as I pushed, but I needed answers.

"Maybe my sister was right after all; maybe it's useless to talk to you reporters," he tried to hide the tremble in his lip as he stumbled over his mention of his sister, "All you can see is the big headline at the end. You never stop to notice the people you may step on in order to get to that story. Do what you have to, but consider yourself warned. Good luck, Elizabeth, I hope you fare better than the others that have come looking."

Before I could say another word he turned and walked away easily melding into a crowd of tourists getting ready to take the next tour. He did not get on the bus this time. I couldn't understand his comments about his sister, but I'd definitely hit a nerve with my guesses. I couldn't believe that this was the family that had been present in my dream. I kept that to myself for the time being. Thomas already didn't like me, no reason to give him more fuel for that fire, but still, it was odd and couldn't be a coincidence.

I am a strong believer in fate, not that I don't believe in free will, I just believe that fate gives us a push every now and again. I was fated to lose my mom at a young age and to be raised by a father that was strong and believed that he needed to instill that strength in both his son and his daughter. He was a single father that raised his two kids while continuing his career as an engineer. He was resourceful and always found a way to participate in whatever interest my brother Aaron and I held. He never remarried and keeping us all afloat had to have been difficult, but he never complained and always worked hard instilling a strong belief system and work ethic in both of us.

Because of this background, I was fated to become strong-willed, even in the face of ridicule, and just stubborn enough to keep investigating and working toward my end goal in spite of obstacles thrown in my direction. Thomas and the Renzen family were an obstacle, at present, yet in my dream, they were clearly important players. I didn't want to lose this tenuous connection that I'd gained, but decided that I'd pushed enough for one day. I now knew where I could find Roger Renzen most of the time, and where I could find Thomas Renzen at least some of the time. That would have to be enough for now.

I took stock of the rest of what I'd learned this morning. There was, in fact, something about the island that needed exploring. Whatever is happening on the island is dangerous. Whatever happened to the Renzen family may still be happening. Why else would Roger and Thomas still be here? If Roger stayed here to remain close to the island and Thomas stayed here to remain close to Roger, then whatever is going on must be known by more than just them. Those houses that are closest to the island must have some inkling of what is happening or at least be able to shed further light on the island's oddities. I would have to canvas those homes, go door to door and ask questions to see what others around the island know. I took a closer look at the map I'd been handed when boarding the tour bus and noted that the homes surrounding the island formed a crescent a mile and half in length. That would be my starting point. I would talk to the locals and succeed where Roger had failed. Not only will that launch my career as an investigative reporter, but it would be a bit of a bonus to be able to get to the bottom of this mystery, especially after the way that I'd just been treated by none other than a retired reporter and his know-it-all son.

I looked again at the map and traced the route that I'd have to take to get back to the island and its crescent of homes. I realized I'd need transportation to get there and looked carefully around. I found a small stand that rented mopeds and headed in that direction. Minutes later I had procured a moped and was finishing up the paperwork when the kid that worked the rental shop asked if I would be using the moped all afternoon.

"Yes, I have several stops to make today." I responded.

"Okay, are you headed in the direction of the island?"

"Yes, actually, that's where my business is being conducted today. Why do you ask?"

"Can you see in the distance, the clouds that look to be pretty far off? Those usually indicate a quick storm. Sometimes when these storms come in, they mess with the electricity all around so if that happens and your moped begins to act weird, you haven't broken it. I just thought you should know. Most workers won't tell the renters and just see what happens, but I didn't want you to abandon the moped or something like that. If it starts acting up, it will stop again when the storm has passed."

"Hmmm, that is strange. Any reason why this happens? Has anybody looked into that at all?"

"Not that I know of, but we usually close the stand when one comes in since everything we deal with here is electronic," he looked up again at the clouds that had seemed to advance drastically in the short moments of our conversation, "it looks like that may be the case today. I would get moving if I were you. Maybe you can make your destination before there are any issues."

I nodded my head and started off. As I was pulling away and merging into traffic, I checked my rearview and noticed that the boy, in fact, was closing up shop. He had pulled a garage door down and all I could see was a large "closed" sign on it though it did look like someone had painted a storm cloud complete with lightning hitting the ground right next to it. If he hadn't prepared me for their possible mid-day closing I would have been shocked. Looking around, it was a warm, sunny day, traffic was flowing smoothly, and the storm that he'd pointed out was moving quickly, but seemed to centralize itself over the island alone. Lightning was lighting up the clouds every now and again, but for now, it remained within the clouds.

It was quite remarkable and something I made sure to take a mental note of. The storm was over the island and didn't seem to be affecting anything outside of the island's bounds. The streets and roadways all around were bright and cheery, but darkness had settled over that island alone. As I made my way closer to the island, I started to notice some other differences that I'd ignored while watching the storm on the island. All around me and very suddenly, there was not a car in sight. Life seemed to come to a halt at this moment and though I was still moving closer and closer to the cluster of houses I'd identified to conduct interviews, I seemed to be the only one moving. Just beyond the next cross street was my destination. I saw that there was a place to park on the road just in front of the home and I set my sights there. There was a small, Mom and Pop store/restaurant on the corner and I noticed that this business, too, had a "Closed" sign in the window and seemed to be deserted despite the fact that it was a warm day in the height of tourist season. I supposed it was possible that this was an older business that had been abandoned, but I didn't think so. I couldn't explain it, but it felt as if the business itself, or perhaps customers that had been recently served, were maybe hiding in there somewhere.

I was about to continue through the "Stop" sign and begin the arc that would turn the moped around and end with me parked in the proper direction for the road, when my moped faltered the first time.

"No, not now. We're almost there." I coaxed.

As if it heard me, it sputtered to life again and I thought I'd make it through the intersection when the engine revved drastically, the headlight flashed once, then the whole thing died and would not budge an inch. If this were a time of high traffic, I'd be a pancake as I was quite literally in the middle of the three way intersection; I was only safe on the side that made up the small lake. I tried a few times, but acknowledged what I'd been told, dismounted, and began to walk the same arc I'd planned on driving a few moments before.

At that moment an especially bright flash of lightning came crackling through the sky. I followed its path all the way to the sands of the island itself and was shocked. In the wake of where the lightning must have hit the ground, it looked as if the air were shimmering. They shimmering began at the ground and rose up ten feet into the air and hung there, almost as if it were a doorway. A figure appeared within the shimmering background and stared up at the sky as if she were waiting for something or someone.

While I could not see her well, at this distance, it was near impossible, I knew that she was a woman. Her hair was held back in a ponytail that fell toward her back as she raised her eyes heavenward. Oddly, I had a feeling of familiarity with the figure standing so far out on the island as though she were also, somehow, standing right next to me and staring at me with surprise or shock. I almost believed I heard my name floating on the air, in the same high pitched, feverish voice I'd last heard sixteen years ago when I'd lost my mother. I looked toward the island again and the door or opening

I thought of my dream this morning and quickly dismissed what I'd heard. It must have been a reflection of that dream and my unresolved issues with my mother. I decided that I was being silly and that I'd just have to wait out this storm as the boy at the moped stand had suggested. I walked on pushing the moped beside me and made the turn so that it would be facing the proper direction for the side of the road that it was on. I was looking around for somewhere that I could stay out of the rain if it happened to move in this direction when I heard a door creak from the home that my now defunct moped was in front of.

I looked up and saw a small girl standing in the doorway. She was looking at me with recognition and surprise though I'd never seen her before in my life. She smiled warmly at me, "You better get in here lady. It's not safe out there."

She was a curious little thing. She couldn't have been any more than eight or nine years old. Her deep blue eyes looked kind of far away and sad, like she's seen too much in her short years. She had darkish blonde hair that was straight, parted in the middle, and cropped to just under her chin.

"Why not, honey? What's happening out here?" I thought I'd see what she could tell me.

"An electrical storm, silly, the most dangerous kind from what my science teacher tells me. Your bike is broken, come in until the storm is over. It mainly stays over there, but sometimes the rain still falls here when it leaves. Grandpa won't mind you coming in. He likes to be nice to strangers."

"Can I talk to Grandpa?" I asked, feeling a sense of familiarity.

Roger, who must have been working the morning shift, walked to the door and looked at me fiercely. He shook his head and looked kindly down at his granddaughter, "Grandpa doesn't like to be nice to all strangers, honey."

"But Grandpa, that's the lady in my dreams, we have to let her in. We have to protect her," she said.

"I thought your dreams only had your mommy and grandma?" he asked in tones that were not quite hushed enough.

She responded in kind, "There are new dreams, Grandpa. She is in the new ones with Mommy. Her name is Elizabeth and she's going to bring them home."

No one spoke for a moment but the shock that I felt register on my face when she spoke my name must have been mirrored in Roger's face at this revelation. He was clearly already dealing with more than he could handle, but now his granddaughter seemed to know things that she shouldn't. He had been on the precipice of allowing me inside, his hand was arcing in a welcoming gesture, but then he quickly made a decision and turned on me.

"Decided to ask around more about that island, huh? Thought maybe an innocent child would be more willing to talk? You really are good, Elizabeth. How did you find out so quickly where I lived?"

I ignored him for the moment and turned my attention to the little girl, "Honey, as long as it's alright with your grandpa, can you please tell me your name?"

She looked at him and he gave a reluctant nod.

"My name is Clarissa Renzen."

The last name of Renzen I had already guessed at, but knowing that this was Clarissa changed everything. I had to talk to this little girl. I had to find out what else she's been dreaming about. Somehow, this meeting was fated to happen, but I'm not sure that I could convince Roger of that.

"Okay Clarissa, it's nice to meet you. But can I ask, how did you know my name? I didn't tell you what it was."

"My mommy told me in my dreams. She said that soon you'd come and that when you did, it wouldn't be long before I'd be able to see them again."

"Who is 'them', sweetheart?"

"My mom and my grandma. They've been away for a long time, but they told me that when I meet you, that means that soon we'd be together."

Roger looked up and saw that the rain was moving inland so he decided to invite me in. I wasn't completely sure he wanted me in their house, but this clear connection between Clarissa and me was definitely disturbing him. I wasn't sure that I was comfortable with this either, especially considering our conversation earlier and the subsequent conversation with his son, but I didn't really think I had a choice. I didn't see another soul around and the wind was really starting to pick up. I took another look at the island and planted myself where I was out of stubbornness.

"I am sorry," my voice soured at his mood, "if I would have known that you lived here, I would have broken down up the road. And to answer your question, no, I did not come here to prey on the innocence of a child. I'm not like that. She noticed that my moped had broken down and invited me in. I was the one that told her we needed permission from you."

"Yeah, well, your moped isn't broken, just paused while the storm is here. It will be fine once the storm passes. Clarissa was right to invite you in as it isn't safe out there when the storms pop up. Are you going to come in?"

"Why isn't it safe?" I pressed.

"Just come in, I'll tell you all about it," he conceded and looked around nervously.

"Thank you, I guess."

"Don't thank me, thank my granddaughter. I would have been happy to leave you out there, but there's very little I wouldn't do to make her happy," he finished with a pained smile.

"Right, thank you Clarissa. With your grandpa's permission, I would like to ask you a little more about your dreams. Is that okay with you?"

"Yes," she looked at Grandpa who nodded, but planted himself firmly.

"You have seen me in your dreams?"

"Yes."

"Do we know each other in your dreams?"

"Not really, but my Mom and Grandma know you. And your mom is there too."

For the second time in the last ten minutes I felt my stomach drop.

"That can't be right. My mommy died in a car accident when I was just a little bit older than you are now."

"Oh, she told me all about that and said to tell you that things aren't always what they seem, and neither are people, whatever that means."

"Okay, well, then I guess it's not too much to tell you that I've dreamed about your mom and grandma too, is it?"

I was looking at Roger, waiting for his reaction when I said it. He didn't look all that surprised, and I began to get angry, "Why do I feel like this is not surprising information for you? What are you hiding, Roger? Why isn't my moped broken? Why will it start again when the storm passes? How are you so sure of that?"

He raised his hands in surrender and responded, "Why don't you make yourself at home first and we'll get into all of the details that I wasn't sharing earlier. Can I get you something to drink?"

"A water, thanks. And along with that, the bitter, cranky, not going to give an inch Roger that seems to have recently vacated your form." I said with a smile.

"Yeah, I know. It happens sometimes. I'm sorry for that. I'll get you your water and maybe when I explain everything you'll see why I'm so touchy. Come help Grandpa, Clarissa. Please don't stare at her like that; it's not polite."

Roger and Clarissa went to the kitchen together and I was left with my thoughts. I glanced around the house and noticed that this house must have been an original on the island. With very few updates to fixtures and countertops it was obvious that Roger enjoyed the antiquity of his home. The wood had been beautifully preserved and must have been shined often.

I sat on a soft, beige couch in the living room while I waited for them to return. The living room was surprisingly modern given the surroundings. There were no curves to this couch; straight, clean lines made up the frame and multi-hued pillows decorated it. Straight ahead was an archway that led to the kitchen that was still very antiquated as was made obvious by the stove/oven combination still sporting boldly curved black knobs. There were stairs going up to my right with a beautiful, polished wooden banister to hold as one took the ten or twelve steps to the top. I assumed the bedrooms must be on the second floor. There was a fireplace on my left and another door that I assumed to be a bedroom or den. The floors were made of a handsome mahogany.

Apparently my guess about Roger's career had been accurate as he had several articles framed and scattered around the room. Some had been noted as important pieces and one even won a pulitzer.

He came back into the room and saw me admiring his work. He handed me the water kindly and then took a seat and prompted me to do the same. I returned to the couch.

"I can see that you're not going to give up on this, so let me tell you a little about myself. I've lived here for quite some time. I know a lot about this place. I also know that it's not safe for you out there. I know that if you had ridden any further on that rent-a-moped, you may have ended up on that island. Most importantly, I know what it's like to be a reporter and have that thirst. I'm a retired reporter myself, as I'm sure you've seen by now. I wrote for the Boston Globe. I'm going to try to save you a lot of trouble and a lot of heartache. That island is not a place that you want to go."

"Well," I said musingly, I was itching to get information about the island, but astounded by how pleasant he seemed now, "I'm still waiting for an explanation for the large change in attitude from a few minutes ago when you were about to leave me out in the storm. What happened to the man that told me that there was nothing on that island that was worth reporting on?"

"There is always something behind nothing; as a reporter, you should know that. Well, clearly you do otherwise you wouldn't be here. Anyway, I do apologize sincerely for my earlier behavior. This little girl always reminds me to curb my temper and be nice to strangers, especially those that she feels she knows somehow, though you are a first," Roger said while gesturing to his granddaughter.

The phone began a shrill ring and I was reminded, again, that Roger liked things of antiquity. He excused himself to answer it. I noticed Clarissa's two curious eyes looking upon me intently. It seemed as if I were an old friend that she was eager to catch up with; like she'd been waiting for my arrival.

"Hello again," I started, "do you live here too with your Grandpa?"

"Yes. Are you here to get them? Are you going to bring Mommy and Grandma back from their very long vacation?" She stumbled over a response to my question in order to ask hers. I could tell that this is what she's been waiting to get out since the minute she spotted me.

I was astounded once again. She was very straightforward and eager. I wasn't sure how to respond to this line of questioning especially since that is not the reason that I have come here. What had been revealed to me in the past hour was beyond anything I could have considered. Clearly, this girl lost her mother and believes wholeheartedly that I'm the key to getting her back. I wondered if she simply dreamed of someone that looked like me, but that couldn't be, especially with my own dream thrown into the mix. Luckily, Roger returned from the kitchen and must have heard Clarissa's questions.

"Sorry about that, my son worries," addressing Clarissa, "This lady is here to ask me some questions about the island, that's all, honey. Mommy is on a very long vacation."

"But this is the lady in my dreams, Grandpa; she told me that she's bringing Mommy back. She told me in my dream," demanded Clarissa.

"Honey, it's just a dream, she may have looked like this lady, but I don't think she was. We've talked about this, haven't we? Now Grandpa needs to talk to her about something very important. Please go to your room for a bit and I promise that I'll take you for ice cream a little later, okay?" Roger seemed very disconcerted by her words.

"Okay Grandpa, nice to meet you," she said to me as she approached the steps and disappeared.

He settled himself in his La-Z-Boy across from me and took a moment to compose himself for what he must have seen as a difficult conversation. I could see him struggling and he definitely was worried about all that Clarissa had said to me. I felt guilty for causing him undue stress and thought maybe I really had crossed a line here.

"I can see that you're upset. Maybe I should go, it looks a lot better out there now," though it didn't, not really.

"No, it's not better and you can't go out there for the very same reason that that little girl you met has to be raised by her old, grumpy grandpa and not her own mother," Roger paused for a deep breath, "Clarissa is my granddaughter. She lost her mother and grandmother two years ago and I don't have the heart to tell her that her mother's not coming back. I stick with the "vacation" story to buy time, but I'm no fool. I know she doesn't believe me, but she keeps up the pretense of belief for now. I know I'll have to tell her the truth and that time is coming up quickly, she's nine years old already.

"It's for that reason that I speak of the island with such contempt. I truly hate that place. There's something wrong out there. I can't figure out exactly what it is, but I'm not leaving here until I do. I just wish I knew how."

His exhaustion and surly attitude were suddenly making a lot more sense, but little else was.

"Okay, you've managed to lose me. Can you tell me the whole story from the beginning and how the island has anything to do with the death of your wife and daughter? Can you tell me the story from beginning to end?" I asked.

"You are astute, aren't you. I didn't say that my wife was with her, but I guess Clarissa did. Well, I don't even know for sure that they are dead. No bodies have ever been found and we've been over and over that island so many times I could probably tell you every shade of sand. This is a picture of them, taken the day they disappeared," he handed me the frame from where it had been sitting just under his wooden lamp, always at his side.

It was a picture in which they both looked infinitely happy. His wife was wearing a long mother-of-the-bride dress. It was a soft blue spaghetti-strapped dress with a sheer jacket. Her hair was pulled into a salon up-

do, soft locks escaping on either side in patterns. She looked as beautiful
as if this were her own wedding day.

It was, in fact, their daughter's wedding day. She was in a fitted gown
that looked as though it cost thousands of dollars. The gown was sleeve-
less; it was plain white and fit her figure perfectly down to the ankles
where it flared out dramatically. Her hair was also in an up-do with pieces escaping in banana curls down either side of her face and accented her
bright blue eyes. She had definitely gotten her eyes, and her small figure,
from her mother, but her chocolate brown hair came from her father. She
had a beautifully beaded veil that she had attached to the tiara that wove
around her hair like a perfectly proportioned snake.

"It's a beautiful picture," I said, "they both disappeared on this day?"

"Yes," he said struggling to hold back tears, "it was supposed to be
the best day of our lives, and it ended in tragedy. The worst part of it is
that it easily could have been avoided. My daughter wanted her wedding
in Boston, but I told her that it had to be here. I told her that my job was
here now and that this was where we were going to be. If only I had listened to her. She was going to Boston anyway, and I couldn't blame her.
It had always been her home."

"You were out here when you were still working for the Globe? Or
had you already started driving the tour bus?"

"I was working for the Globe. I only started working with the tour
bus because my son said it wasn't good for me to stay home all the time.
He said that I had to start getting out and doing something, otherwise I
was liable to go crazy here. I think he was right. Believe it or not, I like
driving that tour bus and meeting all kinds of people. You just happened
to catch me on a bad morning and you touched an explosive nerve," his
face crinkled into a sheepish grin.

"Anyway, I was working with the Globe and was assigned to come
out here to the Vineyard and write about this mysterious island everyone had been talking about. Rumor had it that the island was some sort
of gateway in which, if looking through a telescope during a storm, one
could see a sort of door opening in the middle of the island. Some claim
to have even seen a lady standing in the doorway looking out when it
opens. Sounds exciting, right? That's what I thought. I was really excited. My family and I had been talking about moving anyway, we knew
I was heading toward retirement and had always enjoyed coming out
here to vacation. Our son was already out of the house and we knew
our daughter wouldn't be far behind him. When we came home with
the news that we were moving, there was relatively little surprise. Our
daughter, Madeline is her name, didn't want to move because her boy-

friend at the time, later fiance, lived in Boston, but somehow they made it work. This was supposed to be my last story anyway. I was going to retire once this one was written and published; a fact that I hadn't yet shared with my family. Before we were out here long though, Madeline got engaged and we all got very busy planning her wedding. I hadn't taken a lot of time to research the island yet. I wish now that I had, but their engagement was to be short and we had a lot of people to bring into town. Since I had some time to play with on the assignment, it fell by the wayside.

"The wedding was going to be on that island," he pointed as he said it, "I had spent weeks putting together ferry rides to the small island, getting the florist, caterer, and band set up out there, and setting up so many other details. After a while, Madeline seemed to start agreeing with me, she thought this small island would be lovely for her wedding day, so exclusive. Or that's what I thought.

"The day of the wedding came and we were all bustling around getting ready for the main event. My daughter came into my den in her dress and I just melted. We shared a few words about marriage and what a big day this was and how excited she was. I told her that I was excited for her and that her mother and I looked forward to inviting Mark into the family.

"We got into the limousine and drove to the docks where we would be ferried across. The bridal party went first since there had been a tent set up just for them so that Mark wouldn't see her before she was walking down the aisle. The boats ferried us over and we were all together on that island. I pulled Madeline aside again, still wanting to talk to her before the ceremony got underway; I knew that once that happened, my little girl would truly be gone.

"After some pleasant conversation between Madeline and me, I said the dumbest thing I could have possibly said. I asked her if she was unhappy that the wedding was here instead of Boston knowing that she'd only done that for me and that if I'd given her the choice, she would have chosen Boston in a heartbeat. That put a huge damper on things because, of course, she answered honestly, and my temper rose quickly. I remember looking at her and thinking that she shouldn't be so stubborn when I was the one that wouldn't budge. If it weren't for me, she would still be here today, and so would my wife.

"We argued and I said some things that I wish I could take back. I told her that she could just go to Boston after the wedding and stay there. I will never forget the look on her face. It was as if an arrow had pierced her heart, and it may as well have. She turned from me, hiding and controlling her tears, but she didn't look at me again..........she never got the chance." Roger's eyes filled with tears and he was momentarily overcome by a grievous howl.

"It's okay; you don't have to tell me any more," I said.

"No, I do need to tell you, there's too much built up inside and now it's opened. I have to tell you to protect you. Something good has to come of this. Maybe it's too late for them, but it doesn't have to be for you. I don't want to make the same mistake and send you out there. Just give me a moment to compose myself."

A few moments of awkward silence passed and the shrill voice of the phone started up again. Roger excused himself to answer it. This time I overheard the entire conversation.

"No, I'm fine. Everything's good. You don't need to....you know how I get when.....Okay, well, if you insist, but I have a guest...that reporter from the bus. No, it's fine...we're getting along a lot better now...no, she didn't....I told you I'm fine....see you in a minute."

"You're having company and I'm dredging up all kinds of bad memories, I think I saw your kitchen light flicker on and then turn back off. The danger has probably passed; I better go," I tried to beg off but saw quickly that that was not an option.

"No dear, the danger hasn't even started. See how the storm has centralized over the island? When you finally see it move off of the island, that's when the danger has passed."

I saw what he was talking about and thought again, how strange it was that the storm seemed to head straight for the island when the kid at the moped place pointed it out, then came out of the island just as my moped died, and now seemed to hover over it. And I knew I'd lied about the light flickering. But if Roger's temper and our earlier interaction was any clue, I figured I was in for it when Thomas got here. It was almost as if Roger could read my mind.

"That was just my son. He's coming over. He always checks on me when we have a storm. He tries to take my mind off of things. Also, he thinks I've lost it. He completely believes that his mother and sister were hit by lightning and killed immediately. I have never agreed with him as I'm sure there would have been bodies had that been the case. There never have been so I know that there's more to this.

"When Madeline turned from me," he switched gears and continued the story, "she went out further on the beach to take a walk. Her mother told me she'd wanted some time alone and said she'd go talk to her. The wedding was due to begin shortly, and the two hadn't returned; we were all getting nervous. I knew that I could fix this with Madeline, but couldn't figure out what was taking her and Rose, my wife, so long to return. Mark and I decided to go looking. We searched and searched and the wind picked up, just like it did today before the storm hit. We couldn't find them and many of the guests joined the search. We were yelling their names and the rain began to pour down, soaking us all. Completely worn out and drenched, I thought I saw something at the center of the island. It looked like two women, frozen, unable to move. It was too far to see their faces, but it looked like they were wearing dresses, one white and one blue. Mark swears that he saw no such thing and that it was wishful thinking on my part.

"That was it. We never did find anything that would whisper of their whereabouts. We continued to go out for several days. Mark stayed at the house with Clarissa and me for six months. We went out as often as we could, posted signs, posted on social media, tried everything we could think of, but nothing. Thomas also would help from time to time when he could get away from work, but I think he really just did that for my sake. Mark eventually joined just about everyone else in the belief that they'd been killed. That image on the island haunts me every time one of those storms pops up and my convictions are renewed that they are out there somewhere. Why else would I continually see them? Why would Clarissa be dreaming such specific dreams? It has to be more than just a little girl missing her mom and grandma. My convictions are strong, but my body tires out so easily these days and I have a really hard time getting out to look anymore, but I'm not giving up. So, that's it. That's my story, when will the paddywagon arrive?" he asked with a bit of a smile.

I was so touched by his story that I was just about to stand up and tell Roger that I would devote as much time as I could to help him solve this mystery. However, Thomas, a very angry Thomas, chose this moment to show up. His entrance made all the more dramatic by a quick flash of lightning followed swiftly by ground shaking thunder as he opened the door and threw murderous looks my way.

"I guess you did hold to your promise. You're doing everything within your power to get your story no matter who it may hurt," he had taken in his father's tearstained face, "What are you doing here? I thought my father had been clear with you earlier."

"Thomas, relax. She is here as a guest and as someone needing my help as she was.about to be overtaken by the storm. Her moped died just outside our house. Clarissa saw her struggling and invited her in. She wouldn't even accept her invitation until she'd spoken to me. At first, when she realized that I lived here, she didn't even want to come inside, but it was too late, the storm was here and she needed shelter. We've had a chance to talk and she's not what I accused her of earlier. That was rude of me and I've apologized. I know what it's like to be in her shoes."

I couldn't believe that he was actually defending me. Yes, we'd spoken and I felt we understood each other better, but I didn't expect this. I remembered; however, that I had expected him to treat a reporter with more respect since he had been one before retirement. I was suddenly grateful for him as I turned and saw that none of the fury had left Thomas's face.

"Broke down or not, she's proving to be just as ruthless as you once were. She's sticking her nose where it doesn't belong." Thomas railed.

"That's our entire career, Thomas. Remember that. The ability to 'stick my nose where it didn't belong' paid for your childhood and schooling. She's doing nothing more than what a good reporter should. As I said, she didn't seek me out, she was looking around the island, I assume coming this way to try to interview others, but could go no further. I wasn't going to leave her outside with a moped that we both know is no good to her until this thing passes."

"Uncle Thomas, don't be mean to Elizabeth. She's in my dreams and she's going to help them come home," said Clarissa who'd reappeared from her bedroom at the sound of her uncle's arrival.

"Clarissa, honey, how many times do we have to go over this? Mommy's taking a vacation with grandma. Some day you'll see them both again, but you'll be all grown up by the time that happens. No person can go where she is and bring her back. That's just not possible."

"You're wrong. You've always been wrong. Mommy and Grandma are stuck and can't come back, but Elizabeth is here to get them. Mommy told me in my dreams and so did Elizabeth," said Clarissa.

Just then there was a loud crash that sounded like it came from the island. We all rushed to the window just in time to see lightning striking in several silver streaks in the center of the island. It was like a great electrified hand was reaching down out of the sky and its fingers were making contact with the sandy beach…each one as long as the next.

"Here it comes," said Roger.

"Here what comes?" I asked.

"The doorway that will release them," said Clarissa in a low guttural voice. Thomas and Roger looked as shocked as I was.

I looked out the window just in time to see the door that I had thought was in my imagination before. It seemed to appear out of nowhere and it did not appear to have anyone within or on either side of it. It popped up and stood, on its own, for two minutes, then it slowly faded and there was no more door. It was like there had been nothing there in the first place. I shuddered again at the thought of my dead mother standing at that door glaring across the island. For the second time I refused to let that become part of my conscious thought.

Another quick crash of thunder and the storm was gone. The clouds quickly dissipated, the sun came out, Clarissa fell to the floor unconscious, and as I glanced outside I saw the flashlight on my rented moped flash on and off once. We all stared amazed at Clarissa who began to stir almost as quickly as she hit the floor.

"Clarissa, honey, are you okay?" asked Roger.

"How did I fall down?" she asked.

"We're not sure, honey," I responded, "you just seemed to lose your balance as you were talking about the door."

"Mommy said you'd come, she said so just now. Everything's going to be okay now," Clarissa seemed delusional as she struggled to sit up.

"I'm not sure about your mommy, kiddo, or if you actually heard her talk to you just now, but I'm here to get a story, then I'm going back home to Boston. I think maybe I better leave now," I continued bracing myself for their response, "This all seems to be a little much. Maybe I'll take your advice, Thomas, and leave this story alone."

"You're not going to Boston. You're going to meet your mommy too. Your mommy says it's time for you to come home," Clarissa's voice was now hers. She was so sure of herself it was absolutely alarming.

"Honey, I know what it's like to have dreams. I know what it's like to have mommies go away when you're young and have to wait to see them again. My mommy and your mommy are in the same place," I glanced at Roger nervously, "and neither you nor I will see them any time soon."

"No, we're going to see them soon. That's what my mommy says in my dreams and she always tells me the truth. She even told me that they've started sending you dreams to help prepare you to see her again," Clarissa said.

Three sets of eyes burrowed into mine, two of which silently begged for me to deny this outrageous claim. I have never been one to turn away from the truth though, even when that truth doesn't make any sense.

"She told you that they've sent me a dream?" I asked Clarissa.

"Yes, they've been sending it pretty regularly lately. They were sure you were aware of it, they said you were scared."

"I think bewildered would be a better word," I replied.

"You can't tell me that you actually have had a dream? About them?" asked Thomas with heavy skepticism.

"I wish I couldn't, but yes, she seems to know what she's talking about though I've never met her before today. I can replay the dream for you in detail because, as Clarissa said, I've been having it with increasing frequency lately."

"Okay? Do tell," Thomas said.

"Well, it starts with my mom insisting that I won't want to come with them, wherever they are, because I'm young and full of life. She also says that she doesn't understand what the "Renzen" family needs to be there for. A figure named Dominic, someone I don't recognize, tells her that he can take care of my desires and that everyone is just about ready to join them. Then he stops further objection by kissing her. As they're kissing, he looks up, directly into my eyes, and that's when I wake up."

"A mere mention of our name and you're buying all of this?" Thomas asked.

"The mention of your name, meeting Clarissa who he'd also mentioned, finding out that she has had these dreams too and that somehow our dreams are connected. It makes a certain amount of sense. You have to admit that."

"Not really, what I see is two girls that have suffered great loss and through the power of suggestion, are buying into a story that any rational person would recognize for the sham that it is. What do you really want here, Elizabeth? Is this your angle to keep going after this story?"

"No Uncle Thomas, she is telling the truth and so am I. No one wants to believe me, but Elizabeth does. Mommy says that it's okay if you don't believe me. You'll all see in time."

With that, Clarissa stormed out of the room and the next thing we heard was a door slamming shut somewhere overhead.

"I apologize, Elizabeth. This whole thing has been emotionally draining for all of us, as you can see. We're very divided in our thoughts and beliefs. Whatever Clarissa is waiting for, maybe it will be happening soon, now that you're here. Maybe that's what was needed to set things in motion.

"No apologies necessary," I said and turned my angry eyes in Thom as's direction, "as was pointed out, I know how hard it is when a little one loses a parent. I do know that from experience. I can't even pretend to know how Clarissa's and my dreams could be connected, but I'm not going to deny it because it's scary either. However, your priority should be Clarissa. I need to get out of your hair before I stir up any more trouble. I'm sorry to have brought up such painful memories. The danger has obviously passed and I will not be told no again."

I turned to close the door behind me and noticed both Roger and Thomas looking at me with concern, but neither of them tried to stop me. I was sure that they were worried about what I'd witnessed with Clarissa and what they'd told me, but they were overwhelmed right now. I started the moped, and just as they boy had said, it started right up with no complaint. I drove it back to the roadside stand, returned it, and found myself lodgings for the night so that I could reflect on all that I'd learned today.

Chapter 2

I settled myself into my room at the Harbor View Hotel and replayed the day's conversations. Some I was literally replaying on my recorder, like our less than pleasant encounter on the bus. Other conversations I was trying to write down in my notes before I forgot exactly what had been said. The incredible story that Roger had told me kept rattling in my mind, but most of all, I couldn't forget little Clarissa. At nine years old, seven really, she'd lost the two most important women in her life. It's not unusual for her to have supplied a story to account for their long disappearance. The further from today's events I allowed myself to get, the more it seemed like a ghost story that was emphasized by an after-noon storm.

Still…a storm that the kid in the moped stand seemed to know was coming? A storm that would affect the moped? And what about the dreams? Had I mentioned my own dream first and Clarissa picked up on it? Kids can be very smart when they're calling out for attention. But I just couldn't get her out of my head. Everything else today I could chalk up to a little girl wanting her Mom and Grandma back, but how did she know that I'd lost my own mom? How could she look deep into my heart and know that her predicament and mine were really quite similar? She couldn't;- she just couldn't know those things. I wanted this room to be a much needed reprieve from today's stress. I wanted to take a long, hot bath and forget about it,- her words kept repeating in my mind like a song that is playing on repeat no matter how hard you try to change the station.

As the sun was beginning to make its way toward the horizon I finally decided on the long sought after bath. The jets were wonderful as they massaged the stress out of the twisted knots in my back. The thoughts about Clarissa and today's events were a little more stubborn. However, after a few aspirin and a foray into the world of fiction, I finally began to doze just as the room's telephone announced itself. I jumped out of the tub, wrapped myself in the hotel's robe and slippers, and ran to answer it.

"Hello?" I asked into the receiver.

"Elizabeth, sorry to bother you, this is Thomas. We need to talk."

"Um, how did you know where I was staying? I didn't even know until I left and returned the moped. The kid suggested this place to me."

"I followed you. I'm sorry, and I promise that I'm not some stalker, I just really needed to make sure that you were safe. I wasn't even going to bother when I saw that you'd gotten settled, but then my Dad called and said that Clarissa had more to say after you'd left. They were equally as alarming as the things she'd said earlier this afternoon. I thought you should know because they have to do with you."

"I am beginning to get whiplash talking to you," I complained, "first you warn me away from the island, then berate me for talking to your Dad. Clearly you believe that your mother and sister are dead and I don't know what to tell you there. And now a complete change again? Do I have 'fool' tattooed on my forehead?"

"Listen, we haven't gotten off to the best start, but I cannot deny what is right in front of me. Something is going on more than what even I can explain. I haven't entirely changed my mind and I'm not really ready to believe anything, but I also cannot deny the sincerity of Clarissa. She truly believes what she's been saying and she's been saying it all day so I'm ready to at least be open to the possibility that something more is going on."

"Okay, I can buy that, but why are you calling now? Do you want me to come back out and see Clarissa?" I asked.

"No, she's with me, we're actually down in the lobby. We thought we'd ask if you'd like to have dinner with us and maybe talk some more."

"I guess I'd like to talk to her too. Give me five minutes, then come up to room 118, but I guess you already knew that," I replied, wanting him to know that I was still not comfortable with this stalking business.

I was in a hurry, but I didn't miss the fact that Thomas seemed to be interested, or at least intrigued, by me. He was handsome after all, so after quick consideration, I looked through my suitcase and found a pair of jeans I thought I looked good in and a white tank top/blouse combination which I wore with a black belt around my slender waist. My flip-flops were in the corner; I slid my feet into them and threw my long brown hair back into a quick ponytail, pulling out a few traces of bangs so that they'd frame my face. I had time to make a cursory glance at myself before there was a knock at the door. I grabbed my small purse and opened the door for Thomas and Clarissa.

We left the hotel room and went out for burgers and fries at a small Mom and Pop restaurant nearby. We sat down and a friendly waitress took our drink orders. As we perused the menu, I turned to Clarissa and blurted before I could help myself, "What new things did you tell your grandpa and Uncle Thomas after I left today? Do you remember?"

"I tried to explain," she said.

"Explain what?" I asked gently.

"Explain that your mommy told me that when you were here, my mommy would be coming back."

"I'm confused," I said looking up at Thomas, "this is the same thing she said earlier. I thought you said there was something new?"

"Clarissa, what else did you tell Uncle Thomas? What about the strange man with the green eyes?" he prodded her.

Once again, my stomach took a dive. I hadn't mentioned the green eyes at all. I told them that he'd looked right at me, but I hadn't said a word about those piercing eyes.

"Oh yeah," she smiled then, "this man said you belonged with your family just like my family belonged with me. He said, 'don't worry honey, it won't be long now.'"

The chills this gave me ran the length of my spine.

"Honey, do you remember what you said this afternoon about the door releasing them?"

"Releasing who?" asked Clarissa. Obviously, that part she had no memory of.

"What about my mommy?" I changed course, "do you remember what you said about my mommy?"

"Yes, she said that it was time for you to come home. You would go home to your mommy and my mommy will come home to me with grandma," she repeated.

"When did she tell you this?" I asked.

"In my dreams. She always talks to me in my dreams. Ever since Mommy went away, she's been telling me that she'll be back soon," Clarissa said.

"Have you told your Uncle Thomas or Grandpa about this before?"

"I used to, but they didn't believe me, so I kept it secret and only talk about it in my dreams," out of the corner of my eye, I saw Thomas wince in shame.

"How often do you have these dreams?" I asked.

"At first not all the time, but more lately," she replied.

"Thomas, how often has she talked about these dreams? Have you guys ever had her talk to someone about it?" I asked.

"Yes, as a matter of fact, we have. We know it's odd behavior too, Elizabeth," impatience clear in his voice.

"I'm sorry. I'm so surprised by this I literally don't know what to say. I don't know how she can possibly know these things."

Any further conversation was put on hold and I found myself grateful for a moment to think. The waitress came and we ordered. I stayed pretty quiet from that point and throughout the meal. I had a lot on my mind. I had more to ask, but how much would a nine year old girl really know?

Again, Clarissa shocked me, "When did your mommy go away?"

Apparently I wasn't the only one that had questions.

"When I was close to your age, sixteen years ago," I slowly responded.

Thomas chimed in just in time. It seemed that he was working through an epiphany, "I really think that we need to investigate this further. This poor little girl lost the two most important women in her life to whatever this is and I really don't think she's making this up. Not anymore. Not after meeting you today. Why would she?"

"No, she's not making it up. Glad you're finally on board. The way she spoke earlier today, it's like she wasn't even aware of what she was saying. She's been dropping bits of information on me all day that there's no way that she would possibly know and every time my stomach drops. I'm certain she's not making this up, but I'm also certain that she's going to be needed in this adventure. I don't think we'll be able to find them without her. This can become dangerous for her and you. Are you ready to take that kind of risk with her? And with yourself?" I asked.

"You're talking about going out there? To the island? And bringing Clarissa with? I...I...I don't know. My Dad won't like it and I can't say that I do either; can't we go first, just you and I?" He asked me.

"First of all, I hardly know you, I'm not going to some deserted island without some assurance that I'll be safe, or at least that our fate will be the same. Also, no, I don't think that will work. She seems to be what he's waiting for and I think she'll be the key to finding out exactly where they are and how they can come home. Assuming that all that we've seen and heard today is true, if they really are being held against their will, then their captors will want something in return. And no, I'm not suggesting we hand her over, I'm suggesting we make them believe we are so that we can at the very least, learn how to get to them. I understand your hesitation, but I really don't see another way around it."

Thomas was considering this. From the look he displayed, he was trying to figure out how much danger this would put all of us, especially Clarissa, in. He must have been remembering something from the past because suddenly a big smile crossed his face. It reached all the way to his eyes as he chuckled quietly, but he was keeping this joke to himself.

"My father's never really been the same since they disappeared and if there's a chance that Clarissa's right and I've been blinded all this time, I owe it to her and to them to try this. My father feels so guilty for that argument, but he truly believes they are still out there somewhere.

"As I'm sure he told you, I immediately believed that they were no longer with us, but today's events have me doubting myself. I'm thinking that it's time to find out the real truth once and for all without involving Clarissa if that's possible. But if you want my help and the help of Clarissa in whatever capacity, you have to make me a promise," Thomas said.

"What's that?" I asked.

He was instantly serious, "None of this story ever gets published. You can tell a story about the island and its oddities. You can report on the storms and their effect on the electricity here, you can even report how the entire town closes down whenever there is a storm, but nothing about my family will ever be included."

"Thomas, let's pretend for a minute that I'm actually as shallow as you clearly still perceive me to be," I said with a sigh, "if I were to print that there is a family that lost two of its members during a storm and those two members are perhaps existing somewhere, but no one knows where rather than dead, and in addition to this, my dead mother may also be existing in the same place and wants me to join her, just how quickly would my boss, friends, and/or family show up on my doorstep, straight-jacket in hand?

"No, if we're in this, we're in this together now. I was given two weeks to write a story and get back to Boston. This will come first and if there's still a story left to be told about the island, I'll tell it. Otherwise, I'm sure there are other stories out here."

"Good," replied Thomas, "and I don't think you're shallow. I just recognize the thirst that always drew Dad. Clarissa, Sweetheart, Uncle Thomas will give you some quarters if you'd like to go and play a game while you're waiting for us to finish," he said. She smiled happily, took the offered change, and was off.

He was thoughtful for a moment, and then looked at me, "If you don't mind my asking, how did your mom die? Maybe there's some connection between that and my family."

"It was in a car accident. I don't see how there could be a connection, but you tell me. I was in the car with her that day. We were driving along on the expressway and arguing. My mom was conservative and traditional. I wanted to play baseball and that was not a very girly, feminine thing to do. In her eyes, because I was a girl, I needed to play with dolls, learn to help in the kitchen, eventually become obsessed with make-up, so on and so forth. At the time when I should have been painting up my face in an attempt to use make-up correctly, I was smearing black paint under my eyes to avoid the glare and grabbing a bat and ball every chance I got. I also loved to fish and hike. None of these things were in her wheelhouse so we were arguing.

"It was raining outside and lightning had been striking close to the car. My mom kept telling me to drop it, but I wouldn't let it go. She was turning her head to again tell me that I couldn't be on the team when I saw a flash of lightning right in front of us. I yelled at her to look out and she swerved. She lost control of the car. We spun out of control. We ended hanging off the edge of a cliff with her end slowly falling off. She told me to get out of the car. I was so scared and confused that I was frozen where I sat, but then she said it in a voice I'd never heard before, 'GET OUT OF THIS CAR ELIZABETH'! Those were the last words my mother spoke to me. Lightning struck again, close to my mother's side of the car and quickly I opened the door and jumped out. I fell to the ground as the car, and my mother, tilted and fell. I lost consciousness shortly after that. I was taken to the hospital and treated for some minor injuries.

"Once I was home I insisted we go back. I wouldn't stop pestering my father until he agreed. My mother's body was never found. Everyone just assumed she fell to the ocean below. There wasn't even a search party; she was just gone. And that's the story or how we lost my mom," I finished with glossy eyes.

"I'm so sorry, that must have been terrible," consoled Thomas, "but I'm seeing some puzzle pieces fitting together. What if your mother didn't die? What if they never found her body because there was no body to find? What if the lightning struck your car just like it struck my mom and Madeline?"

"I thought about that earlier today, but then why wouldn't I be with her? Wherever she may have been taken. Your mom and sister were taken together. Why wouldn't I have been when my mother was taken?"

I could tell that wasn't enough for him to dismiss the idea entirely. He was getting excited at the prospect that his mother and sister could still be alive. It was becoming overwhelming for me. I'd reconciled myself to my mother's death over fifteen years ago. I remembered the image I saw on the island and the odd dream that seemed so real. I began to quietly hyperventilate. I put all of my effort into calming myself before Thomas could notice.

"I don't know Thomas, doesn't that seem a little too convenient? We buried my mother sixteen years ago. I never had any reason at all to believe that she wasn't dead. Why wouldn't something else have happened by now? I don't want to spoil Clarissa's hopes," I said, turning to look at her smiling as she played, the panic was rising again, "but she could be seeing anything. I've changed my mind. I don't think I can do this. You know enough now to know what to look for without me. I...I...I just can't. My hotel isn't far. I think I'll just walk from here. Goodnight." I said as I threw down enough cash to cover the bill.

Thomas's jaw dropped as I'd finished. I thought I was going to be able to make a clean getaway. I had only managed a few panicked steps when I felt his hand on my arm. It was firm, holding me in place, but there was no malice in it. He wanted a chance to talk.

"Whoa," Thomas said, "please sit down. If you really still want to leave, I will take you home without an argument, and please take your money back. I asked you to dinner. But what happened? A minute ago you were ready to plow in and solve this mystery, now you want nothing to do with it? For the first time in two years I get a glimpse of hope that my mom and sister are out there somewhere and you're just going to give up?"

My panic started to abate, but I still wasn't sure I could get involved. These were people whose missing family members had left them broken. My case had not quite been the same. My mother and I were not close and didn't understand one another at all. It was one thing when it had just been Clarissa and her sanity; and perhaps bringing some peace to a little girl that was hurting, but this was something else entirely. I felt bad for Clarissa, but I was not the person she had been pinning all of her hopes on. And now Thomas's hopes on top of that. I couldn't be.

"It's just gotten too personal. A family reunion in your case would be a joyous occasion, and together we've figured out the next steps for you to follow to pursue them. There is an opening for you to find them. I'm not sure that I'm the person to help you do that. The reunion, in my case, would likely not at all be the same. My mother was not the type to encourage anyone or anything unless they fit her preconceived notions of what they should be. That was never the case for me. I was always so much like my dad that it grated on her despite her love for my dad.

Sorry, but again, you guys have what you need to get started. You don't need me, no one does really. I'm sorry, but I really have to go and I want to walk. I could use the fresh air to clear my mind."

I left the restaurant feeling awful for leaving this family for the second time today, but I couldn't face this. There was something very creepy and very wrong about what Clarissa knew. It's been sixteen years. That's long before Clarissa was born. My mother was dead and that was it. She couldn't come back. We buried her and I said goodbye. I couldn't go and trudge it all up again; it would be too much for everyone. And what if there is truth to it? What if she'd been existing somewhere for all this time? Why hadn't she tried to find us? It was best that I simply leave it alone.

Half an hour later I was back in my room which was blissfully empty. Thomas must have finally realized that I was serious. I would have a glass of wine and try to forget about today. I tried not to notice that the light on the phone was flashing indicating that some message had been left for me. I raided the mini-bar and found a passable red. I considered drinking it directly from the small bottle, but thought better of it and pulled down a glass, unscrewed the cap, poured, and set it aside to breathe. The light was blinking insistently and I realized, much like the light, I couldn't pretend that today wasn't here. I couldn't pretend that the knowledge I was given today didn't exist. This little girl said some things today that I could not believe she'd been prompted to say. Even the best investigator would have had to have been privy to the inner workings of my mind to come up with the things that she told me. Or maybe I just missed my mom. I couldn't reconcile it, and the light continued to blink.

"Fine," I said to the empty room, picked up the receiver, and dialed in to hear the message.

"Elizabeth, this is Sue. It's been a couple of days since you arrived on the island and we haven't heard from you. I wanted to make sure that you got to the room okay and that things are progressing nicely. Give me a call on my cell when you get in this evening. Talk to you later, bye."

I realized I'd been holding my breath, bracing myself for another pleading phone call with Thomas, and exhaled loudly. Sue was my editor and of course she'd want to check in with me and make sure everything was okay. I felt foolish that I hadn't reached out to them yet. I was just hoping that I'd have more to impress them with when I did call. I had worked as a fact checker and editorial assistant for a year. This was my first assignment as an independent reporter and I wanted to give them something that would let them know that my promotion had been worth it. I did at least have some notes and suspicions to share. There wasn't anything scary about calling her back with what I'd gathered. I made the call, got her voicemail, and proceeded to leave a message detailing today's events while glossing over the harder to believe items. I told her that I'd call again when I had something more solid and felt satisfied that things were moving; however slowly and strangely, in the direction I'd wanted them to.

I gathered my glass of wine, found some cheese and crackers that I'd picked up earlier in the day, and turned on the television. Shortly after consuming my late night picnic, the screen began to get hazy and I caught myself drowsing off once or twice before succumbing.

Faintly, I began to hear the shrill sounds of a voice I had not heard in sixteen years. I looked around and could not make out my surroundings immediately. It seemed that I was in a hastily thrown together room made of what looked like tree bark. I looked down and was standing on sand as though this were a room on the beach. I heard her voice again.

"Elizabeth, you listen to me, it was never about the sports. I always wanted you to be happy. I guess I didn't understand it at the time. You do what you want. Elizabeth, I'm here for you," she said.

"What? Mom? Where are you? Am I dreaming?" I asked both scared and mystified.

"I'm here, honey," she said as she walked into the room through a door I hadn't noticed, "You can be whatever you want to be."

"I know that, I did. Mom?"

It was incredible, I was standing in front of her though she didn't seem to notice me. It was as if she were speaking to the young girl that she saved all those years ago. She looked exactly as she had the day of the accident. She was wearing a khaki skirt down to her calves and a sea blue short sleeved blouse buttoned up the front. Her hair was long, wavy, and chocolaty brown. The top half of it was pulled back into a barrette. I recognized the colorfully striped scarf that was still fastened around her neck as one I'd given her for Mother's Day. Her light brown eyes, not near as big as mine, were warm and comforting. Suddenly, those eyes seemed to settle on me.

"Mom?" I questioned again, "Is that really you? Where are you? Do you know Clarissa, the little girl that talks to you? Are her mother and grandmother with you? Mom, can you hear me?"

"Elizabeth," the eyes that had seemed to find me, swept off and glanced around the room, "my sweet Elizabeth. I'm so sorry. You can do anything you want to do," she said again and started walking toward me.

"Mom, look at me. Can you see me? I'm right here in front of you," I was almost screaming at this point.

"I won't judge you anymore, I promise," she whispered and lowered her head.

"Mom, I've missed you; why can't you hear me? Who are those women with you? Mom, look at me. What's that ringing? Mom, where are you going? Talk to me, please. Mom? Don't leave. Mom?" I asked tearfully as her suddenly black eyes landed full on my face, then faded as the sound of the ringing telephone overtook my dream.

"Hello?" I asked sleepily, practically tripping over my own feet in my haste to not miss the call.

"Lily, there you are," said my brother Aaron, "I called Sue to get the number to your room. She said she hadn't heard from you and I was starting to worry. Why don't you keep your cell turned on? Anyway, I just called to make sure you were okay."

"Yeah, I'm fine. Sorry, my cell is on, but the sound is turned off. It gets too annoying with the noisy notifications every time I turn around."

I could hear the smile in his voice, "You know you can set those so they won't be annoying, right? I mean seriously, for a girl that's grown up in this generation, you should have that cell thing down."

"Ha, ha. Yes, I know you can set them, but who has time for that? Anyway, yes, I'm fine. Sorry Sue worried you. I called her last night and left a message. I did see that she'd been calling me. I've had a busy couple of days, but no solid leads, unfortunately. I'm going to have to start interviewing strangers, I think."

"Why did you sound so breathless when you answered? What are you doing?" he asked.

"Your call actually woke me out of a dream. I was worried I wouldn't get to the phone before you hung up. It was the oddest thing. For years, I haven't dreamed of Mom, but since I've been out here, I've dreamt of her twice. These dreams feel so real too, almost like she's here. Anyway, sorry that I worried you. I know you have to get to work and I need to do the same."

He assured me that he had a few minutes and I asked him about his wife and my twin nephews. We caught up with each other a little bit, but I wasn't about to tell him anything that I'd discovered since I'd been here. He would very likely insist I leave this thing alone. I wasn't ready to do that.

I spent the next two days canvasing the other homes along the crescent of land outside of and across the street from the island. I came up with surprisingly little. Everyone basically said the same thing: they were aware of the little storms and they were annoying, but since the majority of them didn't live there full time, these were vacation homes for most, they didn't really pay that much attention to it. When the storms came in, they hunkered down indoors and found something to do that didn't involve electricity. Once the storms were gone, everything went back to normal. It was weird, but not astronomically so to many of them.

I was waiting to meet a promising lead, a youngish man that lived alone year round just on the far edge of the crescent. He said he'd noted some strange happenings and even said he'd seen what appeared to be a doorway open on at least one occasion. Oddly, he also noted that at times, it seemed that a bolt of lightning would strike down and splinter off through the doorway. It was a small bit of information, but certainly an interesting detail. His name was Tony and when I came knocking at his door, he'd agreed to meet me at a nearby cafe. I glanced at my watch and noted that he was already ten minutes late. So much for Tony and his great insight. If he can't even keep an appointment, how reliable could his information really be?

I ordered myself a cup of clam chowder and a sandwich and waited while reviewing my notes.

"Deary," the waitress wanted my attention, "it looks like someone is looking for you."

I looked up from my notes quickly, scanning for Tony somewhere near the door. I looked back at her, confused, and noted that she was pointing outside at the man whose face was pressed right up against the glass I sat next to, hands cupped around his eyes. Thomas was smiling at me. I smiled back at how goofy he looked and waved him inside.

"Have you come to gloat?" I asked, "I have found very little since we parted ways."

"Are you on a date? The space across from you is set."

"No, I finally found someone that lives here year-round and we were supposed to have lunch and discuss the island. He was supposed to be here a while ago, but no show I guess," I finished with a shrug.

"His loss," Thomas said while sliding in the booth opposite me.

"Not really, this story is not going to write itself and if I can't get more than speculation over lost family members, I may be looking to switch careers."

"Come on, don't be so dramatic. You have more than speculation. You have verified proof that the storms do happen and that they affect the immediate area. You have a family that has been affected by the island itself. If you'd like, there may be a family member that would happily help you fill in the details."

"Accurate details, or further speculation?" I prompted.

"Well, it would likely be speculation at this point, but who's to say that it can't become fact?"

I didn't like where he was headed, "are you suggesting I be dishonest?"

He looked at me for a moment and was about to answer, but was saved by the appearance of my appointment.

"Are you Elizabeth?" the bespeckled man that had walked to the end of the table asked.

"I am. Tony, I assume?"

"Yeah, sorry I'm late. I was having some car trouble and it took longer than I thought it would to fix it. All good now, though," he glanced at Thomas, "do we need to reschedule?"

"No, Thomas is a friend of mine that happened to walk by as I was waiting. Thomas, Tony…Tony, Thomas."

"That's my cue," Thomas said as he pulled his phone out of his pocket and looked at the screen, "nice to meet you Tony. Dad's calling me anyway. I'll leave you guys to it. See you around Elizabeth."

"See you around," I glanced at Thomas who was immediately caught up in his conversation with his father.

"Tony, sorry about that, have a seat."

He sat and looked at me nervously, "Really, I'm sorry I was so late. I'm glad you hadn't left. It's really not like me to be late. I just had the car serviced so I was really surprised that it didn't want to start. I was getting an engine notification and was looking it up, but not finding much help. I was about to give up and call a tow truck; I thought I'd try it one last time and it started right up with no problems."

"It's okay, who hasn't had car trouble, right?" I laughed, surprised by the long explanation, "You said you had some information about the strange events on the island?"

I was all business, subtly letting my annoyance show at his being late. I mean, car trouble? Really? Who buys that kind of excuse anymore? I wondered if I could even trust what he was going to tell me, but he was the only one I'd been able to find, other than the Renzen family, that had seemed willing to talk about it at all.

"Yeah, okay, so you already know that the storms pop up and affect the electronics in a certain range. Did the other family talk to you about the missing journalists? The others that have come out here trying to make sense of it?" Tony asked.

"No," the Renzen's had mentioned this, but hadn't gone into detail, "please continue."

"Well, there have been others that have come out here looking. Other journalists that had been assigned to this island, but some of them haven't returned. They simply go missing while on assignment."

"Hasn't anyone come looking for them?"

"How do you think I got here? My brother went to investigate this island three years ago. I moved here two and half years ago. You do the math."

""Hasn't anyone gone to the police?"

"Several have, but with no evidence and a clear disappearance, there hasn't been much to go on."

The waitress brought my soup and sandwich and asked Tony for his order. He looked up to order and I took him in. He had close-cropped brown hair, longer on top allowing for some soft curls to form. His eyes matched his hair and he had a trim figure. His mouth would worry the stubble on his chin when he needed a minute to collect his thoughts. He did this now as he returned his attention to me and caught me staring.

"Sorry, did you want to order something more?" He politely pretended not to notice.

"No, I'm good. Do you know how many, collectively, have gone missing looking for this story?"

"No, sorry, but it couldn't be that many, otherwise more people would know about it, right?"

I agreed with him with a nod, "Is there anything else you can think of?"

His food arrived and he took a minute to take a bite and chew.

"Not really. Just that I think there has to be a way onto that island other than by boat, as odd as that sounds."

"This whole thing is odd, so that ship has sailed, but what do you mean? Are you talking about some underground tunnel or hidden bridge or something?"

"Not exactly," he thought for a minute, seeming to make a decision, "Fine, this is going to sound nuts, but when my brother disappeared, and I came out looking, I researched any kind of ferry service which there was none. I met a few locals who'd said they'd accepted money to take a person or two over on their boat, but none of them knew my brother. There was nothing that I could find that could tell me how he got on that island."

"Then how do you know he's there?"

"A hunch," he said.

"You mean you don't even know if he ever got to the island?"

"No, but he had to. That's what he was here for."

"Have you ever found any indication that he'd been here? Do you even know if he came out here to the Vineyard?" I was growing exasperated.

"Yes, he told me where he was staying and I verified that he checked in, but never checked out. I asked the hotel manager about it and he'd said that he couldn't divulge names, but there were at least two others that had done the same. They are only one hotel so I began interviewing nearby hotels with just that question. I knew they couldn't tell me names, and I came up with a total of twelve."

"Okay, but that's it? Yes it's coincidental, but there could be a million reasons why someone would abandon a hotel room."

"Too coincidental, though, don't you think? All within the last five years? No one willing or able to investigate further? Come on, you're a reporter, you can't tell me that when the coincidence is at this level, there has to be more to it."

He wasn't wrong, but I wouldn't even know where to start from here. We couldn't get names without a warrant and we couldn't go to the police without expecting to be committed.

"So you see the problem," he said with a smile.

That smile disturbed me. There was something in it that I couldn't place, but it didn't seem genuine.

"Yes, well, I do appreciate you sharing the information that you do have. I'm not exactly sure where to go from here, but you've certainly given me a lot to think about."

"No problem, Elizabeth," he said as he looked at me with another disconcerting smile, took a final sip, looked at his watch, and muttered something about being behind all day.

I called after him that I'd contact him if I found anything more that could help him in his search, but I don't think he even heard me.

"Lunch done already?" A voice took me out of my own head.

"What are you doing back here?" I said to Thomas.

"It's Clarissa. I know that we didn't leave this whole topic on very good terms and I swore to myself that I'd leave you alone, but Clarissa is refusing to eat. That was the phone call that I took as I left you earlier. My Dad was calling to tell me about it and I went there to try and convince her. She said that she will continue to refuse to eat until we bring you back and go after her mother," he shook his head in frustration and apology, "I didn't want to give in to her, but it's been two days and we're really starting to worry. Please Elizabeth, I don't want to sit by and watch her wither away and I don't know what to do. She's very stubborn and she's hurting. She believes that we've all given up. Can you at least come to my father's house and tell her that you're going to do something, even if it means I'm asking you to be dishonest? At least until she gets some food in her belly?"

"And what, then crush her hopes again after she's eaten something? You want me to be the person that goes in there, gets her to eat, then completely pull the rug out from under her? I will go and speak to her, but I am not going to promise her anything that I'm not willing to follow through on."

"Thank you, Elizabeth."

It struck me then. I was trying to place my discomfort around Tony when Thomas came up and distracted me with the news about his concern for Clarissa. When Tony looked straight at me, it had seemed that he was smirking, like there was some private joke that I wasn't getting. I wasn't looking at his eyes, but somewhere, my mind must have made note. The eyes that I looked into were eyes I'd seen before. They were the exact same piercing green eyes that had been haunting my dreams of late.

"Hello, Elizabeth, are you still with me?" Thomas's voice broke through my reverie.

"Sorry, yes, let's go see Clarissa."

"Are you okay? You looked horrified for a minute."

"I'm fine, let's go." I wasn't ready to talk about my epiphany.

Soon we were in Thomas's forest green Jeep Wrangler and on our way to Clarissa. I decided that I would tell her that I would do what I could to get her Mom and Grandma back. It wasn't lying, I am still going to investigate the island after all, and if finding out the truth is what sets them free, it's a win win. Maybe I'd promise her that I'd check in with news whenever I could and follow up on that so that she knows that I'm keeping my word. Whatever gets her to eat is great.

"I hope you didn't spend too much time on your hair," Thomas said as he noticed me trying to calm my tangled locks into a ponytail, "sorry, I didn't think to mention the car."

"No worries," I tried to yell over the roaring wind.

Twenty minutes later and hair in a tangled mess despite the ponytail, we were sitting in Roger's living room. Clarissa didn't want to come out of her bedroom at first; she didn't believe I was really here. Roger seemed especially distraught as he came from her room and told us that she was still refusing to come. I was going to have to go to her.

"With your permission," I said to Roger, "I can go to her and see if she'll talk to me."

He gestured toward the steps in a "go ahead" motion. I turned to head up the stairs when I noticed a little face appear at the top of the steps.

"Elizabeth," she smiled and bound down the stairway, "finally, you're here. Didn't you have a dream a few nights ago? Wasn't your mommy there telling you that you can do anything you want to do? I heard her. I saw your dream, she sent it to you so that you would come back to me."

"Clarissa, how can you possibly know that?" I looked up and scanned Thomas and Roger's shocked faces, "the only person I even talked to and told I had a dream was my brother. There's no way she could know that on her own."

"I told you already. They come and talk with me. That's how I knew it was you when your moped died, remember? I told you that you'd be the one to bring back my mommy and grandma. Your mommy is the one that told me. I told you this."

I had no arguments left. All of my convictions died away with the pleading of this lost little girl. She knew things there was no way that she could have known. Mission accomplished, I now believed her and quietly dismissed all plans I'd made earlier of stringing her along. This was real and I was going to help her reunite with the family she's missing. I was too involved now.

"How is it that she's talking to you? Where is she talking to you from?" I asked.

"I knew you'd believe me," she threw her arms around me, "She said you'd come around. She said that you'd soon see that I was telling the truth and that you and your mommy can be reunited too. Rosalyn said that as soon as Elizabeth appears everything will be okay. I know she's telling the truth."

"Clarissa honey, are you ready to eat something?" I asked.

"Definitely," she said and I could feel the collective output of held breath in the room.

"Okay sweetie, what would you like to have?" Thomas asked her.

"Can I have my favorite cereal?"

"Absolutely, and meals for the rest of the day."

"Okay Uncle Thomas," she agreed with a smile and ran to the kitchen to serve herself.

"Roger, I know this is going to sound crazy to you, but I no longer have a doubt that she's telling the truth. I don't pretend to know how she can be, but the dream she was describing, that was the dream I had two nights ago. She couldn't have known that.

"This is no longer about the story. I have to know what the death of my mother has to do with everything else. I'm in, I don't see how this will come out, but I will do what I can. The question now is, will you allow me to see what I can find without interference?"

He contemplated my request for a minute, looked from me to the kitchen where Clarissa was, to Thomas, shrugged his commanding shoulders and said, "I guess I'm in too."

"Great," said Thomas, "what's our next step, Elizabeth?"

"When did I become leader of this crazy endeavor?" I asked, astounded.

"Well," said Thomas, "since it's your mother that has our little Clarissa convinced that there is something worth going after, I guess that means that you get to take the lead."

He looked at me pleadingly and I smiled back at him, "only if you'll take co-lead."

"Okay with me," he said with a warm smile.

"Roger, I can tell that Clarissa has some part in this and I don't want to involve her, but I can't promise that that won't be necessary. Somehow communication is coming through her and she seems to have something that they want if I believe my dream. How willing will you be to involve her?"

He hesitated to respond so Thomas prodded, "Dad, what do you think?"

"I think it's time we really sit down and talk about what happened the day that your mother and sister disappeared. You see, there is a little more to the story than what I have told both of you. I was hoping not to talk about it at all, but I can see that it's going to be necessary. Once my whole story has been told, then I would say that yes, Elizabeth should be in charge of this as you know your mother best. As for Clarissa, leave her out of it. I don't want to lose her too."

Chapter 3

"What do you mean, Dad? How can there possibly be more? What haven't you told us?" Thomas asked with surprise in his edgy voice.

"We all better sit down and get comfortable. This story will take a little while to tell and needs to be discussed before we go off with the idea that we're going to change the fortunes or misfortunes of your mother and sister, son.

"That day, the day that they disappeared, there was something different about the storm. I noticed it right away because it was almost as if there was something in it that I could feel. When Madeline and I began to argue, I felt something that I've never felt inside me before. I started to get incredibly agitated. When that happened, I started saying things that I didn't mean and have never spoken of since. I felt as though something, something outside of me, were pushing me to say mean things to my daughter. I couldn't fight the urge. I told her that if she didn't like the wedding that I was throwing her, she could be sure that this was the last thing that I'd do for her. I told her that I didn't want to see her again. I was horrible to her.

"I feel so guilty for saying those things. I was angry that she wasn't satisfied with the expensive wedding that I was putting on for her here, but not so angry as to say those things. I...," stammered Roger as he was fighting off tears, "I was the reason that she went for that walk on the beach, away from everyone else. Worse than that, I sent my wife after her knowing full well that there was a storm coming."

"Dad, it was a stressful day for all of us. Everyone says things they don't mean when they're under stress. Madeline knows that you love her and mom certainly doesn't blame you for sending her. You know how Mom was always the peacekeeper. It was just bad luck that they happened to be out there when the lightning struck or whatever happened," said Thomas.

"You can't blame yourself, Roger," I added, "you have to believe that if they weren't taken then, it would have happened sometime. There's more than just bad luck involved with this."

"Yeah, well, that's not all," continued Roger, "that's not the whole story. There was something that I saw when the lightning struck…and someone I talked to. I did see them go. That is why for all of these years I haven't let go of the hope that they'd be back."

"You what?" Thomas reacted.

For a minute no one in the room breathed.

"He saw them go," repeated Clarissa who had come into the room to hear the story, she got comfortable at Roger's feet, "Mommy told me in my dreams that you talked to the lady, Elizabeth's Mommy, when they were taken. She said that you wouldn't come after them. She said you wouldn't be able to do it until Elizabeth came along. She told me that when the time was right you'd tell me what the lady told you that day. Is the time right? Are you finally going to tell me?"

"Clarissa, why didn't you tell me any of this before?" Roger asked, stunned.

"Because you never believed me. You were talking about hospitals. You wanted me to believe that she was never coming back. Now you know that you'll be able to see Grandma again and I'll be able to have my Mommy back," said Clarissa with optimism.

"Okay, before this gets any weirder, I need to know what you saw, Dad, and who you talked to when they were taken. What were you told? And how could you keep this from me?" Thomas had been hurt.

"Yes, okay, the rest of the story coming up. Can I fix either of you two a drink?" asked Roger, stalling.

"Not really thirsty right now, Dad,"Thomas said through gritted teeth, "Elizabeth is keeping very quiet, but I think she and I are equally inter- ested in this event."

"Okay fine, but this may not be easy to hear, especially for Elizabeth," I flinched at that. Why did it seem that everyone around knew so much about me and my family?

"Why will it be so hard for me to hear?" I asked angrily, "If this has something to do with my mother, I have a right to know about it. Please don't mess around with this. It literally took me years to deal with the fact that my mother was gone and we'd parted on bad terms. I always felt responsible for what happened. Do not quit on me now, Roger. Please."

"Okay, okay," he started again, "When the lightning struck and your mother and sister, Thomas, were taken away, it seemed as if they went through a door. It happened very quickly. The lightning came and hit the sand. I watched it happen from where I was still hiding in shame. At the time that your mother and sister should have been writhing in pain, a doorway opened that I could see nothing behind. It was pitch black. In that instant, instead of being electrified, they were pulled through the door. One moment they were standing in front of the open doorway, the next they had backed into it. They were not able to move. Their eyes were wide and begging for help. I was trying with all of my might to go to them in the door, but something was keeping me out. I don't know what, but I could feel the electricity in the air. It felt as though something unseen were moving past me. I would have sworn that I heard a woman say 'Dominic, you're back.' By all rights, that lightning should have struck me down as well as your mother and sister, but this mysterious door happened instead.

Roger took a deep breath and composed himself before he went on.

"The part that will affect you, Elizabeth, is that when they were frozen in the door, a woman came behind them, the woman that must be your mother. She said something to me that I have never forgotten. It has always been the key to getting my family back, but I never knew what it meant until you came here and Clarissa began putting it all together for us. This woman said, 'One day she will come and she is the key to the return of those you love. Do not pass up your opportunity to bring them home.' I can only imagine that you are the 'she' that was being talked about and that, according to her, you are meant, just like Clarissa's been saying, to bring them home."

As he finished he raised his hands in the air as if he were surrendering and in a strange way, he was. For several years he wanted to maintain the illusion that they were dead even though he knew better. He didn't want to believe the woman that spoke to him, but now he had no alternative. Everything he'd been told had been set in motion and he was starting to understand, and possibly hope, that they were, in fact, going to be coming back home. He clearly didn't want to hope, but he couldn't help himself. The small sparkle in his pale blue eyes had given him away.

"Is that all she said? Did she say anything else? She didn't say anything about herself or the way that she died or didn't die or how she got to where she was? Was there nothing else?" I asked, searching.

Roger sighed and pulled a trinket out from behind a clock on the wall, "there was this."

As soon as I saw the necklace, everything else was drowned out. The room became very long and very warm suddenly. I was happy I was already sitting down. I clutched my mouth with my hand so that I could hold back the scream that I felt building inside. This was something that

I had worn without exception every day until the day of the accident. I had lost my locket when the car went out of control and my mother fell to her death. I didn't even know it was missing until a day or two after the accident. I assumed it was gone along with my mother. Apparently, I'd been more right than I knew.

He handed it to me and I gasped. The outer pieces of the locket were decorated in Victorian white gold. The intricate detail still shone out as I pried apart the two halves to find what I knew was inside. Tears fell quietly as I saw for the first time in six years; the image of myself, my brother Aaron, and my mother and father standing together smiling at the camera as my Aunt Ella took the picture. We had gone to the zoo that day and we were standing in front of the butterfly exhibit. I was swept into the memory.

It had been a gift from my parents. They had given it to me for Christmas and I had loved it immediately. Our trips to the zoo were some of my favorites. I remember seeing the little box sitting under the tree and trying to guess what was inside of it. My parents' eyes had both been sparkling as I reached to pick it up. They were waiting for my reaction, knowing that even at a young age, this gift would mean a lot to me.

I tore the paper away from the box and there was a blue, velvety long box under the paper. I pulled the sides apart and saw the necklace inside. I remember telling them that it was really pretty. I was twelve years old at the time.

"Open it up," my dad had said, "look at the picture inside."

When I did, I started crying immediately. My Aunt Ella, my favorite crazy aunt and actually a great aunt, had died of a sudden heart attack shortly after the picture was taken. I sobbed for a few minutes then ran to both of my parents and engaged them in a tight group hug.

"We love you, sweetheart, and knew this would always remind you of her as well as keeping us in your heart," my mother had said as I wiped the tears from my eyes.

I realized that Thomas and Roger were looking at me with concern, waiting for some kind of response.

"She gave this to you?" I managed to croak out through my shaky voice.

"Yes, she said that the locket and owner would be reunited in time. She told me that my family would come back to me soon after the locket found its owner. I have no idea what the next step is, but I have no desire for you to be stuck wherever they are. I never guessed she meant a trade and I don't want to see that happen to you," said Roger.

"I always wondered what happened to that locket. I was wearing it the day of the accident. I even remember feeling a pinching sensation on my neck when we were tumbling around in the car. But I never thought to look for the locket after I woke up in the hospital. I realized it was gone and just assumed it was lost forever. I-I-I have no idea what to think of all of this. I do know; however, what the next step is. We have to go out to that island and figure out exactly what is going on. Like you, Roger, I have no desire to be stuck on whatever plane they're on and the more informed we are going into this, the better. Now you mentioned once or twice to me in the beginning that others had gotten trapped there. Tony, that I just interviewed, also stated that his brother had gone missing there so maybe he could be of some help. But what of the others that have come. Has no one made it back? Hasn't anyone published anything regarding this island? And if not, why don't more people know about it? Haven't their families come looking for them? Or at the very least, their bosses?"

"There have been a few that have made it back, but nothing much has been published. I can only guess why but I would imagine it would have something to do with the fantastical nature of the stories. Without credible proof, their stories would be discounted, the stuff of satire magazines," said Roger.

"That's why I didn't want to see you go through with this investigation. I didn't want to see that happen to you," said Thomas.

"What about the other reporters that have come through? Did you warn them as well?"

"We have warned everyone we've been able to come across, but they laughed it off as superstition, much like someone I know," Thomas pointed out, "and we don't have a list of reporters sent on assignment so we can only warn them off if we happen to meet them before they head out. We've met a few and they conducted their investigations anyway. The only reason we say that some have made it back is because we have seen the occasional story pop up in the headlines, but usually it's just regarding the strange nature of the storms. It's typically a sideline stuck back on page six somewhere."

"So, if I hadn't gotten on that bus the other morning there's a good chance that whatever that is would have taken me already?" I asked both of them. But I didn't need an answer. I thought of seeing that door and thinking, even knowing though I'd denied it, that my mother was standing there. Somehow she knew that seeing her there would be enough to get me out on that island alone and then it would be too late. I shuddered at the thought, but drew my attention back to the conversation.

"It seems that fate wants you here. Actually, I think the storm that came through the day we met was meant just for you. With everything we've seen, heard, and talked about, it seems like it, doesn't it? The storm was bad and it developed just as you were riding along the coast, around the time you came within eyesight of the island. Once you were in the house for good, it lessened in intensity, and ended shortly after. Maybe this was the first of many storms that will wind up until we deal with this problem," Thomas replied.

"How often do these storms pop up when I'm not around? Do they happen all the time? Is there something common to the storms? The guy at the moped stand warned me about the storms moving in which is why I wasn't too surprised when the moped died. Those that are around all the time clearly are used to how the storms affect the area."

I couldn't help it, I was spouting questions and facts as quickly as I thought of them. I didn't want to leave anything out.

"Whoa, slow down there Ms. Reporter. One question/piece of information at a time," said Thomas recognizing my panic.

"Sorry, it's the reporter in me. I think it's probably best to know all that we can before we head into unknown and certainly not understood dangers. Don't you think so?" I looked around the room.

Clarissa looked a little put out and said, "I want to go after my Mommy now. She said that when you came we'd go and get her. Can't we go get her now?"

"In time, honey," Roger replied, "we still have some things that we have to work out. We want to be safe when we go, right? I know it's hard to wait, but we want to do everything we can to make sure we all are together again, safely, right?"

"Okay," said Clarissa, defeated.

We resumed our discussion of what we, as a group, know about the island. Roger and Thomas did most of the talking and I listened and took notes. Though this was now so much bigger than a story, I was still hoping to get one out of this and I wanted to make sure I had a running record of everything that happened before I sat down to write.

Still, I could not shake this sense of foreboding. Something was not right. Though I truly believed Roger and his family's story, I still could not quite get my head around my mother's and my part in this situation. Why would she have gone to some mysterious island instead of dying that day? What was she doing there for all of this time? If this were all true, why hadn't she tried to contact me before now? Who is Dominic? It didn't escape my attention that Roger had said his name during his story. How had I dreamed about the Renzens before meeting them? After seeing the way that they placate Clarissa, I decided to keep the rest of my own dream to myself. Why does this entire thing hinge on the innocence of a little girl who misses her mother?

As these thoughts were passing through my head, I noticed that everyone stopped talking. I looked up and saw frozen faces. Clarissa was gone, but Roger and Thomas looked as though they were both about to speak when their faces took on a stone-like expression. I turned my head to look for Clarissa. My eyes widened as I took in the one person that, other than in my dreams, I hadn't ever expected to see again.

My mother looked just as she had as I slept. She was beautiful and intimidating in the way that she looked at me. It was amazing. A familiar look of contempt came over her as she took me in. Her eyes slightly squinted, her shoulders hunched toward her neck, and she scrunched her nose. She forced herself into a warmer, more erect posture, and got ready to address me. It seemed that I was the only one in the room capable of movement, though I was planted in terrified fascination at the moment. I still hadn't found Clarissa.

I looked up at her and couldn't unstick my tongue from my mouth. My first instinct was to run to her and hug her tight. My good sense told me that the feeling was not mutual so I stayed where I was and continued to look at her.

"Hello dear," she finally spoke, "I want you to know that I am here and I am real. I did not die in the car accident all those years ago though you were probably happy to see me go. It allowed you and your father to really connect, just how the two of you wanted it. You were young, but I would have thought that your father may have looked a little harder for me before giving up when the detectives decided to end the search."

This was nothing like the dream I had. When I finally accepted that this may be happening I thought that she'd be happy to see me when the time came, not reliving hurt feelings. She knew I was closer to my father and I guess that did always bother her, but I thought that would be the last thing on her mind at the moment of our reunion.

I finally found my voice, "Mom? How could this be? I watched you fall and disappear. I almost fell with you but you screamed at me to get out of the car. I didn't want to leave you. There is no way that you could have survived that fall. How did Dad or I have any say in that? Of course we didn't want you to go? We were both crushed. How dare you accuse us of anything less? If you've been alive all this time, why haven't you come home?"

"Oh Elizabeth, do you really think that there is life and death and nothing in between. For a reporter, I'd think you'd be able to work out for yourself that that's not the case. You better open your eyes otherwise I don't see you reporting for long. I didn't die in the actual sense; I was reborn that day. Anyway, clearly I'm not dead, I'm standing here, aren't I?"

Hadn't I always had a problem with the typical life and death explanations? It seemed that she knew more, too. She was in no mood for sharing. The way that she was looking at me now, she had been waiting for this conversation and she was showing me all of the contempt that she'd been saving up.

"What did you do to Roger and Thomas? Why can't they move? Where is Clarissa?"

"I didn't hurt them. I don't see why you care so much though, it's not like they're your family. Maybe you should be a little more concerned about your own well being. I came here to help you. You are about to get yourself into something that is so much bigger than you know.

"That little girl's mother and grandmother are here, that much is true. I have been communicating with her because she believed so completely that her Mommy was coming back. The good thing about where I am is that I have been gifted a little insight into the future of those that I care about. Since I was able to tell that you and Clarissa would cross paths eventually, I started speaking with her. I wanted to know when you'd be coming. Now that that has been accomplished, we can be together again."

"What do you mean, gifted? Where are you? And you still didn't answer one of my first questions, why haven't you come home?"

"I can't explain it all until you've met everyone involved. I will tell you more once you're here with me. That's all I can say right now," she said.

I sensed some impatience in her voice and realized that while she's been given some sort of gift, it's not as powerful as she'd have us believe. She was limited in what she could do. It was an important point, but I wasn't done with this conversation, "what about Clarissa and her family? Don't you intend to keep your promise to her?"

"I mean really, now Elizabeth, are you five? Of course I'm going to keep my promise. They'll be reunited. One way or another," she scoffed.

This was not the woman that I'd known. We'd had our differences, but she wouldn't have been so thoughtless for all those around her, "Mom, how could you? This is a little girl's life you're messing with, not to mention the rest of her family. She has put all of her faith in your words. She believes that her mom and grandma are coming home with her and this will be the end of it. Who are you? This is not the Rosalyn that I remember. We may not have always gotten along, but I never knew you to be so cruel."

Her eyes flashed up at me and for a second, it looked like they were pained, like I'd gotten through to her. Liquid amber turned to stone as she shook her head slightly, "Come here, Clarissa and tell my daughter what I've done for her."

Clarissa appeared out of the shadows flanked by her mother and her grandmother, each one had a hand on one of her shoulders.

"She brought us back together. She brought us here so that we could be together. We are going to go home soon. That's why she gave the locket to grandpa. So that we knew she would keep her promise," said Clarissa.

"I love the innocents. You can get them to do and believe almost anything to accomplish your ends," said my mother with a laugh, "and I thought you were naive, Elizabeth; this one has played into my hands nicely. You are here now; you are with me now," she said this last with more meaning and determination in her burning eyes."

"No, that can't be. We haven't left Roger's house. There was no storm. Look around Clarissa, we haven't gone anywhere. Clarissa, honey, this is fake. She's not really here, they're not really here. They only want you to think that they've already won. Come to me sweetheart, we'll go find Uncle Thomas and Grandpa together. We'll find our way back home."

Clarissa looked confused. Her mother's hand had moved from her shoulder and slid into hers. Her grandmother was still grasping her shoulder. My mother had become a gifted manipulator. She spoke as if she thought I was just going to walk away with her and leave this family broken. Clarissa looked at me and back at her mother. I could tell she was much smarter than my mother was giving her credit for.

"Clarissa, look at me honey," her confused eyes found mine, "they're not really here. Look at your grandpa and uncle. We haven't left the living room. These are illusions to make you believe what she's telling you. She's counting on the fact that you're young and will believe her because you don't know any better. Don't let her win. Come with me, Clarissa and we'll do this right."

"I can't," she cried and twisted in their grip, "They're holding on too tight. Let go of me."

Clarissa yelled at the fake versions of her family. She twisted and flailed violently and began to break free. The two fakes screamed in frustration as Clarissa was slowly defeating their grip. I went to her and grabbed her waist. I yanked and the fakes screamed louder.

I said to her quietly, "bring your head against mine, close your eyes, forget that they're here, and just believe that we're home and everything is as it was."

She did as I asked and suddenly we were jolted back as the pressure on Clarissa lifted. Roger and Thomas, no longer human popsicles, looked at us with surprise.

"What in the world was that?" asked Thomas.

"Oh, you won't believe this," I said angrily as I recounted the events of the last few minutes.

"At least we know how to beat her if this happens again. We know our way back for now. I don't think she could actually take her from here anyway. If she's still on that island, as with the missing reporters, there has to be a reason why. We're going to have to be seriously prepared when we go out to take on the island and my mother. There is something larger than life in her, and we have to find out what it is. That's the only way I can see of getting them back."

"You still want to go through with this?" asked Roger.

"More than ever. That person that I met a moment ago is not my mother and if that's the case, how dare she assume her form. At least she's not the mother that I remember. My mom was a lot of things, but cruel was never one of them. If that is my mother, she used you and your entire family just to get back at me. We will get your family back," I said with finality.

Roger and Thomas had no recollection of the incident. All they knew was that one minute we were sitting and talking and the next Clarissa and I were shooting into a corner as if being thrown.

I looked toward Roger and asked, "what did my mother say when she handed you that necklace? What are you holding back? There has to be more than just an incentive for me to feel connected to my mother again. Roger, what is it exactly that she told you when she gave you that necklace?"

Roger looked at me with surprise, "What do you mean? She said exactly what I told you. The locket's owner would be reunited with the locket in time. Just as you are now reunited with the locket. I gave it to you. What on earth can you mean there was something else?"

"Roger," I began, annoyed, "being a reporter yourself you should know as well as I do that you can't bullshit your way through something that you don't want to tell. I've been trained to sniff out the lies and right now, the air is ripe. Fess up, she said something else. Did she tell you that you'd be trading me for the necklace or what?"

"I think you're going to find yourself being one hell of a reporter, Elizabeth. It took me some years to gain the skill of knowing when others were lying so quickly. Okay, you got me, she said something else, but it doesn't matter because it's not going to happen her way. I won't let it. I can't watch you take risks for my family and not step in when I know that ultimately she wants you there with her. This Dominic has offered her some sort of deal if she can get you onto the island. He believes that once you're there, he can convince you to stay."

I read the meaning in the words that he didn't want to say. Though the words that followed made their way to my ears, my suspicions were getting the best of me. Before I knew it I was yelling at Roger again.

"She did, she told you that when I came for the necklace you'd be bringing me to her and the two of you would trade. She's been feeding you this for all this time."

I knew I was out of line, but I was angry and taking it out on Roger. I had to calm myself.

"You're pretty smart Elizabeth, you have come to the truth of some of it, but boy do you have an imagination. Next, Thomas will have been in on this too," said Roger calmly, "no one is conspiring against you; everything we've told you has been the truth. It's clear to me that you are an important part of this and of course I want my family back, but it won't be at your expense."

"Just as no part of this will be at your family's expense either. You've suffered enough. I'm sorry, I don't know what got into me just then. I think it's become clear that you didn't need to be involved in this to begin with if she'd just come at me directly. I don't even know why she got you involved. I am going out there and I am going to take care of this. And I assure you, your family will be made whole again," I finished as I backed out of the room and turned for the door.

I had almost made it. I was reaching out for the door handle and taking the step that would result in me opening the door when it all became too much. I stopped, took a deep breath to control the emotion inside, and pulled the locket from my back pocket where I'd stashed it. A quiet thought was gaining traction now. If we weren't meant to all be in this together, why would she have given the necklace to Roger? It didn't matter, I shook the thought away, they should not be in danger. I raised my arm and grasped the handle when I heard a sound behind me that chilled me to my deepest core.

"You can't run forever. Facing your demons means facing them like this, on my terms, whether you like it or not. It's time for you to come home and be with your mother."

I turned back and saw Clarissa's eyes rolling back until just the white was visible. I realized with horror that it was her that croaked those words. Her nine year old voice had managed to sound like that of a woman that would be in her fifties now. She looked at me for another moment and Clarissa fell to the floor and began full body convulsions. Her small frame jumped up and down with the rhythm faster than that of a heartbeat. Her pupils remained hidden.

Thomas looked at me with pleading eyes, "for the love of God, make it stop. Do something."

I screamed at the top of my lungs, "YOU WIN YOU CONNIVING BITCH. LEAVE HER ALONE."

Clarissa stopped convulsing immediately and lay quiet on the floor. She gathered herself into the fetal position and began to cry. She remained that way for a long time as we surrounded her, Thomas grabbed her from the floor, hugged her close, and laid her on the couch. Slowly she came around, focused on each of our faces, and came back to us. A piece of her childhood was robbed from her that day and I silently vowed that it would be the only piece that I would allow her to lose. I was going to finish this.

"Come to me sweetheart and this will all be over," came that mysteriously detached voice floating bodiless through the air.

"You win," I repeated, "you win. We will do this, just don't do that to Clarissa again."

There was no reply.

"Elizabeth, we're not going to let her take you," said Thomas.

"Is that what I'm doing? I thought I was writing a story," I said resigned, but with mischief in my eyes, "that's what she thinks anyway and we can use that. If we stick together, and really, she will use anything she can as leverage and you barely know me, I think we can find our way back out...together."

"My teachers always say that teamwork is best," said Clarissa.

"Well those are some pretty smart teachers. As long as we work together we have a good chance."

We would have to come up with a plan and there were still some outlying houses to visit. Roger and Thomas both agreed to ask around those people that they knew just on the off chance that someone had some insight we weren't aware of. We agreed to give each of us a few days to do some canvassing and meet for dinner in town.

Chapter 4

As the morning of our approaching meeting dawned, I was feeling a little overwhelmed and somewhat upset as my further interviews had turned up no new information. I decided that a morning run would help set my mind at ease. My wandering thoughts and emotions led my running track right to the perimeter of the island. I ran along and stopped briefly to survey the layout of the land and any possible access between the island and the stretch of land that surrounds it. About ten feet ahead of me there was a brief section of grass and sand before the water engulfed everything. I stepped off of the pavement and onto the small embankment determined to see how far I could go before the water got too deep.

I felt a new electricity in the air, the same way I always felt when I was getting ready to enjoy a good thunderstorm. I looked up and saw the clouds coming in. They hadn't been there only a moment ago, but they were coming on strong. It was moving of its own will and the entire area above the island alone became engulfed in gloom. I looked across and saw the door begin to open in the center of the island.

I was being pulled; I started to feel my feet rise from the ground as though I was going to walk forward though I had no conscious intention of doing so. My thoughts began to head in that direction. I could take care of this whole thing and end it for all of us. I wouldn't have to risk anything more happening to Clarissa and I could bring Thomas's sister and mother home. I didn't need to get attached to Thomas and if I ended this thing on my own, I could write my story, go home to Boston, and move on with my life. I wouldn't come out of this on the losing end.

I looked across into my mother's piercing eyes and thought better of it, "Not yet. I'll come when I'm ready."

I somehow put myself back on my own two feet and the clouds dissipated quickly. The greenery surrounding the island again began to dance back and forth in the dainty breeze.

I began running again and completed my circuit of the island. There was one area that seemed to be pretty shallow. I took off my shoes and socks and walked into the water, allowing the chilly waves to cool my overheated body. A little at a time, I walked further until I was chest deep in water. I tried to assess the remaining distance to the shores of the island and decided it was a short enough distance to swim. This could be my starting point.

It certainly seems like I'm the main player here and there really was no need for anyone else to put themselves in harm's way. Still, this was not the time for rash decisions. I had affairs to set in order, phone calls to make, and subtle, sneaky goodbyes to say just in case things didn't go as planned. I backtracked out of the water and dried myself as I headed back to my room.

To my surprise, when I opened the door and walked in the room I found Thomas inside waiting for me. This unnerved me. I couldn't say I was exactly happy that he'd broken into my hotel room.

"How'd you get in here?" I asked.

"I know the right people," he smiled at me, "really though, I thought I'd come back to see what you were able to find today and arrived just as you were setting out on your run. I figured I wouldn't bother you and stayed here to wait instead."

"Wasn't the plan for all of us to meet for dinner at six? You can't wait until then?" I was a little annoyed at being caught post run, looking like a drowned rat, "Why are you really here?"

"I can't resist your charms," he flirted, "do you always sweat so profusely when you run?"

"No, I got caught in a storm," I corrected him and noticed his alarm, "no worries, all is good, just my mother trying to mess with me. But if I wanted guests earlier, I would have called."

I was attracted to Thomas, and clearly he'd noticed, but I wasn't comfortable with him just showing up and finding a way in.

"O-kay," he said, drawing out the word, "I guess maybe I misjudged. I'll get out of your way. I guess I'll see you at the restaurant… but am I mistaken, or haven't we been flirting?"

I looked at him as he clung to the doorway looking adorable, but my good sense guarded my weakness, "Guess you were mistaken. See you at dinner."

He left and I had to sit down. I couldn't help but think about him. Yes we'd been flirting, but I didn't have room for feelings right now. After what happened on my run, it was clear I had to keep a clear head if we were going to come out of this on the winning side. I did like Thomas, and yes, he liked me too, but it was just more than I could deal with at the moment. I may not come out of this victorious; I may not come out of this at all. I couldn't get any deeper into whatever this was.

I took a long shower and let the warm water drain my body of its current stresses. I'd made a decision to go alone and once I was showered, dressed in my favorite jeans and T-shirt, and talked to a few people, I'd be on my way. I began my round of phone calls. An hour or so later I'd talked with my father, brother, and workplace. I told them that I'd been looking into this island and was investigating further, that it had led to some interesting facts that I was trying to get to the bottom of. Without sending up any red flags, I told them all that I loved them and planned on seeing them soon. I left a note for Thomas at the front desk thanking him for his help, promising to do all I could to bring his family home, and telling him to stay out of it. I put my things neatly into my suitcase and placed the suitcase on the bed as if I were checking out and left the room.

I was reaching for the door when I heard a light tapping on the other side. I took a deep breath knowing, intuitively, who would be on the other side, and opened it. Thomas was standing there looking like he'd been rehearsing what he was going to say. He looked at the state of my room, at my outfit, and the fact that I had a small backpack in my hands, and deduced what I'd been about to do.

"Where are you going with that? It's almost six."

"I thought we'd agreed to meet at the restaurant. First you break into my room and now you're here again. Are you checking up on me? Am I on Thomas watch?" I said, exasperated.

"Do you need to be?" he asked, eyeing the packed suitcase on the bed, "Just like that? You were going to disappear? You were going to go without so much as goodbye? Did you even think about how Clarissa would take your disappearance?" There was no mistaking the hurt in his voice.

I hadn't thought about that. I figured I'd be back before she had a chance to get too upset, but I had no real way of knowing that.

"I left a note for you; I figured you'd be the one to come looking for me. I have every intention of coming back. No, I guess I didn't think how Clarissa would take it, but then, I figure I'll be back before she can even notice.

"I'm really sorry that this happened to you and your family, but this is about me and her. I can't let you lose more of your family, or lose them permanently because of her. I'm going to handle this. Now let me go."

"You don't know that this is all your mother's doing. I can see that the hurt between the two of you goes both ways, and I think it's blinding you to a few things. How do you know that she's manipulating everything? Have you noticed that she's mentioned Dominic twice now.

That's the guy from your dreams, right? She also mentioned others and so has my dad. And, I don't want you to go alone. I know I'm not crazy, I know that we've been enjoying being in each other's company. At the very least, let me go with you."

There was a pleading tone in his voice. I was very tempted to give in and let him come with me. Yes we'd been flirting, I'd already admitted that much to myself, but it was more than that. I felt very comfortable with him somehow. I wanted to be selfish and bring him along; to not feel the fear of walking into this alone, but I couldn't. If I did that, she'd have another person that she could hold against me. She has already made it clear that she's willing to do that.

"I can't let you do that. I have no idea what's going to happen when I get over there and look what she's willing to do to Clarissa. Your father has already lost his wife and daughter. I'm not ready to let him lose his son too. You stay here and tell Roger and Clarissa what I'm doing. Wait at the restaurant and I'll be back before you know it. If I'm not, you can probably guess what happened," I moved closer and past him intent on heading for the island.

"I'll just come after you," he called toward my back, "You'll have help whether you like it or not."

"Why do you even care?" I turned to face him, "Whether we're there together or not, it's me that is going to allow your sister and mother to come back. That point has been made very clear."

"I can see that subtlety is not going to work with you. In case you've missed it with all of the flirting, I care about you. I know it's only been a few days. I know it sounds dramatic and over the top, but I'm not ready to let you walk out of my life when I've just found you. If I can't make it any more clear to you, maybe this will," he took a step toward me, saw that I wasn't going to protest, ducked his head to my level and pressed his lips to mine. He let his hands drift down my back and deepened the kiss. After a long minute he pulled away, looked at me and said, "Do you get it now?"

"Yes, but don't you see, this is why I have to do this alone…"

I trailed off as Thomas stopped my words with another urgent kiss.

"No, this is exactly why we're doing this together. Safety in numbers, right?" He smiled at the fact that I'd raised no objection to his kisses, "So, I guess we were flirting, huh?"

My resolve was gone. I couldn't deny that I was terrified of going to that island alone and I no longer wanted to.

"I hope you're a good swimmer," I said with a smile, "Let's go eat. I'm starving. And yes, we were flirting."

"What do you mean good swimmer?" Thomas asked as he took my hand and led me to his car.

"I was doing some reconnaissance today when I went running. I went into the water and found that it was pretty shallow for quite a distance. The rest is swimmable," I said.

"Sounds like fun and all, but I have a better idea, let's take my boat."

"I didn't know you had a boat," I replied.

"See how much help I can be? And what happens when you don't try to take on everything all by yourself?" Thomas said and laughed.

"Okay big shot, help me get to dinner."

We sped away in his Jeep and were at the restaurant in less than ten minutes. We joined Thomas's family who were already there waiting for us. As we sat eating, talking, and sharing with Roger what we'd decided, Clarissa dropped another bomb on us. She told us that her mommy had brought her the door in her dreams once and she went through. She said she was there for a little while and it was just like being on an island. But she always came back before she woke up. My interests were piqued.

"Clarissa, why didn't you tell me you could go in and come back?" I asked.

"My Mommy told me not to. I wasn't supposed to tell you that I can come and go through the door. I'm also not supposed to tell you that your mommy wants to come home too, or at least she used to. She can't do it by herself either," said Clarissa.

I was starting to get used to feeling shocked when Clarissa had things to say. However, I was exceedingly glad that she was ready and open to share. After what happened to her earlier, she was seeming a little more herself.

As we emptied our plates we discussed the specifics. We decided that we'd make our entrance on the island tomorrow morning. Roger and Clarissa would come along to help us put the boat in the water and see us off, but they'd stay on the main island for now. Clarissa was a little put out that she couldn't come with us, but Roger didn't mind at all. He stifled her protests with a promise of ice cream.

It was a sketchy plan at best, but at least it was something. After a bold glass of red wine and a custard dessert, we decided to call it a night.

"I really meant what I said before you know, about caring about you," Thomas said as we got into his Jeep and sat for a moment, "But why did you act so strange when I met up with you at the hotel earlier? It seemed like we were getting along so well until then; well, except at very first when I will admit I was pretty rude. But it seemed like all of a sudden, out of nowhere, you were hurrying out and pushing me away as if I'd done something wrong," said Thomas.

"I had a million thoughts jumbling through my head at the time; I just wasn't sure how I was going to proceed with this. Plus, you'd just broken into my room; that was slightly alarming even though I knew why you did it. When you called me on the flirting I wanted to tell you then how attracted I was but I was afraid of how all of this might turn out.

"When I first went for the run and ended up at the island, I was trying to clear my head, but the clouds started to gather. I decided then that I was going to do this and almost hopped right into the water to swim to the shores of the island. I decided though, that I better set my affairs in order first, you know, just in case. Then you found me, just as I was getting ready to go. I just wasn't expecting it, that's all," I said.

"Well, I'm glad I caught you in time," he said as he took my hand and wove his fingers through mine, "There's something you should know about me, totally unrelated to mysterious islands and family that has disappeared. If I didn't think that something could come out of this, I wouldn't have even bothered," he pondered quietly, continued, "What would you think about coming home with me rather than back to the hotel tonight?"

"I think that's a very practical suggestion since we'll be setting out so early tomorrow," I smiled.

He grabbed my other hand at that moment and bent down to kiss me again. There was something about him; something I knew was worth whatever we were getting into. His kisses were unyielding but soft. His arms held me close, and then drifted down my back. He pulled back and revealed a toothy smile.

"Let's go," he said, "we'll stop by your room and get your stuff."

"Umm, not necessary, remember?"

"Oh that's right, you were all packed up and ready, weren't you?"

"Yep, and I threw that bag in your Jeep so I'm all set."

We drove for fifteen minutes before arriving at his place. I was excited to spend some time with him and not think about what we'd be facing tomorrow.

When we got there, Thomas went to his little kitchen to open a bottle of wine. I was sitting on the large, brown microfiber couch in the small living room that made up most of his studio apartment. I realized this couch must double as his bed. Then I noticed the tell-tale folding cushion that made up the futon bed when needed. The walls were a sea of white. If I didn't already know that he'd been here longer I'd say that it looked like he'd just gotten here, or was getting ready to leave. There was no sign of him 'settling' here.

"Do you really think that's wise?" I asked, referring to the bottle of wine, "We need to be sharp tomorrow."

"A glass won't hurt though, will it?" he asked with a seductive smile.

"I suppose not."

We sat on his couch and drank wine and talked. He told me more about his mother, sister, and their family history. I found out that they had always lived in Boston until Roger's big story/retirement idea. He said that like his sister, he'd always wanted to return to Boston, but didn't feel right leaving his Dad and niece. He didn't want to be away from them, but he felt stuck here. It was great at first because it was new and it was beautiful, but home had always been Boston.

"What about you?" Thomas asked quietly, "you know so much about my family and our past. I feel like I barely know you at all."

"Well, you know all about my mother and the accident. My father, brother, and I struggled emotionally for a few years after that. My dad really did love her. She wasn't really a bad person. All she wanted was for me to be more girly, but my natural inclinations were more aligned to the things that my dad enjoyed…sports, outdoorsy adventures."

"If you ask me, you've turned into quite a beautiful woman. She should be proud of that, right?" Thomas said.

"You would think, but who knows. It still seems like that same problem is lying with her wherever it is she is all these years later.

"Well, my brother went off to college, got his degree, got married, and is now living happily in Charlestown. He has a little boy that's three years old and he loves to come and see his Aunt Lily, my brother calls me that. My dad never remarried. He never really got over her. He's a retired school teacher. He gardens in his free time.

"I, obviously, became a writer and work at a small publication out of Boston that would desperately like to become a large publication out of Boston. I've been working there now for a few years; I started when I was still in college working summers and any other free time I had. I hope eventually to become a columnist or something like that for a nationwide newspaper and that's pretty much why I took this assignment."

We continued sharing stories into the night until the wine ran out and made us tired. We dozed off, him lying against the pillow at the end of the couch, me lying against his chest. It felt warm and safe like an evening in front of the fire. We fell asleep holding each other. When we woke, we saw the sun beginning its trip above the horizon. It was time.

Chapter 5

We both decided that an earlier start would be better. With a little luck, we would get there in the morning and be back in enough time to enjoy a welcome home lunch with Thomas's reunited family.

"I'm going to go out and get the boat ready to go, you enjoy the rest of your breakfast," said Thomas as he kissed the tip of my nose.

I sat with my bowl full of cornflakes and stared out the window at the bright, yellow sun. My eyes were on the sky, but my mind drifted toward simpler times. I thought about my mother and father when I was a little girl. They were happy together. They would have continued to be happy together. I was pretty young, but I remember times that they would laugh together, trips to the beach where we'd enjoy a day on the sand and in the water, and even a vacation that plays on the edges of my memory. A trip to Disney World where I was still young enough to be pushed in a stroller. I remember belly laughs and getting on rides. I remember being in awe of the parades and smiling at my parents who'd smile back at me. Many years later, Dad was missing Mom, but doing the best he could; my brother was a teenager and I was on the brink of being a teenager myself, twelve years old. It wasn't perfect, but it was a happy home.

My thoughts shifted to the accident. I wondered what had happened to her as her grip could no longer cling to that dangling car all those years ago. I began to question if she truly was still here with us; what was holding her there, wherever it is that she's gone? Clarissa said my mother couldn't come home either, that she was stuck there, but that she no longer acted like she wanted to come back. Why couldn't she come back? Why did she suddenly not want to? I remembered my dream again and how Thomas pointed out that there could still be a lot that we didn't know…like who Dominic was. The Renzen family was real; Dominic must be real too.

"Earth to Elizabeth, are you still here?" I heard from a distance.

I shook my head and looked at Thomas. His face was three inches from mine and it was showing concern. His charming blue eyes were worried and I realized he thought I crossed over again or had been taken like Clarissa had.

"Yeah, I'm still here. Sorry to scare you. I was thinking about the past and about the things Clarissa has told me about my mother.

"I thought something happened again. I thought she came here and had you in her grip."

"I guess it just hit me how much this was affecting me. I'm getting a little scared about what we're about to walk into," I admitted.

"Me too, so what do they say…no time like the present…boat's ready. You ready to go?"

"Yep, let's get to it," I replied.

I got up from my seat, took my half-eaten bowl of soggy flakes and dumped the contents into the garbage. I followed him out the back door and got into the open door of the Jeep with Thomas waiting just outside of it. I was in the process of buckling my seatbelt when I looked up and noticed that Thomas was still standing next to the door, "You don't have to do this, you know. It really isn't worth your life," he was more serious than I'd ever seen him.

While there was a small part of me that wanted to book it back to Boston and forget any of this had ever happened, it was much too late for that. This was real. Thomas was real, and my mother…well, maybe she was real maybe not, the jury was still out on that one. But I couldn't avoid it and I couldn't run from it. I wouldn't let Clarissa suffer because of it either. As she and Roger came into view, I knew that I wouldn't let her down.

"Maybe," I said, "but that little girl has a much longer life to look forward to and I want her to be able to enjoy every moment of it. Besides, you saw what happened to her when I made my mother mad. I'm not going to let her get hurt."

With that, Thomas closed my door, spoke with Roger briefly, got in and started the engine. He looked at me once, concerned, then threw the Jeep in gear and we were off. Roger and Clarissa were right behind us. The feel of electricity in the air intensified as we came closer to the island. There were no clouds in the sky, yet, but I could feel her. That's what I came to associate these feelings with, the arrival of my mother. I could feel the strength that she possessed. It was oppressive, as though she was already trying to restrain me. Thomas pulled up to the island pointed far out to the east where the inevitable clouds were gathering. Roger pulled up next to us and we all got out to prepare ourselves for the journey.

Thomas started, "It's coming, this may be a bumpy ride in," we both noticed the water getting choppy as the wind began to pick up.

"Don't kid yourself, she's coming and she's going to do whatever is possible to make this difficult for us." I responded as the clouds came in amazingly fast, blocking out the bright sun.

Thomas turned the Jeep around and began easing the boat into the waiting water. Roger waded in while Clarissa waited on the shore. By the time the boat was floating and we were disconnecting it from the trailer, the wind whipped and lashed at us. I held onto the boat while Thomas pulled the Jeep and trailer from the water. He ran back and after some close capsizing calls, we both managed to board. We were already soaked from head to toe when the rain began to fall. The fierce wind continued and as the engine roared, the waves became threatening.

Roger ran to Clarissa, picked her up, and brought her back to us to say goodbye.

"Good luck you two," said Roger, "looks like this isn't going to be easy."

"Nothing worthwhile ever is," I replied with a smile, "Clarissa, honey, I will bring them back to you."

"I know," she said as she cringed away from the rain. Suddenly she threw her arms around me and hugged tight, "I love you."

I was shocked by those words, but returned the hug and the sentiment. I felt like it may be true.

We said our final goodbyes as we navigated our way toward the island. Before long, I saw the door appear. Lightning flashed and there it was. We were feet from the opposite shore when the engine stopped and I remembered how my moped had died just as abruptly. She came to the threshold of the door and I saw Rosalyn, my mother, the woman from my dreams, again. She opened her arms as if she were getting ready to hug me.

"Welcome home, Lily. I've been waiting for you," she spoke the words that were dripping with contempt, from the shore.

"This is not my home. I hope you haven't planned on me staying." I shouted at her.

"As you wish, Elizabeth; I really thought we'd be able to work this out," she said and turned into the nothingness behind her.

We pulled out the oars and paddled the boat forward. The storm grew even fiercer in intensity. The waves were almost impossible to navigate. Water kept flowing into the boat and we kept shoveling it out as fast as we could. Thomas did the best he could to stay on top of the waves and it seemed like we were making it when lightning flashed threateningly in the sky.

"We better get there right now. That lightning comes down on us and this is all over," said Thomas.

"Why would she want this?" I shouted to no one in particular. Then I had an epiphany. She wanted me on the island, not Thomas. He was in more danger than I first realized. Why didn't she just bring his mom and sister then and make a trade? She must need all of us or didn't think he'd be willing to trade, "she wants us to turn away, or more accurately, she wants you out of the picture. Whatever is happening, she needs me over there, just me, alone."

Thomas looked at me as he processed my words. The hard set look in those gorgeous blue eyes had just the right amount of defiance to ease my worried mind. He had doubled his determination to make this happen. With a final push we overcame the waves and made the shore. The lightning only appeared once or twice more and stayed in the sky. We pulled the boat well onto the land so that it would be there when we returned.

The island itself was calm as we took in our surroundings, despite the storm that had just erupted. The sand was wet and cool and the sun began to peek through the now receding clouds. In the distance I saw what looked to be a new mass of gray forming and sparking every now and again. I figured it wouldn't be too long and we could finally walk through the door and solve this mystery.

The island didn't look too different from what I'd imagined. There was sand beneath my feet, warming up now under the glare of the newly freed sun; tall trees that seemed to clump together as though they were family, and the lulling sound of the waves breaking against the shore. I didn't hear birds in the distance and got no sense of other animals that may be brushing through the trees. It was Thomas and I on this island, all alone.

"It's quiet, unbelievable after such a storm. You would think that things would start to come to life again, eerie." Thomas's words echoed my thoughts.

"That's just what I was thinking, too quiet. Should we explore a little before the blanket of clouds is upon us?" I asked as I looked toward the sky.

"Yeah, maybe, at least then sitting in this spot won't seem so creepy."

We got up and headed for the trees. We welcomed the chance to let the air dry us a little bit, at least for the time being. We entered a small path leading into a dense patch of trees. We decided to make that our road map, keeping to the trail so that we always knew where we'd come from. We wanted to make sure that we didn't miss the door when it opens this time.

It was your typical hike through nature with the exception of the lack of living creatures. There were oak and walnut trees as well as other species that I couldn't identify. The low growing bushes were leafy and some had stickers; others had mysterious berries, the kind that you were taught to avoid if you'd spent any time in nature as a kid. We avoided touching any of it until we got a better feel for what was going on in this place. We came to a clearing and stopped at the edge to get a better view. As we entered I began to hear something that made me freeze where I stood.

"Lil, Lily, where are you? Mom said you were coming. Rhonda and Sheldon need me, Lil. I want to go home," came the calls in the voice of my older brother.

"No, please say you are not this selfish," I called out to the air as I turned and dragged Thomas with me. The clouds had come again and the rain had begun to fall.

At a pace that was slightly slower than a run, a confused Thomas and I went back along the path until we came out from the trees and I could see her standing by her doorway. I saw her, but not my brother Aaron.

"I need to go home, Lil," came a mocking voice that sounded exactly like my brother, "Pretty good, aren't I?"

"No, not really, pretty ridiculous," my face red with anger, "it's time for this to end. That's what I'm here for."

"We'll see," she said simply and turned to disappear, but then thought better of it. She twisted back to look at me and continued, "I am powerful over here Lil; I have people that depend on me like you never did. They look up to me. Only I know where Rose and Madeline are."

She disappeared then. My eyes met Thomas's and I was a little surprised to find them worried again.

"We have to find them. You first?" he asked as he gestured towards the door that still stood as if it were waiting for us. I wondered just how long it would stand there, then decided not to chance it.

I grabbed his hand and we took a step forward together, "we're in this one together, remember?"

"Yeah, that's right," he smiled at me and I could feel the quick pace of his pulse. Oddly, I felt ready for this.

As we left our world and entered the new one, the first thing that both of us did was to turn our heads and look behind us. It was almost as if we hadn't gone through any doorway at all. Everything looked the same. As we crossed the threshold there was a shot of cool air and my ears popped a few times. Other than that we couldn't tell we'd gone any-

where. I saw the outline of the door and a shimmering effect that made
the doorway itself seem to dance slightly, but when I turned back I saw
the same part of the island that I'd just been looking at.

I figured Rosalyn would be standing on the other side of the door
waiting for us to come through, but she was gone. She was nowhere to
be seen.

"Is this a trick? Have we left?" I asked.

"I'm not sure. I felt something change as we walked through, but I
can't explain it. It was as though I was going up in a plane, but with cool
air passing through my body, then we crossed and I felt the same as I did
before we crossed through so I know something happened, but I'm not
sure what."

I turned again and saw the outline of the door was still there. I took
a few steps toward it. I stretched out my hand toward the threshold and
found that it would go no further than the edge. Suddenly, the shimmering opening disappeared.

"Listen," said Thomas, "hear that?"

"The birds," I responded, "they're all over here. How weird."

"Yeah, really weird. The trees look the same and so does the sand. I
wonder what draws the birds here, hmm…" Thomas drifted in thought.

"Food, of course; look," I said as I watched birds flit from tree to tree
and gather berries that hadn't been present on the other side.

As I looked more closely, I started to notice other differences as well.
Not only were there birds here, there were also people. I was shocked to
see actual people starting to come out of the shrubbery. They were staring at us as if we were aliens from another planet rather than two more
people coming through the door. The one that must have been elected
"speaker" walked toward me with fear in her sharp green eyes. She must
be in her mid to late thirties. She had short, brown and curly hair that fell
graciously along the lines of her face.

"Who are you? How did you come here without her?" She asked.

"Who is 'she'?" I wasn't sure how much I wanted to reveal just yet.

"Her, Rosalyn, the leader of our community. The one that teaches us
to be who we really are," she spoke as if I were the one that wasn't quite
right.

"What is your name? How have you come here and how long have
you been?" I began.

"I am Theresa. I don't know how long I've been here," she said
sounding defeated, "I couldn't count the time after I'd been here a few
weeks. Our watches stopped working soon after we arrived and there

is no cell service wherever this is that we are. So there's no real way to keep track of time.

"I was a reporter sent here to find a story and also to look for some other reporters who hadn't come back. I had spent some time getting a little bit of information but it seemed that there were dead ends everywhere I looked. Finally I came over to the island itself to see what I could find and didn't find anything more. I was about to give up and head for home when the storm struck and I've been here ever since. But when I came through, Rosalyn was waiting for me and made this place sound so great that I didn't even attempt to leave for quite some time. By the time I figured out what this really was, it was too late. I haven't been able to find my way back," she finished with a sad smile.

She looked utterly defeated. There was no sparkle in her eyes; she had given up hope of going home. If she was the most recent to cross over and she was already this defeated, the others would likely feel the same if not worse.

"I am Elizabeth and this is Thomas. We have come to help; to try to get everyone out. We're confused though and I'm not sure you can help. We thought Rosalyn would be waiting on the other side of the door when we arrived. She's been waiting for us to come so I'm very surprised she's not here gloating that I've crossed over. Is it possible that she doesn't know yet that I'm here. We saw her on the island as we struggled to get to shore. She spoke to us. She knew, at least then, that we were coming. How could she have vanished and not realized we'd be here in minutes?"

"She must have been using one of the new tricks that Dominic has taught her. Astral projection. She's been bragging about it for weeks. She can make a version of herself appear and apparently this image looks very real, but she's not actually there at the time. If that's what she was doing, it makes sense that she's not here now. She loves using her new toy, but it knocks her out. She likely was asleep before you even made the shore. She will be here soon though, I'm sure of it." Theresa explained.

"Who's Dominic? How does this projection thing work? Is she conscious when she sends herself out?" I asked her as another one of the flashes from my dreams almost made my knees buckle.

"He brings the storms," she explained, "we don't ever see him come, but he has come to us from time to time when he needs something. The projection, like I said, is an image of her, but yes she's conscious at the time so she's aware of what she's saying and doing."

"Wow, she can do that? I have seen the projected image a few times lately. How does Dominic bring the storms?"

"We're not allowed to know that," said Theresa suddenly hedging, "we're not even supposed to know much about him."

"Well," I said, reaching for a new topic, Dominic was clearly off limits, "I suppose we can work her not knowing that we're here yet to our advantage. If she doesn't know we're here, we can hide from her for a while and figure things out. That is," my eyes met Theresa's, "unless you plan to turn us in?"

"Our main objective is to try to get off of this island and go back to our lives. Somehow that witch has been able to make our loved ones forget us. That's why there hasn't been too much news about ten...well, I guess twelve now people that have gone missing in the same location over a period of five years."

I turned to Theresa and asked, "What has she done to you here? Why don't you overthrow her? There's a lot more of you than there are of her."

"She brought us through the gate. She promised that things would be better than before; that we'd live a happier life. See, she used to come back and forth from the island. We'd meet her and get close. She always wanted to know the reporters and how happy we were in our lives. Those that were pretty content were left alone, but those of us that were fed up and didn't have too many ties in our personal lives, one at a time, were taken. She would set it up with our bosses telling us all the time that she was going to take us to a retreat where we could hone our craft and gain an audienceship and by the time we returned from our "trip", they would see our value and allow us the creative freedom that we all wanted.

"Our bosses bought into it, paid their outrageous fee, and then once they had us here, they'd go back over and erase us from the memory of anyone that knew where we were. And then she and Dominic have simply used us for our connections to the outer world and to help build their empire here on the island. But she hasn't brought anyone over since the mother/daughter pair that they made their personal project. That's why we were so surprised to see you. Every time they planned on bringing someone new we'd know about it because we'd have to build their hut and gather food and supplies for their arrival."

"How have you figured all of this out? If she has mind controlling powers, wouldn't she want you to stay in the dark?"

"Her 'treatments' aren't as effective as they once were, but she doesn't know that. We listen a lot when she takes us to her home."

"What treatments?"

"Treatment is not a pleasant experience, let's just say Rosalyn knows a lot about pressure points in the human body and how they can be used to cause pain. It's her way of making you more amenable to the way of living here while also blotting out your own memories until all you know is life on the island…at least for a while. But once you begin gaining control of your mind again, it's too late. You no longer have any power to fight against her. By then you've been starved and tortured and it's clear that if you want to live, you have to get with the program. If we are caught doing things for ourselves like trying to grow food or allow her to know that some of our own memories are coming back, that person is taken away and given treatment again until that person is again completely compliant. It took us a few painful situations to realize that we should keep to ourselves anything we're doing to try to better our own situation."

"So you haven't entirely given up?" I asked.

"Not entirely," Theresa admitted though fear was still clear in her eyes.

"Relax Theresa, we're on the same side. I'm not going to say a word," I said.

"Okay, I'll try to relax," she said, but the way she kept looking all around told me otherwise.

"That's fair. Are you the leader of this group, then? Do the others look to you for help?" I asked.

"They come to me for help with their problems. I've had some luck talking to Rosalyn in the past so they think that I can do better for all of us," her eyes darted again, "And we better get moving, I'm sure Rosalyn knows you're here by now. Her naps don't usually last long. Let's get among the others."

As I met the other captives, I found it was absolute. Every person that she brought over that threshold had been a writer. They'd all been here for a story about this mysterious island. They were aware of nothing that happened. They would be standing in one place observing the oncoming freak storm that would happen with no warning, then the next thing they knew, they were in this place. They only knew that they'd find themselves with a place to live, clothes, food, and bare necessities, but with no idea of what they were doing here. I even spied Tony, but noted that he didn't seem to recognize me at all. I remembered the green eyes that he'd had when we met and wondered who all could project?

There were ten of them altogether, as Theresa had stated. Each one was now involved in this little resistance group that was trying to find anything that would allow them to go home. They all looked haggard and worn. Each of them had sores popping up around their mouths. The ones that had been here the longest, Jim and Paul, though Paul came first, were an extremely important part of this little resistance. Those two had been here for the entire five years. The next three came within a month of each other, all working for separate publications. Jerry, Nisa, and Ruth and they'd been on this little island for almost four years. Theresa, Steve, and Rick were all members of the illustrious Boston Globe and have each been here about two and a half years. The last two were Rose and Madeline who, as was explained earlier, never joined the others, but rather were always with Rosalyn, though they did have huts to themselves that they would use only occasionally. They had been there this morning and Rosalyn had come for them and they hadn't been back.

When that news made Thomas stiffen in fear, Theresa reassured him that this was not unusual and those two had always been treated better than the rest. They were fed better, also had rooms in Rosalyn's compound, and were constantly at her side.

"They are important to you?" Theresa guessed.

"Yes," he replied quickly, "Madeline is my sister and Rose is my mother and I have spent the last two years believing them to be dead. Thank you for making me feel better about where they are right now."

I thought it best not to share how I was related to Rosalyn for the moment. I didn't want to risk our tenuous friend leaving us. Instead, I noted that she hadn't said the name Tony, though I saw him when we arrived with the group.

"I met someone in my interview process that called himself Tony who had claimed that he knew about the island. I saw him in the group of people that came forward with you. The interview didn't reveal much, but now I'm wondering if there is no one here named Tony, who I was talking to?"

"Likely you were talking to Dominic. Another little trick of his and something else I'm not supposed to know. He can alter his looks so that he doesn't resemble himself...and that would mean that he was here, among us when you arrived. Rosalyn has to know you're here. I wonder what's keeping her?

Theresa led us on a journey to what passed as her home. We walked along a path that led us into the thick of the forest. With very few words to one another, we zigged and zagged through trees and other green fragrant plants and we finally found the clearing.

At first it seemed to be the same clearing that we'd found in the middle of the woods on the other side, but then I noticed the huts. Theresa guided us quickly through to hers. It was a rustic relic of what must have been a thatch home. Looking at it from the outside made me think of the three little pigs and the first two with their meager huts that couldn't stand up to a strong wind. Theresa explained that these only held up during the storms because they were buried so deeply within the safety of the tall forest trees. On the outside the thatch and mud were thick. They created rudimentary walls for the shelter of their occupants. The main entrance was made from the bark of trees. Someone had sanded the wood and created door handles by taking long pieces of cattail, lacing them through a small opening in the door and tying slip knots on both sides. There were no locks on the doors. If there were windows at all in the huts, they were rudely cut and torn away. There was nothing over them that would lend protection from the elements.

When we entered her home, body odor overtook the olfactory senses quickly. Instinctively, both Thomas and I immediately raised our hand to our noses and tried to turn from Theresa's gaze. We caught each other's eyes beginning to water and knew we couldn't hide it from her.

She looked down at the floor and quietly spoke, "there's no soap for cleaning and waste is starting to pile up near our homes; the water alone will only do so much in the hot summer sun. If you want to go back outside, I'll understand.

Thomas looked at me and we silently agreed this was a friend we wanted to keep.

"No," he said through gritted teeth, "it's okay. We're sure it has to be hard here. What more can you tell us about life here? What do you do all day?"

"When Rosalyn's not here watching our every move, we talk, play games, eat together, some of us even have dates, though they're pretty simple," said Theresa, red-faced.

"Do you remember much about life before you got here?" I asked.

"No, Rosalyn took that from me. When you first get here she makes it a priority for you to forget where you came from. I remember a lot now, like the fact that I was a reporter, and many things from my past, but at first it was almost all gone. What I remember now comes in waves," Theresa said.

"What about when you came? What do you remember about when you first came over?" I asked.

"I don't. I was there, and then I was here, in this house, standing in the center of it wildly looking around. I remember darting out the door, running past the few others that were waiting to make a new friend, and intending to swim back to shore, but I couldn't get past the doorway, no access to the water. When I gave up trying and turned back, Rosalyn showed up and took me to her home. It gets fuzzy after that."

"So somehow she took your entire memory of life before you got here including the process of her taking you?" Thomas asked.

"Yes," Theresa said.

I caught Thomas's eye and saw that he was in as much agony as I was. Neither of us wanted to offend Theresa, but we just couldn't stand it anymore. We excused ourselves acknowledging that we wanted to get some fresh air. This was the truth and Theresa graciously accepted it. I could see the shame in her eyes as we both got up and rushed a little more than was necessary to get outdoors and away from the stench. It was very difficult to stand in there and breathe in the reeking fumes of human sweat, sex, urine, and excrement.

There was a slight breeze which was irresistibly refreshing. We both breathed deep and decided to walk a little away from the hut so that we could talk. Theresa was watching us from inside, but she no longer had the look of doubt on her face.

This ability to project herself was a bit disconcerting. I could understand manipulation of the mind, but how does one send a 'version' of their 'self' to talk to or threaten others. It didn't make any sense. It sounded like Dominic helped Rosalyn do a lot of these things. What was he that he had this kind of power? And where were we if not on the same island we'd come through? I was about to express these concerns to Thomas when I noticed that I'd gotten about five paces ahead of him.

Thomas was staring straight ahead of us. I followed his gaze and realized immediately why he couldn't move. The two women walking toward us were still dressed for a wedding. Madeline's gown had gone from cloudy white to pale, mucky gray. There were several rips in its seams from prolonged wear. Rose's dress had fared no better. As Thomas stood gaping at the approaching figures, a single tear spilled down his cheek. They seemed to have the gait of relatively healthy people. Theresa had been right; these two were given privileged treatment compared to the others.

"It's okay," I said to Thomas, "they're real. They are here. Clarissa has been right all along. Go to them."

"What if they're like Rosalyn? What if they're bitter and angry and don't want to come back? What will I tell Clarissa?" Thomas whispered.

"I don't think so; if Clarissa has been right about everything else so far…I don't think they want to stay here," I said encouragingly and took his hand in mine, "talk to them."

He listened, "Mom?" Thomas's voice was shaky.

"Thomas, is that you?" Shouted the figure from a distance, "Is that really you; but...but you never believed Clarissa."

"I know Mom, I'm so sorry," said Thomas. Tears streaming freely now, he let go of my hand and began to run toward them.

Thomas, Rose, and Madeline were like freight trains headed toward each other. They collided as arms encompassed one another. There were tears all around, including my own. Everything that that little girl has been through has been true. Here was the proof standing right in front of me. Madeline and Rose were now reunited with Thomas after two long years, but what did this mean? Why were they okay while the others suffered? There was still much that needed to be talked about. This is who Thomas needed to be with now. I was beginning to sneak off into the shadows.

"Hey, Elizabeth, where are you going? After all this don't you even want to meet them?"

"Of course I do," I could tell he was offended, "but this is your re-union with your family. I don't want to get in the way."

"Never would you be in the way of anything when it comes to me," said Thomas smiling and taking my hand in his, "Mom, Sis, this is Elizabeth. She's been helping Clarissa, Dad, and I make sense of all this. She's a reporter that was sent here to do a story on this island and it turns out she got much more than she bargained for. We have a ton of questions for you two. Are you able to talk?" He asked, excited now.

"You mean she's the daughter of that woman that holds us here," said Madeline with hardly a glance my way.

"I'm sure you're angry about what's happened to you here, I would be too, but that woman is no more my mother than she is yours. Biological-ly, she did give birth to me, but what she's become is not who she was."

"Elizabeth is the one that convinced all of us to come out here and look for you guys. Don't blame her, Maddy." Thomas said.

She looked at me again and decided she wasn't being fair.

"Sorry," Madeline said, "but it's been awful to be stuck here. To watch Mark walk away from you guys; to watch Clarissa over the last two years knowing I'm not really a part of her life. It's been unbearable."

"You could see all that?" asked Thomas.

"We have been given a window into your lives through Clarissa. She has never once stopped believing that we were coming back, so it was easy to work into her thoughts, both conscious and unconscious. She believed us right away when we told her what had happened. We were always able to check in with her. She told us that Mark had left and that Thomas didn't believe our story.

"I don't blame you, Thomas," she added quickly, "I probably wouldn't have believed it either. But Clarissa seems to be sensitive to thoughts of others; she tends to believe the unbelievable easily and have faith in it. That's why it's been so easy to communicate with her, she didn't resist when we started talking to her. Rosalyn gave us that ability and we've used it to keep her hope alive. That's why she knows so much."

"Rosalyn gave you that ability?" I asked, confused.

"She has a way with the mind. She seems to know how it works and works with it easily. She taught us how to communicate with Clarissa. That's why she's the one who's giving all of the treatments. She knows how to be very convincing," Rose explained, speaking up for the first time.

"It's Rose, right?" I asked politely, "I have spent the last few days getting to know your husband, son, and granddaughter and as I'm sure you've gathered, I've become a bit attached. Roger has told me everything that he was able to regarding the events surrounding the day that you came to this island, but if I could get your perspective, I think it would help."

"Well, if he's told you everything, then he's told you about the argument between himself and Madeline," I nodded my head in confirmation, "but he had no way of knowing what happened after that. I went after her to talk to her and hopefully find a way to make peace between the two. When I found her the storm had already gathered overhead. It was about to start pouring down on us and I was trying to convince Madeline to come back to the bridal tent. She was due to get married shortly and all she kept thinking about was how badly her father's words hurt. After lots of talking and convincing her that her father was truly sorry for what he'd said, we were just about to start walking toward the tent when lightning struck two feet from our noses. At that moment, a door opened and a woman stood there staring at us. I'll never forget her words, they were eerily accurate. She said, 'I know you love him, but we can bring him here.' This was the first of many lies.

"Madeline had seen Roger hurrying toward us. She grabbed my arm and forced me through the doorway. When we arrived on this side I tried to turn around immediately and come back through. I was scared, but Madeline held tightly and leaned in to whisper, 'She told me that this was necessary in order to live a better life.' She went on to tell me that she and Rosalyn had been talking for months. Rosalyn promised her everything she could wish for. She would be able to give Clarissa a stellar childhood if she crossed through the doorway. She would be prepared to attend the finest schools and once she was ready, she'd be allowed to cross back over and make her own successful way in the world. To make a long story short, she was lied to, but convincingly so. My daughter is no fool and I can't pretend to know exactly how she was convinced or if she wasn't just so caught up in the moment that she saw an escape and took it, but she seemed to gain clarity just after we'd gone through the door. The look on her face was like she'd just woken out of a dream.

"I told her that she couldn't trust Rosalyn and her eyes told me she already knew that. We tried to come back through the door, but found it impassable. Rosalyn told us, once we finally turned back to her, that it was only a matter of time before you came here and once you were here, we'd be released to go home. I'm not foolish enough to believe her, but is that what you've come for? Have you come over here to join your mother?" Rose asked.

It made me cringe to think of this deceitful person as my mother, but I couldn't deny the facts.

"I am her daughter, that is true, and I have come here willingly, but not to stay. I came with Thomas and we're here to get everyone out. I am not like her. Whatever happened to her when she got here must have made her like this. I will spare you the details, but I believed my mother to be dead for the last sixteen years up until a few days ago, now I'm not sure what she is. However, having said all of this, before I give up all hope and leave this place without her, I'm going to have to be convinced that there's no way to fix her. I hope I can count on some help in that endeavor," I said, surprising even myself, but thinking of my own father and brother.

"You've got all the support you need," Thomas spoke.

"Of course," said Madeline after a quick glance at Rose, "we wouldn't have any thought of leaving here if you hadn't come. Of course we'll do all we can to help you. I have to warn you though; she is a very cold person. I don't know how she was before, but she is not going to be happy to see that you've come to take her away from her kingdom. She used to talk about making her way back home, but she hasn't brought that up in a long time."

"What does she do to the others when they cross the threshold? We met one named Theresa and she seemed to have only hazy memories about life before coming here. Do you know what that's about?"

"Unfortunately yes, your mother has grown quite angry over time.

When we first arrived here, she was happy to have someone new to share her space with, but she still missed her life. Dominic…I don't know if Theresa knows about him or said anything…but he's the one that brought her here promising her a place of her own and those that she would lead, but she longer for home. She talked to us often of her husband, son, and her unruly daughter," Rose started and Madeline picked up quickly avoiding my reaction to Rose's words.

"When we asked her how she maintained her health all this time, she told us that Dominic allowed her to go to the main island once a month; most times he accompanied her and they would shop for a month's worth of supplies. She would survive off of them until the next trip came around. He was actually very good to her in the beginning.

"She filled her time at first with simple thoughts of survival and ways that she might get back home. When others started arriving on the island, Dominic told her they'd just buy more supplies and that these others could be useful in building her kingdom that he'd promised her so they began to set up huts for them. When she realized that this was all a sham, though, she began to get angry.

"Dominic still hasn't told her everything and that has made her mean to those that had been brought over. She told Dominic that she would either have companions as well as those that she could lead like he'd promised or she would take her own life. He agreed to her demands and the two of them began to plan to get us here. It didn't take her long to realize that there were people in the distance, especially those that were staring back at her; she got the idea to bring them over to this place. She couldn't do it from here to the main island though, they had to be on this small island for it to work. She found the more that she stared, the more that she could break into their conscious thought. Once that was done, and Dominic had gifted her some clairvoyant abilities, it was an easy trip into their thoughts and she could direct those the way that she liked. We were the last people that she pulled through, in addition to those that Dominic pulled over, she specialized in the reporters coming for a story. My Dad was one of those, as I'm sure you've heard by now.

"What Rosalyn didn't like about my mother and I was the fact that we were both independent strong women and she couldn't control us well. Her mind games did not have the effect on us that she'd planned. After a while, she found it was better to keep us close and use us to help keep the others at bay than it was to work against us. She made us a part of her compound giving us a nicer place to live than was planned for us originally. She also fed us more than she has fed the others and with better food.

"I have a theory as to why her treatments aren't working on us though. I have this feeling that Dominic is somehow pulling back from her. She is slowly losing some of the ability that he gifted her and that is also making her angry." Madeline finished.

"Theresa, the woman that we met first, was reluctant to talk about Dominic. She mentioned that they weren't really supposed to know anything about him. Is there anything you can tell us?" I asked.

"Ah Theresa, always saying more than she should," Rose said with a sad smile, "Rosalyn is very protective of him and won't allow anyone to see him more than necessary. We haven't seen him much, but I can tell you that he is the reason that Rosalyn can do what she can. As Madeline said, he's gifted her these abilities."

"What I don't understand is how she gave Roger my necklace. How did she know that I'd be coming here two years later? Back then I hadn't even graduated from college and had no idea where I'd end up. I came close to taking a job in Chicago, but then got offered the job at ECN and decided I'd rather stay close to family."

"Remember," said Rose with perfect knowledge of the necklace I was referring to, "she knows how to alter your perception. She didn't give Roger that necklace two years ago; she only made him think that had happened then."

"But he did have the necklace." I said, confused.

"Yes, he did, and she was the one that gave it to him, but she did that as soon as she found out you'd been assigned to this story, not two years ago. She's very good at working with the mind. She knows more about it than anyone I've ever known whether she's losing some of that power or not. She's very good at what she does."

"What about the others? What has Rosalyn done to them to make them the way they are?" asked Thomas.

"Well, I'm not sure exactly what happens, but when they are brought through the door, they are sort of hypnotized and Rosalyn carts them off to her home. We're not allowed in there during these sessions, so we couldn't tell you exactly what goes on, but when they come out they stammer and seem drunk. They are taken to their new home and we see them again in a day or two when they come around and start adjusting to their surroundings," said Madeline.

"So that's what I have to do," I said, "I have to get in there when she's having one of those sessions and find out what she's doing. That's the only way I can think of to stop her."

"I don't hear any screaming or discomfort when those sessions are going on, so I couldn't think it would be more than mind perception alterations, but we'll see because we're all going in," said Rose.

"You don't have to do that. You've escaped the worst of what she's capable of and she's my mother. If I can stop her, I will, but you have a family; one that's very eager to get back to you," I said.

"So do you," Rose said with a smile, "so let's not argue over something small. You need us and we're going. You don't have to beat yourself up; it's not your fault."

I looked up in the sky and sure enough, another storm was approaching. I couldn't believe there'd be another today. It was coming on strong and fast.

I did not feel her appearance nor did I feel her arms encircle my temples, but I could not mistake her voice, "good job keeping her calm ladies. Thank you for your service. You may take Thomas with you, for now, but I'll want to see him too."

I felt myself losing consciousness as the clouds covered the sky like a blanket.

Chapter 6

When I woke I was lying on my back on a small cot. There were life-less eyeballs staring back down at me. I started from my sleep and sat up quickly. How long had I been sleeping? To whom did these eyes belong? Thomas and I had found Madeline and Rose and we were trading tales of what we knew and I remember the clouds. Right, the clouds had come in fast and I could keep my eyes open. I had been standing, but I staggered and sat heavily on the ground after hearing her voice. I couldn't concentrate on the conversation anymore. Rosalyn had finally caught up to us.

I scanned the room. The cot that I was on was rudimentary. It had been haphazardly thrown together from petrified wood and skins of animals. The eyes that I had seen had once had visions of predators and food all around them until they met with my mother or possibly Dominic. They were now decorating the mattress on which I slept. I did not see any of my companions from earlier in the day.

"They are gone, it is just you and me now," came a disembodied voice through the walls.

"Mother, it was never you and me. You and me was a dream you had along with raising a little show pony that wouldn't be of much use except to be married off to someone that would gain you more wealth or power. This isn't the sixteenth century and no matter what you do to me or my friends, you will not gain the kind of power you truly want."

Oh Elizabeth, have you not seen the puppets that live here by my good graces? They exist because I have spared their lives. You haven't yet figured out that I control everything here? Where are your friends, Elizabeth? Where's your newfound heartthrob? How did you get here? Why don't you ponder that for a while," she responded.

"You're not in control of everything. You wouldn't have any of this without Dominic," I said.

"Yes, dear, how very perceptive you are, but still entirely too believing. The others know nothing of Dominic except that he exists and that's all they've been able to tell you, so don't try to throw me off with any silly little knowledge you've gained from the others here. It will do you no good," she said threateningly.

She had not yet entered the room, but I knew she must be near. I could feel her desire to come at me, to make me pay for being alive for so long. I know that she is a master at mind games. I thought she was playing another of her mind tricks and I could return to where I belonged as I had done in Roger's home, but it was no use.

She had taken me while I slept and brought me to her home. I tried to replay the memory of earlier in the day and stopped when Rose resolved to help me get to the bottom of this. After that I don't really remember. Madeline and Rose had been wrong, or lied.

I took in my surroundings. The room was sectioned off from the rest of the oversized home. Rosalyn's home was like the others, but she must have added on a few times because there was a door attached to the room's opening. I could feel a breeze coming in through the cracks in the door; therefore the room must be on the exterior of the home. There was enough space in here to house a bed and some storage equipment that looked like dressers. The walls were just as they came; pure bark. There was no decor at all. The floor was a simple dirt floor in which you may find the occasional weed pop up.

"You can look all you like, but you're going to have to get through me in order to come out of this house," threatened Rosalyn with a smooth, sure voice.

"Is that what you told the others? That they were confined to quarters and could only go through you? Did you keep telling them and pressing where it hurt until they believed you?" I asked.

"You'll find suppressing things is a powerful way of manipulating others. Half starved and dying of thirst, people will believe just about anything you tell them. Of course, peppering the room with mind numbing serum doesn't hurt either," she said as she entered the room with a devilish grin.

"What do you mean 'I'll find'?" I asked. "You actually believe that you're going to convince me to stay in this loony bin with you and those poor creatures. Your time is done. I'm going back to my life along with the others that you convinced to come over here. You can rot in this place."

"Oh, I think you'll find that hard to do, Elizabeth," came another voice from an outer room.

My mother looked at me and smiled as the door opened. In walked two people that should have surprised me. Instead I found myself laughing hysterically as they came through the door.

"Oh you are good; 'we're going to do this together. We're going to find our way back home,'" I mocked.

Agitated, Rose said, "What are you laughing at? We have the upper hand now. You did us a favor by bringing Thomas here. That's just one more reason for Roger to bring Clarissa here and come over too. Once we're all here, no one will leave. We'll all live here as one big family. You really thought that we were going to plot against Rosalyn? The one that freed us from our imprisoned lives? That is funny."

"Where is Thomas?" I asked, concerned.

"He's in a room a lot like this one. He's learning the value of this place and being with Rosalyn. We are loyal to her and she takes care of us. We are her right and left hand. We do everything for her and in return she spares us the mind games. Madeline is with Thomas right now teaching him that this is the best way for us to live; that the life he had on the other side was empty and lonely. He is better off here with us," said Rose.

At that I leapt up and raced forward only to be mercilessly pulled back by the ropes that were binding me to the bed.

"You bitch," I screamed toward Rosalyn, "I won't even call you mother anymore; even at your worst, you were never this vindictive. You're going to allow them to take the power of free will from Thomas and God knows who else just to keep them here with you? How selfish have you become? What happened to you? Why didn't you die?" I asked.

"Because I'm strong, that's why, stronger than you could believe. I was not the little housewife that I played while at home with your father. I was strong enough to say, 'I'm not going to die' and make the choice to come here. It was offered and I accepted. I was lonely when I first got here, but it wasn't long before nosy people started snooping around. Those nosy people had to pay the price to come be with me, but now they have and I have built a real family. This family comes to me when they need things; they worship me," she explained.

"What loyalty do you have if you have to continuously brainwash others to remain loyal? What kind of attachment do these people feel if they run away and cringe at the mention of your name?" I asked.

"Theresa is a deserter and she would no longer be here if it weren't for the fact that you were coming. She served her purpose. You let your guard down and I was able to take you and Thomas. He will be given back to his family, but you will stay with me, with your family," said Rosalyn.

"Hey Rosalyn," I said with open defiance, "If I was really your family you'd want what was best for me and what would make me happy. This is still the same argument we were having all those years ago. Unbelievable. Don't you dare call me daughter again, you hypocrite. You, Rosalyn, are not my mother. She died several years ago in a tragic car accident. You are an empty shell of a woman with nothing but contempt to keep you going."

"We'll see," she said as she closed the door and walked out followed by Rose and Madeline.

I looked for routes of escape but could find very little. I analyzed the ropes and found that they were little more than scarves. I began to hear painful grunting noises from next door and decided that Thomas's sanity may be on the line. It was time to get out of this room and show my mother what happened to her willful, stubborn little girl now that she's all grown up.

I leapt out of the bed and slipped my unusually small wrists through the holes that bound me to the bed. I pressed up against the wall next to the door to try to see through the cracks. A sliver of light in my room caught my eye. I saw a small crack from the bottom of the walls which went up a few feet. Sunlight was blazing through. If there was a way to surprise the woman who thought she knew it all, this was probably it. I scanned the room for anything that could help me widen that crack without setting off any kind of alarm. There was nothing helpful here. If I was going to burrow out of this dismal room, I'd have to use the strength of my two sets of fingers. I went over to it to see what kind of hold I could get on the wood. Using all of the strength of my hands, I pushed my fingers as far as they would go which wasn't far. The top digits were not bending enough to get a good grip. As I flexed the muscles in my fingers and pulled with all I had, a few small pieces of bark came toward me. With a smile I returned my fingers to their former position. I was now able to push them through to the first knuckle. This was progress. I yanked again and more bark came flying toward me. Chunks of tree landed piecemeal all over the room. I did this over and over as quietly as possible. Within a simple five minutes I had pushed to the outer edges enough to stick my head through and see that there were no guards watching the perimeter of her home.

Before I squeezed myself through the hole I created with fingers that were now sore and streaked with blood, I gathered up as much of the bark as I could. I brought it over with me so that I could try to at least cover some of the hole I made as I went out. It wouldn't take her long to find the hole, but I didn't want to help her.

As luck would have it, Thomas was kept in a room that had a window.

Since the weather was warm, the window was free from any type of covering. Once I'd pushed myself outside and haphazardly repaired the hole I'd made, I carefully stepped around the structure. I reached the window and ducked down just as Rose turned and looked outside. I trembled, fearing that she'd seen something, but then knew she hadn't seen me when there was no alarm raised. I was getting ready to spring inside and grab Thomas and make a run for it when I realized the advantage I had. I was getting the insight that I needed. I was finding out what it was Rosalyn was doing to her captures to "retrain" their way of thought. Granted she was not trying to erase his memory, but she was trying to alter it.

Drifting through the window I heard a melodious voice that couldn't be Rosalyn's but somehow it was, "Thomas, why did you come here?"

"To find my mom and sister," he replied dreamily.

"Good Thomas, no one came along with you. You decided to come all alone so that Clarissa would have a chance to be with her mother again. Right?" Came that sweet voice again.

"Yes…no…I don't know," struggled Thomas as reality and suggestion merged.

"No, Thomas, you do know," she said as he let out a grunt.

I decided to risk a peek. She was physically doing something to him. I had to know what it was. I looked up and quickly ascertained that all attention was on Thomas. He was placed in what looked like a dental chair. He was leaning back though he looked anything but relaxed. His eyes; however, looked far away. He'd been hypnotized. Rosalyn's hand was against his head and her thumb placed strategically just under his right ear. From my brother's years in karate I knew that area held one of the many pressure points and saw how Theresa said Rosalyn would use them. I guess pain is a pretty convincing argument. They had made some progress; he was convinced that he'd come here with the intention of finding and joining his mother and sister, but I turned out to be a wrench in the works.

Though it took every ounce of self restraint I had to watch this awful treatment, I took a minute to fully assess the situation. Again I took note of the hypnosis and Thomas. His eyes were not darting all around looking for a way out as mine had been. They were stark still as though there was something of great interest about two feet in front of his nose. I realized that my mother must have become a gifted hypnotist in her time here.

As I was taking all of this in I saw her ask again if he had come alone only for him to stumble over the answer. I watched as she took her thumb and pressed hard. Madeline stood next to him trying to hide the anguished expression in her eyes. He grunted again. As he did that I noticed something out of the corner of my eye.

He wasn't staring straight ahead into nothing, he was staring straight at me; and he winked. I couldn't believe it; he was allowing this to happen to him.

I sunk down and sat on the lush grass that surrounded the little room. I realized he must be doing this because he knew they wouldn't really hurt him and we needed to know what she was doing to people. The afternoon sun was hot on my back so I shifted further into the shade of the shrubbery. In doing so, I noticed movement nearby. I turned just in time to see movement about ten feet away and heard the "psst" sound. I could hardly believe my eyes when I saw Theresa appear from the trees surrounding Rosalyn's home.

"What are you doing here?" I whispered as I drew nearer to her.

"Be quiet and come here. They're going to notice you're missing and Thomas is not going to get help if you make a lot of noise," she said, annoyed.

I stayed in my crouch and continued my steps until I met her.

"I just saw him in there and he winked at me, he's not really under her spell. He's faking it so that he can find out what she's doing. I was about to break in there and free him when you came along."

"Glad I made it," said Theresa, "it's not that easy to run in there. She can get to you. I will help you get him out, and then we'll go back to a place I know…oh, and it's not as bad as you think, they're not really bad, just making her believe that they are, Madeline and Rose I mean."

"How did I get here?" I asked, contradicting her claim.

"They didn't betray you. Rosalyn was coming, so they allowed her to hypnotize you and take you away; they knew they'd be following," she explained.

"But I don't remember even seeing her. Wouldn't I remember that much?" I was confused.

"Madeline and Rosalyn have this silent mind connection," began Theresa, reminding me immediately of Clarissa, "so when Rosalyn told Madeline that she was coming for you, Madeline convinced her it would be best if you ended up in the compound not knowing how you got there…there'd be no fighting. It sounds bad, I know, but she knew this was the best way to protect you. Rosalyn was coming anyway."

I was still very confused. For now it seemed I was safe and that was something. Theresa wouldn't have come just to turn me back in. But soon the alarm would be raised when they realized I'd gone missing.

"Well, for now, I'm glad you're here, but how strong can she be if you're able to overcome her training methods and Thomas is able to fake his way through his?" I asked.

"Stronger than you think," she responded quickly and seriously, "I can work around her because I've been here longer. The human brain is much more powerful than you realize and it puts up its own defenses when it comes under attack. What she's doing is only 'convincing' to the brain for so long. Eventually it stops listening to the manipulation and memories come back. I don't have all of mine back yet, as I've told you, but it is getting clearer every day. We're all getting stronger mentally but she keeps us in such poor physical shape that there's not much we can do to fight against her. With you and Thomas here, it's a different story. You have full use of all of your faculties and if we get to Thomas in time, he will too."

"So how do we break Thomas out? How much more will he be able to resist?"

"If he's smart, which I get the feeling he is, he won't resist. He'll convince them that he's been 'fixed' and he'll walk out of there shortly and come looking for us. Let's go see what's happening there now. I've seen her work, she wastes no time."

We crept back up to the outside window just as she finished, ".... good Thomas, you're making progress. You've come here to be with your mother and sister and soon your father and niece will join us too. You go on and find your room. I'll be there shortly to check on you," she turned to Madeline and Rose and said, "I need to talk with both of you; I still need your help today."

Thomas left the room and I decided to stay under the window for another minute.

"You two are going to have to help me keep Thomas convinced. He seems to have really taken to my daughter. She's going to be harder to break. She was always stubborn and never really saw things my way. She will resist more than he did..."

I realized that they were coming for me next and decided that I better get out of there before they found out I was missing. I crouched below the window and moved along the side of the house. I quickly disappeared into the foliage of the surrounding trees where Theresa was waiting for me with Thomas.

I ran into Thomas's waiting arms and he encompassed me. I looked him over and he looked to be okay. We found a safe retreat since our disappearances would soon be discovered. We could not go back to Theresa's. Rosalyn would be sure to come there. Theresa convinced us that of the others, there was one that Rosalyn had no idea had turned on her. She always kept quiet and did as she was told.

"Are you trying to get me in trouble?" Shauna asked.

"No," responded Theresa as we stood outside Shauna's hut, "we just need a place to talk and didn't know where else may be safe. She's going to be frantically searching for these two. We won't be here long."

Thomas told us everything that had happened since he'd been taken into that room. Rosalyn did a lot of talking while they thought Thomas was hypnotized. She made it well known that she needed something or someone from Rose and Madeline and that was how they were getting the treatment they were. Once Roger and Clarissa had been brought over, all bets would be off.

When Thomas finished, we asked him if they'd hurt him badly. He assured us that because of who he was, they wouldn't hurt him too severely. They were trying to convince him that I did not exist and that he was only here to be with his family. He kept up a pretense of resisting for a while because he was worried if he broke too soon they'd see right through him, but eventually he said he had come alone. That's when they left him alone and let him go. There was a room set aside for him somewhere, but he never went to it. As soon as he came out the door Theresa saw him and called him over.

Theresa and I filled in the blanks for Thomas from there. I told him about my escape from the room where I was being held. Theresa and I told him about sneaking under the window and listening in.

"Yeah, you about gave me a heart attack when I saw you by the window," Thomas said to me and smiled.

"Sorry, I couldn't resist," I said, "I had to know what they were doing to you. I remember being told that usually only Rosalyn was in the room during treatments. I didn't know what was happening and I had to find out. She must be out searching by now, we should probably keep moving."

We carefully peered out of Shauna's door and saw nothing but trees, "Thanks Shauna, we're out of here. Hope to have some good news soon," Theresa said.

Shauna nodded sadly and watched us leave.

We headed for somewhere that we could sit and talk. Soon, we found a clearing that seemed like it was made just for us. There were a few trees laying across the ground rather than standing tall. We used those to sit on.

"I should go alone," I argued once we'd begun.

"Why? Why should anyone do anything alone? We don't fully know what she's capable of. Dominic is there, we don't have any clue what he can do," Thomas tried to reason with me.

"That may be true, but I'm her daughter…she won't…" but I couldn't finish. The truth was that Thomas was right. We don't know what she's capable of and that woman is not my mother, not the woman that raised and cared for me. I really wasn't sure what she would and wouldn't do anymore.

I came out of my reverie and noticed we were one teammate short. She hadn't gone far though, I could see Theresa's outline in the distance.

"Theresa," I called after her in a loud whisper, "what are you doing? Where do you think you're going?"

"I'm getting you the information you need. Stay there," she hissed and disappeared.

I didn't know what to think. Should we follow her? Should we listen and stay put? Theresa knew Rosalyn better, did that mean we should just let her go?

"Let her do what she will. She's been here a long time, let's use that to our advantage. I'm sure she knows her way around."

I knew there was nothing more that we could do right now so I settled into Thomas's lap and waited.

Chapter 7

When Theresa still hadn't come back after a very long time, Thomas and I decided to at least move position a little closer to the compound. If we could get close, maybe we could find out what was happening. If Theresa was stuck in there with her, we'd have to find a way to get her out. As we made it to the fringe of the trees outside of her compound I saw the room that I'd been held in. I recognized it immediately because of the hastily repaired bark wall that I'd mutilated. From what I could see, there was no indication that any alarm had been raised. I hoped that meant that Theresa was still in there undetected. I didn't think I was close enough to hear anyone inside, but suddenly I heard Rosalyn's voice. She was speaking to someone, maybe Dominic.

"Theresa," she said more to herself, "that girl's been trouble since she got here. Okay, I will have to deal with her personally."

"Didn't you tell me that you'd recently educated her?" came the voice I recognized from my dreams.

"Yes, I'm not sure why she's here again so quickly. I'll work that into my questioning," Rosalyn's voice sounded nervous.

She left and there was no longer a purpose in listening. I was worried about Theresa, but with Dominic there, it would be harder to get in there to get her out. We'd have to bide our time and wait to hear their voices again.

Thomas and I sat in the protection of the trees keeping an eye all around us. We couldn't hear much from inside so we passed the time staring into one another's eyes.

"Tell me more about you," I said to Thomas.

We sat facing each other and he took a deep breath, "Well, let's see. What else is there to tell? I was born and raised in Boston as I said before. I went to school, went on to college, became an apprentice to an architect, and before I left to be with my dad, was promised that I could come back any time I wanted. I freelance as an architect now, but have made several good connections that will have me doing pretty well when this is all over and I can finally move," Thomas said with a note of impatience.

"It's been hard for you to be here, hasn't it?" I asked.

"It's not that bad," he smiled, "I was just so worried about my Dad and Clarissa after the disappearance that I couldn't stay away. They are my family. I thought they were the only family that I had left; I couldn't abandon them to misery. It would be better if I came and tried to distract them. That's, at least, what I thought. I guess I didn't need to do this after all, though it did bring me to you."

"I'm sure glad you ended up here," I smiled, "for my own selfish reasons. Meeting you has made everything else worth it."

He looked at me with pure contented happiness as he leaned in and pressed his soft lips to mine.

"You're really planning on coming back to Boston?" I asked.

"Now more than ever," he said, "I always knew I belonged there, and now I know why."

The passion that had been simmering now was overwhelming. We leaned toward each other, kissed, and we embraced each other, deepening the kiss.

"Well, I suppose he's really in love," I heard a somewhat familiar voice say from somewhere near.

I didn't want to look up. I didn't want to lose this perfect moment and I knew that we'd dropped our guard. My hands began to shake as Thomas responded to his mother.

"Let's just say that I'm happy with where this is headed," he said while smiling at me, "but yes Mom, you're right. I don't want this to end. Is that going to be enough to get all of us out of here or are you still intent on using Elizabeth as bait?" Thomas wasn't ready to trust that I wasn't in danger.

"Who said we were going to use her as bait?" Madeline had genuine surprise in her voice.

"Are we forgetting the whole lock us up in separate rooms and torture the memories out of us until Rosalyn gets what she wants?" Thomas asked.

"We had to do that, Rosalyn was watching, but she's got a new pet now. She knows that more than anything else we want our family back together. She is using that as leverage against us just like we are using Clarissa as leverage against her."

"You're using your daughter and granddaughter as leverage? Clarissa, who is desperate to have you come home, and you're using her?" I said, incredulous.

"Relax Elizabeth," said Rose, "it's not what you think. We're not putting her in any danger because we will not leave her to Rosalyn, but as long as Rosalyn thinks there's a whisper of a chance that that may happen, we continue to be above punishment. Believe me, what she did to Thomas was extremely mild. Before she realized the potential that Clarissa had, we were going to be getting the same kind of treatment. It was only when she realized there was another voice breaking through Madeline's mind, one that she couldn't recognize, were we elevated to beyond treatment level. She decided then that she wanted Clarissa here to use her special gifts. Rosalyn didn't build this little empire herself, she's had help and having Clarissa on her side would only serve to expand her abilities. I think she's trying to even the score a little bit. It does bother her that Dominic holds power over her."

"Yes, we already know about Dominic," I said, annoyed.

"We have told you of his existence and what we know of him, but even we aren't privileged enough to know everything. We know that he gifts her some abilities, but we don't know how much she's capable of or even how much he's capable of. We don't know Dominic's plans. I'm pretty sure that even Rosalyn isn't privileged enough to know that," Madeline said.

"She truly does believe that she is the ruler and these "subjects" are here to do what she'd like with. He lets her think that. He let her believe that she was the one that would conjure the storms at will and she was the one that was able to manipulate minds, but it's not true. Dominic feeds her his power in order to feed her obsession, but without him, she's no different than you or me."

"How do you know anything if Rosalyn guards him so closely?" I asked.

"We pay attention, every time a storm pops up, he's mysteriously here, on this island. She couldn't leave the island without him. Little things like that add up to Dominic having ultimate control," Rose finished.

"How powerful is he?" I wondered aloud.

Madeline was going to respond, but Rose cut her off, "We can't be sure that he's not listening right now, Maddy. Perhaps we shouldn't be going any further?"

"He's not here just now," she responded.

"How do you know that?" I asked.

"Clarissa's clairvoyance had to come from somewhere," she responded with a small smile, "I only noticed it when I got to this island and wanted to communicate to her that I was okay. I am able to communicate silently and I know whose thoughts are closest, far away, and not around at all. His are away so while he's been here communicating with her, he's not close enough for us to have to worry. It's something that runs on the female side of our gene pool because Mom has it too though she doesn't like to use it. Clarissa, she, and I can all communicate among ourselves without anyone being the wiser."

Madeline glanced quickly at Rose to be sure she hadn't said too much, but Rose seemed content.

"Okay, spill, clairvoyance aside, what exactly is everything that we know about Dominic?"

"Before we talk about Dominic and what we do know, we have to do something about Theresa. Rosalyn still has her in there and she's been leading the resistance. We risk a lot keeping her in there. We need to go after her," said Madeline.

"Won't that put you in danger?" I asked, "She still thinks you're working with her."

"Rosalyn doesn't know that we have come. She thinks we're on the hunt for you," Rose said quietly, "I will go back and tell her that Madeline is following a trail. You go to Theresa's home. Madeline can fill you in about Dominic there. After I get the information we need, I'll tell her I'm worried about you and want to find you. I will meet you at Theresa's."

She suddenly looked sad. I got the impression that she didn't think this was going to work. She paused for a moment, "I'm a little worried about Theresa. She's already been through so much and I'm sure Rosalyn will not hold back this time, especially with Dominic calling her on the frequency of treatments needing to be increased. I hope we can get to her quickly," Rose added glumly before leaving.

I tried not to picture Theresa writhing in pain as Rosalyn found her pressure points and exploited them. The wince that I imagined on her face made me wince and suddenly I couldn't stop the torrent of emotion leaking out of my eyes.

I was silently berating myself for the grief and anguish of every person stuck here. Every one of them should be home with their friends and families, living their own life. They should not be stuck here in Rosalyn's game and while my rational mind knew I didn't put them here, I couldn't help but feel guilty. If I would just forfeit my own life and stay here, everyone else could go home. They could have lives again. This dangerous situation could come to its end tonight.

Thomas was reading my face, trying to comfort me and turn off the tears. He must not have liked what he saw.

"This isn't your fault," he said, "I may not be clairvoyant, but I can tell what you're thinking. I won't let you do it. Bad things happen all the time and it's no one's fault; we have to do what we can from this point. We can't worry about what led up to this."

"I guess my 'put on a brave face' tactics aren't working so well... you can see through me even in the darkness," I said pointing out that there was no more daylight to see me by, "I'll try to remember that, but I won't say that I won't feel guilty. I can't lie to myself like that. I'll try to set the guilt aside. And I won't run off and do anything unexpected, I promise."

"That's my girl," he said as he gripped me in a warm embrace. I hadn't noticed that I was getting cold until that moment.

I shivered once, kissed Thomas quickly and said, "let's go to Theresa's and wait for Rose's return."

Thomas and I got up and he threw one arm around his sister's shoulders and one arm around my shoulders and we set off. We walked in silence, lost in our own thoughts as we made our way to the small community of huts.

It wasn't long and we were sitting quietly among the familiar stench of Theresa's dirt floor. Thomas and I leaned against one another for comfort and prepared to hear the tale that would finally shed some light on this ever changing parallel universe.

"So, Dominic," began Madeline with a worried look, "everything that you've never wanted in an enemy and the only real way to end this nightmare."

Chapter 8

"In order to really tell you about Dominic, we're going to have to start with the day you believed your mother died," Madeline said.

"Don't be concerned," I lied, "that day hardly bothers me anymore."

She gave me a sympathetic look and continued with the story.

"Well, after your car finally stopped moving and she knew it was the end for her, her one concern was that you made it through safely. At the same time, she was jealous. You were going to live. She wouldn't stop screaming until you jumped from the car and let her go, but when you did, her thoughts in a split second turned to her demise.

"She became angry that not only was she losing the chance to raise her daughter as a proper little girl, but also that it seemed that you were going to win. You'd be free to hang out with your dad as much as you want and become Daddy's little girl like you'd always wanted and that she'd been fighting so hard against. All of this occurred to her almost instantaneously and that's when he showed up. It must have looked like a flash of lightning hit your mother. Dominic had flown to her side and asked her if she wanted to live. Without thinking, she said yes and they flew off to this very island," Madeline finished.

"Wow," I said, tears flowing freely, "I knew we'd always disagreed, but I didn't know that she resented me."

Thomas's arms tightened around my waist and I laid my head on his chest, "It doesn't sound like she resented you as much as the fact that you'd get to live…without her."

I nodded my head and motioned for Madeline to continue.

"The worst is behind," she said, "that was the hardest that you'll have to hear.

"Okay, so he brought her here. When he did that he told her that he would be able to give her ultimate power. She'd be able to rule this entire parallel universe with his help. She claimed that she was leery of accepting his offer at first, but instead of giving him an outright 'no' she wanted answers. Your mother never… What?" she asked.

"Please stop calling her that," I said through clenched teeth, "her name is Rosalyn."

"Oh, okay, sorry," she went on, "Rosalyn never was good at hiding her ambitions. Dominic had chosen wisely when he came to save her because he knew that she'd have to be capable of some inhumane treatment and she'd do it to gain the kind of 'power,' the kind of 'love and respect' he was selling her.

"She asked him questions of himself. Pretty typical stuff like 'where did you come from? Why did you choose me?' and he guided her through the answers like the smoothest salesman on the block. He told her that he was extra worldly and she had nothing to fear from him. He convinced her he was an angel and had been sent to her to set things right in her own life. He was telling her the truth in a way. He is an angel, but the one question she never bothered to ask him was what kind of angel he was. She took him at his word that he was sent down from the pearly gates. It never occurred to her that he may have been sent up through the door that indicated that all hope had been lost."

I was looking at her questioningly. She noticed.

"You're wondering how my mother and I know?" she guessed.

"Yes," I admitted, "How can you know these things about Dominic if you're not working with him? You said you're not supposed to know so much."

Thomas gave me a look that said that he thought we were past this mistrust.

"After what we put you through earlier, I'm not surprised at your reaction. I am, however, going to see to it that I earn your trust back," Madeline said with a sad smile, "We know these things because we pay a lot more attention to Rosalyn than she thinks we do. Since she has taken a liking to us due to the uncanny ability of my daughter, she has let us in on a number of secrets that she wouldn't have had she known our true intentions. She's the one that told us how Dominic originally brought her here, but we figured out for ourselves what kind of angel he was…or is it demon? Minion? I'm not really sure, but he sure wasn't what he was promising her. The first ten years or so of her being over here Dominic had to train your mo…Rosalyn how to be a leader. He had to give her the gift of mind alteration and once he did he had to show her how to use it. She was a monster in training I guess you could say. Dominic planted a huge garden behind Rosalyn's home and showed her how to tend it, promising her that before long there'd be people to do that for her."

"Is that his ultimate plan, then? Is he trying to create a special little piece of Hell on Earth or Earth's parallel universe?" I asked.

"That's at least part of it, but it seems that Earth is not enough for him. He's hoping that if he can gain enough power on this side of the divide, he'll be able to overthrow every powerful being…there will be no heaven or Hell, just Dominic and those that follow him. At least, that's what we've been able to come up with on our own, though we don't know for sure. There's been some idea of him going back to where he came from to rule also."

"You've heard him say these things then?" asked Thomas with a flush of anger and concern, "you've actually been close enough to hear him say this?"

"No, there's something else, some part of Rosalyn's gift that I didn't tell you about. In her training, Dominic realized she'd need others to help her find the people that they would bring over to spend eternity with them. Since he knew this, he knew she'd have to have the ability to share her gift. He taught her to do this also. The thing that works to our advantage is that she doesn't seem to realize that she's given it to me, or maybe it was something I already had. She knows that I have some ability, but she has no idea of the scope of it. She knows nothing of the fact that I can hear her or Dominic.

"She already told my mother that she was planning on giving her a great gift and since I've been with my mother all the time I was able to tell her that the gift was the mind altering and reading ability. It was good that I knew that too because our mother," she looked at Thomas when she said this, "was scared half to death and began contemplating ways to attack Rosalyn when she told her this."

"Really?" Thomas said with a smile, "she would attack Rosalyn?"

"She would do anything to have her family back in one piece," said Madeline a little sadly.

"What do you mean by that, Madeline?" asked Thomas.

"It means that she's been thinking about sacrificing herself in order to help us get out. She thinks that if she can keep Rosalyn busy, we can find a way to get ourselves, at least, if not everyone else, through that door."

"No," Thomas said, "I won't let her do that."

"I don't see how you're going to stop her, she just told me to go," Madeline said, shaking her head slowly.

Rose didn't want to go talk to Rosalyn and pump her for information. She wanted to martyr herself so that the rest of her family could be whole again. I looked at Thomas with wide eyes and his face mirrored mine.

"No, what are you doing? Maddy, how could you let her do that? We have to go get her now," Thomas's face twisted into fury.

"She didn't tell me what she was doing," said Madeline calmly, "she was thinking it as she struck up a conversation with Rosalyn in order to get her to leave Theresa alone."

"Is Theresa is okay?" I asked.

"Alive anyway and that has to be enough for now," Madeline said.

"You can't communicate with her without Rosalyn knowing, can you?" Thomas asked.

"No, if I were to do that she would be like a lifeless doll; Rosalyn would know that something was happening."

"But she wouldn't know what?" I asked.

"It wouldn't take her long, she'd start looking for the weak link and she'd know it was me."

"I don't need long. If we get closer to her home, then you make your mother hear your thoughts…think as long and hard as you can, it will make Rose look catatonic. Rosalyn's suspicions will rise and she will go out to investigate. When she's clear of the house, I go in and get Rose and Theresa. By the time she comes back we'll at least be back together again." I smiled with approval of my own plan.

"No way," said Thomas, "I just found you; you don't think I'm actually going to let you walk right into the heart of the danger, do you? If you're going to get two people out, you're going to need help. I'm coming with you."

"And leave your sister out here to fend for herself when Rosalyn does track down the mind waves? I don't think so. I'll be taking the risks," I said with finality.

"It doesn't matter; we're all in grave danger. This does sound like something that may have a chance at working. You do realize, though, that when that happens, she's going to know the truth of it all, she'll know that my mother and I are working against her," said Madeline.

"Not if you and Rose are safely back at her home. She knows that I am out here somewhere. She doesn't know what all I'm capable of yet. She doesn't know the full extent of what Dominic is capable of. Once you two are back you'll convince her that there must have been some glitch. Once that's done we'll have some time to figure out the mystery of that door." I finished, but then thought of a question, "So, Dominic comes to the island every time there's a storm?"

"Yes, he comes and goes a lot and every time he's here he knows what we're up to. He has similar abilities, far greater than ours, I'm sure, but he can't communicate silently. He can; however, read what's going on in your mind. He is also quite a manipulator, it's very difficult to resist him once he's made up his mind about things. It is possible, but difficult.

"When we sense a storm coming on we very consciously guard our thoughts by purposely thinking of other things. That is why we can talk about this safely. He's not here just now." Madeline said.

"How do you know when he leaves?" I asked.

"I can read it in his thoughts."

"So, if Clarissa is key to getting everyone back through the door, why don't you just convince Rosalyn to bring her over, then trick her and run with everyone?" I asked.

"Once Clarissa is on this island, she has no intention of letting her go," Madeline said darkly, "she likes the fact that Clarissa has not met Dominic, is not one of his subjects, but seems to be able to read people anyway. She's fascinated by that and wants to study her and I honestly don't know what Dominic's plans are. But I won't allow her to do that anyway. If I have to spend an eternity here, she will not take my daughter."

"I understand, I don't like to ask this and of course I wouldn't want her to do that, but out of curiosity, why can't she just do it without you? She's been able to pull several people over here against their will. Why not Clarissa?"

"She can't. Simply put, Clarissa won't let her. Every time she's come close to convincing her, Roger is there and talks to Clarissa making sure she stays grounded in reality. He's just so sure that we're coming back that he's always been able to convince her of that." Madeline said.

"Good thing Roger is stubborn," I said with a smile.

"Good thing that Clarissa is still so young. I'm terrified that Dominic will try to convince her to come if Rosalyn decides to open up to that possibility, but so far he stays out of it. He's convinced that Clarissa will come in time and time is all he has. He's not worried which I think will work to our advantage. We just have to keep our thoughts away from Rosalyn's mind. We'll have to be even more careful about that than before," said Madeline thoughtfully.

"Okay," she continued, "if we're going to do this, you two had better go. I will stay here and wait for your return. We will quickly fill Rose in and she and I will leave. In the meantime, you two and Theresa can figure out what our next step is."

Thomas and I went out the door as Madeline started gathering all of her concentration and focusing on it. I thought I felt her whisper 'good luck' as we began our expedition. It wasn't far from Theresa's hut to Rosalyn's compound. It would only take us five minutes to make the walk. I hoped that would be enough time to get Rosalyn out and looking for us. Thomas must have had the same idea.

"Stop, wait a minute," he said casually, taking my hand.

"What?" I asked.

"We don't want to get there too soon. She has to see my mom lose consciousness, then have enough time pass to actually leave the compound and go looking for the cause," he said, "besides, I wouldn't mind stealing a few minutes of alone time."

"Once she sees that Madeline is doing this, won't it spoil the whole thing?" I repeated a nagging worry that hadn't gone away with our conversation.

"Not as long as they convince her that Madeline wasn't aware of this ability. That shouldn't be too hard as she doesn't even understand her own abilities fully, it seems. If she did, we would never be able to get away with what we have. Either that or Dominic is lessening the intensity of her control. Rosalyn will know what is causing the reaction, but she won't know who's causing it. This will cause her to go hunting.

"She may even think that Dominic gifted Rose with an ability without telling her. Right now, she thinks she's the only one that knows all about Dominic. With her busy trying to figure out what's going on, we can reconvene at Theresa's and figure out how to get us all out of here."

We started walking again and approached the front entrance, "How do we know she didn't already leave?" I asked.

"We'll have to hope for the best and be patient." Thomas said.

We saw the front door open and Rosalyn stepped out. She turned back for a moment and was doing something to the inside of the door. When she turned again she had a wild and concerned look in her bright, brown eyes. She was definitely being cautious, before she went too far she seemed to be staring into the beyond. She was clearly scanning all around, likely both visually and mentally, looking for the one that was responsible for Rose's slump. Thomas and I skirted behind a large tree as she looked in our direction. She took some tentative steps forward. She must be assuming that Dominic had something to do with it because she kept looking up at the skies.

As soon as it was clear that she'd finally left the compound, we exited the trees and it was now my eyes dancing all over the place watching every movement and listening for every sound. The path to the door seemed to stretch forever, but we made it without incident. Thomas stretched out his hand to grasp the handle, but it would not budge. He looked at me with a startled expression. We weren't counting on any kind of locks on the doors. I glanced up and to my left and saw a window had been carved out not far from the ground. We walked over to it and determined that if Thomas gave me a boost, I could crawl through.

"No," Thomas sounded angry, "I don't want you to go in there alone. What if there's some sort of trap?"

"It's the only way. We don't know what kind of lock she has on that door and we don't have time to argue about it. Let me shimmy through that window and I'll get the door open. We're talking seconds here. I won't be in danger," I pleaded with him.

"Fine," he said gruffly, "but be quick."

He bent down so that I could sit on his shoulders. He easily lifted my weight and brought me to the window. I gasped when I saw Rose sitting there lifeless.

"What's wrong?" he asked.

"Nothing, it's just that I've never seen anyone sit quite so still in my life," I admitted.

I crawled through the window and immediately went to the door. There was a long piece of a very thin log placed strategically through the door lever that would not allow it to be opened from the outside. I wondered for a minute how Rosalyn was going to get back in or how she lodged that log in the first place, but figured it was something to do with her "gifts". I dismissed the thought before it could lead to a line of fears that would set me panicking. A shiver ran down my spine as I processed the very thing I'd just decided to dismiss and took the log out of the levers. I opened the door to see relief wash over Thomas's worried face.

"I'll get my mother," he said once he'd entered, "you go get Theresa. This place creeps me out, let's make this quick."

"I'm with you," I agreed.

I started calling Theresa's name and heard a muffled response coming from one of the rooms toward the back. I began to pick up the pace as the muffled sounds grew louder and more defined. I opened the door and saw Theresa's shocked and pained face. I was unpleasantly surprised with all that my mother had done in such a short time.

"What are you doing here, Elizabeth? Your mother said you were with Dominic preparing for the exodus. What are you doing?" She asked, confused.

"What exodus? I haven't even met Dominic. I'm here to get you out," I said, concerned.

"The exodus with Dominic; the trip to his home where we'll all live together, happily," Theresa said wistfully.

"We've got to get you out of here," I said urgently, "We have to get you away from her. Every second you're here she's poisoning your mind. Please come with me."

She still hadn't recovered, though she began to mumble so something was getting through to her, "Leave? Why leave? Dominic....everything... down below... all we.."

"Theresa, look at me," her eyes drifted to mine and stayed, "Are you telling me that Dominic plans to take all of us? No matter what?"

"No matter what," she said a little drunkenly, "he's going to take care of us and he'll show his father..." she drifted off.

"Theresa," I yelled inches from her face, "snap out of it, we have no time. Rosalyn will be back at any moment."

She looked at me strangely and I could see the battle going on behind her eyes. She was lost, but hadn't completely given up yet. She'd been listening to Rosalyn for so long, years of reinforced brainwashing with a recent boost from Dominic to amp up the believability were confusing her, but she was still in there. I used that.

"Theresa," serene tones floating all around her, "We have to go now. Remember our plans to leave the island and go back to the lives we've left behind. Rosalyn is telling you lies as is Dominic. They've been lying to you for years and you know it. It's time to break free from their head games. You figured her out a long time ago, you can do it again. I have faith in you."

Slowly, I could see her win the struggle and come back to herself, "Whoa, what happened? Nevermind, it's not important, let's get out of here."

"Oh thank God," I said as I directed her out of the room. We came through the hallway and found Thomas cradling Rose in his arms.

"We have to leave things as they were," Thomas said, "we have to get that log back in the door. We can't let Madeline and Rose pay for this."

"Not a problem," I replied, "Let's go."

As we neared the exit we froze, Rosalyn was earlier than expected.

Chapter 9

"Forget it, let's go," said Thomas quickly as he took my hand. He was carrying Rose and I grabbed for Theresa, "it's too late to set the stage. We can come up with explanations later."

He opened the door a fraction of an inch and saw that she was coming straight up the path.

"*Back door*," I suddenly heard whispered. I didn't wait to find out who'd said it.

"Follow me," I cried.

The group looked surprised, but did as I asked.

"*First hallway on your left*," I heard the voice again.

I followed and the rest followed me. Our strict adherence to silence was rewarded as we heard voices from the front of the house.

"Rose is gone?" asked Rosalyn of the empty room around her.

"Dominic," she whispered to herself, "he's not going to like it if I can't control my own people."

As we paused to listen, I noticed a new tone in Rosalyn's voice. The confidence was slipping. It was plain that she was as afraid of Dominic as much as she was awed by his power.

"If he thinks I'm losing my hold on Rose…" She started.

"We better move quickly," I whispered, realizing that Rosalyn was setting out again to find Rose.

"*Down the long corridor and turn right*," came that strange voice again. Again, I didn't argue.

We twisted and turned as the voice in my head commanded. The others were shocked that I knew where I was going, but followed silently. We all knew the entire idea would be out the window if Rosalyn found us here; especially with Rose in our arms unconscious. Finally I was directed to a tunnel that led underground. It was here that I started to get suspicious. What if Dominic was here? What if it wasn't Madeline leading the way as I'd been suspecting? What if this was a trick to get us somewhere we had no hope of getting out of? Rose began to stir in Thomas's arms.

"*Can't do both*," I heard an aggravated voice in my head, "*Elizabeth, go*."

"Thomas, why are you here? What's going on?" asked a confused

Rose.

"Mom, shhh," he replied, "we're getting you out of here."

"This was your chance," she replied sadly, "I told Madeline to go."

"She heard you," Thomas assured his mother, "but we're not going anywhere until we can all go. We'll figure this out."

"Oh, your sister never did listen to what was best for her," Rose said, "What happened anyway? One minute I was talking to Rosalyn and the next, you are here somehow rescuing me."

"Madeline broke into your thoughts. That's what got Rosalyn out of the house and away from you which gave us our chance. Now we're trying to find our way out of here and it seems like Elizabeth is leading us, like she knows where she's going somehow." his voice turned up an octave as he finished his statement.

"Put me down," said Rose.

Thomas complied and we all stopped moving. Rose took a look around at our underground tunnel. Her face was intrigued and her eyes questioning as she tried to absorb all that had happened.

"Elizabeth," Rose looked directly at me, "how did you know to come down here?"

"I don't know," I responded, hesitant to declare where my weird knowledge was coming from, "I guess I've sort of been directed in my mind. As we walked, I just knew where to go."

We already knew about Madeline's ability to silently communicate, but I didn't know and couldn't believe that that would extend to me, I wasn't sure I was ready to believe it.

"Hmm," she said, deep in thought, "weird. Madeline, Theresa, and I are the only ones that know of this tunnel. We have spent several months working on it when Rosalyn was otherwise occupied. This leads us almost directly to Theresa's. How remarkable that you'd be able to find this on your own. These feelings that you were getting, the ones that were telling you where to go, are they coming in the form of words?"

"Yes," I admitted, "yes, it's as though someone is talking to me…can we walk and talk? We really need to get out of here."

"Okay, but we're in no danger now. Rosalyn knows nothing of this tunnel," said Rose with a superior air.

"That may be true, but she knows that when she left you were co-matose, nor responsive at all, now she sees that you're gone. Don't you think she'll be coming for you?" I asked.

"I suppose you're right. At the very least she'll be out looking. Okay, let's walk," she went on, "Tell me exactly what happened that got you down here. I have to be sure that it's still safe."

I started to explain, "When we heard Rosalyn coming back to the compound, we knew we needed a second exit. That's when I started hearing a voice that directed me. When I first left it told me to take the hallway that I never assumed would lead anywhere. As it talked, I listened and led everyone to where we were when you began to stir. As you did I heard the voice say 'can't do both'. I have my suspicions, but I can't be sure." I finished.

"What are your suspicions?" Rose asked with a knowing smile.

"Well," I said hesitantly, "it sounded to me like Madeline's voice. It seemed that somehow she knew we were in need of help and she was able to direct me through, but since you've woken, I've heard nothing."

"Her gift is more pronounced than we realized," said Rose, excitedly, "this is good news. Rosalyn still has no idea that Madeline has this ability."

Theresa remained very quiet as we walked along, but slowly was looking more at us than she was at the sky or somewhere else that could cause her no more pain.

Rose was almost exuberant with this new knowledge. She had an eager smile on her face. The tunnel slowly began to brighten as we walked further. Rose was like a child; she was so riddled with excitement. Our plan had worked. We'd gotten Rose and Theresa out of that horrible place. We would have to sit down with Theresa when we made it to safety. Her demeanor concerned me and I wanted to make sure she was still fully on board with our plans. I could only imagine what she'd suffered and wanted to take that pained look away from her.

"There," Rose said, breaking my wayward thoughts, "Can you see the steps?"

Crude stairs had been formed out of the dirt that was now rising to the surface.

"Did you and Madeline do all of this?" I asked in amazement.

"Not all of it, Theresa gets credit for the steps and about half of the tunnel. We told her where to start and she met us in the middle. It took us a long time to do. We couldn't ever dig when Dominic was here and we could only dig at night when he wasn't. Rosalyn started wondering why Madeline and I were so tired all the time. We had to make things up like we were starting to have bad dreams or our thoughts of our family were depressing us. That didn't do much good, though. Once we'd given her that excuse several times she got tired of hearing us and gave us treatment. It wasn't pleasant and we didn't quite 'forget' as quickly as she wanted us to." Rose finished.

"Oh, I'm so sorry. I thought you were no longer subject to treatment because of your status," I said.

"Usually we are, but we'd gotten in too deep with our cover by that point. There was nothing to do but endure it. To deny it would walk us down a path of questioning that we'd both like to avoid. We thought it better to just deal with her 'therapy' and be done with it."

"So let me get this straight," I said as we edged closer to the opening, "Thomas, you, Madeline, and Shauna have all broken free from the bonds of her treatment? And she's not aware of that with any of you? What about the others? Are they also placating her as you search for a way out?"

"Almost everyone here is placating her," said a voice from behind us. I jumped then turned to see that Madeline had joined us from above ground.

"Her hold can only last for so long, but none of us want her to know that because then she'll just treat us again until she's done permanent damage. We all have a silent agreement to make her believe she's getting what she wants while we meet secretly in places much like this one to plan a way out. So far we've been unsuccessful, but you've brought with you the first glimmer of hope in quite some time," Madeline said as she turned to me.

"Me? What do you mean? I thought Clarissa was the key to opening that door and letting everyone out. How does me being here have anything to do with that?" I asked, confused.

"We just had the most successful experiment yet," Rose said as Madeline's eyes twinkled.

"What's going on?" I could feel my cheeks heating up as my frustration began to show.

"Well, we were just able to completely pull the wool over Rosalyn's eyes, weren't we? She has no idea what's happened to Mom and she's scared," said Madeline with a smile, "Dominic is the one with the power and now we know that for sure."

"How does that help?" I asked, confused.

"Well, we know that with all of her threats and her 'treatments' that no longer work, she is idle. The real problem is Dominic. He's calling the shots, so it's not her that we have to fear, it's him. This helps give us direction," Madeline explained.

"I get it, we need to find a way to get to Dominic," I said.

"That's right," chimed Rose, "and after what your mother had planned for you and the fact that she knows you're here…well, that can work to our advantage."

Afraid to ask, I croaked, "What is it that she has planned for me?"

"She wants you here, with her and Dominic. She has some real hero worship thing and she sees you three being a family here. She figures he can have his domination over the others as long as she gets the family she's always wanted on her terms." Rose answered.

"What then," Madeline hissed in my head, *"does this have to do with Clarissa? Why don't they leave her and my family alone?"* I voiced the same question.

"Clarissa's just a perk," Rose admitted, "and I'm not sure I fully understand what they want her for yet, but from what I can tell, since she does have some clairvoyant ability, they want to see what else she's capable of. They want to see just how far in the future she can predict and how close she'll be, but this is speculation. I don't fully know, but I do believe it has something to do with her natural clairvoyance. I do know, though, that they believe that she'll be useful in baiting the hook and drawing others into the little dominion that they're creating here."

A new idea was forming in my mind, but it would be dangerous and I didn't know if I could get Madeline and Rose to agree.

"It's okay, get out of that hole," Madeline was paying more attention to my stress levels than I'd noticed, *"and no, she's not coming here until I know she'll be getting out."*

"All right, all right," I grumbled and looked at Madeline, "let's go for a walk."

All eyes were on me as I realized I'd responded aloud to Madeline's thoughts.

"Well," I looked at everyone, "Madeline can see that I'm stressed. I need some fresh air."

"How?" Thomas responded, "Rosalyn can be anywhere. We're all stressed, but isn't it safest to stay underground and out of sight. She knows nothing of this place."

"She's not looking here right now. Mind connection, I'm feeling more confident of it all the time, she's elsewhere and all of this new information has my head spinning. You can stay if you like, but I need to breathe and think."

I walked up the stairs and squinted my eyes to adjust to the light. I was hoping that what I told them was true, that she was far away looking elsewhere, and I thought I was right, but this was so new I didn't know if I could trust it. It was quiet behind me at first, but then I heard a shuffling of feet as Thomas, Rose, Madeline, and Theresa decided to follow.

I edged into the trees using them as a natural cover and allowed myself to enjoy the silence. I knew that if there was real danger Madeline, if not me, would be alerted to Rosalyn coming near and I'd be able to duck and cover. I needed to think about how we could get Clarissa here and use her strange clairvoyant ability to get everyone out. How would I convince Madeline and Rose in the first place? I had just about made the fringe of the trees when Thomas caught up with me.

"What do you think you're doing?" You can't leave the cover of the trees," he said, panicked.

Suddenly I was angry, "The hell I can't. I am not going to act like some rat in a trap. I want to go walk by the water to clear my mind. I know that Rosalyn is not a problem right now. An oncoming storm will be our warning if Dominic decides to show up. I. AM. GOING. FOR. A. WALK."

I turned abruptly and left, not really sure what brought on the anger. I needed a moment to think by myself. My heart began to race as the trees thinned and the clear sand of the beach was upon me. I took a cautious step and felt nothing out of place. I continued to walk slowly and could feel the eyes of the others on me, watching carefully.

"You're more like her than you know," I heard though no one had spoken.

"Shut up," I responded feeling the depression and desperation threatening to overtake me, "I'm nothing like her." A tear escaped the corner of my eye as I crumpled to the ground and sat facing the water. It seemed so calm.

"Elizabeth," Thomas had come up behind me, "are you okay?"

"No, not really okay," I admitted as a wave of tears kept me from explaining. "I just don't get it. We didn't get along, that much is true, but I never hated her. Everything that she's doing is driven by her pure hatred of both me and my father. What did we do?" I asked childishly.

"I think you have it all wrong. I think she wants to hate you for your individuality and your devotion to your father, but I don't think she really does. I think she's incredibly jealous. I mean, look at you. You're everything that she couldn't be. You are independent and you have strong individuality. She wanted a different life for you, but she's been watching you make a success out of the life you've chosen. She feels shunned; like her future for you was not good enough. And it wasn't, not in your eyes. She's striking out and it's not fair to you. It's not fair to any of us, but it's not your fault either. This doesn't all fall on your shoulders. She's the one who's made the decisions that she has. And frankly, you don't know that whole story either, and maybe you never will, but the enormity of this does not rest on your shoulders."

I started to open my mouth to protest, I was tired of being told that it wasn't my fault when it clearly was, but he stopped it in the best way possible. His lips found mine and stopped my protest. He deepened the kiss and the passion between us became palpable. He held me in his arms and kissed me again.

He pulled back and looked at me, "Is any of this convincing you?"

"It's nice and don't get me wrong, I'm in this with you, but it doesn't change the facts. If it weren't for me and my refusal of my mother's old-fashioned ways, no one's life would be in danger," I said as I looked out at the water and noticed the other edge of the shore where life seemed so much simpler.

"There are not many people that will agree with everything that their parents do. That's called growing up and that's what most parents want for their children. They want to see them become independent and successful. Your mother…oh, sorry, Rosalyn," he corrected himself, "has things all wrong. Her jealousy has taken over her good will. Maybe you and she would have been fine had she lived through the car accident, but this Dominic has poisoned her mind beyond all reproach. I'm so sorry that you have to be put through this, but I hope you realize that I'm not going anywhere. I will be here to stand beside you through this and I hope I'm not too annoying because I'd like for you to want me to stick around."

"Even after all of this?" I asked, shocked, "even with the miles of baggage that come with me?"

His hands reached up and gently caressed my cheek as his thumb whisked away the tear that had fallen onto it.

"Baggage is such a negative word. I'd rather look at it as a past. A past is something we all have and there's bound to be good and bad in everyone's past. I'm not worried about that," Thomas said, smiling.

"Well," I was feeling a little more confident, "I have an idea as to how we can get out, but it may be dangerous."

Actually, the plan was becoming crystal clear as Thomas helped free my mind of the guilt that I felt. I was ready to share it and put it in motion. We had to get Clarissa over to this side of the little island. We had to talk to her without alerting Madeline to her presence here. I couldn't be the one to do it. It seems that Madeline has taken me under her wing, perhaps because she knows that her brother cares for me, but I was constantly in her thoughts. This meant that I would be able to hide nothing from her.

"Elizabeth, are you asking me to take what little family I have left and bring half of it, the most vulnerable and desired half, and put her in the most dangerous position possible?" Thomas argued after hearing me out. "I'm sorry, but I'm with Madeline on this one. We can do this without involving her; there has to be a way. If Rosalyn or worse, Dominic, had any idea that she was here, that would be the end of it. My father would be completely alone and I truly don't think that he'd survive that kind of loss. How can you even ask me to agree to this?"

"I know the risks and believe me, it kills me to put Clarissa in this position, but I don't see another way. When we came through that doorway, I felt something, you did too, and what we felt was some sort of divide, like something was sealing around us. I knew that we would not be able to get out. Remember, we tried and couldn't go past the barrier. But Clarissa, whatever her clairvoyance does for her, it's enough to open the door at will. She could bring all of us back through.If we have any hope of getting ourselves, your family, and the other captives out, I don't know how to do it without her."

"No, I'm sorry. I won't do anything further to hurt my family, even at the cost of all those that are currently here." Thomas was serious and I could see that wasn't going to change.

"Okay, fine. We'll think of something else."

Chapter 10

Thomas would not budge, that was clear, but Clarissa was our only way out. I didn't know what else to say that would possibly convince him, but it was clear that I wouldn't be changing his mind today. I couldn't allow his devotion to his family ruin the only way we had to escape. She was the key; this was something that I knew without a doubt. I would have to do something that could mean the end of this fragile flirtation that has the possibility of becoming so much more. I really liked Thomas; dare I say I may even be headed straight into the path of love.

If I went through with what I was thinking about, I may lose him. If my plan worked, would he take that into account or consider me so selfish that he would be completely disgusted with the lengths that I'd go to? Those were my choices then, betray Thomas with my best intentions in mind and perhaps lose him, or not put little Clarissa in danger which could ultimately end with us stuck here indefinitely. I only hope that he'll see that I have no choice.

These thoughts plagued me as we walked slowly to the underground meeting area. Thomas and Theresa were talking strategy. Thomas had faith that when he spoke to Madeline and Rose again, they'd be able to tell us something useful. I listened to him talking to Theresa about the world outside of these confines. Most of it she remembered well, but in order to keep her truly vulnerable, there were still some memories that she was repressing, likely due to the fact that those memories would make her miss home and try harder to resist what was happening here. Thomas was asking her all kinds of questions in order to prod at the holes in her memory which would lead to her frustration from time to time, but Thomas took it well; he never lost patience in those moments.

I made a decision, Thomas was becoming more important to me by the minute. I didn't want to lose him, yet I could not see this working without Clarissa. I knew that if I could convince Thomas that Clarissa would be unharmed and able to return home when all of this was over, he would go along with it, but I didn't know how to convince him.

"*Lie*," I heard Madeline say in our new, silent way.

I couldn't believe what I was hearing. She had definitely been against this before and now she wanted me to lie to her brother. Was she finally agreeing with me that the risk was worth it so that we could finally flee?

"*Yes, find a way around Thomas and meet me on the beach,*" she said.

He and Theresa were once again engrossed in a plan to do some reconnaissance work the next time Dominic decided to pay a visit so I figured I'd not have trouble getting away for a little bit. It worked better than I thought; he didn't even say anything, just distractedly waved his hand when I told him I was going up.

I walked slowly through the trees and got that same tense feeling when the trees began to clear and the open beach became visible. It was after midnight but the moon shone bright so I could see Madeline as she stood, waiting for my arrival. There was a look of longing as her eyes stretched to the other bank where her daughter was safe in her bed; hopefully not having any bad dreams. I summoned my courage and left the safety of the trees.

"What's going on, Madeline?" I asked, curious about her change of heart.

"I know how Thomas is, that's all," she replied, "he's going to have a hard time doing what we have to do to get out of here. I know I told you that I wouldn't consider this earlier, but I've been paying attention to your line of reasoning and you're not wrong. She can come and go, if there's trouble, she can just leave, at any time. He's not going to want to put Clarissa in harm's way, but I am also agreeing that there does not seem to be another way. I've been thinking about this for years and I think I've come up with the exception that we've been looking for. I think I've figured out what we can do to get us all out of here with Clarissa in tow, but it does mean her coming over here and I'm not sure that we can fully let Thomas in on those plans."

"I was thinking of that a lot in the last hour or so," I admitted, "But I have a very different dilemma. I really like your brother. I may even be feeling the beginnings of love, though I know how early it is to think that. Anyway, I'm afraid that he's going to think of me as ungodly selfish if I give up hope that there may be another way. I don't want to lose what we've started here together. Like I said, I know we've not been together long and the beginning of the relationship infatuation can be strong, but I feel a deeper connection. Am I being incredibly selfish by even thinking about this right now?"

"No, not at all, I remember what it was like to feel that way. I remember feeling like I'd walk through fire to stay with Mark. When he asked me to marry him, well, it was the happiest day of my life..." she trailed off, "We would have been truly happy, you know?"

I could feel that at this moment, if I wanted to keep her, I was gaining the sister I never had. Madeline and I were bonding, connecting; I knew I could tell her anything.

"I know you would have. If there was anything I could do to change how things happened for you there, I'd do it in a second," I said.

"It's too late for that. Mark did give up and move on and I had to let him go. I couldn't really expect him to keep waiting around while I wasted away here with no way out. I'll just have to start over when I get out of here; I'm not ready to give up on love yet. Look at you and Thomas. Under other circumstances, you may never have met or you may have simply been another person on one of Dad's tour buses; but instead you and he both were in the right place at the right time and were prompted to speak to one another. Your lives were already connected though you didn't know it. Tell me fate didn't have something to do with that?" she snorted a sad laugh.

"So you do understand why I don't want to deceive him?" I smiled.

"I do, but this will not be your doing, it will be mine. I'm her mother and whether or not my brother agrees with us is immaterial. He can be mad at me. I haven't seen my brother in a very long time, as you know, but when I did see him last, he was only moderately happy. He had just started working and was excited about that, but there wasn't really anything else for him to be excited over. His friends were starting to get married and have families of their own, and I could see the envy in his eyes when we'd talk about them, but he just hadn't found that person yet so he was sticking to work at the time. Since I've been reunited with him through you, I've seen a light in him that did not exist before. You have literally lit him up and whether or not this is love, I can't say, but whatever it is, it's as strong for him as it is for you. As someone who's already had to lose that partnership more than once, I don't want him or you to lose what you have. I know that my daughter is the key to our survival and to our escape. I, as her mother, will reach out to her and communicate that it is time that she come here and join us in order to bring us home. You know that I can communicate with her and I'll have to make sure she knows it's really me and not some ghostly copycat, but I'm certain I can do it. I will be convincing," she said.

"You don't have to do that," I responded, trying to sound grateful.

"I am his sister, he may be mad at me for a while, but our relationship will survive. Besides, I'm the girl's mother and I have decided to allow her to come over here, but we have to be very careful about this. We have to make sure that she comes when it's safe for her to be here. I don't want to take the chance of Dominic paying a visit and discovering her here; that will make escape near impossible. This is between us alone. Go back and tell Thomas you're feeling better and join him and Theresa in making plans. Dominic will be here soon and Rosalyn's made hints that he wants to talk to you directly. This is truly his project and I'm sure he's going to search for you as soon as he gets here. It'll be best to meet him head on and do what you can to hide your plans. He will be rooting around in your mind so it's important that you not even think about the plans that we've made while he's here," Madeline said.

I felt my legs go weak. I knew that he'd come for me eventually, but Madeline said it so matter-of-factly and we've spent so much time planning for our escape, I began thinking that maybe we could get away with never having to see him. It was unnerving that I'd soon be in the spotlight having to guard my thoughts the whole time. I found myself looking to delay his arrival.

"How do you know he will be here soon?" I asked.

"See those clouds," she pointed off to the shelf of darker black on the horizon, "That's not how the storm front looks when it's just the weather passing through. He's not in any hurry tonight, though; it's unusual for him to move so slowly, I wonder what it means."

I could almost see what she meant; through the light of the moon, it was clear that there was a storm coming, but it also looked to almost hover out in the distance. Indeed it was moving slowly which was not like anything we've seen so far. Usually there will be a blanket of clouds, much like the one we're seeing now, but the foremost clouds will form the front and stand out fluffy and bright as if they were leading a charge.

The difference tonight was subtle. The band of clouds was smaller, seeming to only stretch the distance of the island. They would light up from time to time whereas usually that wouldn't happen until the storm was right on top of the island. The lightning stayed within the bands of clouds for now, but each flash threatened a certain intensity that was at once thrilling and terrifying. Madeline was right, the clouds moved slowly like the clouds on a windless day though there was a noticeable breeze. My mind threw itself into overdrive and my eyes widened... scared absolutely stiff I turned to Madeline.

"What's wrong?" she asked.

"What if he's been listening?" I stumbled.

"Oh," her face relaxed, "it doesn't work that way. He has to actually be here to hear us. This is our warning that he's coming. I just don't know why he's coming so slowly, but it has nothing to do with us. Trust me."

"Well," she backpedaled, "maybe not nothing. It may have something to do with you. I'm sure that by now he knows that you're here. He may or may not know that you've gone missing, that's something that Rosalyn probably would want to keep from him as long as possible. I'm betting she's delaying him somehow. She must be buying some time."

As if in answer to her question, we heard a strange ruffling in the trees. I looked up, panicked and noticed that Madeline looked confused, but not alarmed. The footsteps were coming closer but hadn't yet breached the edge of the forest.

"Do you know who that is?" I whispered to Madeline.

"Yes, don't worry. It's just my mother and Thomas, they've come to share information," said Madeline, "remember, what passed between us about Clarissa stays with us. Hi Mom, Thomas, have you talked to Theresa?"

"Yes," Rose said suspiciously, "she is just finishing up her plans for Dominic. You know he's coming."

"Yes, I see him moving slowly, but I'm not sure why. Why isn't he speeding through the night like usual?" asked Madeline.

"I heard Rosalyn ask him to take his time. She's trying to buy some time to find Elizabeth and Thomas before he gets here. She doesn't want him to lose faith in her. Especially Elizabeth, since you're here, she knows this would be another instance of you winning over her. She would be utterly defeated." There was a glint of hope in her eye as we silently communicated.

"If I understand you correctly," I started out sounding braver than I felt, "you'd like me to go to Dominic when he comes and act as though I were trying to replace Rosalyn. You think that if we do that I will be able to eventually overthrow him and get us all out of there without having to involve Clarissa at all?"

I envisioned the future that she'd imagined for me and grew angry. I knew from the look in Madeline's eyes that this was exactly what Rose had planned for me. I remembered what I had been thinking earlier; better to put myself in the path of danger rather than that sweet little girl.

"What are you talking about, Mom?" interjected Thomas who apparently shared my feelings, "Why would you want Elizabeth to do something like that? Don't you understand the danger? Why would you ask her to do that to herself?"

"It's not her, Thomas," I said quietly, looking at him, "it's going to come down to Clarissa or me. Which do you prefer?"

"How do we keep coming back to this?" He said, frustrated, "Those cannot be the only two options. What about what we've started here? Am I supposed to just stand by and watch as Dominic comes and tampers with your mind? As he burrows further and further into your mind and shreds your very will, I'm supposed to be okay with that?"

I felt the others back away to give us some privacy. This was something that I knew, from the moment I almost went on the island alone, I would have to handle. If that meant losing Thomas, that might be the price I'd have to pay. He'd be able to move on. This is about my mother and myself and I had to make him see that.

"Thomas, as much as I've enjoyed the time that we've spent together, and as much as I may be developing real feelings for you, I can't keep ignoring what brought this all on just because you want me to. We want everyone to go free, right? With no mistakes and no one being forced to stay here against their will?"

"But that includes you, doesn't it? Or have you decided to stay?" he asked, hurt.

"I'd like it to include me, but I'm not sure that there is another way. Madeline and I were ready, against your wishes we were going to call Clarissa over here and make an attempt through her. Now I don't have to hurt you like that and little Clarissa can have her family back."

"Though I understand why you're doing it, don't you think I'd be equally, if not more hurt, by you allowing yourself to be our sacrifice? First my mom tried, now you. How will I live on the other side knowing that you are the reason that I am alive and also the one person I'd never be able to see again? You think I'm just going to say, 'oh well, it could have been nice?'" I could see he was getting angry, "I don't know where this is going yet, but I do know that I have real feelings for you and I feel like this is something that can go somewhere if we give it a chance. That can't happen with all this talk of sacrifice. I won't allow you to suffer while the rest of us go free."

Suddenly my heart felt like it was wide open. I knew how I'd been feeling for him, but hearing that he was feeling the same made what I had to do that much more difficult.

"Oh Thomas, I am feeling the same for you, exactly the same and this scares me more than you know. Instead of looking at this as a sacrifice on my part, be my rock. I'm not intending to stay here. I'm intending to go back with the rest of you, but maybe we have to go along with this in order for it to work. Be the person that I know I'll have to come home to when all of this is over. Be the one to keep me sane even in the moments that it seems that Dominic has won. I have to be the one to do this, but our time is up either way. Once he gets here, they'll find us in no time, and then the torture will begin. If I truly can convince Dominic that I'm as selfish and self-loathing as Rosalyn, I can get out of this too. The one thing that I do know is that Dominic is coming and if he finds out Clarissa is here, it's all over. If we try this first, we may succeed without having to involve her."

"You're right, you're so brave," he leaned down and kissed me fiercely, "I can do that for you. I can be the person that you can always depend on; even in the darkest moments. You and I will do this and I will be with you every step of the way, no matter what happens."

"Thank you," I said, "but Rosalyn has to think that I've come to her on my own. She has to believe that I've finally accepted her vision of our future here. That's the only way I'll be able to convince both her and Dominic that I'm ready to be what she wants me to be.

"If she's worried that Dominic will find her weak because she was thwarted and can't find us in such a small place, then I'll use that to my advantage. When Dominic arrives, I will come out and meet him. I will make myself sound just as greedy as her. When I have him convinced, he will take me to her and the real test will begin. You have to be out of all of that. I don't even want him to know that I care about you. I'll have to guard my thoughts while he's here carefully," I continued almost to myself, "If he realizes that you're here and that I care about you, he may try to bring you on board or worse, take you out of the equation altogether."

I looked out at the water desperately and suddenly felt insecure. I thought to myself, "*I don't know if I can do this; if I can be so convincing knowing that I may be looking at my own death or at the very least my removal from ever having a real life.*"

"*You can, you'll find it gets easier in time,*" Madeline's calm voice came floating through my mind. Her thoughts mellowed me and I was able to relax slightly. I looked over to see that Madeline and Rose were both looking at me now. What I was being asked to do was no different than what they've been doing for years now. They have been here pretending to be working with Rosalyn. They'd been able to spare themselves the mind-altering 'treatment' that Rosalyn performs by deceiving her. They've also gotten treated more humanely than the others. I would have to work with them and have them show me how to do that before Dominic could make his appearance. Perhaps his slow arrival will give me the time I need to become convincing.

"Let's go join the others and get back underground," I finally said to Thomas, breaking out of my reverie and staring into his trusting eyes.

"If I'm going to put on a convincing show, I'm going to need to practice while I can."

Thomas seemed convinced that I was calm enough to rejoin the others and begin planning our strategy. He was also relieved that I was ready to get out of sight again. We went back under the canopy of the trees and I already began to feel safer. I told everyone that we would all stay underground as much as possible until Dominic's arrival with the obvious exception of Rose and Madeline who needed to get back to Rosalyn's side.

After some lessons in the art of being convincing to both Dominic and Rosalyn, Madeline promised that she'd keep in touch with me through whatever psychic connection we had and let me know the progress of Dominic. She said that with the way that he was moving, she figured we'd at least have a day before his arrival. She knew that they'd be spending most of their time on the 'hunt' for us. Rose and Madeline both would be assigned to lead separate parties which would be going on wild goose chases. They would let us know when they were coming near so it appeared that they'd searched the entire island and no one would know that they were giving us silent messages to move as they approached.

"I won't let you go hungry. The food may not be great, but it's just for a short time. Dominic will be here soon and then the real games will begin." Madeline said and she and Rose disappeared.

Thomas and I were together in a small underground area. Something about knowing we would not be able to leave for what could be as long as a day seemed to make the walls close in around us. I began shivering and Thomas tightened his arms around me in an attempt to keep me warm. He was trying to ease or at least share some of my stress. Exhausted, I finally dropped off. I fell asleep sometime during the cold early morning hours and I dreamed. Thomas and I were together. I could sense that our bond had strengthened somehow though neither one of us was wearing a ring. We were gazing into each other's eyes, but were distracted by a voice in the corner of the room.

"You can't do this," said the hurt child's voice, "you promised me they'd come home."

I turned my head then to find the voice and saw Clarissa huddled in the corner of the room as if she were lying under blankets. Her eyes were closed and I immediately realized that she was dreaming.

"But Clarissa," I responded, "you are home, honey. Look around, all of your family is here now."

As I said it I took inventory of the room. Rosalyn was there with a defeated look on her face. Roger, Madeline, and Rose were there also. The latter three were standing together with large smiles on their faces which didn't quite seem to reach up to their crimson eyes.

"We're all family now, and we'll always be together," I said softly to her.

"You promised, Mommy promised, she said it was time for you to come home," as she said this she opened her eyes and pierced my heart. I panicked realizing what had happened and how it had all gone so incredibly wrong.

"Clarissa, how did you get here?" I asked.

"I came on my own to show you," she looked incredulous, "don't you remember, you told Mommy that I was the key, but then you changed your mind and went there for yourself. Dominic took you and didn't give you back, he won. You came out, but so did they and look at them, look at their eyes. Look at what you have done!"

"Stop," I yelled, shaking my head and closing my eyes. As Clarissa had finished talking, they all started coming at me, Rosalyn included, "Please, stop!!!"

I continued to scream over and over until I heard Thomas's panicked voice, "Elizabeth, Elizabeth," he called trying to wake me.

"I...I...I...this is not going to work," I said in a terrified voice, "I think I may have just seen our future and it's not good."

I was trembling again as I saw the last scene of my dream playing on repeat in my head.

"Whatever you saw, let it go. You're frightened, as you should be, but that doesn't mean that this won't work. Remember, you can be convincing, every bit as much as Rosalyn is, you just have compassion to go along with that and that's what is bringing this dream and all the worry that you have. We need to make confidence replace those insecurities," he said as he kissed my forehead, "we'll start in the morning. Rest now and try to sleep."

Thomas's words worked to calm me and I quickly fell back to sleep and knew nothing else until the daylight started to peer through the entrance of our underground escape.

That morning I was inundated with plans and instructions for how to handle the onslaught of Rosalyn and Dominic. Rosalyn would be harsh, at least until I could get her to believe that I was joining with them. I could already hear that impatient yet righteous tenor of her voice as she would mock the interests that I still held to this day...*I told you those things weren't for you, well, you had to learn sometime*...it would be hard for me to hold my tongue on that subject, but I would do it. I kept telling myself that though the dream of the previous night poisoned my thoughts.

Though I knew nothing of Dominic, Madeline and Rose gave me the feeling that he would be the real problem. He had the ability of manipulation down well. He was very charming when he wanted to be and he was well aware of his talents so he'd be leaning on them. On top of being charming, he was able to appear in the form that was most appealing to those he wanted to sway. He was able to flit through your mind and see what was most appealing to you and present himself in that way. He would have your attention, and often your acceptance, before you even thought twice about what you just agreed to. There were very few on the island that have actually been in Dominic's presence. That was reserved for those that were most resistant to Rosalyn's teachings. Only Theresa and Shauna have met with him. Both took a lot of coaxing to bring them out of the mental state that Dominic had left them in.

The clouds were becoming more ominous and a fine mist began to fall slowly through the sky as the morning progressed to afternoon. Madeline checked in with me and told me that Rosalyn was still lost as to where we could have gone. She had no idea that there were any underground tunnels and she was starting to think that maybe I'd gotten too close to the water and taken Thomas with me. Madeline said that Dominic would likely be here by nightfall which meant that we had to iron out the logistics of the plan. We'd been working so much with what I'd say to Rosalyn and Dominic; we hadn't really talked about the others.

Theresa had noticed, "What about preparing the others to leave or isn't that part of the plan anymore?"

"We should prepare them to leave," I tried to cool Theresa's temper, "but we don't know what's going to happen yet and under pressure and pain, we don't know what can be said. I think it's best that we keep this to ourselves for the time being. At least until we have a feasible escape plan. I can't imagine there'd be a lot here that they'd want to take with them."

"You'd be surprised," she gave me a look.

Anyway, we need to get Rosalyn to believe and Dominic to think that I'm more capable than her. All the while, I'm somehow going to have to hold on to my real purpose while Dominic does his best to alter my mind. It's going to be a miracle if this works, but if it does look like it's going to come out that way; you have my word, Theresa, no one will be left behind, not even Rosalyn if I can help it," I added mostly to myself.

"*When* you succeed," Thomas exclaimed, "we will all come out of this and go back to our lives having shared an interesting, yet frightening experience that we'll likely never forget; we are tied together now by this strange bond. It's not like we'll ever really be able to talk about what happened except among ourselves unless we're looking to spend our time locked up in a different kind of place…"

"Elizabeth," continued Thomas, "did I hear right? You're planning on bringing Rosalyn back with us too?"

"I owe that to my father and brother at least. My father still believes that he loves her and I want him to know what kind of person she really is. He has always thought that he lost 'a gem' as he says, when he lost her. My brother also does not realize what she is like. They should be able to see this for themselves," I said, coldly.

Thomas, Theresa, and I planned and schemed and discussed exactly how this was going to work. When the rain really begins to fall, that's our clue that Dominic will be along shortly. During that time I will go to Rosalyn and make myself known. I will tell her that Thomas and Theresa were safe with Rose and Madeline; that I convinced them of the truth, which is 'life here is preferable to anything that would happen out there.' I would convince her that I was working on Rose and Madeline and trying to convince them to bring Clarissa over. Since I'd already met little Clarissa I'll let on that I'm making some headway in that direction, though I'm far from getting her here yet.

In the meantime, Dominic will make his arrival and see that I've come forward. When he begins to question me I'll tell him that I came here of my own free will. Rosalyn will try to convince him that she was the one that brought me here, but I'll stay firm that I decided on my own that the way to be happy was to come here and join Rosalyn and Dominic in their efforts to create a home that will dominate others. They will be suspicious at first, but I will put on my best, most convincing voice and stay firm in my story.

Thomas and Theresa will have their own role to play. No doubt Rosalyn and Dominic will hunt them out and ask them to confirm my story. They will also have to convince Dominic and Rosalyn that they are on board.

Since Rosalyn is aware of Thomas's feelings for me, we'll convince her that it's over.

"This is going to mean some real convincing, Thomas, are you okay with that?" I asked him.

"I'm not excited about it, but I'm willing to do what has to be done in order to bring all of us out of this," Thomas said stiffly.

Theresa looked off as one of the others popped their head in and nodded his head quietly with a smile.

"Thomas, Elizabeth, let's let the scheming go for a little bit and enjoy what little time we have left."

"What do you mean, Theresa?" I asked. "What are you talking about?"

"A gift," she said smiling, and pointing at a small opening I hadn't noticed before, "we've prepared a little bit of privacy for you. You're going to have to be someone you're not for a while, enjoy some time being who you are, with each other."

I was stunned into silence, but couldn't contain my gratitude for her kind words.

"Theresa, we are hardly the only couple here," I said, "but we thank you."

"You are taking the risk and we wanted to do something to show our gratitude. It's all of our lives at risk and we want you to know we appreciate what you're doing. We'd do more if we could."

"Theresa," Thomas stopped her, "this is touching. Please send our gratitude to everyone else."

"Well, time is short," she said, "I will send a warning whistle when you're out of time."

We turned from her, joined hands, and headed to the prepared space. There were a few steps down that led into another small cavern lit by daylight making its way through a few crude openings at the top covered loosely with pine needles. We were altogether amazed at what they'd been able to put together for us. There was a large blanket on the floor with a few feathery pillows placed on the far side. There was a small, hand woven basket that was filled with cheese, crackers, a few apples, and shockingly, a bottle of red wine. I remarked to myself that I'd have to ask Theresa how there happened to be a bottle of wine here. The food was understandable, but the wine was a treat I wasn't expecting. There were two cups fashioned out of tree bark that someone had tried to smooth over, but the edges were still quite sharp; one had to be careful sipping from this wine glass. Someone had even filched some candles and somehow they were lit and created a warm, glowing light. This was a very romantic moment for us both.

We went and sat on the blanket and looked at each other allowing all of the repressed fears to come to the surface for a moment before burying them again.

"Well, this was really nice of them," started Thomas.

"Yes, it really was. I'm surprised they thought to do this for us. It's not as if they don't have anything riding on this. I think it's sweet though."

"Just don't forget," Thomas said sadly, "you have just as much riding on this as everyone else, maybe more, so don't let anyone convince you that you're not worth saving. If you don't mind, I'd like to see you come out of this too. I know you feel like you have to sacrifice for them, but I'm really counting on seeing you again and spending every moment possible at your side when we all come out of this together."

"I won't forget," I promised, wondering how honest I was being with myself and him, "I will do everything in my power to come back to you. I will find a way to hold onto myself long enough to break through their hold on everyone here."

His face was inches from mine now as he spoke, "When you leave, my heart will be going with you and I won't be whole until you bring it back."

Our lips met then and moved together softly, but I wasn't going to let him end it this way. I pulled away from him and his eyes met mine with confusion.

"I don't know what's happened in the last few days, but I do know that no man has ever made me feel the way that you have. The first few times we met you drove me crazy; I thought I couldn't get away from you fast enough, but I found myself going over our conversation in my head. When you came back, I was overjoyed. I know that whatever happens my time with you has been the happiest of my life and will continue to be when all of this is over," I tried to sound confident, but was sure my wavering voice was giving me away, "I will also need you to hold onto my heart while I'm away."

I kissed him as I finished my last words. His soft lips met mine and the intensity flared. His arms felt good as they wrapped around my body and his fingers traced my spine. As our bodies mingled together it seemed that this small room would not be able to hold the intense passion that we felt for one another.

We lay quiet, exhausted, with our bodies twined together; the picnic blanket now wrapped us in a cocoon. I was enjoying the illusion of safety as I lived in the moment, but I could hear the pitter patter of raindrops as they picked up in intensity. I knew it would be minutes before Theresa arrived to tell us that it was time. I would have to walk away from this man that I was falling in love with, possibly for good. I curled myself into him as a child may look for the safety of their parents' arms. He tightened his grip on me for a quick minute.

"I'm guessing you're hearing the same rain that I am," he said quietly.

"I am, I'm sure Theresa will be here soon," I sighed.

"In that case, now would be a good time to give you this," he finished as he pulled a small, felt bag out of his pocket.

I looked at him, shocked, "What is that?"

"I've had this feeling, like something big was coming, since the first minute I saw you sit down on that bus. I had a feeling about you even then. When I decided to come with you out here no matter what that meant, I brought a little something that means a lot to me just in case things went the way I'd hoped for them to. Since they have, I want you to have this," he said as he handed me the bag, "It belongs to my mother and I always loved it when she would wear it. I'm now giving it to you in the hopes that having it and wearing it will keep me at the forefront of your mind and heart."

I opened the bag and saw a small, silver chain. It was delicate and it held an intricately designed silver heart, "It's beautiful. I've never seen anything quite like it. Is it an antique?"

"I'm glad you noticed. Yes, it's an antique piece. My grandmother's mother gave it to her when her father, my grandfather, died. She thought it would help her through the tough time she was suffering.

My grandmother gave it to my mother and my mother, believe it or not, gave it to me. I know it sounds funny to give a son something like that, but she always knew that I'd want to give it to someone that was very special to me; someone that had potential to become a part of my family," he said with steady eyes.

"On Thomas, I love it and I'm so glad that you've chosen me to give it to. If I had something with a weighty meeting like that to give back to you, I would in a second. Thank you so much."

I threw my arms around him and kissed him passionately, and then, like the omen that I knew was coming, we heard the whistle that signaled the end of our little heaven straight in the middle of our own hell.

"It's time, Elizabeth," Theresa's voice came from above, "You better get moving. Dominic will be here any minute now."

I suddenly felt anguished at the thought of having to leave the safety of Thomas's arms. He took my face in both of his hands and kissed me hard. He released me and we both got up, got dressed, and prepared to part ways.

"I will stay with you as long as I can be sure that I will go safely unnoticed. I don't want to leave your side," Thomas admitted.

"I know, I want you to stay with me too. I'm glad you'll stay with me for a while though.....coming Theresa," I called out after I heard an impatient sigh from outside.

We came up from our seclusion and I thanked Theresa again for giving us a bit of normalcy in this messed up situation. She told me that the rest of them had decided to hunker down at Shauna's hut since she won't readily be suspected.

If I were going to convince Rosalyn that Thomas and Theresa were 'on board' I'd have to give them time to get to Madeline and Rose so that they could verify our stories. Theresa also reminded me that I would have to guard my thoughts very carefully from here on out. If Dominic even gets a glimpse of what we're planning to do, all hope will be lost.

We walked in silence for a while, Thomas's fingers interlaced through mine for as long as we could possibly stay that way. All too soon, though, the trees started to thin again signaling the clearing that was near. This clearing reminded me of the river Styx, no one that passed through this arched dome of trees was likely to make it back to the other side.

Dominic was here to do one thing and that was to build himself a group of disciples. He would make them put of the facade of the worshipful like so many Christians attending mass on major holidays, yet they'd be forced to pay him homage on a daily basis.

Ever closer came the moment that I would have to leave all those that loved and cared about me and walk alone through those gates and straight up to the door. I wondered who would be there first, Dominic or Rosalyn? Or would they come together so they could work as one in taking my mind and warping it?

We stopped walking and I gazed at Thomas with pained, but loving eyes, "I guess this is as far as you can go. It's not going to take long for Rosalyn and Dominic to come looking."

My eyes did not leave his as I directed the others back. I kissed him fiercely and ran my fingers through his hair as I held tightly as I could to him. The tears had sprung up in my eyes as I broke off the kiss as suddenly as I'd started it. Tears were now welling in his eyes as well.

"I will be here, whenever you can get away, and whenever you need me. I love you."

"I love you too," I couldn't believe our first declaration of love would be here, but we'd all but said it in the cave anyway. I backed away and steeled myself for what would be coming as I stepped out into the open air.

Chapter 11

I mustered all of the courage that I had and I continued the journey to the edge of the trees without looking back. I could not look back. If I allowed myself one weak moment, I would go running back into Thomas's arms and he would do nothing to stop me. It was as hard for him to watch me go as it was for me to leave; I would not now double that pain for both of us by looking into his longing eyes. Thomas and Theresa both had their parts to play as Rosalyn would not linger long once I had come to them.

When I went through those doors I would ask for Dominic. I would not give her the satisfaction of thinking that she's won entirely. I would find Dominic and tell him that I am ready to join his cause. That would satisfy him enough to take some suspicion away from me. Since he can override everything Rosalyn can do, I better do a quick job of convincing him.

"*He's here,*" I heard Madeline's voice in my head. I knew he'd be able to hear her say that too, but he wouldn't know that the thought was directed at me so he'd just assume that she was thinking it toward Rosalyn or Rose. I started guarding my own thoughts as though they were on trial in front of a firing squad.

They knew I was coming, Madeline had told them as much. They'd have to believe that I was coming with perfect confidence. I walked directly toward them and tried to envision myself talking with Dominic. That would let him know immediately that that was what I was here for and hopefully he'd come looking for me before I could find him. Unfortunately, luck was not on my side. Before I could reach the door, Rosalyn opened it and stared at me with a smug look in her deep brown eyes.

"So, you finally decided to stop running," she said as she looked around me, "where is your entourage?"

"I'm here alone and I'm not here to talk to you, Rosalyn. Where is Dominic?" I stared at her, deadpan.

"I don't really know that that is any of your business," she responded, "maybe you've gotten too close to Thomas. I know that Madeline and Rose want to protect him, but I don't think there's any point. With Dominic here, it's not like anyone can resist him," she couldn't entirely disguise the sadness in her voice as she said this.

She was watching my reactions closely and I knew that I had mis-judged my enemy. She was more formidable than I thought. She was trying to root out the real purpose of my arrival on her doorstep. She'd tried to enter into my thoughts before and was able to in my dreams, but in my waking mind, I was too strong for her. She was not about to give up.

"Well, maybe it was Madeline," she said, fishing again though coming up empty. I could see her frustration growing, though she worked to keep her face smug, "she and Rose have some sort of plans to overthrow me and try to put her pathetic little family back together."

My face wavered for a moment at this. Madeline and Rose were so sure that Rosalyn knew nothing about their plans. I felt a moment of panic. She didn't miss it.

"Ahh, I'm coming closer to the truth," she said, reclaiming her smug posture, "well, we'll have lots of time to talk about all of these wonderful developments now, won't we?"

"I'm not here to talk to you," I said through gritted teeth, "and you're avoiding my question. Where is Dominic? It's him that I want to talk to."

"So sure of yourself, are you?" she asked, "well, it happens that Dominic is doing a little work right now. He's busy rounding up Thomas, Madeline, and Rose, and that traitor Theresa. We've decided that it was time we had a talk with all of them."

I was sure she was telling the truth, but also sure that she was looking for a reaction. I hadn't expected anything else. I knew they'd want to question all of them and that we were all in danger of being treated. But Clarissa was still nowhere in her thoughts which made me feel smug.

I wouldn't give her the satisfaction of seeing me react the way she was hoping. She hadn't mentioned anything about the latest set of plans that we'd been talking about so I held on to the hope that she knew nothing about them. I made sure that my mind was busy with other things. I held my posture and my face steady and allowed her to search for a reaction that she was not going to get. Her face gew sour as she realized that she was not instilling fear into me. My confidence seemed to make her angry and she decided on a new course of action.

"So, Thomas is your boyfriend, is he?" she asked snidely, clearly enjoying the reaction she was so sure this would bring about.

"No," I countered, remaining calm, "that ended before it really began."

I tried to sound bitter to give her the impression that things had ended badly. Hopefully this would be enough to get her to leave him alone. We'd been over this story many times and I knew he'd be able to confirm what I was telling her now when he was under her hypnotic gaze.

I went on when it was clear she was waiting for an explanation, "Thomas decided that he'd rather be with one of your zombie girls."

"Really? Which one?" She sounded almost giddy. We'd also prepared for this part. We picked the one that we knew she'd be the least suspicious of.

"Shauna," I said, trying to sound cold and jealous.

"Well, isn't that interesting," she said smiling, clearly enjoying the jealousy that I was displaying, "so what about you, do you get to end up alone?"

"Guess so," I replied with a smirk, "just what you were hoping for, right? Now that I'm alone, there's nothing to go back for anyway."

"So is that what made you change your mind about us?" she asked.

"Yep," I said, sounding sad.

"Well, we'll see what Dominic says about that. It seems he's back."

She was clearly happy to get away from this little conversation. She was not intimidating me at all and that was something she wasn't used to. She didn't like the fact that I came here of my own accord, which was, of course, our plan. This was only the beginning.

I trailed along behind her as she stormed out of the room clearly upset with the lack of fear that I felt. I quickly and lightly traced the shape of the heart on the necklace as I walked behind and tried to keep my thoughts away from Thomas. I would only allow myself the slightest graze over the intricately designed heart hiding so close to my beating one when no one was looking.

"She is asking for you," Rosalyn said flatly as we entered the room that held all of the pieces of my heart, and I got my first eyeful of Dominic.

I tried to remember his ability for deception as I looked over his flawless features. His eyes were a piercing, intense, emerald green. His dark brown hair fell around the sides of his angular, yet pale face. He was larger than life, yet only slightly taller than Thomas. His muscles billowed through the black t-shirt he was wearing. He turned the full force of his gaze in my direction and showed his bright, white teeth in a smile that could melt a room.

"Well, hello there Elizabeth," he said as if we were old friends, "I've heard so much about you already. I feel like I know you. Rosalyn, darling, please take Theresa to the kitchen and feed her. This poor thing looks like she's about to starve."

They left the room and I realized that Dominic was putting on a show of his own. He wanted to impress me. I suddenly had a good feeling about everything.

Turning back to me slowly and unleashing his full manipulative force, Dominic spoke, "Sorry to hear that things between you and Thomas didn't work out. You would have made an attractive couple."

They were already testing, making sure that our stories add up.

"Yes," I said returning the smile he gave me, "it is too bad. It hurts to see that he seems more taken with Shauna."

It took everything in me not to dwell on the pained look in Thomas's eyes. I had to remember, just as Thomas did, that we're doing this to keep ourselves alive and in one piece. It killed me that I couldn't even attempt to make Thomas feel better by looking at him, but the ruse was the most important now and we had to follow through on it.

"Well then," Dominic said with indiscernible eyes, "now that our awkward reunion is out of the way, let's get to business. Thomas has decided to rejoin his family and stay here on the island. Apparently, he, too, as Elizabeth has mentioned, has struck up a new romance with one of the girls here. Thomas, I hope you're happy as well. So now, we can all be one happy family in our quest to bring others out of the gloom of life on the other side and show them the joy that is life with us."

As he continued to talk I realized that now was as good a time as any to start down the path of usurping Rosalyn's place by Dominic's side. I had these thoughts almost unconsciously and worried for a minute that I'd be caught, but Dominic was preoccupied by his eager vision of the future here.

"Dominic," I called softly, matching his easy tone, "may I have a word with you alone please?"

"Yes, my dear, why don't you wait for me there?" he asked as he pointed to the room that I'd just come out of.

"*No Mamma no*," I suddenly heard somewhere far in the back of my mind. I grimaced as though in pain and Thomas caught it with his eyes. I looked back at him and ever so subtly nodded my head in an effort to explain to him that I was okay.

"Aren't you supposed to be waiting for me, dear? In the other room?" Dominic noticed my hesitation.

"I just wasn't sure which room you pointed to." I said, covering my tracks.

"We'll see," he said and pointed again.

I walked toward the room on the left as he'd pointed out. He followed just behind me, "Now, what is this all about? Why do you want to see me in private? Can't you say what you need to in front of everyone?"

"Don't you know?" I prodded, "I thought you could read the thoughts of everyone here."

He smiled as he prepared his answer, "Oh, my reputation does precede me, doesn't it? Rosalyn said you seemed awfully well informed about me and my abilities for someone who hadn't met me."

He was fishing too, just like she had done. I didn't let my face or my voice betray me, "people do talk, you know."

"Well then, what was it that you wanted to see me about?" he asked.

"Oh, no, you still haven't answered my question," I pressed, "you should know if your reputation truly precedes you. Why don't you tell me?"

"Fine then," he snapped, "I was trying to listen to everyone at once and it became too much. That's all. Now, one more time, what do you want to talk to me about?"

I couldn't believe how quickly he'd lost that cool, confident exterior that he'd held. He didn't like the fact that I'd noticed so much, nor that I felt comfortable pushing him for an answer.

"Rosalyn," I said, satisfied that I'd learned so much already, "I think I could do better for you."

"Really?" his mood settled and his eyes piqued in curiosity, "she never spoke that highly of you. She always said that you'd want nothing to do with what was happening here. She said you were far too much of a humanitarian to allow something like this to happen. Convince me. Why do you think you can do better than her?"

"First of all," I started off strong, "If Rosalyn truly wanted to be a leader, would she allow her people to suffer so? Most of them have festering sores because of the malnutrition that they've suffered. Their homes reek with human waste. If you want to create a city of those that worship you, shouldn't you give them something to worship? I know the mind alterations are necessary so that people don't go to extremes, but should they really be treated like disposable garbage too? Eventually, they will find a way to overthrow you."

I could see the cogs moving in his mind, he was imagining what it might be like with me at his side instead of her…so far so good. I was growing more confident as I continued. I began to pace around him so that his imagination could get the full picture.

"Rosalyn is losing her control. She couldn't find me. This is such a small place and she had no idea after a full day of searching. She's supposed to be the one with the powerful mind link; yet she couldn't even find me. I'm her flesh and blood. I think you deserve someone that has won over the people and someone that is stronger than she is. I can fill that role for you."

He was lost in his musings so it took him a moment to realize I'd stopped talking. He composed himself to respond, trying to sound disconnected, like these thoughts didn't excite him, "It's something I'll take into consideration, but since we just met, I'm not entirely sure I'm ready to risk it. Still, you make some good points and it's an intriguing idea."

"You'll be getting what you want, a stronger leader that can track down others and do your bidding without mistake. I don't need to brainwash everyone, I already have their trust. I'm younger and my senses are sharper than hers," unexpectedly I found myself visualizing this future and liking what I saw. I cast that thought out of my head as quickly as I could.

"Like I said, I'll keep it in mind, but now I wonder if you'd do something that may show me just how serious you are in your intentions to join us?"

I was worried, but I knew that I'd be tested, "Yes?"

He came right up to me now and brought his face just inches from mine. I could see the evil that lurked under the perfected surface. I saw hints of the crimson hiding behind the green in his eyes and they held me in a steady gaze. I realized what had brought him so close. This was his first attempt to hypnotize me.

I had to make him believe that he'd succeeded. I planted the picture of the necklace Thomas had given me in the center of my mind and I kept focus on it. I felt my eyes get heavy and my voice get sleepy, but my intellect was still mine. I could almost feel the weight of the miniscule chain that hung around my neck as I focused all of my thoughts on that one picture. I expected Dominic to know that I was picturing this, but either he did not, or he just tossed it aside as some trinket I received. Either way he did not bring it up.

"If you're going to take her place, you're going to have to administer the lessons that she administers now. Rosalyn's already told me what a humanitarian you are so I know it will take some time for you to be able to do this effectively. I want to provide you with some practice.

"Thomas is being brought into a room. Rose and Madeline are with him," silently I breathed a sigh of relief at this news, "Rosalyn is administering and they are watching over Thomas since he's escaped once already. I need you to pay attention to the treatment and watch carefully what Rosalyn does.

"Rosalyn's usefulness is coming to an end, you're right about that; I will be paying very close attention in the next few days to see what you do..." his barely veiled threat trailed off.

"Show me the way," I said to him blankly.

He took my arm lightly and we walked along a short hallway with two doors. Thoughts of Clarissa's little voice tried to creep through to the front of my consciousness, I pushed it out of my mind as quickly as possible. I thought about my brother Aaron who was probably just about frantic by now since he hadn't heard from me in several days."

"Don't worry, Aaron will see you again...someday. Sooner than you think, actually," Dominic chuckled.

I flinched as I realized Dominic had been reading my thoughts very clearly and wondered why, if I was staying here, I'd see Aaron again. Again, he responded to my thoughts.

"He'll come here looking for you, not that it will change anything," Dominic said with a smile.

I kept my horror in check and followed along trying to think of nothing at all.

We finally made it to the room that held all of my cohorts; they tried not to notice the desperation in my face. Thomas was already staring straight ahead, faking the hypnosis as he had done earlier in order to escape this very room.

Dominic passed here and looked at me before speaking quietly. He gazed into my eyes for a moment, then spoke with a soft voice that could easily be mistaken for a man agonizing over something, "You know, I didn't pick this either, but I can't think of a better way to spend my time in this place than with such beauty. Thomas is a fool for not realizing what he had."

His hands traced the outlines of my face as he made his little speech.

"I am going to have to speak to Rosalyn for a few minutes, and then I have to be getting back below. It seems that a search party is planning on coming to the island to look for you. We can't do anything while they're here, so I must go for now. Please, don't forget me while I'm gone as I'm sure I'll be thinking of you every moment that I am away," in a very unexpected move, his lips met mine as he finished speaking and before I knew it his tongue worked to part my lips.

I had plenty of kisses today alone, but none quite like this one. His forked tongue made for a very odd sensation as the two edges met and parted ways. He looked intensely at me for just a moment when he pulled away, and then his eyes went directly to Thomas.

I suddenly knew what he was doing. Our test was still not over. He wanted to see if he could provoke a reaction from Thomas, but true to his word and not wanting to blow his cover, Thomas remained unmoved. Dominic must have been concentrating on Thomas's thoughts as he kissed me, but they had not betrayed him. We were still safe in the facade that we were putting on for them. I realized that Dominic had said something about leaving and decided to press my luck. I was ready this time when Dominic returned his gaze in my direction.

"Well," I said soothingly, reaching up and placing my hand on his chest, trying to look adoringly at him, "that was something. How long will it be until those lips return?"

"Oh, not long I suppose. A few days; however long it takes for them to give up on their search. Please remember that when they get close enough for you to see them, they won't be able to see you and by the time I return you should have made your intentions clear," he said as he nodded toward Rosalyn.

"Yes, that won't be a problem," I said, batting my eyes flirtatiously.

"I'll see you sooner than you think."

I took that as a warning and decided that we couldn't relax just yet. Madeline would be able to tell us when Dominic was out of hearing range, and then we could talk openly. I was beginning to feel like a marionette just waiting for someone else to pull the strings that would have me dancing across stage again. This was the role that I'd agreed to play and I would play it. Now was not the time to back down.

"Mamma, please, you said you'd come home now. Where are you?" I heard Clarissa's panicked voice again. I looked up and saw that Madeline was already staring straight at me trying, unsuccessfully, to hold back the tears in her eyes.

"Can't talk now, work to do," Madeline did her best to make it clear to me that Dominic had not turned off the 'ears' yet. I understood and gave her a slight nod. She continued talking quietly to Thomas.

I was ready to put on a show for Dominic as I knew he'd be watching at least in the beginning before he went and talked to Rosalyn. Madeline began as she heard Rosalyn do earlier.

"Thomas, why did you come to the island?" she asked with her voice full of meaning.

"I came," he responded sleepily, "to…to…to find someone, I think her name was Elizabeth."

He was laying it on thick and I could tell he also realized that Dominic would be listening. Just like before he didn't want to 'break' too soon.

"Mom," Madeline said looking at her with cold, hard eyes, "I don't think your son quite got the message yet. Please remind him."

She took her thumb and forefinger and placed them at the crux of where the neck and shoulder meet. She increased the pressure on both of her fingers until she saw his reaction. His face twisted in pain and I could hardly restrain myself. I took comfort from the fact that this was an act. Dominic was still watching. We had to continue in this way constantly asking questions and exploiting pressure points until we got the responses we desired. Finally, after what seemed like hours, though I don't think it was actually more than one, Madeline was speaking in my head.

"He's finally gone, we can stop this now," I looked at her.

"What about Rosalyn?" I asked timidly.

"Her thoughts are too caught up in Dominic's visit for now. He gave her a lot to think about as he shared what you told him today. He's playing both sides of the fence until he's sure what course he'll take," sighed Madeline.

"Why hasn't she come after me yet?" I asked incredulously.

"She's not ready. He really hurt her with his insults and she's grieving for his high opinion of her; but I'm sure that it won't take her long," as she finished, Thomas opened his eyes and looked at me lovingly. I didn't deserve him.

"I'll tend to Rosalyn's wounded ego," Madeline said, "I'll warn you if her thoughts are going to go to yours. I doubt it though, I think she's going to come at you head on," she saw my wide eyed expression and she gestured with her hand in the universal hands out gesture to stop, "I'm not telling you this to scare you, I just want you to be prepared for what's coming."

She left the room and Thomas and I were left alone. I could feel the pained expression in my eyes as I looked at him. I felt like I didn't deserve those looks of adoration he was throwing my direction.

"Do I get another chance with those lips today? Or are you saving them up for more important matters?" His voice was joking, but I didn't see that joke in his eyes.

I hurriedly kissed him then. I wanted to take advantage of every moment that we had together. I sat on a stool that was placed next to him and rested my chin next to his muscular chest. I stared at him for a long time in silence trying to think about what I could say to him, and then I looked up into his bright gray-blue eyes and was swept away. Tears had begun to fall from my eyes and I couldn't quite compose myself to start.

"It's okay," he said as he rubbed my back, "I know this is hard for you, but you're doing great."

"I'm not worried about me," I said finally able to speak through the sobs, "I had to kiss Dominic knowing that if I didn't do it our cover would be blown and who knows what would happen to us then. Dominic is testing me and testing you too. He's looking for our reactions. Rosalyn's going to do the same thing as soon as she gets me alone. All I can do is think about your necklace. I feel like if I can envision that then at least it's sort of like you are the person that I'm kissing."

"Listen, don't be so worried. Of course it's hard for me to watch you kiss and flirt with someone else, but don't think I missed the few times today when your hand went to my heart hiding next to yours. That is your necklace now," he said with unimaginable patience, "I'm glad that that is what you've chosen to keep in your mind while you're doing deplorable things like kissing other men."

I smiled at his playful mood, but couldn't hold it for long as I remembered why my thoughts had to be hidden from Dominic and Rosalyn both. My face went rigid as stone as I replayed the panicked voice that I heard in my mind. Based on Madeline's nod from earlier, I'm sure I'm not the only one that heard it, but what could it mean?

"What is it, Elizabeth?" Thomas asked, concerned.

"Well, there was something else that was happening as I was putting on my ruse that I had to push to the back of my mind for her safety. It seems as though I might be sharing Clarissa's dreams. I explained to him in detail what I had heard and the fact that I believed that Madeline was aware of it too. I had to admit, this part of the puzzle was no longer fitting. Didn't she know that I was going to help her get her family back?

"If even Madeline knows and can't make sense out of it, I don't think there's a lot we can do right now. We couldn't even go back there and get her if we wanted to," Thomas responded.

"That's what scares me. What if she decides to come here by herself? She's smart, she could easily figure out how to get here, she wants her family back more than anything. What if she sees something in one of her dreams that makes her come here by herself?" my voice was growing more hysterical by the minute.

"Slow down, Elizabeth," Thomas said, "you're getting way ahead of yourself. Clarissa's dreams have been very vivid since this whole thing started. It doesn't mean that she knows something that will make her do anything. It just means that since you share this psychic connection with Madeline, perhaps you simply share this characteristic with Clarissa too.

Come here miss doom and gloom."

He said this last as he pulled me down into a kiss and a warm embrace.

"It's going to be okay, Elizabeth. We will win this together."

"Thank you and I know that. I suppose, somewhere, it's in there. I know that we'll get through this," I said miserably as I held him. We stayed like that, just holding each other and appreciating the stolen moments. Soon though, Madeline's voice was back in my head telling me that Rosalyn was on her way. I jumped up and Thomas fell right back into his acting mode. He stiffly rose from the bed and was pretending to stretch out his muscles as Rosalyn rounded the corner.

"I need to talk to you," she said, clearly annoyed, "hallway, now. Thomas, lay back for a minute. Don't go anywhere."

I couldn't turn my head to look at him as I marched out of the room. I had to stay calm and even as possible as I steeled myself for her wrath.

"What is it that you told Dominic? Exactly, I want every word," she said, accusingly.

Fishing again, "Why does it matter? That's between Dominic and me."

"He's shielding his thoughts from me, he's refusing to let me in on your conversation, but after he left you, he came to talk to me; he was less than happy. I want to know what you said to him," she was pouting now.

It would be better to play along with her now. Dominic's behavior toward me had shaken her.

"I didn't tell him anything he didn't already know. I told him that I had been hiding out and thinking about what I could do to get myself out of this situation. I had been contemplating how to get back home, then I came to the realization that I am home. My place is here with you now. I told him that my desires had changed and I wanted to stay here with you and him. I also told him that the subjects that he was hoping to rule needed to be better taken care of," I slipped that in to give her something to be upset about.

"Why did you say that? Those people are well taken care of," she actually looked surprised.

"Really, what are those sores that are popping out on their faces? It's called malnutrition. You don't even give them anywhere to dispose of their own waste. They are dirty and smell bad and they know it. You are keeping them alive, but they are hardly well taken care of."

"Fine," she said, calming, "I'll see what I can do to improve conditions for them. Maybe he'll be happier with me when I do that. He said we're going to have some visitors tomorrow; a search party for you."

"Yes, he told me too. I'm sure Dad and Aaron will be here, but he said they won't be able to see us. Don't you miss them at all?" I was trying to understand her choice.

"Honey, it was this or death, what I feel or what I wanted is long gone and forgotten…still," she said contemplating for a moment, and sounding a little like the mother that I lost, "it will be interesting to see them again. Your brother was always so worried about you."

Suddenly I was sure that she was putting on an act as much as the rest of us. I just wasn't sure if the act was for us or for Dominic. Either way she was starting to let her guard down. She really could be a caring person when she wanted to, but it seemed she'd let go of that person a long time ago. Now I was wondering though I didn't get a chance to bring it up. She turned and gestured for me to follow. We went back into the room where Thomas sat on the bed waiting for us. The brief flash of the person that had been my mother was now gone. In its place was the cold-hearted, grasping person that I now only knew as Rosalyn. Whether we were still a couple or not she knew I'd have feelings for him and her pettiness was getting the better of her just now. I guess I couldn't expect her to completely change just like that. She grabbed onto Thomas's shoulder and squeezed. From the anguished look on his face, I was guessing she'd found another of those pressure points.

"So Thomas," she said, slightly releasing the pressure, "what is it that you are here to do?"

"I am here to be with Shauna. I am happy and don't want to leave her," he said almost too mechanically.

"Hmm, and what about Elizabeth here, didn't you two have some sort of thing just a few days ago? Don't you care for her anymore?"

"I'm just not into Elizabeth like that, she understands," he said with a little more feeling.

She gave his shoulder another little squeeze and his anguish turned to genuine pain. His face was red and sweat beads began to stand out on his forehead.

"I'm not sure I should believe you yet. Neither is Dominic. We'll be watching," she threatened as she finally let go. Thomas's face was instantly relieved and I kept my eyes steadily on her. Of course she'd be wanting to see Thomas's pain reflected in my face, but I wasn't about to let that happen. This game had just begun and we were winning.

Rosalyn brushed past me and I went to Thomas quietly. Madeline was there in an instant blocking my way.

"Get out of here," she said with a knowing look in her eyes.

I didn't hesitate. I left the room with the understanding that this was, again, a test. Rosalyn wanted to see if I'd comfort Thomas or follow her out. I followed.

"Aren't you going to make sure he's okay?" She asked when she sensed me behind her.

"Madeline's there. She can do that. I need to know where I'll be staying, " I told her.

"There's an empty room down the hallway there," she said as she pointed off to her left. I've been reserving it for you."

"You knew I'd come?" I asked, surprised.

"I had a feeling," she allowed, "I'm wondering about something. If you came here with Thomas and met his family, what was the point of you coming on the island? If you're really here to join us, why did you come in the first place and what made you change your mind?" She sounded genuinely curious.

I made a split second decision. I pulled the locket out of my pocket that Roger had given me. She gasped when she saw it.

"Where did you get that?" I could hear confusion and anger creep into her voice, "I would swear I had it with me when I came here. In fact I'd been keeping it in your room, but a long time ago, it disappeared."

She didn't bring up Roger and neither did I. Dominic could have sent out Rosalyn's spirit self to give Roger that necklace for all I knew. Rosalyn's surprise seemed genuine.

"Well, Clarissa convinced me to come, that you already know, but when I got here and began to see all of the possibilities…it's like a new beginning. No school debt, no credit cards, no worries. Besides, it's not like anyone but Dominic will get what they want. Why fight it?" I was being convincing, but I needed the personal connection, "I know we weren't getting along when the accident happened, but I always missed you, Mom. I had to go through my whole adolescence with only two males in the house. What I wouldn't have given to have a female person around to guide me through those awkward years."

"Yes, well," she said trying to regain the coldness in her voice, "we would have been fighting the whole time. Maybe it was just as well."

I was incredulous again and I couldn't control my temper now, "Just. As. Well? Just as well that your entire family was torn apart and grieving after the accident? Just as well that Dad never really recovered from losing you? Just as well that Aaron had to go through life without his mother to guide him? How can you even say that? How can you actually be so selfish?"

"And you're not? Aren't you doing the same thing by coming here now?" She asked.

"Yes, I suppose I'm being selfish now, but my brother is a grown man and my father stopped living life a long time ago," I said accusingly.

That seemed to get her. I saw the flash of regret settle over her features as I described the one person she did care about.

"I'm truly sorry that your father had to suffer. I'm sorry about what you went through, and I'm sorry that I was so horrible that God decided that I wasn't good enough to live any longer. Dominic and his path is my choice now.

"Dominic's vision is going to come to fruition," I thought I noticed sadness in her voice as she said this, "and I will be here with him to rule over all of those that are here with us. I have given myself over to him. Here my thoughts and beliefs are valued and not mocked which was often the case with you. Your father always took your side, too. He never supported me. Here, I truly am treated like a queen," Dominic has been feeding her that lie for so long that she seemed to believe it.

I wanted to tell her that Dominic had kissed me and was hunting a suitable replacement for her. If she only knew what was really going on here, maybe I could change her mind and convince her to come home. I knew that words would not be enough. I knew that if I were entirely honest with her right now and told her everything that Dominic had told me, she wouldn't believe a word of it. She was too disillusioned by his hypnotic eyes and melodious voice. She would turn on me full force. No, I had to go along with this for a while. I had to continue allowing her to believe that I came here to redeem the years that the two of us had lost.

I extended an olive branch reaching just between admission of Dominic's plans and my plans to bring her home, "I might question Dominic's intentions for the future a little more, I worry that he has plans that he hasn't shared with you."

Plainly struck by my words, "I need to be alone for a little while, it's getting late anyway. Why don't you go find Thomas, Rose, and Madeline. They're your friends now; go spend time with them. They can fill you in on what happens here daily."

I was more than thrilled to do exactly what she said. I wanted to talk with Madeline about Clarissa and as soon as we were sure that Rosalyn was asleep, we could do that without fear. And, of course, I wanted to see Thomas. Though it couldn't have been pleasant for him today, I was so glad that he was a part of this. Knowing that he was close by made me feel like I could do anything to get us out of here. I rounded the door into the room where I'd left him and smiled as I took in his anxious face wondering whose steps he heard in the hallway. Immediately he beamed back at me and all was right with the world again, at least for the time being.

"Oh thank God, I was sure she was going to take you away and not allow you back," he said.

I noticed that Madeline and Rose had rejoined him here as he waited for me. I noticed that Madeline had been crying.

"What is it?" I asked, worried about another tragedy.

"It just gets to be too much sometimes," Madeline admitted, "hearing Clarissa today and knowing that she's confused. I just want to be able to go to her. If I could bring her here I could comfort her."

"I panicked too when I heard her voice," I tried to sound sympathetic, "you have to have faith that Roger will never let her do anything that would put her in danger. I believe that."

"Yes," she said sniffling, "you're right. At least she still has him."

"She still has all of us," I reminded her and took a stab at being play-ful, "we're just on extended holiday."

She forced a smile and rolled her eyes at me, but at least seemed to cheer slightly. Madeline assured us that Rosalyn had dropped off for the night, so the four of us went to camp out in my new room. I suddenly felt like an eleven year old having a slumber party.

I began by filling everyone in on what happened with Dominic. I told them that I didn't have him totally convinced, but he was certainly inter-ested in my desire to join them. I told them what he had told me about replacing Rosalyn and we all shared a horrified glance. Rose and Made-line were taken completely by surprise.

Dominic had always had little pet names for Rosalyn and there was definitely a bond there, but it was more of a partnership than anything else. Madeline was worried about him using his desire in a romantic way as a trick and something to upset Rosalyn with, but we decided that that was unimportant for the time being. Finally, I told them about the search party arriving tomorrow. I relayed the message that we'd be able to see them, but they'd have no idea we were here no matter how loud we could yell or any other signals we could give them.

Everyone immediately began talking about ways that we could signal the search party, but I was quite certain that Dominic would be very thorough. He wouldn't want anyone ruining what he's built here so I don't see him leaving it to chance. Dominic would not be here for the duration of their stay so there would be no storms or anything like that to tip them off; they'd simply find nothing. It would take them a day or two to entirely search the island and if I knew my Dad, which I did, I was certain they'd drag the lake, at least what they could. This gave me an idea.

"This is a necklace that ended up in Roger's possession," I said as I pulled it from my pocket for the second time today, "I showed it to Rosalyn and she freaked. This is only a theory, but if I can get this into the water, it's possible that it could land somewhere that it could be found by someone on the other side. I don't think that door extends beyond the surface and it certainly wouldn't go to the bottom of that little lake even if it did go down some. If my dad were to find it and recognize it, it may go a long way to making him realize that we are, in fact, here, even if he can't see us. Of course it may only prove that I was here once, but I don't think that will be enough of an explanation for him. I don't know how much it will help, but it's worth a shot…"

I trailed off as I had another idea, a much more far fetched idea, but possibly one that could even give our search party a little direction.

"Has anyone come up with any type of writing utensil here? Is there a way to…" My idea trailed off as the others started picking up on it. I saw Thomas realize what I was getting at and hsi smile widened as he took a pen out of the front pocket of his shirt. I couldn't believe the luck…I couldn't believe, I, of all people, didn't have a pen with me anywhere, then I remembered the hurry we'd been in and our adventurous road in and forgave myself a bit.

Thomas also pulled out a receipt from his pants pocket that he'd saved from a gas station. It was perfect, just big enough.

I took the pen and the paper and quickly scrawled a note in the hope that if they did drag the lake, my Dad would recognize it and pick it up. In that case he may open it and find a bit of hope.

Dad, we're here on the island, though you can't see us. We can see you. Wait for a storm and a door to open, follow through, but be careful. Not sure how to get back. Please come find us. P.S. Rosalyn is alive.

I felt bad asking him to come find us knowing what could become of him once he entered that door, yet I knew that once he saw Rosalyn for what she was, he'd be free of the ghost that's been haunting him all these years. Or maybe they'd be able to reconcile. Either way, he'd finally be able to move on and begin living again.

I carefully folded the note into a very small square and placed it in the center of the locket. I snapped the two pieces together so that the note was trapped inside. I sent up a silent prayer that everything that made this seem desperate would work in our favor. I prayed that the seal would hold and no water would get inside the clasp. I prayed that somehow the necklace would work its way under any kind of door that divides whatever world we're in from our own. I prayed that the picture inside, one happy family, would stay intact so that it could be recognized.

Aloud, I said, "I need to get to that water tonight. Once the search party makes the shore, I'm sure that Rosalyn will be watching my every move. I need to do this tonight while she's sleeping."

"I'm coming with you," said Thomas.

I wasn't about to argue. I knew our alone moments would grow fewer and further between as our ruse intensified. I was actually surprised I was already able to spend time alone with him after all of our heartfelt goodbyes earlier.

"Let's go," I said to him, to the others, "we'll be back soon. Please let me know if you get any indication that Rosalyn's on the move."

"I will, but I think you're safe. She's feeling very uneasy about Dominic and his plans right now," Madeline responded.

Quietly, we left the room, made our way to the door, and exited without stirring any suspicion.

"This is going to be hard for you tomorrow, isn't it? Seeing your Dad and brother so closely and not being able to contact them, I mean."

"I feel like I'm doing something to reach out to them," I responded with a shrug, "I feel like, if they find this necklace, at least they'll know that I'm out here somewhere. And if they don't find it, at least I'll know that I did everything I could to help them find me. Yes, it's going to be difficult, but I will be able to find comfort in what I've done. It's a long shot either way, but I've done what I could."

We both continued down the path silently. He could tell that I was caught up in thoughts of my Dad and brother and their arrival tomorrow, but his feet began to slow as we were reaching the edge of the trees and onto the open sands of the beach.

"Don't we want to get there tonight?" I asked a little sarcastically.

"Yes, but I wanted to ask you something first. It was something you sort of glossed over earlier when you were telling us everything that happened," he said.

"Okay, ask away," I said, confused as to where he was going with this.

"Well, I know that you and Rosalyn talked and she knows that your father and brother will be here tomorrow. Does that hold no persuasion for her? Does she not care that she will be able to see them again after all of this time?" He asked and I thought I could see the direction of his mind. It made me nervous.

If Dominic could make Rosalyn forget the love of her life so completely, and the children that they shared, wouldn't he be able to do the same with me?

"Rosalyn didn't know what was coming. She knew she was going to die and she was feeling extremely bitter and resentful about it. Dominic used that. He played on her feelings and did what he could to make it seem like he was giving her everything that her 'other' life had denied her. I have none of those qualities about me and I'm going into this knowing exactly what kind of enemy I'm up against," I tried to reassure Thomas.

"I just hope you still feel that way after you see the looks on the faces of your father and brother, especially if they find that necklace," he said as he gestured to it, "I'm not sure you're ready for that."

"If it gets to be too much for me, I'll turn away. I'll walk back to the compound claiming a headache or something like that. She'll have to know that this will be hard for me to watch."

"That's what I'm afraid of," he replied, "sounds like something she would get a kick out of."

"Come on, let's get this thing sunk," I said, rolling my eyes and grabbing his hand as I stepped forward.

We left the relative safety of the trees and were on the beach. I walked right up to the water's edge and was about to fling the locket when Thomas surprised me. I must have been very caught up in my imaginings of my dad or brother finding the trinket because I didn't even hear him come up behind me.

Suddenly his arms were wrapped around my waist. I turned to look in his eyes before I could fully get my head around, he drew my face in and kissed me hard. His intensity surprised me, but I was elated. Already to be back in his embrace, the only place I wanted to be after saying our goodbyes; it had to be a good sign, right? I pulled away from him for a moment as I thought I caught something on the distant shore in the corner of my eye. Thomas looked at me concerned.

"Elizabeth? Elizabeth? What's going on? What's ove…" He couldn't finish the word as his eyes followed mine and landed on the small outline on the opposite bank. Standing all alone in the distance was Clarissa. She was at the water's edge. I could see her as if she were standing right next to us.

"*You have to keep your promise. You have to bring them back to me. Don't let him win.*"

"I won't let him win, sweetheart. Please go back to your grandpa. As long as I'm in control of my own thoughts, he will never win," I thought and said at the same time.

"*That's what Rosalyn said,*" she said sadly, lowered her eyes to the ground, and turned to go back home.

"I'm not Rosalyn," I tried to reassure her.

"So much for a romantic stroll on the beach," Thomas said, disappointed.

"Let's get this done," I said, my thoughts now on Clarissa and her sad eyes.

The necklace was already in my hand. I took it and threw it as hard as I could. It seemed to make a pretty good distance before it plunked into the water and settled below.

"Okay, job done, let's go," I said shortly.

"Wait a minute," Thomas pleaded, "I knew we said this earlier, but we may not have much time left to spend together. Are we just going to stomp off and not enjoy the stolen moments that the situation presents us with? I'm not ready to go back."

"I'm sorry, I'm just so freaked out about what Clarissa said. This is starting to come apart at the seams, or I am, I'm not really sure anymore," I said, reaching my boiling point.

"Slow down, and please share for those of us that aren't clairvoyant. What is it that Clarissa said to you?"

"I explained to him Clarissa's words and seemed pretty at ease about the whole thing. He said there was a very easy explanation which was that Rosalyn would promise Clarissa just about anything to lure her onto the island. True to kids' natures, Clarissa would naturally want to help and that would be the end of us all. Rosalyn would simply pull the blanket right out from under Clarissa and she'd become one of the brainwashed laborers; here to serve those in charge.

I allowed him to calm my nerves. He kissed my lips and my throat and I found myself deliciously distracted, my fears melting away not being able to withstand the fire that was suddenly ripping through every inch of me. When he felt I was calm enough to go on, he led me back to our underground haven. The blanket from this afternoon was still laid out on the ground where we'd left it.

As we approached it he looked at me with a sparkle in his eyes. He raised and lowered his eyebrows a few times and I could no longer resist. I no longer wanted to resist. I suddenly turned on him and wrapped my body around his. I craved the warmth and safety of his arms. I took advantage of this moment that I never dreamed we'd have after meeting Dominic.

"We're going to have to get back there," I said after our breathing returned to normal, "if she finds us gone…I don't want to think about those treatments again."

"Yes, I suppose you're right. We should be getting back. Here, let me help," he said as I'd already started gathering my clothes. As his head popped through the top of his t-shirt, his eyes gave away what his smile was trying to conceal. He was terrified. Whether it was losing me, losing this fight, losing his entire life to this place, or a combination of all of those I could not tell.

"You know, you don't have to be so brave all the time," I stated the cliche as old as time itself.

"Yes I do. I've had to be brave for myself, I've had to be brave for my father and niece, now I'm adding my mom and sister to that list. But most of all I have to be brave for you. Just as you hold in your head a picture of that necklace, I also have to keep something in mind in order to stay positive. What keeps me going is you. I picture your sweet face when I'm trying to focus on being hypnotized. It gets me through so that I never really lose consciousness."

"I'm flattered, and I love you too," I said with a smile.

We walked back quietly lost in our thoughts. I knew tomorrow would be hard. Even if I was lucky enough to have my brother or father find that necklace, would they really be able to understand what it meant? If they hang around and wait for a storm to come through, then what? Did I just sentence them to the same fate that is staring me in the face? I didn't know, but I wasn't sorry I'd done it. There was something that told me it was the right thing to do and I usually like to go with my intuitions.

We approached the hallway that would lead us back to my room, Thomas grabbed my hand and squeezed. It was amazing how much comfort I got from that small gesture. I found myself almost believing that this may all turn out okay. The odds were still incredibly against us, but perhaps the tide was turning?

All my guests were gone when we returned. Thomas already had a room arranged for him; he went there now. We all slept and prepared for the time when my family, friends, and loved ones would be out looking for me. I knew I'd have a very hard time just watching, but was sure that

Rosalyn wasn't bluffing. Mine will not have been the first search and rescue mission and mine will go away just as empty handed as the prior ones had. But maybe I'd be able to give them a moment of hope in their doubt and frustration. That was all I could do; or was it? I was thinking of this psychic connection and wondering if just being here was enough to make my voice amplify when needed. I couldn't help but try to send the message to my father that they'd have to drag the lake. I never thought in a million years he would have heard me, but I never would have believed a lot of things until my ill-fated first writing assignment as an independent reporter landed me here.

"Why not?" I whispered to myself as I reached out with my message.

Chapter 12

"*Drag the lake*," was the last coherent thought I had before I drifted into a fitful sleep. I had been trying to send my message over and over in the hopes that Benjamin Milton would somehow be part of this weird psychic connection that has made itself known since I've been here.

Daylight was drifting in through the crude window. The sun was shining bright…too bright. How long had I slept? I sat up with a start and quickly got to my feet. Rosalyn was there, waiting for me to get up. She wore a smug smirk on her face, yet her fingers ever twisting the small tissue in her hands told a different story. She was nervous.

"Finally getting up?" she asked suspiciously, "Have a late night?"

"Just a lot of dreams," I said.

"No visitors last night then?"

"A few friends stopped by to check on me, nothing more. You told me to go find Thomas and the others and I did and we visited a while. They wanted to see how I was adjusting, but otherwise, a quiet night. So, are you ready to see them again?" I was genuinely curious how she would take this.

"See who?" she asked.

"Who do you think? You haven't seen your husband and son in over a decade and you're not the slightest bit worried? I see you twisting that tissue over and over…" a thought occurred to me then, "why do you have that tissue anyway? Are you concerned that you may actually feel something when you see them?"

"I will feel nothing," her reply sounded very practiced, "They are not my future, they are my past. Dominic and the home I've created here are the only future I want."

"Very convincing," I said sarcastically.

"Butt out, Elizabeth." She said, frustrated.

"Not a problem, I don't want to be around you for this anyway." I turned to leave the compound hoping she didn't hear my voice catch as I rounded the corner. I just couldn't see why she couldn't admit, at least to me, that today's going to be hard for her too.

I walked out into the open air and steeled myself for my family's arrival. I continued down the path until the trees cleared and the beach opened itself to the warm, sunny day. Though there were often small boats out tooling around, I immediately spotted the two that were headed to our small island. I counted as they got closer and saw that one boat held six passengers and the other held five. I was shocked that my dad would be able to pull that number of people together for this search party.

The boat that held the six was made up of my three cousins and their wives. Paul, Tim, and Henry and I had grown up pretty close and I liked all of their wives. I was the youngest of the cousins and the last remaining single person among us though they'd all gotten married within the last five years. The other boat held my Dad and brother, of course, but also included my two uncles and my grandmother. I was awed that she'd made the trip out. This was no place for an eighty-five year old to be; what could my dad have been thinking?

Suddenly Thomas, Madeline, and Rose were at my side. Knowing that Rosalyn wouldn't be far behind, I knew I couldn't reach out to Thomas and run to his arms for comfort the way my entire body was urging me to. I could see in his face that he wanted the same for me. If he could, he'd be at my side in an instant hugging me while I cried on his shoulder. A silent tear fell down my cheek as I realized that knowing would have to be enough for now.

"Who are they?" Madeline asked curiously.

I started with my cousins and their wives, "Henry and Paul are twins. They are a year older than me, but we grew up close. We went to the same schools and our parents were friends so we often were thrown together. As we all grew up and became our own people, we have tried to remain close through monthly gatherings. Interestingly, Henry and Paul had a double wedding as they both found love at the same time. They married very different girls, Rita and Kris, but they all get along well.

"Tim is the third cousin in the boat and their brother. He's always been a little different than them, but not in a bad way. We also grew up close; he was just always interested in different things than his siblings so he was often off on his own. He has that loner tendency, but seems content with it. He likes to read and write a lot and loves the computer and other technological gadgets.

"Terri is his wife and she's a reflection of him. It's interesting that two relatively solitary people could fall in love, but that's what happened. They're often hanging out doing their own thing together. I guess being in each other's presence is enough to keep them happy.

"In the other boat, the tallest, is Tim's Dad, Rex. My other uncle, the dad of the twins, is Matt. Just like myself and my cousins, my dad is very close with his brothers. Actually, my dad's side of the family is unusually close for having that many different personalities among them. We get in arguments occasionally, like any other family, but nothing breaks these familial bonds permanently, not even Rosalyn, which brings me to my grandmother.

"It's pretty obvious which one she is. Unusually healthy for her age, but has always fit into our family like a glove. My dad and she hit it off at once, from the stories they've both told me. She was ecstatic when he proposed to my mom, so happy to be joining his family. She really liked my dad and his brothers."

During my haphazard explanations, Rosalyn had arrived.

"Wow, look at all your father's family here to find nothing. And…is that…no, Mom came along?" she was genuinely surprised, and a little angry, "Don't they know how old she is? What's the matter with them?"

"At least you two agree on that," Rose said.

"I'm sure she can handle it," I threw in, she's a tough old bird. Not sure how you're so cowardly Rosalyn, maybe grandpa was the coward."

I still couldn't believe how nonchalant she was being about my dad and brother and it was making me angry. I was childishly lashing out, but I couldn't help it. I never knew my grandfather, but I hadn't heard good things so I felt justified.

"That was below the belt," she said glaring at me.

I stared daggers back at her, too angry to speak.

"If the two of you kill each other, what will Dominic have left to do but kill the rest of us?" Rose started quietly, but continued with confidence, "Will you please stop now? You may not like it, but we're all in this. Rosalyn, must you be here? Are you intentionally trying to make this harder for Elizabeth? I thought the two of you were supposed to be trying to act civilly toward one another. Wasn't that the directive Dominic gave you both?"

"Rose," started Rosalyn, turning her anger from me, "Are you actually asking me to leave when it's my husband and son out there?"

"No," I said before she could respond and make this worse for herself, "no one is asking you to do anything. I'm going to walk further up on the beach and see what I can see. They've begun the search and I'm going to watch all I can. I am asking you, Rosalyn, please leave me alone…please."

"Fine, wander away and leave me be with my family of followers.

Thomas, shouldn't you be with Shauna or something?" I flinched at those last words. Apparently our civility of last night was long gone. Rosalyn was jealous of the friendships I'd formed in the short time I'd been under her supervision.

"Uh," Thomas stuttered his response, "I am here for my mother and sister. Shauna and I aren't really…getting along right now."

"Well, you do go through girlfriends quickly, don't you? Maybe I'll have to go see her a little later today. Perhaps she needs a shoulder to cry on," she said. I caught her scanning the room for our reaction and knew we'd pass this test without trouble.

I let her taunts fall off my shoulders as I walked away, looking back only once at her and was very surprised to see that tears had surfaced in her eyes. This only confirmed my suspicion that she was, in fact, in there somewhere. I turned my attention to the group getting closer with every moment and walked further out toward them.

Before long they'd made the shore and were beginning to unpack. I noticed that they had brought enough food and clothing to last themselves for a few days. I smiled knowing that they wouldn't give up soon.

They were setting up tents and foraging for dry wood so that they would have a fire to come back to when the day's chore was done. I noticed some extra accommodations and heard my brother's voice travel as he responded to my cousin's question about the same thing.

"If we find her at night she'll need somewhere to sleep. It doesn't take up that much room; it was hers when she was younger. She'll barely fit in it, but she should have something," Aaron said sadly.

I recognized it. I had bought it when a group of my friends and I had decided to go camping for the weekend. He was right, if they had found me, I probably wouldn't be able to fit in it anymore. It was comforting to know that Aaron went over the top to make sure that I would have everything I need.

I watched as they left camp together to explore the island. The group stayed together until they had a little better idea of how big the island was. It was just a few hours later when they ended up back where they started and the divvying up began. One group would go off to the west and another would go to the east. The final group would cut right through the middle. They would meet once they'd completed their area and report on their findings.

I didn't know how they'd known to look here, but I figured Aaron had something to do with it. He was so used to me calling so often and it has been a few days since we talked. I told him what I was researching, though nothing about what I'd found out. He had an idea of where I was.

He probably put the whole search party together.

I watched my dad carefully. The lines of worry were etched deep into his forehead, but this was not what caused me the most pain. As he passed inches from me without knowing it, I truly took in the expression in his eyes. It was that of a hopeless man. He was trying, unsuccessfully, to bring himself to believe that I was out here. Tears were often right on the edge of his eyes, but he willed them back with a deep breath for cover. His usually shaven beard was growing and I noticed for the first time they gray peppered in with his usual brown. It made him look old; far older than his years. He was doing everything he could to stay strong for the others.

My father willed himself to rise from his crouched position and looked toward the others, Okay, let's get a move on. Daylight's wasting."

How many times had he said that same phrase to me? How many times had he seen me wasting time instead of doing some outdoor chore? Or instead of getting ready to go camping? I remember being so annoyed by that, but at that moment, he couldn't have said anything better. A wave of nostalgia hit me as I thought of those last moments before my mom and I got in the car on that fateful day. My father had said, 'come on you two, daylight's wasting, get done and get back here.'

That was the last time we were truly together. Everything unraveled after that. Even after we'd mourned her death, things were really never the same again. My father never truly came back to himself again. My brother and I felt helpless as the weeks and months passed and our father's suffering only seemed to grow. It sort of felt good to have him speak so nonchalantly about what he was about to do.

I didn't know which group to follow so I decided to stay where I was. I sat on the soft sand and watched them leave. I sat quietly and let the tears flow freely when it was too much for me to handle. Vaguely I was aware that Thomas was standing close by watching me. Once I was all cried out I felt tired. I closed my eyes and allowed myself to drift.

I had my arms wrapped around myself as if I were cold. My eyes opened and I couldn't tell at first if I were dreaming or not. I was cramped from being balled up. I decided to get up and give my muscles a good stretch. As soon as I'd done that I saw them coming toward me. Aaron, my dad, all of my cousins and their wives were coming toward me with their arms open, ready to embrace the one they thought they'd lost. We all hugged, one at a time, then everyone together. I was relieved and elated. My family had come to find me and somehow they did.

Then I asked, "Where's grandma?"

My dad replied, "she's where she belongs now," as he pointed.

I followed the direction he was pointing with my eyes and saw what would make me shudder in horror every time I thought of it for the rest of my days. My grandmother, along with my new family, Thomas's family, was standing together hugging one another too; including Clarissa. The smiles on their faces were as plastic as the little toys that come in kid's meals. Their expressions appeared to be frightened. Dominic was standing with them and all of their eyes glowed red.

"See," said Dominic, as friendly as ever, "we can both get what we want. That's not a bad compromise, is it?"

I looked at Thomas and saw that his eyes were glowing red too, "Go home, Elizabeth," he said to me, "your part in this story is over. We'll see you on the other side."

I screamed until I'd woken myself fully from my nightmare. I looked around and saw Madeline and Rose coming toward me.

"What happened? Are you okay?" Madeline asked.

"Bad dream," I replied loud enough to smooth the concerned look on Thomas's face, and quickly turned my face toward the water.

I stayed quiet for a while and waited for the search parties to come into view again. I started to hear their voices.

"...haven't seen anything, just woods as far as we could see. Maybe one of the other groups had more luck," I heard my Dad's voice.

"I'm here," I whispered weakly, assuming that he'd hear nothing.

"What was that? Aaron, did you say something?" he asked.

"No, I didn't say anything. You hearing things, old man?" Aaron asked jokingly.

Everyone got still for a moment and excitement shot through my chest like a bullet. I tried again.

"I'm here," I said with a little more volume, concentrating on them hearing me.

"Anyone hear something a minute ago?" My dad addressed the whole group so I knew he hadn't heard the second time, but noted that he looked in my direction with a smile.

A small flame of hope was kindled. It couldn't have just been a coincidence. I vowed to keep talking to him; to try to get him to hear me again. If he could hear me, maybe I could lead him here. That thought brought comfort, but sadness as well. What would I do if I brought him here, or worse, all of them? Their lives would be in jeopardy and they wouldn't know how to get out of here any more than I would. My depression deepened and I longed to be back in Thomas's arms.

The search party continued on and hope had been kindled in my father's eyes. They looked different than they had just a few hours ago, more hopeful. He had decided not to give up on what he'd heard.

The next day continued much like the last. Even after we were all supposed to be sleeping, I was too distracted to spend any quality time with Thomas. We would meet in what we were now referring to as our favorite corridor, but it was a wasted effort. I was so busy going over and over the things I'd seen and heard that I wasn't really giving Thomas the attention that he was craving. It was beginning to wear on him, but he was trying not to show me that. On the third night, just after they'd decided to drag the lake in a last ditch effort to find anything, Thomas and I were again alone.

"I can't believe that she can stand there day after day watching them and not say anything, not try to do anything to reach out to them. I can't believe how cruel and unfeeling she is," I droned on.

"We've been through this before Elizabeth; Dominic has long since removed any longing she's had for your father, your brother and you too, apparently, at least all the reasons that she'd want to go back to her old life. She's only been able to hold on to the anger she felt for you," his anger and frustration was breaking through.

"What's the matter with you?" I asked him suddenly, catching his tone.

He was taken by surprise, not expecting me to focus on anyone other than myself.

"I guess I just miss you. I want to be the one to give you comfort after your trying days," he said sadly.

I felt guilty; I knew that everything he said to me was true. I had been awfully unfair as he has never wavered in being here for me and he's allowed me to unleash on him night after night.

"I'm sorry," I said, dropping my eyes to the dirt, "you're right. It has to be hard for you too. I see you watching me from where you're standing with Madeline and Rose. I see the longing in your eyes. I wish I could show you the same, but she's always watching."

"You're talking about what Rosalyn can see during the day, I don't like it, but I know why it's necessary. What I'm talking about is the night when we're together. Shouldn't we be enjoying each other in the few moments when that's possible? Or have you tired of me already?" Thomas asked sadly.

"Oh Thomas, I'm so sorry. I'm just so worried about everything," I said feeling miserable. I took a deep breath and changed course, "you're right. I won't talk about it anymore, okay? I'll leave the daytime to the day. Better?"

"It'll be better when this is all over and it's just me and you. I'm sorry, I promised I'd be strong for you. You don't need to be bothered with this."

"It's okay, I'm glad you're not holding it all in. For now, let's just hold each other. Let's shut out the rest of the world and just be," I said.

"That's all I ask," he said with a winning smile as he drew his strong arms around my waist and met my lips in a soft, urgent kiss.

We stayed like that for a long time, enjoying the comfort of being in each other's arms. I don't think either of us actually slept, but you couldn't really say we were awake either. We were merely content to be together in that moment. Faster than we'd like, the dark night started to fade into the first light of dawn. We were forced to let go and begin the facade again. I rushed to my room before anyone had a chance to wake and threw myself on the hard cot just seconds before Rosalyn made it in to wake me.

"Come on Elizabeth, it's time to put on a pretty face for Daddy," she said, laying on thick sarcasm, "maybe he'll see you today."

"Maybe you don't know as much as you think you do," I muttered under my breath.

"What was that?" She looked angry.

"Nothing important. They're dragging the lake today. When they don't find anything, I assume they'll leave," I said, quickly changing the subject.

"Yes, about time too. None of the other search parties went on for four full days."

I was dreading going out there to see their faces today. On the day of their arrival, there had been hope. When I was able to reach my father, that hope had blossomed into expectation. By now, that would be all but gone. I continued to try to call out to him again, but to no avail. Other than that first time, there were no indications that he could hear anything that I was trying to say.

Their supplies were almost down to nothing and though I knew it wouldn't take them much to go over to the mainland and get some necessities, I also knew that this was not part of their plan. They had jobs and lives to get back to. Today would be the end of their search. Dominic would be elated. To be entirely honest, I was also ready to get this show on the road. Having to watch this day in and day out had certainly taken its toll on all of us, but it had a way of bringing about my stubborn side. I would bring them out of this, all of them, no matter what I will have to sacrifice in the process.

"Dad's called in just about all of his favors on this one, huh?" I mused.

"He must have had something to hold over his brothers, he never had this kind of turn out for me," she said, hurt.

I looked at her and shrugged my shoulders. It would be safer to agree with her now, "I guess he must have."

As we walked out to the beach my mind drifted to the clue I'd left him. I was beginning to worry. What if he found the necklace under Rosalyn's careful watch? If that were to happen she would know that I planted it there for them. I tried not to panic as I saw our whole elaborate plan unraveling. I imagined Rosalyn's face as she recognized the locket he'd be holding in his hand. I saw the horror and betrayal that her face would display and I cringed into myself. Had I really been that stupid? If he found it of course he'd call everyone over to analyze it. When that happened, she'd want to know what it was too and would go right to it. Then it's all over, for all of us.

"*Remember, we're in this together, Elizabeth. If it looks like he's found something, I'll create a diversion of some sort. I will find a way to drag her from the search. I'll be sure to stay close to her today,*" Madeline was in my head sending the comfort I so badly needed.

"*Okay, and thank you,*" I responded.

By the time we reached the beach there were large hoses protruding from several areas. The water was being pumped into a large basin that it would be pumped right back out of once they searched the floor of the small lake. They couldn't search the entire thing, but they cordoned off the distance that they'd decided to go and let the sandbags do the rest. They'd sandbag a section at a time, and search. It was quite interesting to see some of the things that they did find out there. There was an old AM/FM radio with a small television attached, a pair of boots, and so many coins. I couldn't imagine how some of the debris had gotten to the floor of this little lake, but there was much to be found. I remembered the area in which I threw the necklace and it seemed that they'd get to that section last. I sat down to settle in for a long day of interesting, but hardly relevant, finds on the bottom of the lake.

Rosalyn, Madeline, and Rose were close by, but I could not find Thomas. I thought of all of the reasons why he wouldn't be here. He knew today was crucial. He knew that this was exactly what I'd been waiting for. I had to work to keep these worries to myself as I knew that Rosalyn would be paying extra attention to me and my thoughts today. My hand made its way to the locket that was hidden next to my heart. I needed that tough and unbreakable belief today and Thomas's necklace, my necklace, held me steady as I watched the frown on my father's and brother's faces become more and more pronounced. They were beginning to doubt. I had to do what I could to give them some sense of hope….at least enough to get them through the day.

"I'm here not even a mile from where you stand. You can't see me, but I'm here."

I willed the words to them and saw that spark of hope return to my father's eyes just seconds later. I couldn't be sure that he heard some or all of what I'd said, but I was beyond excited when I saw it. He began working harder, moving faster, but was very thorough in his searching.

After several hours of the same, they reached the final area of the lake, the sun was beginning its descent, but they were determined to finish the lake today. The same process began as before. The pumps were pouring water into one area of the lake while everyone worked to move the sandbags to the next. Once that was done, they began pumping the water out of the final area. Once the water was down satisfactorily, they began to search. They took every ounce of water out and searched the ground below. It was obvious that I wasn't there, but they were looking for anything, any clue to where I may be. I was beginning to get nervous that they had missed it or perhaps it had gotten buried in the sand below, but then I saw my father stop and bend down. He was grabbing at something with his hands, looking intently. My mind caught up with me at once. I flashed a warning to Madeline and she did not disappoint.

"Rosalyn, Rosalyn," came a very convincing moment of clear panic from Madeline, "it's Clarissa, she's talking to me again. Come here, I have to tell you now, you know how it fades."

Rosalyn was torn for a minute; she wanted to know what my father had found, but her curiosity and her burning desire to bring Clarissa to this island was stronger. Madeline knew well what she was doing and I appreciated her all the more for her giving spirit. I didn't have time to show it before they were out of sight though; I was now watching my father's face closely. I was looking for the recognition that I was sure would come when he realized what he'd found.

"Aaron, come here," my father called.

"What is it, Dad? Did you find something?" Aaron responded as he darted to our father's side.

"I may have," he said as he drew the necklace into his hand.

I couldn't hold back the smile that was on my face. It worked. He found the one clue that I was able to get out to him. I could only hope now that the note inside was still intact and that he'd be able to make sense of it.

"Yes," I whispered to myself knowing that Madeline was keeping Rosalyn busy. I couldn't celebrate completely though. Thomas was still nowhere in sight. He hadn't come out to join us all day and I began to worry. I stood up straight and peered around, but there was no Thomas.

That concern fell to the back of my mind though as I watched my father open the locket and find the note. He read it over and finally set it in Aaron's waiting hands. His knees buckled slightly. I remembered the last part of the note I had included. *Rosalyn is alive.*

All of those years of loss and healing and I just pulled the rug out from underneath him. He was dumbfounded and it was hard to read his expression though I stood only feet from him now. Was he in pain? Was the small hope turning into greater hope? Was there belief and truth? I couldn't decipher his thoughts, but the tears in his eyes were clear enough. When Aaron came to hug him a moment later, there were tears in his eyes as well. I had certainly rocked their worlds with this information.

I walked away toward the beach trying to hold my own sobs in. I wanted to crumble right there, but I had to go back before they started pouring the water back in and I knew that once I went down, it would be a while before I would be able to pull myself back up. I could feel the misery overtaking me, but fought to hold it off. I turned to look at them again though I knew my heart, already in pieces, would be shattered.

"I'm sorry," I whispered to them as I turned my head.

Before I could fully turn away, I saw recognition light up their eyes. They looked at each other and then all around them. I had done it again, I was sure of it. I'd gotten through to them. Their eyes fell in my direction and my mouth gaped.

"Do you see something?" Aaron asked, squinting his eyes.

Our father's eyes were also squinted like he was trying to see something more clearly.

"I don't know," he said thoughtfully, "doesn't it look like the air is sort of shimmering over there? Like something is standing there?"

"Something or someone," Aaron was getting excited, "well, it's not her, but what is it? It looks kind of tallish...sort of like the outline of something. Look over there, there's more."

Aaron was pointing directly to where Rose was standing. But where was Thomas? This was too much. They were seeing us. It wasn't us, but it was enough.

They were coming toward me. The outlines that they had seen made them curious and they wanted to check it out. I saw Rose back away; Madeline was on her way back to us, but I stood my ground; just as curious as they were as to what would happen when they stood next to me.

I hadn't seen Rosalyn arrive, but she was suddenly there, yanking my arm.

"Let's go," she said harshly, "that's enough of this game. They have gotten close enough."

I stood for one second longer, resisting, "Wait, I want to see what they do."

"Fine, wait and see, but they will find nothing. I am taking the others back to the trees. They will be leaving tonight, Dominic will come back, and all will be as it should be," she was clearly shaken by the length of their stay and what they were seeing.

As the two of them were a hair's breadth from my arm I couldn't help but reach out. My touch went unnoticed. Though I could feel my father's arm as he searched the empty space, he could not feel my hand. Rosalyn was right, there may be a shimmer for him to see, but we were not really here so there was nothing for him to find. I threw my arms around him and hugged him fiercely anyway. Then I did the same to Aaron. My sobs were uncontrollable now. I backed away and fled. I turned to go and I noticed Rosalyn staring at both Aaron and my father with a wistful look in her eyes. This was another confirmation that she hadn't crossed over entirely. I made it almost to the edge of the trees when I decided to turn and sit. I had watched them come, I'd watch them leave too.

"I would have sworn there was something there," Aaron said, "just a second ago."

"There was, I know what I saw," answered my father, "I'm just not sure what it means. I do think, however, that maybe instead of heading out of town tonight, we should stay one more night, and then head back for the main island in the morning. There's no sense in breaking down camp now. I need to go back to the hotel where she was staying and ask a few more questions."

They walked off as they finished up their plans for the remainder of their stay and I was alone. I replayed today's events in my head several times over. I wondered what it was they saw that brought them close to me. I knew they said something shimmering, but was that all? Why could they see it now and not before? Why could they hear me at times and not at all at other times? These questions were plaguing me as the sun settled behind the horizon. I had no idea how long I sat there thinking, but suddenly the moon was up, throwing a bright light across the sand. I saw a figure approaching the place where I was sitting from the beach. He couldn't see me, this I was sure of, but until he entered the light, I didn't know to what extent my brother came to believe what he saw today.

"You're out there. I know; I saw it today. I will not rest until we find you, wherever you are. Thank you for that note. Dad cannot stop going on about the possibilities. He knows what I somehow knew for years. She never really left us, did she?" Aaron finished his silent monologue.

"No," I whispered, but he did not hear me.

"We will be back. We are going to gather information, but this search is not over. Do not worry, we're not giving up. I won't let that happen."

I knew he was telling the truth. At that moment I knew that there was nothing he wouldn't do to keep me safe. I knew that he'd believe whatever was necessary to bring me back. I felt hope. He turned to go back to his camp and I turned to hide myself in the trees. The emotion was too much and the tears came freely. I hadn't made it very far when I saw a movement just inches from me.

"Elizabeth, I'm here," Thomas said as I ran into his arms. I sobbed freely and he stood steady waiting for me to get it all out.

"Where were you today?" I asked when I finally found my voice again.

"Right here, watching you. I knew that it would be especially hard for you today. When I saw them find the necklace, it took everything I had to stay where I was, but I didn't want to make it doubly hard for you. I almost came right out of the trees…he'd never know I was there, but Rosalyn might have been watching, so I remained here."

"How do you know she's not watching now? This is quite a risk to be taking," I said through my tears.

"I asked Madeline to make sure she was sufficiently distracted before she went to bed. I'm pretty sure right now Rose, Madeline, and Rosalyn are opening a bottle of wine and lamenting over the unfairness of it all."

That reminded me of my curiosity on the day that Theresa had set up a date for us in the underground.

"Where do they get wine?" I asked.

"Everyone else is stuck here until Rosalyn says different, but Dominic has granted Rosalyn the ability to come and go one day a month. She makes a trip to the main island to get necessities and sometimes throws in some extras too.

"You meant to tell me someone snuck into Rosalyn's stuff to get us that bottle of wine?" I was feeling angered by this.

"That was my mom, she really does like you a lot," Thomas said.

"Good, I like her too and I love you. Thank you for thinking of me today."

"I decided being there for you today was worth the risk…plus I know what a bottle of wine and three women can do; we'll be lucky if they get out of bed tomorrow," he said jokingly.

"Aaron promised they'd come back," I said, and looked down at the leaves on the ground, "I'm not sure that they should."

"I know, I heard what he said. If…when," he amended, "they do come, we'll be sure to get to them as quickly as we can."

I spent a long time in Thomas's arms and eventually we made our way down to our tunnel. The whole world would change tomorrow with the departure of my search party and the return of Dominic. But tonight we had each other and we enjoyed every minute of it. Just before dawn I made my way back to my room and Thomas went to his. Though we'd said it before, this time our 'goodbye for now' seemed more final. As I drifted into an uncomfortable sleep, I envisioned the heart that was hidden next to mine. I knew that that part of Thomas would be what would get me through whatever was to come.

Chapter 13

I slept soundly for several hours. By the time I woke up the search party had returned to the main island. Rosalyn came to announce that to me as if it were the best news on the planet…or wherever we were. I knew that Dominic would be here soon. Now that the island was clear of interlopers, he had no reason to stay away. I decided that I'd go for a walk and see what I missed while sleeping half the day away.

"Madeline," I said when I found her outside in the garden, "what's happening?"

She looked up at me with worry, "Thomas is in for treatment. Alone with Rosalyn."

"What? Why?" I asked, suddenly scared that we hadn't been careful enough.

"Rosalyn noticed that he never came to the beach yesterday. She's questioning him now," she replied and there was no mistaking the sadness in her voice.

I gasped thinking of last night, but Madeline must have read my thoughts, "she knows nothing of where either of you were last night, but I'm not sure he'll be strong enough not to tell her. She can be very convincing when she wants to be."

"Translation, she can inflict a lot of pain until she gets what she wants," I said smugly, "Where is Rose?"

"Standing outside the door. Rosalyn won't let her in, but she refuses to leave. She's listening as much as she can and she keeps hearing whimpers from Thomas; it's eating her up."

My knees buckled; I could hardly hold myself up straight. We'd become too careless. She'd been waiting for it but I thought we'd done well. Once the guilt washed through, anger came in its place. Dominic had ranked me almost as high as her. If she could take him in there and torture him to find out what information he was hiding, I could surely go in there and stop this madness. Before Madeline was aware of what I was doing, I stormed off toward Rosalyn's favorite treatment room.

"Elizabeth, no," I heard fading in the distance, but Madeline's attempt to stop me was half-hearted at best.

I walked furiously not thinking about what I was doing. I came within sight of Rose and she saw the determination burning in my eyes. She was not about to stop me.

"Elizabeth, what are you doing?" Rose said as she saw me coming near. She'd clearly been sent the message that I was on the way, "Do you want to make it worse for him?"

"I'm not going to stand by and let her torture him," I said loud enough for her to hear me.

"Let it go, Elizabeth. She promised she wouldn't hurt him too badly," I could see the struggle in her eyes; she wasn't entirely convinced that Rosalyn had been true to her word.

"Please Rose, do not make me shove you out of the way. I am going in there and she will hear what I have to say. This will not make it harder on him; she will not hurt him anymore," I said this quietly though I was sure her attention was focused on me now. Good, less pain for Thomas that way.

I begged Rose with my eyes for another minute and she finally decided that I was serious. She moved to the side and I pushed my way into the room. Thomas's eyes were far and away and it didn't look like he was faking it this time. Rosalyn's eyes were inflamed, as was her temper.

"How dare you interrupt me while I'm in treatment," she spat at me.

"How dare you treat someone with absolutely no reason," I fired back, "Thomas has been nothing but compliant and you have no right to be doing this to him."

"You don't get to make decisions around here. Thomas was not at the beach yesterday and I want to know why," Rosalyn explained angrily.

"Have you told him what you want to hear yet? Is that why you have him under? Shouldn't need brainwashing or mind altering if you're actually trying to get him to tell you the truth."

"I know that the two of you are still together. I see the way he looks at you. He didn't come to the beach yesterday because he was waiting for you," she pointed her finger at me in wild accusation.

"Have you stopped to think that perhaps he misses me? He told you that he and Shauna aren't together anymore; it's only natural for him to cling to the last relationship he had. Maybe he didn't come to the beach yesterday because he got tired of watching the same thing day after day. Unbelievably, maybe he had some compassion for me and didn't want to watch me suffer anymore. It could be any of those things, but what you're doing to him now only proves that you're trying to give him the answer and make him believe it," I ranted.

In that brief moment I saw his eyes twitch and I knew he was back with us. I glared at her just as much as she glared at me.

"Fine, I was about finished with him anyway. I will wake him and he may go," Rosalyn said, ceding defeat.

"I think that sounds like a wonderful idea; Rosalyn, my pet. You weren't being fair to him. Elizabeth was right to stop you," said a soft, confident voice from behind me; a voice that oddly set my heart fluttering.

Dominic? How could he be here? I heard no storm. I thought he always brought a storm with him. As my panic began to wane I realized that I'd been hearing the rain all along. My anger had been burning so strongly and my heart thumping so fiercely in my ears I'd missed it.

At the same time that she snapped her fingers, Rosalyn turned her head to look at Dominic. Thomas quietly smiled at me. I was tracing the lines of the heart he'd given me. Thomas knew I'd come here for him, to save him and that was all I could give him. It was enough. A second later I turned my head to Dominic.

"Now ladies, what is all of this about?" Dominic asked, sounding like a doting father.

"Nothing," Rosalyn said sharply, "Thomas, you can go."

He scooted quickly out of the room and Rose went with to comfort him. Dominic was standing between Rosalyn and I and I noticed the emerald green color of his eyes once more.

"What's the matter, my pet?" Dominic said to Rosalyn, "You look angered."

"I'm fine, really," she said trying to compose herself, "my wayward daughter and I were just having an argument."

"Over Thomas?" he asked.

"Where her loyalties lie," she looked at me.

"And where do your loyalties lie?" Dominic turned the full power of his gaze on me and immediately my brain went fuzzy. It took a lot of effort to pull myself to the present and recognize the danger that I was now in.

"With you, of course," I lied, "We just had a rough time with my dad and brother. It's over now and they're gone. We can pick up where we left off."

"Hmmm, that sounds about right," Dominic said suggestively.

"Yes," Rosalyn threw herself back into the middle now that tempers had cooled, "it's time we get back to business, right Dom?"

"Please don't call me that," he said to her and I caught the surprise in her face before she could mask it, "I'd rather you just call me Dominic.

Now," he continued, changing the subject, "let's talk about what happened over the last four days."

Rosalyn and I took turns filling Dominic in about the search party. We talked about the countless hours they'd spent looking under everything on the tiny island. We told him that they dragged the lake but hadn't found anything of interest.

"They didn't, did they Elizabeth?" she asked, remembering that Madeline had pulled her away from the search.

"Your attention was somewhere other than the search for even a minute?" Dominic asked, clearly upset.

"Yes, well, Madeline was having some issues with Clarissa and since we need that little girl here I thought it was pretty important," she said trying to explain her blunder.

"Nothing is as important as doing the duty you promised you'd do. That should take precedence," Dominic was not happy.

I saw my chance and I took it.

"I was there for every moment of the search. I saw that there was a moment when my dad thought he'd found something, but when he called my brother over to look at it, they both decided it was nothing and threw it back on the ground. When he finally had to admit defeat he cussed himself a blue streak. I never knew he had that kind of language in him; I thought that kind of talk only ever came from one of my parents," I said, throwing in that last stab just for Rosalyn.

"That's a good girl, Elizabeth. You're catching on fast. I knew I could count on you. See Rosalyn, sometimes we need to step back and let a fresh pair of eyes take over for a while. They bring such wonderful insight," he said as he stroked my hair and stared into my eyes.

"Yes, I suppose you're right," said Rosalyn, defeated again, "I'm sorry to have failed you in this, Dominic."

"That's okay, my pet, we all make mistakes. Why don't you go get some rest. You look tired."

"Oh, okay, I guess I can use it. I'll be in my room if you need me," she said sadly.

"That sounds good," he said dismissively, keeping his eyes on me as he spoke.

"Now that she's gone…," he whispered in my ear just seconds after she'd rounded the corner. He moved his lips to mine and kissed me softly, "Didn't you say something about wanting to have these lips back?"

"Yes, I did," sounding not quite myself, even to my own ears, "but I've had a very hard morning and would really like the opportunity to clean up and rest myself a little if that's possible."

"Of course," he said, sounding more than a little disappointed, "don't take too long, though. I'd hate to think that Rosalyn is actually correct in her suspicions regarding you and Thomas."

"I'll be back before you know it," I said smiling and touching my finger to the tip of his nose.

"Okay then, I'll see you in a bit. In the meantime, I'll see what Rosalyn is fussing about."

I detected the not so subtle threat in his statement and decided that like it or not, I'd have to return to him shortly. I walked out and was headed to my room when Madeline caught up with me.

"Thomas wanted me to thank you," she said with a gleam in her eye, "he said it had started to get pretty intense, so he owes you one."

"No problem, tell him I said 'you're welcome,'" I said and gave her a wink.

I left and headed straight for my room. In reality, adrenaline was coursing through my veins. I couldn't stop my mind from frantically playing out each scenario that I saw coming; none of which I was looking forward to. I needed to decide how to handle what was happening.

I sat on my cot and closed my eyes. One thing was for sure, Dominic was trying to seduce me and I was having a very hard time telling him no. I wasn't entirely sure that I didn't want to be seduced by him. I couldn't deny that there was something about him, buried deeply beneath the surface, that called out to me in more than just a carnal way. On the surface, I had no desire to end my relationship with Thomas, but I could not deny that my arms were currently longing for Dominic. I shuddered and tried to shake off these feelings, but I couldn't just ignore them either.

I gave up on that and turned my thoughts to my father and brother. Had they seen the door open when Dominic arrived? They were on the main island by then, but were they in viewing distance as I had been so many times? Was it possible that they didn't leave the island at all and came through with the opening of the door as I'd directed them. And if so, have I sentenced them to life in this place?

Finally I thought of Clarissa. Dominic has more than enough ability and power to do what he wants without her, so what is his real objective? Why does he want her here so badly? Why has she begun to doubt our intentions here as she relayed the other evening? Is she truly getting snippets of possible futures in her mind or are these simply her fears? We hadn't heard anything from her for a while which also concerned me.

All of these thoughts were making my head spin and soon I found

myself drifting. I slept a dreamless sleep and woke to Dominic's sooth-
ing voice.

"I couldn't wait anymore. I didn't realize how hard these last few
days had been on you. You must have been exhausted."

"I was," I admitted, "the nap helped."

"You miss your father, don't you?"

"And my brother," I added

"Yes, him too. What if we could bring them here?" he asked.

I sat up with a start, luckily, he took it as excitement, rather than the
bone chilling fear that had run through me.

"Relax dear, that couldn't happen for a while."

"Oh, well, good, I wouldn't want to take them away from their lives.
They are both so happy."

"They came looking for you, though, didn't they? Wouldn't they be
happier here? Don't you want them near you?" he asked.

"Not at their expense," I answered with feeling.

"How could it be an expense to be near you?" he asked, "I thought
you liked it here. Or at the very least you liked me enough to want to
stay."

"Yes," I amended neatly, "that's what I want, not what they want.
They need to have a choice, just like I did."

"You're so right. Your mother is right about you; you are a humanitarian. I'm afraid that's going to cause you more pain here than you should
have to feel. Though maybe you're rubbing off on me some. Where I
come from selflessness is barely heard of. Too bad they thought of that
far too late in their lives. Of course, without them my father wouldn't
have a dominion at all, nor would I be able to come from it to bring it to
this little corner of the world."

"Where would we be without that?" I said, placating him with a
smile.

"It's true what they say, you know," he replied seriously, "there does
have to be a balance. For each right, there has to be a wrong. I can't help
that what provides that balance is looked on so negatively in a regular
human life span.

"You're right, balance is necessary, everything does happen for a reason, just like there was some reason that I had to lose my mother at such
a young age." I said, looking for his reaction.

"Exactly," he said, satisfied that I was understanding, "that misery
that you suffered then brought you to the joy that awaits you here when
you finally take your mother's place at my side. She has long been a
companion, and that's been great and all, but my desires for you go be-

yond companionship."

"Have you told her? Does she know what all you intend?" I asked, suddenly knowing that I needed to stall for time.

"Told her of my plans for you? Not exactly. I'm giving her hints and leading her down the path. Like when I told her not to call me Dom. I've never done that before, but now it's time to make that separation. I'm letting her make the ultimate discovery. I think that will be easier."

"Easier for who?" I was pretty sure I knew the response, but I wanted to hear him say it.

"Well, for me, of course," he said as if I were being simple, "I told you, selfishness comes with the territory when you come from my home."

"Well, just like a man," I said, trying to keep my voice even.

"Oh, no, darling, we're all the same. Our wants and desires are valued far above those around us. That's part of why we have to come and go so often. If we stay around each other for too long, we start fighting amongst ourselves and things can get out of control quickly. It's much easier if we come up to the surface and find others to join us, though I can't remember a group ever being so troublesome," he said with half a smile, not realizing that he'd just let me in on previously unknown information.

"Is that what you're doing here? Are you creating a group of people to take down with you when you go? You're not going to give Rosalyn anything, are you?" I let an angry edge color my voice.

"No," he said, ignoring my outburst, "but I'll give you anything your little heart desires."

"And I should believe that, why?" I asked.

"Because you are the thing that I want more than anything right now," I didn't miss the qualifier, "You are what I'll be after from now until I bring the group down there. Only you, Elizabeth, will be immune to the cleansing that takes place once you arrive," he promised smoothly.

"And what is that cleansing?" trying to keep him talking and finding myself suddenly fascinated.

"The fires that burn you free of your sins. They make Rosalyn's treatments feel like child's play." Dominic answered.

"Are we talking about purgatory?"

"Something like that, Dante didn't have it all wrong," he said with a smile.

"Is this what you told Rosalyn? What did you use to convince her?"

"No, I never promised Rosalyn the chance to avoid her fate, I just promised her a longer life than she was being given at the moment of her choosing," I could see he was telling the truth.

"You mean, as she was terrified, falling to her death, you offered her a way out and she took it?" I asked.

"I can see how you'd take it, but it was her decision. She wouldn't have felt the impact, just drifted off, but that was her decision and her choice. She was clear on how this would come out," his answer was short now; I'd touched a nerve.

"As do I. I know exactly what I'm getting into and what I will be getting out of it," I said, reeling him back in with a smile.

"Good, I'm glad to hear it."

"I have to ask though, why me? What is it about me that makes you want to pick me above any other that you might be bringing down with you?" Curiosity made my eyes sparkle.

"As any person that will sit on a throne, I need someone to sit by my side. Help me make decisions, make sure that I make the right ones for the right reasons. You will help me rule over all of the souls that come into our realm. That's the task that I've been assigned and later, I'll likely sit on a larger throne so it's good practice."

I ignored the mention of thrones for now, "But you told Rosalyn that you weren't going below. You said you were creating this little dominion for yourself to have here on Earth."

"Do you actually think you're still on Earth? Elizabeth, darling, haven't I taught you anything yet? When you walked through that door you walked into a parallel universe. One so new that it does not even have a name, but one that was created just for this purpose. It mirrors Earth in every way, but you are on an ethereal plane…one that is sort of floating in between.

"And no, in answer to your question, I am not keeping the group here. This is a placeholder until everything is ready for our descent. Rosalyn just needed to hear that she'd have a place and a group that she'd be in control of. That's what got her to agree to come with me; the promise of ultimate control over the people that we'd get to join us. She has had that now and now it's time for the new chapter to open and sadly, she's not going to make it to the final act, at least not in the way that she'd hoped," Dominic said with a small chuckle.

I held my tongue for a moment, absorbing all of this information and trying not to react to this horrifying plan. I composed myself before I spoke again.

"So what is it about Clarissa that makes you want her here so badly?" I asked, trying to sound casual.

"She's special," he said and gave me a very stern look. He would say no more about her and clearly, she was a sensitive subject for him. I directed that thought to something I'd analyze later and changed the subject.

"I've had so many questions for you and you've been answering them so patiently; what is it that you'd ask of me?"

"Besides spending eternity at my side? I didn't know that I could ask more of you."

"I didn't think I was being asked."

"Of course you have a choice. If you so choose, you may enjoy the same fate as the others, or you may enjoy eternity as my queen. The choice, ultimately, is yours to make."

"That's twice now that you've talked about it as if you were the ruler down there, I thought that position belonged only to your father?"

"My father believes that too. I'm sure you must be hungry," I'd hit another sensitive spot and squirreled that thought away for further analysis, "Why don't we get you something to eat." Dominic asked, closing the subject for now.

I was ready to drop the somber tones for the day, too, "Okay, what are we eating?"

"It's a surprise," said Dominic, regaining his light, flirtatiousness, "I thought maybe we could enjoy some time on the beach together."

"Sure," I said, not wanting to disagree with him now, though cringing on the inside. Why would he want to take me right back to the place where I was just grieving for so many? Then I remembered his statements of selfishness and let it go. He was not interested in what would upset me. I painted on a happy face and followed his lead.

We walked together through the compound. He had one arm wrapped around my waist as we sauntered through the crude structure. We passed Rosalyn's rooms and he stopped when we were right in front of her door. He leaned down and kissed me gently. He deepened the kiss when he parted my lips with his tongue and Rosalyn grew furious. She walked right to her door and slammed it as hard as she could.

Satisfied with his work, Dominic chuckled and pulled me along next to him as we continued around. It looked as though we'd be having a light lunch right on the beach. If he wasn't so creepy, I'd almost have to call this romantic…if only. He could spout sonnets to me all day long, but I was well aware that the lines he was feeding me moments ago were not true. He manipulated her to believe that she'd be running things even though there was no romantic tie between them. He was clearly a gifted manipulator as I'd been warned.

"Oh come now, you can't have so little faith in me. I was entirely honest with you just now. I've always been honest with Rosalyn as well, I just never included the whole story. She has been given power to rule, she has done with it what she liked, I just never told her that it would eventually come to an end. I figured she'd have to realize that at some point, but she never did on her own. That's why I've started to give her hints to help her make that realization.

"Darling, she was a step on the way to find you. That's not something I shared with her because she would have tried to keep you away. I couldn't have that. It was always you I wanted. Since that day I saw you struggling for life and trying to help you mom, I knew it would be you I'd put at my side. I couldn't take you then, I have waited long, but now it's time; time for you to come with me.I am so hoping that I can make you see how much you desire this too, but the time to vacate this place is coming near."

I replayed the last sentence a few times and understood the warning it was meant to give. If I came along quietly, he'd be kind to me, maybe even grant me a favor or two. But if I tried to squirm out of this, he'd make me pay.

In response to my thoughts he simply said, "we understand each other then."

I sighed as we reached our destination. There was a little table made from a felled tree, complete with two tree stumps; one on either end of the table, to use for seats. I shuddered thinking of those that had to labor over this. The food was already laid out on the table.

"This is a treat that no one gets without me," Dominic said excitedly.

As we took our seats at the table I smelled the dainty medium-rare slice of steak taking up residence on my plate and making my mouth water. Dominic had one on his plate as well. Our lunches were complemented with steamed carrots and sliced potatoes on the side. Any of those living outside of this nightmare would be begging for a meal like this one. I grabbed my glass of wine with a little too much force and some of the contents came sloshing out onto the table.

"Careful now, you don't want to waste that. It's not often we're able to bring so many bottles," said Dominic.

"Sorry," I pouted like a little girl not getting her way.

He led me to my seat and waited quietly while I sat. He then went to his side of the table and did the same. He began eating with fervor. It made me wonder about how his life was away from here. I took a small bite of my steak, swallowed, and then posed the question.

"What do you normally eat? You know, when you're not here?"

"Oh, just the same kinds of foods that you do, only I don't have to eat very often."

"Really, not often?" I was stunned.

"Being who I am, I just don't have the same need for food as normal humans, but when we go below, the need for food will be wiped out entirely," he said, explaining.

"Oh, what else is different down there from up here; beside the whole souls being cleansed thing? What do you do when you're there?"

"Well, my father oversees everything, but there are millions of residents to keep track of, so I guess to make a comparison that you'd understand, I'm sort of a supervisor. I go to all of the different levels and make sure that all is as it should be."

"How many brothers do you have?" my meal forgotten, I was fascinated with how open he was being.

"Oh, I stopped counting a long time ago. There are at least twenty of us, but I'm sure I'm grossly underestimating things. My father is very amorous and has the entire world at his fingertips. When he procreates, he brings the offspring down here to be raised. Most of the time the child is considered "dead" to the world above, but my father "rescues" them before they expire and hands them off to be raised when they get here.

"Am I the first human that you're going to bring with you? Have you brought others down with you before?" I was curious if he really knew what he was up against.

"Only one other time," he said in that finalizing voice which made me realize that this was not a topic that was open for conversation.

I could see it though. There had been another that Dominic had brought down, possibly an entire group. When he took her and the group and presented them to his father, she must have been charmed and led away from Dominic. Likely he was powerless to stop this from happening. I decided to chance a question.

"Did you bring a group the last time too, then?" I asked, catching him off guard, "It's obvious what happened Dominic, did he take from you from a whole group of people or did you just bring her down?"

"Just her," he admitted, "but it doesn't matter, it's not going to happen again."

"So, if I'm the one you want this time, why is it so important to have Clarissa?" I asked, not sure if he'd respond this time, "Why is she special?"

He was apparently in the mood to share, "She, my dear, is the one person that could turn the tide on my entire plan. See, when I took her mother and grandmother, I didn't realize that she existed. When Madeline started communicating with her through her dreams, I started to see what the problem may be. As her dreams and communications grew stronger, I realized what she was capable of. The only thing keeping her there right now is that she has no idea of her strength and her certain belief that her mother and grandmother are coming back for her. That grandfather keeps her pretty close too. Kind of ironic that she's the one that convinced you to come, isn't it?" he mused.

"Yeah, ironic," I rolled my eyes at his smug smile, "but you keep dancing around the question. What is it that she can do that would bring your plan down?"

"As long as she's not here, or if she comes before she realizes her strength, there is no problem. She is the only person, besides me of course, that can walk in and out of the door between universes as she pleases. She only has to decide to bring others back with her and they will be free to go," he raised his arms, palms out, to the sky as he explained.

"How do you know that others can go back with her?" I asked, trying to hide my excitement at the possibilities.

"I know because she believes and since she believes completely free of bias, she can see what others cannot and that's why we want her with us; the most dangerous foe is one that knows more than everyone else. If she's with us, we can control what she does."

The truth of this weighed me down more than the meal. Even if I made it into Dominic's good graces, I wouldn't be able to be the one to pull the door down and free everyone. We truly needed Clarissa to do this. The thought was depressing and Dominic could clearly see, without picking thoughts out of my brain, that this was not making me happy.

"This is not something that you want for her, is it? To be here among us and come with us below?" he asked with genuine curiosity. I decided to be honest.

"No, I believe she deserves better than that."

"Better than being with us? Whatever could you mean by that?"

"Dominic, this little girl has barely had a chance to live and most of her young life she's been traumatized with the loss of her mother and grandmother," I couldn't believe how blind he could be, "I know that you're a selfish being, you've explained that, but she's a child, an innocent. I can't believe you'd ask her to give up her entire life's span."

"Yes, and as a child she won't burn long and she'll have what she wants when it's over. She'll be reunited with her family, just as I've been promising," he tried to appease me.

"That's not good enough, not for her." I said risking our fragile peace.

"Are you disagreeing with me?" he said, anger raising the pitch of his voice.

"Yes, I suppose I am," I said, "I won't help you bring her over."

"You will if you want to remain by my side and spare yourself the cleansing," he threatened.

"Maybe it's a price I'm willing to pay," I said and put my fork down. I wouldn't take another bite.

"It's not something we have to decide right now," he said trying to smooth his tone again, "we can talk more about it. I'll be here for a little while.

"Where are you going?" I said, trying to sound concerned.

"I can't neglect the underground for too long," he said.

"Don't you have brothers?" I asked, trying to regain the playful mood from earlier.

"Yes, but they have responsibilities too," he smiled at my joviality.

"When are you planning to take us?" I asked.

"It won't be long now. I have to make a few more lone trips down, then we'll have a field trip," she said with a laugh, "a very long field trip."

"What are you waiting for? I mean, other than the whole Clarissa thing," I dared to narrow my eyes at him.

"I'm making sure that everyone will have a place to go, and every place is ready for the person coming. Part of my job is also creating room for those that are joining. Why? Are you in a hurry to get there?" he teased.

"Just want to know what my new home is going to be like," I said smiling, "and what I'll be doing when I get there."

"Your job will simply to be with me. No digging or rearranging for you…and certainly none of the less pleasant jobs," he said with a shudder.

"And what are those?" I asked.

"Making sure the cleansing process is going forward. Not all of it is automatic. Not everyone just sits in a pit of fire. There are things to be tended to that require hands and muscle. My brothers and I do those things.

"And do your brothers have someone that they call queen?" I asked.

"Not all of them, the younger you are, the more work you have to do so you don't get as much time to come up," he explained.

"So what happens when an area fills up? Is there always room for more?" My curiosity was getting the better of me now.

"They don't fill up because after a person's cleansing has been completed, they are released into the light, and that, my dear, will be your job," he said.

I thought of another question, "So is it true? Do people actually sell their souls to get things that they want on earth?"

"Didn't you?" he responded.

"Not for anything on Earth," I smiled.

"That's true," he smiled as he got up, "you've hardly eaten anything. Aren't you hungry?"

"Not really, more interested than anything," I lied convincingly, "I've eaten enough."

"Well, I've given you more than enough to think about for one day and work must be done," he said, sighing, "I've got to get back to Rosalyn. I know she's hurt by my behavior, but her job's not exactly done."

"What is she doing now?" I asked.

"Her final mission will be the one that decides how long you're here. She needs to get Clarissa over here. I'm giving her a few more chances to get it done successfully. If she fails, well, she already knows," he said, purposely letting that idea dangle.

A shiver ran down my spine. Clearly he was postulating, making it clear that he can even punish those he holds in the highest regards when things don't go his way. I couldn't imagine what would happen to her if she did fail, but I could guess whose shoulders it would fall upon in her place. I was suddenly glad that she thought I hadn't done exactly what I said I'd do. If I start her doubting, then maybe she'd be strong enough to save herself.

"You really don't try to shield a lot around me, do you?" Dominic asked, "What is it that you told Clarissa you were coming here for? If you're truly in this, then saving Clarissa means bringing her here," his voice was rising as he said this, "I thought we'd just been over this."

"Yes, and nothing was decided and no, I'm not going to back down no matter how scary you become. She belongs over there. I don't want to talk about that any more tonight. How long are you going to be occupied?" My outburst brought a bright gleam into his eyes, he was excited that I'd not wilted and followed his command. He settled himself for a moment before responding.

"For tonight anyway," he said and took two large steps toward me, lowering his face to be even with mine, "but I'll be thinking of you every moment."

He brought his lips to mine and kissed me roughly. He let his arms drift down my back until they finally rested on my waist, suddenly he pulled back and smiled at me with such passion that it brought back the desire I felt for him despite my feelings for Thomas. For one moment I wanted to grab him, push him down on the ground, and ravage him.

"I'll see you tomorrow," he said and left me to my musings.

I sat at the table for a while. My appetite returned so I decided I might as well eat this rare food. I replayed tonight's conversation. I had learned so much. I finished my food and decided to take a walk. I slowly made my way to the compound and my room. I was intensely interested in what he'd told me about Clarissa. I knew that I'd have to talk to Madeline about it and decided to broadcast the request.

"Madeline, I need to talk to you," I whispered quietly to myself, pushing the thought away from me, then I added, "It's safe."

As I waited for her to come, I thought about his words. Clarissa is the one person that could turn the tide on his entire plan. All we'd have to do is get her here and she could begin to bring the others back. How many people could pass through that door without them knowing about it? It was risky, but it was the best I had for now.

Perhaps we could test the theory by taking one of the lesser known individuals, one that stays quiet and out of trouble, and pass them through at our next opportunity. Yes, we'd have a trial run if I could convince Madeline to call out Clarissa. At worst, I'd be punished for my part in it, but the person would be free to return their own life. I could take comfort in that. Maybe in time I could learn the secret of that door; I knew there was more to it than Dominic had told me, but I was nowhere near trusted enough for that kind of information and I didn't know how much time I had left. I'd have to really turn on the charm.

"You wanted to talk?" Madeline questioned from my doorway, bringing me out of my thoughts.

"Yes, I had a lot of alone time with Dominic today and I learned a lot. I wanted to share some things with you and ask you a favor," I said.

"I already heard some of it. I turned my thoughts to yours as I was getting close to your room and I really don't like where they were headed," Madeline said, growing protective of her family.

"I don't like it either," I wasn't sure how true that was, "but I'm going to have to gain Dominic's complete trust and he's already working on the seduction angle. Do you see another way?"

"No, not exactly," she admitted, "just promise me you'll try everything else you can think of first. At least that will be something to comfort Thomas."

"I promise you that. All other avenues will be explored before I go down that road," I said.

"Okay, so what did you want to talk to me about?" she asked, happy to change the subject.

"Clarissa," I saw her eyes go dark, but she composed herself quickly.

"Go on, what did he tell you?"

I relayed to her everything that he'd told me. I stressed the part about Clarissa being the only one that could get us all out of here. Then I told her about my idea. The test that I wanted to conduct the next time Dominic came back from one of his trips. I flinched as I watched her face consider what I was proposing. She didn't immediately refuse, which I took as progress, but she wasn't exactly getting on board either.

"Elizabeth, I want this to work as much as you do, but as long as you're going to have to break my brother's heart anyway, don't you think you could influence him enough to release everyone, including yourself? You know I don't want to make it a suicide mission, but if Clarissa gets caught here…." she was unable to finish.

"…she'll be able to race right back through the door," I finished for her, "and it would be a suicide mission for me. Your brother's broken heart I can live with, even if it means I'll lose him. At least he'd be alive and so would the rest of you if this works."

"And if it doesn't?" she asked, considering now, "What happens to all of us if we're discovered or everything doesn't go to plan? Also, what about you? If this does work, he'll have to know that you helped us. Have you thought of what he'll do to you?"

"If it doesn't work, it will be no worse for you than it would be if we did nothing. For myself, yes, I think he'd be mad, but he has other plans for me anyway."

"What other plans? Elizabeth, what did he tell you?"

"He wants me for his underworld queen. He told me he decided that the day he took my mother. He said that everything he's done since then has been all leading up to what's happening now."

"Then why doesn't he just take you?" She asked angrily, then realized what she'd said, "sorry, I don't mean to put this on you."

"Believe it or not, I asked him that. He told me he had taken one other down that way and his father had stolen her from him. He didn't want that to happen again so he figured if he brought a group along, his father would be appeased and wouldn't take what he'd already claimed."

"You are kidding me," she said, shocked, "no one else is safe from this? Not even Rosalyn?"

"No, not even her. He told me he's letting her down slowly. He kissed me today right in front of her. He has absolutely no shame and admitted to being incredibly selfish," I was actually starting to feel sorry for Rosalyn, she's been deceived for so long.

"Do you believe the things he's telling you?" She asked quietly, daring me to say yes.

"No," I said honestly, "I know he'll say anything and stop at nothing to get what he wants. But I also know that if I don't play his game, he'll stop playing altogether and simply take us all as soon as he has space. That's what he keeps leaving for. He has to move the souls along, oversee the process, and make room for the newcomers. This is the only way I know of to keep a shred of hope of getting out of this alive."

It was her turn to ponder. She'd have to decide what to do about Clarissa. If our test worked, we could begin working on getting everyone out. Her biggest argument against it was starting lose weight even in her own mind given that Clarissa is able to come and go as she pleases with no help from anyone. That set me thinking again. If Clarissa can choose to walk in or out of the door at will, can she will the opening to accommodate more than one at a time? We won't know anything if we can't perform the first test.

"I think you're right. I think it's time for a test. I can fear for Clarissa all I want, I'm her mother, but there really is nothing else. I can see that now. The longer that you have to keep up this charade, the more it hurts Thomas and I don't want him to hurt any longer than he has to," she said with finality.

"Thank you," I said sincerely.

"At least I know that no matter what happens, Clarissa can walk right back out. The tricky part will be getting her away from Roger. We'll have to do this at night so he'll be sleeping. How about midnight tonight?" she asked.

"Okay, I think that should work," I said somberly, "go tell Theresa to pick someone to go home, someone that's out of Rosalyn's eye, that she pays no attention to."

"How exactly is there going to be a door available?" Madeline asked, "If Dominic is here, there can be no door. How can we do this so soon?"

Just get the others ready. I'll make sure there's a door. If I don't come back, you'll have to try to continue the plan without me," I said with strong resolve.

"No, Elizabeth, if you're thinking what I think…," she said, panicked.

I cut her off, "What choice do we have, really? If we do nothing, nothing is going to change. Besides, it shouldn't be anything permanent."

"You're right," she said, "time for action, not words. What do you plan on doing?"

I smiled, "I'm going to tell him that I want to see my new home."

Chapter 14

"Your new home?" Madeline repeated.

"That's what he wants for me, so I will request that he take me below so I know what to expect.

"What if he doesn't bring you back?" she asked, horrified.

"Then you will have to continue the plan without me. Continue to work with Clarissa to get others back home. You'll have to move quickly though because he doesn't plan on being here too much longer," I warned.

"Are you sure about this?" she asked.

"I am if you are."

"Okay, I will work on communicating with her. I will tell her to expect the door tonight at midnight. She will have to get herself to the island, but it's something she's done before, she knows how," she saw my expression change and hurried to reassure me, "she will be perfectly safe."

"Tell Thomas I love him." I said as Madeline turned to leave.

She turned back, "of course."

If this was going to work I'd have to go to Dominic soon. I took a few minutes to wrap my head around how I would approach this so that it didn't sound suspicious. I didn't care who they decided to send home, but fervently prayed that this test would work. I took a deep breath, and went in search of Dominic. He'd told me that he had to spend some time with Rosalyn because she still had a job to do so I was heading in the direction of her room when I was surprised. Dominic was sitting in one of Rosalyn's "dentist" chairs. He was looking wistfully through the window and had his eyes closed. He hadn't sensed my presence so I backed off into the shadows and took a moment to observe him at his ease.

His lips were moving slightly, though no sound was coming from them. It looked as though he was speaking to someone. He gestured once with his hand back toward the rooms where we were all staying. I looked carefully at his face and was surprised to notice that a small track lined his face beginning at his eyes, as though he'd been crying. Suddenly, a new tear formed and began its descent down his long cheek and fell silently to the ground. The room suddenly became bright, filled with an unnaturally bright light, brighter than the sun, then darkened just as quickly. Dominic was still, but began blinking and I realized that whatever had happened, it was over now.

I cleared my throat and made a few loud steps before coming out of the shadows and making my presence known. It was only when he saw me approaching and smiled a huge, toothy grin that I realized it was me he was waiting for.

"Well, finally, I find you on your own again," he said pleasantly.

"Dominic, I didn't expect to find you here. I thought you said that you'd be with Rosalyn tonight," I didn't want to give him any indication that I'd seen or heard what had just transpired.

"She was a little angered by that display that we put on outside her door. She wasn't as compliant as usual. I'm giving her some space. Are you disappointed to see me?" He seemed genuinely concerned.

"No, I was coming to find you, actually, but now I'm thrown a little off guard. You told me earlier today that you were ultimately selfish. I'm surprised you'd give Rosalyn that opportunity. Why the sudden change?" I asked.

"It must be your humanitarian influence," he lied smoothly, "why were you looking for me?"

"I was thinking about our conversation this afternoon and was wondering about my new home. I'd like you to take me there so I can see it for myself," I said.

"Really? Would you?" He drew out the words to show his surprise at my request.

"Yes, I would," I said, confused.

"And what about the others? Do you no longer care about what happens to them? Besides, it's not ready yet."

I understood, "I don't mean I want to leave forever. I just mean it will make an easier transition for me if I know what to prepare for," I said as I stroked the side of his face.

"You mean you want to see the different levels? Meet my father? That sort of thing?" he asked, amused.

"Something like that," I said while I put my hands on both sides of his face and leaned in.

"Okay," he said when he pulled back, "I have to tell Rosalyn that I'm leaving and coming back. Maybe I'll let on that I'm giving her a chance to cool down. Though I don't think she'll like to hear that you're coming with me."

"Don't tell her," I said automatically, sounding much braver than I felt.

"If you say so, I'll be back shortly and we'll be on our way," he said.

He left quickly and I sent a silent message to Madeline. I could only hope that she'd been able to get to Clarissa.

"*She's in agreement, she will be waiting at midnight, try to come back,*" she silently answered my thoughts.

Dominic returned before I knew it and we were off.

"How will it feel for me? When we start flying, I mean." I asked.

"Don't worry darling, I won't let you fall," he winked at me and held out his arms. He looked almost giddy as we prepared to make the trip to his home. I settled myself into his arms, and he lifted my weight easily.

"Ready to go?" he asked.

"Lead the way," I responded, trying to sound calm.

We were in the air in a second. The wind rushed through my ears and I kept my eyes closed and my face turned toward Dominic's chest.

"Don't waste the best part of this," he chuckled, "enjoy the view."

I opened my eyes and looked at the view in its entirety. In just moments we'd made our way up to the clouds and were drifting like a low flying airplane. The ground below looked like a carefully sectioned off frozen dinner. Each section was surrounded by either water or paths worn into the ground.

"If we're not on Earth, why does it look so much like it?"

"It is a place that co-exists with the Earth. It's hard to explain, but it's like it's there and it's not. That's why you can't see the divide until I show you the door."

"Really?" I asked, thrilled that this topic had come up, "You mean the door is always there?"

"Yes," he said smiling, it always has been, at least since it was created. Most people just don't realize it. Like I said before, you have to really believe to realize it's there and most people wouldn't believe in something like this. People walk on through it all the time, but it leads to nowhere unless that's it's intention."

"Why is it only a one way door, then?"

"It's a quirk in the door itself. I have to concentrate in order to see the door, just like anyone would, and once I go through it, it sort of freezes in time; only until I make it to the other side," he explained.

"So that's why someone like Clarissa can come and go as she pleases. She can easily see the divide and has more reason than anyone to want to. Her clairvoyant abilities heighten that sense and lend themselves to more than just the mind," I surmised.

"Yes, Clarissa seems especially sensitive to the obscure," he responded.

"Gotcha," I thought quietly, and then thought of another question, an idea.

"What if you didn't go through the door? What if you only stayed within the threshold, would it stay closed then?" I asked.

"I guess it would; I never thought of that," he responded with an indulgent smile.

"If we're going down below, why are we still going up?"

"Silly girl, in our universe, up is down. You first pass the pearly gates before you move on to the dark ones."

"And those would be in outer space?" I asked, still confused.

He laughed lightly, and then pointed ahead of us, "No, another door, see it coming?"

And I did. Among the clouds I noticed a small rectangular section of blue sky replaced by a dull shimmer. We were heading for it at full speed. As we went through I felt that same almost wet sensation that I had when we went through the door on the island. There were no actual pearly gates, but there was an area that was blindingly bright. We passed that quickly and Dominic glanced at me with a nod. His realm came next. It was much darker, but there was a pale sun shining over it.

As we settled to the ground I took in my surroundings. I felt like my eyes weren't big enough to take in the scenery around me. The ground was rough and sandy. The sand was deep beige and riddled with pebbly rocks. There was absolutely no greenery, no grass, trees, nothing green at all.

There weren't crispy tree trunks all around with branches twisting themselves toward the sky. There wasn't fire randomly popping out of the ground. There were different rooms spanning hundreds of miles. Each room's punishment was more severe than the last. Souls were assigned a room when they arrived based on the sins they committed in life. The more severe room was the one that they started with. The more severe their sins, the longer it took them to complete the process.

When the soul has been properly rid of all of its human weakness, aka sins, it is released to enter into the heavens and stand before the gates where it waits for another judgment.

"So all souls, good and bad, come here before they are released?"

"All souls of those that have ever sinned, yes. But what you're seeing is the starting line for the worst of the sinners. Most of them go through punishments that would barely feel like punishments; it would be more like sloughing off an old skin and putting on a new one," she said, placing a finger under my chin and looking at me directly in the eye, "those areas are days away and I got the impression you didn't want to be away that long."

"Oh, right, no. I just want to see where we'll be and then I'd like to get back, tonight," I said.

"Then tonight it shall be," he said with a sad smile, "but we better not dawdle. Let's go find my brothers."

We looked through a few of the rooms and found one of Dominic's brothers. A short man was pouring some acidic substance into a stream that was flowing.

"Hey there, brother," called Dominic, "waters getting too complacent again?"

"It seems to happen faster all the time," he said while eying me with ill-concealed contempt, "I thought you weren't due back so soon."

"This is my brother, Sanje," Dominic said to me, then gesturing to me and turning to his brother, "and this is my Elizabeth. She wanted to come see what she can expect from her new home when we come over to stay."

"Father will not be pleased. They are not supposed to see until they are brought," Sanje said seriously.

"Father doesn't have to know," Dominic said.

"Ever the defiant one. You picked a good day, at least. Father isn't here. He and the others have gone on a gathering mission. They needed everyone. Seems like July is a popular month for death," Sanje said casually.

I gasped as I realized what he was talking about and tried to smooth out my features before I was noticed. Too late.

"You're going to have to become less sensitive if you're going to stay here, my queen. I think it's good we take some time before coming back here permanently. You need to build a thicker skin," Dominic said.

Despite myself, I was beginning to believe that he truly held me above the rest. I tried to push that thought away, I couldn't allow myself to feel anything for him, not even sympathy.

"So, you're Elizabeth?" Sanje was eyeing me, "tell me about yourself."

I settled in to tell him about my while Dominic stood patiently. He literally wanted to know everything so I started with my earliest memories. I worked through my childhood, the loss of my mother, my special bond with my father, my devotion to my brother. I continued describing my job with the ECN newspaper. All of this seemed so far away now.

"What about your time on the island?" prompted Dominic, "You've gone into great detail about everything else in your life, but have said nothing about recent weeks."

"You mean the happiest weeks of my life?" I asked playfully and smiled at Dominic, hoping that was enough to excuse my blunder.

"Yes, those weeks in particular I'm interested in," Sanje clearly wasn't the forgiving sort, "Dominic's filled us all in with the many familial issues you have. Are you sure that this is what you want to do?"

"Yes, of course," I replied immediately, "This is the path that I've chosen."

"I don't like the look in your eyes. You aren't really going to do this, are you? You're leading my brother on and will leave him. You should just keep her here now, brother," he was shooting eerily accurate accusations at me.

"No, I certainly am not leading your brother on, but Dominic's right. I'm not quite ready to come yet, not until I settle things with my mother," I said.

Dominic interceded, "I'm not ready to make this a permanent visit. Let's just leave it at that, shall we?"

"Okay, brother," Sanje said with a smile that didn't reach his eyes, "Good to meet you, Elizabeth."

Sanje left to go work at another level. I could tell he'd had enough and I had the uncomfortable feeling I'd made an enemy instead of a friend.

"Oh, don't worry about him," Dominic was reading my mind, "he's just extra protective of all of us. He has given all of the women that anyone's brought home the same questions."

"I don't want him to dislike me," I said.

"He doesn't dislike you. You should see the hard time he's given some of the others. He went easy on you. It must be because you're so convincing," he said with a smile.

"I think I'm ready to go back now," I said, wondering if time worked the same here as it did where we were.

"Yes, I'm beginning to think you've spent enough time here," said Dominic, who didn't seem as flippant about my conversation with Sanje as his words would imply.

As soon as we'd decided to go Dominic pulled me up into his arms and we took off. I held on to him as we soared through the sky and made our way back to the island. As we passed through the atmosphere I saw the storm form around us.

"We're actually causing this to happen?" I asked.

He smiled and raised his eyebrows, "Yes, interesting, right? It's our speed. The atmosphere just can't keep up so the moisture is drawn to me and the speed brings the lightning."

"Fascinating," I said, "does the lightning affect you at all?"

"Is it affecting you now?" he asked, raising one eyebrow.

"I guess it is, I feel energized, like I'm ready to do just about anything," I smiled.

"Anything? Really?" He drew out the word suggestively.

"Well, maybe not anything," I felt the blush rise in my cheeks though Dominic wouldn't be able to see it.

"The feeling will wear off. Once we are safely back on the ground and the lightning disappears you'll feel like yourself again. You must be tired, it's been a long day and it's after midnight."

"After midnight?" I asked, panicked, "Is it really that late?"

"Just after," he replied, "probably only by a few minutes."

"How do you know?" He wasn't wearing a watch.

"When you spend as much time as I do outside, you start to pay attention to all of the clues," he said.

I tried not to think about what was happening on the island, but I couldn't help but wonder who they'd chosen to go through the door. I was flipping through images of each of them wondering which would be the most innocuous. I didn't get to think too long before Dominic interrupted my thoughts.

"Why are you thinking of those on the island?" he asked.

"Just wondering which level they'll go to when we bring them below," I lied.

"Oh, I could probably guess for most of them, but you didn't get to see many of the rooms. The good majority of them would go to the less difficult rooms, the ones that were days away," he said.

"Would Rosalyn be allowed to go there?" I asked, sincerely wondering.

"No, I don't think so. Rosalyn has inflicted some of the worst types of pain on others; that has to be atoned for. She will likely be closer to where we were."

"Wasn't she following your command, though? Wouldn't that count for anything?" I asked.

"She was, but again, choices. She made the selfish choice more than once."

"Seems awfully unfair," I muttered, "how long would she have to be there?"

"For several decades. It's kind of hard to explain, but when a person, or soul, I guess, is going through cleansing, their sins become somewhat visible around them, sort of like a visible aura. Once that aura is completely burnt out, the cleansing is complete. The more difficult the cleansing, the longer it usually takes. Those that go to the easier rooms may not even be there a year, not that time there is the same by any stretch of the imagination," he said.

"How is time different? Have we been gone longer than it seems?" I asked.

"No, not when we make quick trips like this, but for those that are there to stay, crossed the river Styx and all that, time speeds up considerably. What a day on earth is would equate to decades down below."

I noticed we were starting to descend from the clouds and began to see land. I saw the door on the beach as clear as day, and I watched Clarissa grab the hand of someone that I could not recognize, though he sort of looked like the individual I'd interviewed before making the decision to come over to the island when all of this started. Dominic was turning his gaze toward the beach so I distracted him with an urgent kiss.

We touched the ground just inside the compound and Dominic asked, "What was that for?"

"For taking me…and for bringing me back," I replied with a smile.

"May I walk you to your room?" The perfect gentleman.

"You may," I said, smiling at the formality.

We walked along together and he slid his hand into mine.

"This is going to be great. I think taking you there was a really great idea. I can't wait to bring everyone!" Dominic said and I could see his planned future playing itself out behind his eyes.

"Yes, it will be. You were right about the tiredness though. As soon as we touched down I felt that exhilaration fading and now I'm just plain tired," I said, hoping he'd take the hint.

"We certainly don't want you to be bereft of your sleep. Go on my darling, get some sleep and I'll come find you in the morning." He said. He was clearly disappointed that I hadn't invited him in, but he didn't show it. He stood in my doorway, stared into my eyes and stroked my cheek. He leaned in for a kiss and was gone.

I turned into my room and curled up in a ball on my cot. The tears started almost immediately. All of the bravery that I'd displayed all day seemed to be releasing itself through my eyes in a watery fashion. I kept quiet as I didn't want Dominic to come wondering what could be wrong and I certainly wouldn't share with him how terrified I was of ending up in that place with him for eternity.

I dreamed again that night. Probably the worst dream of my entire existence. We were back at the palace of darkness and Dominic and I were overseeing the return of a recent expedition. I saw the faces of those filing in and realized that I knew them. As the numbers dwindled I saw the last two faces. They were those of Roger and Clarissa. They, too, were given their assignments and moved to where they were supposed to go.

I made my way around and found the room that was reserved for those with fewer sins to weigh them down. I found Clarissa there. I looked at her confused because not only did she seem to not be undergoing cleansing, she was also carrying a small baby in her fragile arms.

"Here you go, Elizabeth. I took good care of him just like you asked me to," Clarissa said.

"Thank you, sweetheart, you did a good job. I can't believe you brought so many," I said.

"Dominic promised that if I got everyone I could go home," she said and her eyes suddenly were glaring, "but Dominic lies, just like you."

As she finished that last sentence she glared into my eyes and the horror became real. The baby that I was now holding was his son and I had lied just as convincingly as he had taught me. I was the one that committed the ultimate betrayal and brought Clarissa here. I started screaming and did not stop until I realized that my eyes were open and I was alone in my room. Dominic must not have been far because he rushed in and was at my side as I woke up fully.

I knew it would be far too risky to ask to talk to anyone right now, so I let Dominic comfort me after I lied to him about my dream. A situation that did not make me feel much safer.

"It was just a bad dream, darling. It was nothing. I am here now and everything will be just fine," he soothed.

He had no clue how terrifying this comfort was, but I could not turn it away so I sat in his arms and tried to calm myself. My hand returned to the necklace hiding under my shirt, and I calmed slightly. He did not miss that action, or the resulting slowing of my pulse, but he didn't bring it up.

A few minutes later Rosalyn came into my room, and then several minutes later Rose and Madeline turned up. They told Rosalyn that they heard my screams from across the island and came to make sure that I was okay.

"You look much better just being in their presence," Dominic remarked, noticing how I'd relaxed so much more than with him in the room.

"Yes, it's good to see them again. We've become pretty close since

I've been here and it's comforting to know that your friends will come for you when you need them," I looked meaningfully in their direction.

"Maybe you should have a day to yourself, you and the girls," Dominic said, "I will take the boys on an island adventure. What do you say?"

"I'm not going anywhere with that traitorous little waif," came Rosalyn's harsh voice.

"Fine," he replied curtly, "stay here and sulk. Thomas and I and the others will be gathering provisions in the forests. Girls, I suggest you spend the day on the beach."

He was clearly concerned with my dream and the way I had physically relaxed only when Madeline and Rose had entered the room. As much as he wanted this, I could tell that this is something he wants me to do willingly, not against my will. Whether or not he's willing to push, I think I have my answer in his prior actions, but I did find it endearing that he cared at all. I pushed the thought away quickly though I didn't miss his smile.

"Rosalyn, are you sure you don't want to come with us?" I asked, trying to reach out. I realized now just how much she'd been duped.

"No dear, I have no desire to celebrate or relax today," she said in a tone I couldn't decipher. It seemed she was somewhere between anger and defeat.

"That's nice of you to offer, Elizabeth," said Dominic, "but clearly she doesn't want to join in and she does still have a job to do too. Let her do her thing and you can do yours. Hasn't that been the way it's always been with you two? I think I may have been mistaken about the two of you forging a friendship; I'm starting to feel like I'd have better luck asking for the moon," Dominic rolled his eyes.

"If you were, that wish may have been granted before a friendship would," I said matter-of-factly.

"Ha," Rosalyn steamed and left the room.

"Are you seriously trying to get me killed?" I turned on him after she left.

"Madeline, Rose, please go down to the beach. Elizabeth will join you shortly."

They exited the room with worried glances. I tried to smile reassurance after them.

"No one, and I mean no one, is going to hurt you while I'm here," Dominic said mistaking my sarcasm for true fear, "I will not let that happen. I don't care if she is your mother, if she makes it necessary; I'll take her out of the equation for good."

"Okay, I believe you," not wanting to upset him further, "I will try to remember that before I talk about Rosalyn."

"Don't think you have to fear her for an instant. She doesn't know how much you mean to me yet, but she will," he said and I saw true anger in his eyes. I was almost worried for her.

As he walked out of the room, I realized that I had caught Dominic in a lie. He told me that he'd only promised Rosalyn the place that she was in now, but I think her real anger and hurt came from the fact that he was taking me down below. Something he never did with her. I know their relationship was all business, but seeing him favor me, especially when she felt that my father had done the same, couldn't be easy for her. Suddenly I understood her ire much better.

I left the compound and went in search of Madeline and Rose. They were both looking for me with anxious eyes and relaxed when they saw me. When I got close enough to them, Madeline looked carefully toward me for a moment, and then away as if she was listening for something.

"What did he say to you in there?" Madeline asked.

"He thought I was scared of Rosalyn and he wanted to assure me that I had nothing to fear," I replied flatly, "What's the deal with Clarissa? Who did you send? Did it work?"

"We have a lot to tell you. Let's get to the underground," Madeline said.

"The underground? What if he comes looking for me?" I asked.

"He won't. He's staying with her for the day and tonight. He wants to see her make some progress with Clarissa so they're strategizing. I'm kind of keeping one ear open for how that's going, but I know they'll be busy for the night. Even though she's feeling a little upset by how close you and Dominic are, she still follows him around and is constantly seeking his approval. Sometimes you fall so well into that role that I get worried," Madeline admitted.

"I think that's a good thing though, right? If I can fool you I can certainly fool him," reassuring her.

"Yes, that's right," she said, clearly still uneasy.

We walked together then to our underground hideout and as we were approaching the entrance I saw Thomas. His eyes were pained, but he tried his best to smile when we came into view. I ran to him and threw my arms around him in a tight hug.

"I'm okay," I assured him, "I wouldn't have gone if I didn't truly think he'd bring me back."

"I was so worried, you didn't even say anything to me, you just went," he said and I could tell he's been wanting to say this for some time.

"The moment didn't present itself, that's why I asked your sister to speak for me. I'm sorry I couldn't come on my own."

"I am too," he wasn't entirely ready to forgive me despite the circumstances, "don't do it again."

There wasn't much force behind his words and I knew he was speaking more out of fear than a true command. He knew I couldn't always promise open communication if this was going to work. He looked at me a moment more and his features softened.

"I just don't want to lose you," he said and he leaned in and kissed me softly.

"I'm not going anywhere," I said and kissed him again.

"Well," he was looking at me with concern, "I'm not entirely sure how fine you're going to be when we get down there." He gestured to our underground hideout and turned to Rose, "did you tell her?"

"Tell me what?" I asked.

"No, I didn't. She's been through so much, I didn't want to, but we can't put it off anymore," Rose said sympathetically.

"Well, it seems the other day when your search party left and Dominic returned, two of the party did not return with the boats. They stayed here and waited on the island as you'd told them to in your note, for a door to open, which it did last night."

My heart plummeted to my stomach. My Dad and brother had done it. Had Rosalyn found them? Dominic was with her? Had I led them to their deaths?

"Tell me…" my voice was thick with despair.

"Better to show you, actually," Thomas said and turned around to enter the underground.

I looked at Madeline, suddenly afraid, "are you sure it's safe?"

"Yes," she said, repeating what she'd said earlier, "Dominic is well occupied tonight."

I turned and walked forward. Thomas took my hand and led me down the few crude steps we'd come to know so well of late, and then I saw them. My father and brother had done exactly what I'd asked them to do and now they were stuck here, just like the rest of us. I couldn't help the tears that came, unbidden, and the blubbery "I'm so sorry" and "you should have gone back" that escaped my mouth in the next moment.

They both stood and I ran to them, wedged myself between them, and wrapped my arms around them both. We stayed that way for several moments while they tried to calm me. They were really here, they had come to be part of this with me.

"It's okay, Elizabeth, we're here," said my Dad.

"I know, and you can't believe how incredibly grateful I am, but you shouldn't be. It was selfish of me, I should not have told you how to get here. Now you may never get back and it will be my fault."

"Elizabeth," Aaron started, "I know you don't believe yourself to be selfish and of course we would come for you; that's what families do. You wouldn't have asked for our help if you didn't need it. Don't you think we know that? You need us, we're here. We will get out of this, together."

"Have you been filled in on everything since I got here?" I asked.

"Yes, enough for now," said my father, "but let's not talk about that for the moment, huh? Relax and tell me what happened since we talked last."

I knew he was trying to settle my nerves. I started with the morning that I arrived on the island. I told him about Roger and how harshly he spoke of the island on that fateful bus ride. I told him about Thomas and I couldn't keep the blush off my face as I talked about him. Dad noticed and had a lot of fun with that; Aaron joined in too after a little bit and soon we were all laughing.

I went on to tell them about coming to the island and all that had happened in the week and a half since we'd arrived here. I told them about watching the search party and being amazed by all that had agreed to come and search. I didn't give too many details about Dominic and his plans for me, but they seemed to know that part anyway as every time I brought up his name my father's frown grew deeper. I finished by telling them about the amazingly strong little girl that was Clarissa.

"So, I didn't get an answer before. What happened with our little test? Did Clarissa come? Did she get the person through? Who was it that went?" The questions fell right on top of each other.

"We took two actually, but you haven't met them. One of them, Tony I think, seemed to know who you were. He said he thought you'd interviewed him before he was taken."

I did remember, "they were brothers right? So Tony found his brother Paul?"

"Yes, that's right. They'd both pretty much stayed off of Rosalyn's radar, so we figured it would be safe to send them through."

"And...?" I asked.

"And it was a success. She was able to allow them through and to go back through herself. There was a moment of absolute terror when we saw a flash of lightning hit not ten feet from where we were standing.

That could only have been you two arriving. We thought we'd been spotted for sure, but no one came back for us so we knew we were okay," she finished.

"What did you tell Clarissa?" I asked Madeline.

"I told her that we wanted to try an experiment. She had to get over here on her own, that part you already knew, but if Roger had any idea he'd probably stay up all night just so she wouldn't go.

"Once she arrived here, after you'd left, I told her all that was happening. I left nothing out," Madeline said, surprised as thoughts of my dream floated to the surface and made me cringe, "once she again believed that we were all working together to get home we told her about the experiment. We told her what she had the ability to do and that we wanted to try to bring someone back to the other side to see if it would work. I told her she could tell her grandpa nothing of this. Then, we saw the storm arriving and knew you were on your way. You had great timing too; it was just a little after midnight when we saw the first flash of lightning."

"That was the part I was most nervous about. When Dominic said something about it being after midnight I almost panicked, but I held it together because he said something about it being just after midnight. I realized we'd be okay. I asked him how he could tell the time and he just said something about traveling a lot and being able to read natural clues," I added.

"Yeah, I guess he doesn't get a lot of sleep," Rose said, "Rosalyn would always complain that he'd keep her up really late at night when he was here. Did he say anything about why he's been so deliberately mean to her lately? Not that I should care, but I guess I sort of feel bad for her."

"Actually, after spending time with Dominic today, I feel very bad for her and she's been nothing but mean to me since my arrival. Dominic explained today that this is his way of letting her know that he's not going to make good on his promises. He has every intention of going back on every promise he's ever made to her. Since she was so upset by my noncompliance, she jumped at that," I tried not to look at my dad as I explained this though I could feel his eyes on me, "now he's decided that he wants me to be his queen. He said he's doing it in small steps, but is keeping her focused on completing her final task of getting Clarissa here. I'm so sorry Dad and Aaron."

"Sorry for what, baby?" my Dad asked.

"For having to show you all of this, for having to show you what became of her in the intervening years."

My dad's faith in her and belief in the good in people shocked me, "Honey, he's been deceived in the worst possible way. Do you think she'd actually be able to do this to strangers if she had survived that accident, let alone her own daughter? This Dominic pulled the wool over her eyes at her most vulnerable of moments. She was weak and agreed to his terms; and yes, she's become power hungry since then, but that's not her. That's only what he's done to her."

"Dad, you can't possibly believe that's still her in there," I started.

"But she didn't die because of him. For that I am grateful, maybe now I'll have a chance to bring her back to herself," my dad finished in an echo of thoughts I'd had more than once since I'd been here.

"What good will that do? We'll still be trapped here."

"Don't lose faith," Aaron said reassuringly, "we've done a lot of talking here tonight. We may have a way to make it back out of here."

"What do you mean? What are you thinking?" I asked.

"Madeline has been carefully watching Clarissa since she left," Rose started, "that sweet girl has so much compassion for others. When she brought the brothers through, they were still very confused and she would not leave them until she was certain they knew how to get home successfully. When she was certain, she lied to them that she had to go back and meet her grandpa who was waiting for her.

"They were a little shocked, but a little while later they gathered their strength, found the spot that led them closest to the other shore, and swam for it. They made the other shore and began finding their way home. I'm a little surprised they had the strength for the swim, but desperate times and all that. If we try to do this in a massive fashion the next time, we're going to need to get off that beach much more quickly. That means that one of us, one that's aware of the plan in its entirety, is going to have to go with them. Did Dominic say when he was planning on going back below?"

"No, but while we were there I met his brother Sanje and he was surprised to see him return so soon. Before we parted ways, Dominic told him he'd be here for a couple days this time. He also said that Rosalyn has a job to finish before he brings all of us below. That job, of course, is to get Clarissa here with us so that his plans cannot be ruined. Once she's here, I see no reason for him to keep us here any longer, except that he said I needed to develop a thicker skin for the home that I would be living in and he wanted me to have time to do that," I said.

As much danger as I knew I was in, I was almost in a panic for Clarissa. If she's successful the next time, will there even be a next time, it will be obvious that people are disappearing; especially with a more notable person gone. We won't be able to cover up the absence long. I figured Rose would be the one to go with the next group, or maybe Theresa. She hasn't been around as much since this has become a family affair, but I wouldn't want to forget how much she's given. How would we even be able to make the last exit? These thoughts were swirling in my head and I felt my panic rising, but then Madeline's voice was there too.

"Your panic is reflecting my own quite well. If we handle this carefully, there shouldn't be any reason for them to know anything until the last exit."

"How? They're bound to notice if their small army of compliant souls are suddenly missing. I figure we can cover up for a little bit, but it won't take them long."

"We've been talking about this tonight. We're going to create a diversion rooted in a Pro- Elizabeth versus Pro-Rosalyn division among the captives. We will make it known, loudly, that some of us like Rosalyn's leadership and some of us are happier with the way things have been since Elizabeth's arrival. That should create enough of a diversion to keep them occupied for a while. We know that Dominic doesn't really care what any of us want, but he is starting to care about what you want, in spite of himself.

"You, Elizabeth, will naturally start complaining about Rosalyn's followers. When Dominic makes his return and those that are Rosalyn's followers leave…Dominic will simply think that they have finally quieted because they'd have to admit defeat. After that we will have to act quickly to get the final group through. Dominic will be more than suspicious, but that's where you'll come in. You will have to do everything you can to keep his attention, and then you'll have to break away from him and come for us. We'll be ready and waiting and by the time he gets to you, it will be too late. We'll have to move fast to get off the island, but we'll get across and we'll be free of this mess."

"In order for this to work, we're all going to have to be very convincing," I stressed, "If it will work, it will only work by a hair's breadth. Everyone will be in danger."

"What's that "if" word you keep using, Lily? Aaron teased, "We will all do our parts. For every one of us our lives are on the line."

I choked up again knowing that their lives, my father and brother, wouldn't be in danger if I hadn't left them that note. My father recognized my guilt.

"We didn't have to walk through that door Elizabeth; we had a choice. Your brother and I both come into this knowing we may not be coming out. We've reconciled ourselves to that. Do not feel guilty, nothing could keep us away from this," he comforted.

"If you didn't know you couldn't have come," I said quietly.

"Then I wouldn't have such an exciting story to tell my grandkids," he said with a smile.

We spent the rest of the night talking among one another about my father's and brother's arrival here.

As we were talking I looked very carefully at my brother. He has a wife and child at home and he came anyway. Part of me wanted to hit him upside the head for taking such a risk. Another part of me was profusely grateful for his presence. I couldn't reconcile one part with the other so I settled on asking him.

"Why did you come?"

"I love you; of course I would come see what I could do to get you out of this situation. Don't you want me here?"

"Of course I want you here, Aaron, but you have a wife and child to think about. What if the worst should happen? Who will take care of them?" I asked.

"I'm not worried about the worst happening because it's not going to," he said smugly, he and I shared the characteristic of being stubborn.

"You can't know that," I said.

"No, but I can believe it and I do. We will make this happen. You have to have a clear picture in your mind of the outcome of this situation and keep it there.

"Madeline's made it clear what you're prepared to do if it doesn't look like we'll be able to get out together and I'm here to tell you that's not going to happen. Thomas loves you and you deserve to be loved; by someone who will give you everything you want, not Dominic and his false promises," Aaron said.

"I think there's more to Dominic than anyone knows, but you don't have to worry about me falling for him. I'm very clear on my purpose. He is very smooth and charming, but I see right through that," I said, brightening a little.

"That's what I'm talking about. Look for those positives. That's what will get you through even your darkest hour. Let's go join the others."

We did and discussed how we would approach this. I told them I thought Dominic would be here for another two days. We'd use the time to create the separation of loyalty that we'd been discussing. By tomorrow afternoon, it should be widely known that a division was growing amongst the people. This would give them something else to worry about and keep them distracted and busy.

As the sky began to go from dark to the first shadows of light I made my way, exhausted, back to my room. I fell onto my cot and slept a dreamless, peaceful sleep. As I began to wake sometime well after the sun had had a chance to warm the air, I began to hear the first rumblings of the disgruntled choosing of sides.

Chapter 15

As I became fully awake I heard Dominic's soft voice outside my window. He was addressing the crowd that had formed just outside of the compound. We'd talked about this in the early morning hours. We didn't want Dominic making any rash decisions, just enough to distract him from his purpose.

"I understand this can be upsetting for some of you. You've followed Rosalyn for so long and her feelings have been hurt. I can see that, but there always comes a time when things change. This is all this is, a change in leadership. It's not even really that; Rosalyn will simply be sharing her leadership role," Dominic said smoothly.

"I will not listen to the other," said a voice from the crowd, "she doesn't provide us with food and a place to live."

"You will not be given a choice," a gentle warning.

"Fine, I may have to listen to her, but I will always value Rosalyn's opinion over the other," amended the speaker.

"How can you value someone that lets your faces ooze with malnutrition?" Another voice asked, "Maybe Rosalyn brings the food, but Elizabeth makes sure we get our full share and stay strong and healthy."

I heard a murmur of agreement from several voices in the small crowd. They were putting on a good show.

"This, ladies and gentlemen, is not a democracy. You have no choice in the matter," Dominic said keeping his voice calm and even, "you may like or dislike my choices, but they are mine to make. That is all there will be. Go back to your chores; you will be the only ones that suffer if you do not."

The murmur died down and the crowd started to dwindle. They had planted the seed of doubt in Dominic's mind without angering him. At least it sounded that way. I would find out soon as I heard his footsteps coming toward my room.

"Well, sleeping beauty has awoken," he said with perfect composure.

"Yes, I heard something outside, is everything okay?" I asked.

"Everything is just fine," he said soothingly, "once in a while the subordinates have to be reminded who is in charge, that's all."

"What was happening"

"It seems that in the short time you've been here, you've gathered quite the little following. I can completely see why anyone would want to follow you," he added with a smile, "but some of the others are holding onto Rosalyn's leadership."

I faked a surprised expression, "really, I have followers already?"

"Yes, it never takes people long to realize when a good thing comes along," he said, flattering me.

"Those that are loyal to Rosalyn, what are they saying?"

"They wanted to make their opinions known and tried to shoulder a little power saying they'd only listen to her. I gently put them in their place and reminded them that I am the one with the ultimate decision making authority."

"I guess you have to do that from time to time with a large group of people," I said.

"Yes, it's part of the job description," he chuckled quietly, "best be prepared for it. It's part of your future too."

"Okay," wanting to be agreeable, "what are we doing today?"

"I don't know. What would you like to do? Rosalyn is off trying to accomplish her task and everyone here has a job to do. We have the day, but I'm leaving tonight," he added.

"So soon?" I asked, genuinely surprised, " I thought you said you'd be here two more days, not just one."

"The sooner I prepare the area the sooner we can go home and drop this charade. Besides, my father asked to see me," he said reluctantly.

"Will your father know that I've been there?" I asked.

"Not if Sanje kept his mouth shut. We've returned here and I won't bring you there until I'm sure the same won't happen as last time. I don't think he realizes how deeply my feelings go, or maybe he just doesn't care, but I figure I better work on preparing everything. If the dissension among the subordinates gets bad, we'll be making our exit," he said with a sad smile.

"This saddens you," I said, curiously.

"If we go too soon, he's bound to take you from me. I need the time to work him up to it," he said.

I saw my chance.

"Well, don't waste another minute. Get there and prepare him already," I said smiling.

"He won't be back until tonight. I already asked Sanje. I'm going to leave right after dinner. Until then, though," he said, brightening, "we have the day together."

He pushed the bangs that had escaped from behind my ear back in place and I felt desire rush through me again. I had no conscious desire for him, but my physical desires were overwhelming. I figured he must have something to do with that.

"You don't have to resist it, you know. You could just go with it. It makes it so enjoyable when you let me mentally tease you first," he whispered in my ear then kissed me roughly. I still hadn't gotten used to the feel of that forked tongue. I had to admit, I kind of liked the sensation; so different from anything else I'd felt.

"What do you mean, first?" I asked, breathing harder; desperately trying to maintain control, "Don't I get a say in when this will happen for us?"

"Of course you do, darling," he was taken aback, "I just thought with all this time to ourselves today, what else is there to do? Maybe I was mistaken in thinking you wanted this just as bad as I do?"

My body was on fire and I wanted to give in, but I couldn't. I promised this would be a last resort and we weren't there yet.

"What are you struggling with, darling? I don't have to be a mind reader to see, in your eyes, that you're struggling with something. You are here of your own free will, aren't you?" He was spitballing, but managed to land glaringly close to the truth.

"No, no, it's not that, Dominic. Of course I'm here of my own free will. It's just that…well…" I hid my face in his chest.

He picked my chin up with his finger, kissed me softly, and looked at me questioningly, "It's just that what? This isn't something new to you, what are we waiting for?"

"I just…I'm just not sure I'm ready to give this to you too," I said, grasping for a reasonable explanation.

"You're going to sit by my side for eternity in the darkness, right? How would withholding this make any difference whatsoever? There is more behind your hesitation," I could tell that I was upsetting him now, "I am all for agreeing on when and how this happens. I will not achieve you through force, I'm just trying to understand why now wouldn't be as good a time as any."

"Look, make fun of me if you will, but I do believe that there are some things that should be done in special moments, at least for the first time. I don't want to look back on our first time and think of the place where I was taken by force, faced to confront my mother, and watched as my brother and father looked for me knowing that I wasn't there to be found. I would much rather have a memory that closes out one chapter of my life and celebrates the choice that I made for the rest of it."

"You are making an insane amount of sense, I suppose," he said, defeated, then kissed me again with more passion, if possible, than before.

"You're not making this easy," I said truthfully.

"I'm not trying to," he admitted, but then he stopped and held me in his arms, "As much as I want this, you are right. It will be better to wait until the day that we leave. I can wait another week I guess."

"A week?" I questioned him.

"That's the timeline I gave Rosalyn. I gave her an ultimatum. I told her that if she could get Clarissa with us; at that time she would share, in title only, the spot of queen with you. This is a promise I have no intention of keeping, you see, don't worry about that," he said lightly, "and if she can't, we go without Clarissa at a great cost to my personal pride."

"Why don't you just go get her yourself?" I asked.

"Don't you think I've tried? I've come to her in many forms; her mother, you after she met you, even Roger, but she's a very smart girl. Whenever I've disguised myself in her dreams, she always seemed to sense, somehow, that I couldn't be trusted. You have that same quality, you know," he said, appraising me.

"What do you mean?" I asked, shocked.

"The day that you spoke to, who was it? Paul, I think, I was there. I was feeding him lines to tell you and the two of you had a pleasant conversation, but you noticed too much. I could see that plainly on your face."

"I do remember that," a little concerned that Dominic was aware that he had been chosen to go home, "there was something about him that just seemed a little off. I chalked it up to concern over his brother."

"Yes, well, what your intuition was trying to tell you was that the person in front of you was a sham. It's designed to protect you, but only if you listen to its warnings. Since your intuition has not told you to stay away from me, I don't understand why you still don't trust me."

"You are the epitome of someone not to trust, Dominic. You must see that. You lie to everyone to get what you want and you're completely shameless about it."

"But I always tell you when I'm lying. I would think that that would earn the trust you find so hard to award me. I don't keep things from you. Have you caught me in a lie yet?"

"Not catching you in one and you not lying are two different things, Dominic. Just because you're trying to gratify my loathing for my mother by openly treating her badly, that doesn't win my trust," I said, knowing I was taking a risk with this kind of honesty.

"Does it bother you the way I treat her? I was under the impression that you were enjoying it almost as much as I am," he said.

"No, I wouldn't say I am enjoying it. I am bold enough to admit that I take some small gratification in seeing her angry, but that's not the same as hurting her. She hurt me, beyond anyone that's ever before, but I would never want her to suffer."

"Then I'll quit being so insensitive. And you might as well blame me for many of those deplorable things she's said and done. I prompted her to do most of them, but I won't be so insensitive to her anymore, how does that suit you?" he asked.

"You can be a little insensitive," I said with a playful smile.

"That's what I thought," he said, returning the smile, and then gently kissing my lips.

I still had desire for him, but it was not the burning desire that I had to consistently push away. He decided not to push that issue today. He let his hands drift over my shoulders, down my back, and he softly traced my spine as we lay together discussing the future.

"What will it be like, when I'm there permanently?" I asked.

"As my queen, you will be treated just as you should. No pain will ever come to you. No lie will ever touch my lips when I'm with you. My father and brothers will adore you and protect you just as much as I do, but they will not interfere with us," he amended as though I had been afraid of that.

"What will I do though? I can't just sit around day after day, won't I get bored?" I asked.

"Oh no, darling, there will be plenty to occupy your mind. The sinners that are being released to the brightness, once cleansed, have to give final confession before they leave and it will be your job to hear them and grant or deny that final passage," he explained, stroking my back.

"How often will I have to turn someone away?"

"Most of the time they cannot even come before you unless they have been released, but mistakes do happen. If you catch someone in a lie, you must condemn them to the level set aside for liars and they begin the process again," he said.

"Is that my only job?"

"No, no, it's not all work, work, work down there. You'll find we're fond of having fun too. And then there's procreation," he added as an afterthought.

"Procreation?"

"Yes, the continuation of the bloodline. We cannot leave it all to our father. He's quite old you know," he said, "If you couldn't guess, I'm eager to get started."

"I could guess that," I said while I kissed the tip of his nose, "soon."

"Yes, soon," he agreed, "now your turn. You never really have explained to me why you're so ready to give everything else up and spend eternity with me."

I wasn't ready for this one.

"Well," I stalled, "I guess it's because I have never really felt like I belonged anywhere else. I've never found anyone that was my equal in every way the way that I've found with you. Does that explain it well enough?"

"Yes, I understand not fitting in. I have issues in this area myself and a lot of siblings that don't get me. You're awfully young though. Didn't you think maybe your fit was still coming?" he asked and I could tell this question left him feeling vulnerable.

"Not after I met you." I reassured him.

We lay quietly for a long time speaking only occasionally. The sun seemed to move in the sky so it must have become afternoon. I was strangely comfortable lying in his arms. That thought scared me so I redirected my attention to my necklace.

"That's a beautiful heart," he said quietly, "you think of it often."

I panicked but controlled myself quickly and remembered to breathe.

"It was a gift from my grandmother," I lied, "the one on my father's side."

"I guess that explains why you always think of it with such love and devotion," he said.

"Yes, she was a very special person whom I loved very much; I miss her," I admitted.

"I'm sure she misses you too," he said, "Well, I suppose it's time that I'm off. I need to get a status update from Rosalyn before I go below."

He sat up and pulled me up next to him. He cupped my chin in his hand and kissed me softly again.

"I won't be gone long. Look to the skies for my return," he said.

He got up and left and I found myself alone with my torn thoughts. I couldn't imagine why his leaving would hurt me. I couldn't imagine wanting to be back in his arms. I especially couldn't imagine having his child. I couldn't imagine any of it, but I couldn't deny my feelings completely either.

Had I begun to feel something for him? These conflicted emotions I was having, I was sure they were all mine and it scared me. I loved Thomas, that hadn't changed one bit, but was I still in love with him? I couldn't fathom that I could fall out of love so quickly. I couldn't think about it anymore. I decided on a solo stroll on the beach to clear my mind.

I walked along the fringe of the compound, and meandered slowly toward the water, taking my time. I was replaying the day over in my head and realized how comfortable I felt lying in Dominic's arms. Yet, I kept envisioning the heart at the bottom of the necklace and felt it lay so close to mine. I was in love with Thomas. I was sure of it, but where were my emotions leading me?

"He knows what he's doing," came a voice from behind, the one voice that could pull me further from my ponderings, "he's taking control of you in every way he can and that's why you're thinking of leaving me."

"Thomas," I finally looked up, worried that he shared the gift of clairvoyance. Even in the failing daylight I could see the anguish on his twisted face. I ran into his arms, he didn't push me away though I was sure I deserved it. Instead his strong arms squeezed around my middle and held on tight. I squeezed back and my mind suddenly became clear; the conflict was gone. How could there have been any conflict in the first place?

"Oh Thomas, what's happening? I love you, I'm in love with you. Seeing you now I have no question in my mind. My resolve to leave with you is just as strong as it was before Dominic came. How can I be having these thoughts?" I realized Madeline must have been watching after Dominic left and relayed to Thomas what I was thinking.

"Because that's what he wants. He's begun his mind games. You went to him willingly enough, but he doesn't completely believe your affections. He's working inside of your mind to make you start meaning the things that you've been saying," he said sadly and dropped his gaze.

"He's not going to win, you know that, don't you?" I asked. I suddenly felt desperate.

"I know that, but you asked me to make sure that you stayed on the path that we've talked about. That is what I'm here doing. I love you and you love me. We are going to be together when this is all over and Dominic will just be a moment in time. Someone that we can forget when enough time has passed."

"I'm sorry; I just get so confused when I'm alone with him. The second that you were in my sight, all of his lies and my false feelings evaporated. That has to mean I'm holding my own, sort of, doesn't it?" I asked, scared that he would turn from me despite his declaration of love.

"I think it does," he said with a smile for me, "and no matter what, I'll always be around to clear your head. I promised that I would be here for you and I mean to be."

I reached up and kissed him then. I was slightly confused when he began to push me away, but understood quickly.

"Rosalyn is coming," he whispered and he disappeared into the trees.

I turned and faced the direction Thomas had indicated, waiting for her arrival. I would meet her head on, no matter how angry she was with me. I walked toward her approaching figure.

"I'm sure you know that Dominic is gone. He had a commission for me that I must get done. I only have a week to make it happen."

"What's that got to do with me?" I asked.

"We need to get Clarissa over here. Both you and I know that Dominic wants her with us and now we have a deadline. You've gotten pretty buddy buddy with Rose and Madeline. I figured you could help make that happen."

"I could if I wanted to," I said angrily, "not sure I'm so inclined to help you though."

"I'm done with the anger," suddenly she sounded very sad, "we're going to be much better off if we work together. If you don't think Dominic will turn on you as quickly as he's turned on me, you'd be mistaken. I can't be angry about it anymore. We were a great team and really got this place up and running, but now he wants a teammate that he can take to the next level. A teammate that he can make his queen and for some reason, you've agreed to it. Now I just want to stay in the game for as long as I can be useful," for the first time, I saw clear terror in her eyes.

"And you'd be okay with this kind of existence? For all of eternity?" I asked her, wondering if this may be my moment.

"Yes, I am. If this is the way that Dominic has deemed it, then this is how it has to be. I trust him completely and I know he must be doing this for a reason. I'm not going to question his judgment.

"*Agree to it,*" Madeline said in my head.

I was confused, but if Madeline wanted me to agree to it, I would do what she said. There had to be a reason behind it.

"Fine, I will help you, but as far as Dominic is concerned, I've seen no proof that he'll eventually turn away from me. And I don't plan to do anything that will displease him." I threw in for her benefit. It did not have the intended result.

"I don't know that it's up to you, really," she said sadly, "but you can find that out for yourself. I need you to work with Madeline and the others. Find out if Clarissa's been having dreams.

"Every time I try to invade Clarissa's subconscious a kind of wall comes down and won't let me talk to her. If I can't break into her sub-conscious, I certainly can't break into her conscious thought like I did when you were there. Communications have gotten fuzzy with everyone. I'm even having a hard time with your thoughts, but I think Dominic's doing that. Find out what's causing this blockage and get back to me. Dominic will be back within a day or so and I need to get this figured out."

I now understood why Madeline wanted me to agree to this. I had free license to talk with Madeline, Rose, and Thomas. We didn't have to guard our conversations anymore. Dominic had more of a hand in this than she realized. He was taking away the gift he'd given her.

"I will let you know what I find out," I said.

She nodded and left the room. It felt like a great weight was lifted off of my shoulders when she walked away. I was granted permission to think again. I didn't have to guard anything for a while. I set off to find Thomas with a much more positive look at the possible outcome of this whole situation. I hadn't gone far when movement in the trees distracted me again. Thomas was there, just feet from where Rosalyn and I had been talking. I smiled a huge toothy grin at him.

"You heard the good news, right?" I asked.

"You are incredible, you really do put on a good show, and yes, I did hear that you've been assigned to us," I wasn't entirely sure if he was complimenting me or not, but I wouldn't let paranoia spoil the moment.

"Did you miss the part that she can't 'hear' us anymore?" making air quotes with my fingers to indicate the hearing went beyond the abilities of the ears.

"No, that's wonderful too." he said with a quiet smile.

"Should we go down and talk to the others?" I asked not really know-ing what to do next.

"Could I steal some time with you before we tell the others the good news?" he asked somewhat sadly.

"Of course, there's nothing I would like more," I said and smiled but inwardly terrified of his quiet mood.

"Where are we going?" I asked.

"Staying under cover, there's a comfortable little place that I've dis-covered here, above ground. I've been coming here when I need some space," he said.

I let him lead me there in silence. I still couldn't completely read him. I knew he was staying strong for me, but was sure it was hard for him to listen to me talk about Dominic. I wasn't sure it hadn't become too much.

We walked to a small clearing with leaves all over the ground and the air seemed cooler here. There was a felled tree that lay on its side. It worked well as a backrest. I noticed the blanket that we'd used in the underground tunnel on the ground. I went to it and sat down, but Thomas walked away from me and sat on the felled tree.

"Thomas," I started as I looked at the ground. I couldn't bring my eyes up to meet his, "I'm so sorry. I know Madeline is letting you know everything that is happening between Dominic and me and I'm sure it's becoming unbearable. If you brought me out here to end it, I can save you the trouble. I won't blame you if you want nothing to do with me anymore."

I started to take off the necklace that he'd given me so that I could give it back to its rightful owner when I felt his arms grasp mine and stop them before my fingers could find the catch. He caught me up in his arms, kissed me softly, and looked straight into my unsteady heart.

"Don't even think about taking the necklace off," he said as he looked deeply into my eyes, "You've been misinterpreting my silence and brooding. I'm not going to leave you when you need me the most. I'm worried about you. You went with him the other day and I was terrified, not that you were leaving me, but that he may not bring you back. I am being strong for you, as requested. Now that we can safely talk, I want you to be able to get it all out."

My tears then came out in sobs. Everything that I hadn't allowed myself to feel, I was feeling now. For a few minutes I couldn't talk. All I could do was sit there and cry as Thomas held me. He stroked my hair and was steady. He let me get it all out. I eventually lifted my head, finally able to talk. He had a different idea.

He reached down and kissed me. He started with my lips, but let his kisses drift all over my body. Before I knew it, that intense passion that I was feeling earlier was redirected toward Thomas. A fiery shock worked its way through me and I groaned with pleasure. We moved as one and the intensity of my feelings worked their way to the surface. My kisses echoed his; passion igniting time and time again until each of us had no more to give. We lay quietly when we were both supremely satisfied and held one another close.

"We have to get Madeline to talk to Clarissa pretty quickly," I said sleepily while laying in Thomas's arms.

"Why? Did Dominic say something about when he's planning on taking everyone? Concern coloring his voice.

"Yes, he said a week. I'm not sure the Elizabeth supporters versus Rosalyn supporters were a good idea. He said that he gave Rosalyn a week to work on getting Clarissa over here and if she couldn't do it by then we'd just go without her. But I also need to talk to Madeline for another reason. It's about Clarissa."

"What about her?" Thomas was immediately on the defensive.

"Well, we still need her, but not for the same reasons as before. She does have the ability to come and go as she pleases, but it's not anything that she can do, it's more about what she can see.

"Dominic explained that the door exists all the time. It doesn't come and go. It's a matter of concentration. If one concentrates enough, they can find it. Clarissa can simply see it and therefore come and go anytime she wants. If she can do it, so can we, with her help. She can lead us to it and we can go through."

It took a minute for Thomas to bring his jaw back to the closed position.

"This is good news," he said, wanting to smile, "this means you can drop the charade, doesn't it?"

"Maybe, but not yet. It's still not as easy as us just walking out of here. There's Rosalyn and Dominic to think about. If we do make it through they'll come after us. We have to find a way to defeat them first."

"Well, it may just be Dominic that we have to defeat," Thomas said softly.

"What do you mean?"

"Your Dad's gone to see her," he said quickly then shrunk away expecting my response.

"He went to see her? She knows he's here? What about Aaron, did he go too? Why would he do that?" I asked no one in particular.

"He thinks he'll be able to get her to come out of it. Aaron is not with him, he didn't know until it was too late too. Your dad makes a good point though. Dominic has thrown her aside lately. If we can get her on our side, she'd strengthen us considerably."

"You agreed to this?" I asked not hiding my hurt and anger, "You agreed with him that this was a good idea and just let him go without talking to me or at least Aaron?"

"I know it's a risk, but your dad understands that too. We all agreed that the benefits would far outweigh the risk that he'd take. He didn't think that she'd hurt him," he said, trying not to anger me further.

"Who is 'we'?" I asked him.

"All of us minus you and Aaron," he said.

I tried to absorb this without getting up and going directly to get my father. He was putting himself at more risk than he realized and it wasn't necessary. Rosalyn was not going to be able to get us what we wanted so even if she did decide to switch sides she'd be just as stuck as the rest of us. It was incredibly risky letting her in on what we were doing seeing that she'd also have to know that I was lying to Dominic.

"Did he tell you what all he was going to tell her? Like why was he here?" I asked.

"He was going to use your disappearance as the catalyst for him coming here explaining that when the search party left he and Aaron agreed to stay behind and look for a little while longer. Then when the storm came and they saw the door materialize out of thin air, they'd gone through. Once they got to the other side they started the search again and met people that had been able to fill them in on what was happening here so they'd come in search of you. Instead of finding you they'd say they found Madeline who told them about what happened since you'd gotten here and once your father heard that Rosalyn was still alive he'd made plans to find her and so he did," he finished, satisfied with the story they'd come up with together.

"He's not going to say anything about seeing me?" I asked.

"He couldn't; you were supposed to be with Dominic all that time," Thomas said.

"I guess you're right. So where's Aaron, or where will she think he is?"

"With you, of course, he'll explain that Aaron stayed with Madeline and Rose when he left and she already knows that she's assigned you to us. She's realized you'll be having a little reunion with your brother."

"What could he have been thinking?" I repeated more to myself and shook my head. I unlaced myself from Thomas's arms and sat up, thinking about the danger he was putting himself in.

Thomas felt my discomfort with this and was visibly disappointed in my negative thoughts about this outcome. He sat up next to me.

"It is possible, you know," he said as he kneaded my shoulders softly, "possible that she does still love him under that grasping exterior."

"How could she? There's so much of her that's truly gone," I said remembering her thoughts and words since I'd come, " I don't know if there's enough of the person that was my mother left to remember the things that were really important to her."

"You're too hard on her, I think," he said carefully, gauging my response. He went on when I just looked at him incredulously, "most of what you've seen is Dominic's influence. I've had some time to talk to your father and he told me what she was like; how even though she was frustrated with you, she was still so proud of you and your brother. Dominic did take her at her most vulnerable moment and he did it for his own gains, but he also offered her the chance to keep living, to breathe another day. Do you really think she had any kind of idea how he was expecting her to live?"

This made me think about Dominic's admission to me about his influence in her actions and my convictions began to waver.

"She may have chosen this over death, but I see your point. I suppose I have been hard on her; not that she hasn't given me plenty of reason," I said a little defensively.

"No, she hasn't exactly been nice to you, but after all, as far as she knows, you're the reason Dominic isn't delivering on his promises. Don't think he didn't manufacture that for his own gains, also. I'm sure she already knows or has some idea what will happen to her if she disappoints him. I'm guessing that none of the rest of us will have it too easy if Dominic gets his way."

He was asking and my face could not deny the truth. He cringed. "No, no one will get off easy. I may not have to go through the cleansing process, but I will have to procreate."

"Procreate, is that what he called it?" He was angry.

"Yes, carrying on the bloodline, to be exact," I was equally disgusted.

"You will not be a vessel for his progeny," he said suddenly, "and what would they do, go on and continue as he has?"

"Something like that," I admitted, "Apparently he and all of his brothers find queens to bring home and serve the purpose of procreation along with deciding when a soul is ready to move to the next step in the process."

"And what happens to you when you've served your purpose? What happens when you can no longer bear children and all you're good for is allowing souls to pass on; a job that anyone can do."

I shivered at the thought, "I didn't ask him."

He looked down at me again and gently stroked my face, "I know; I wouldn't want to know either."

With that he kissed me and before I knew it he was everywhere. I wasn't about to resist.

Chapter 16

Thomas and I joined the others back in the underground. Theresa had joined in and she was talking to my family animatedly about the plans moving forward. Aaron's face echoed my anxiety. Our father had not returned from his confrontation with Rosalyn and I was sure that he was playing out several scenarios in his mind, just like I was, none of them resulting in the happy reunion of our parents. I ran to him and threw my arms around his middle and squeezed. We stayed like that for an entire minute, feeling one another's fear. I pulled away and looked at him closely.

"Well, thank God you're here," he said.

"For now," I reminded him, "this isn't over, and as scared as I am for Dad, Thomas makes a good point. If anyone has a hope of bringing her out of it and back to us, it's him."

"Yeah, that's what I keep telling myself, too, but I'm not quite ready to forgive everyone for allowing him, even encouraging him..." he couldn't finish as fresh tears were welling in his eyes.

"Thomas, you didn't tell me Aaron was this upset," I said.

"Sorry, I was being a little selfish," he said with a smirk, "I didn't want you to run from me right after I'd gotten you alone."

My eyes narrowed as I sent a glare in Thomas's direction. He put up his hands, palms out, and walked away.

"Aaron, you know how stubborn Dad is. Even if they hadn't encouraged him to do this, do you think that would have stopped him? It was always my intention to bring her home with the rest of us once I discovered that that was an option, maybe this is the best way to make that happen." I said, trying to soothe the worried look off of his face.

"No, I'm sure it wouldn't have stopped him, but I would have been looking out for it. I would have waited until he thought he had his chance, and then I would have stopped him."

"He would have been expecting that too. He would have found a way around you. If nothing else, he'd come right out and tell you he was going to do it. One way or another it would have happened. All we can do now is hope that he's been successful." I said.

"Yeah, okay, I don't really want to talk about it anymore, let's move on and think about how we can be helpful," Aaron suddenly brightened up.

"Madeline and Aaron have done a lot of talking," said Thomas, "she's probably told him more than she should have,"

Thomas scowled in Madeline's general direction as he finished his last sentence and she looked up, smiled, and winked.

"The mood is so much lighter here, despite the worries and sibling quarrels, it's happier here. I miss that," I said.

"We're here to serve, Lily," Aaron said teasingly.

Thomas gently brought us back to reality, "all of us siblings in one room, we're easily distracted, but if we have a week to deal with, we should get moving on our plans."

"A week?" Rose, who had been quietly enjoying the sibling rivalry, spoke up.

"Yes," I answered, "That's why Dominic left now. He was intending to stay longer, but he was afraid that the subordinates that were claiming sides may get worse; he wants to be out of here before that happens."

I saw those words affect each person in that room. We had been so sure that creating the two sides would be helpful to our cause.

"Do not feel guilty. At least we're doing something. Maybe the week deadline will turn out to be a good thing. How long can this actually go on anyway? At least now we're forced to act even though it's sooner than we may have done it. One way or another this will all be over in a week's time and we won't have to wonder anymore," I said, trying to infuse some positivity into the tension-filled room.

"Madeline," I continued, "you're going to have to communicate with Clarissa and you're going ot have to do it soon. She's going to have to be ready to bring a group through that's pretty large. Like, all of us."

"All of us, really?" Madeline asked, "How?"

"Well, we still have some planning to do, but we've found the secret to the door," I said.

The hope immediately emerged in the room and Aaron shook his head, "Lily, you couldn't have led with that news?"

I gave him a smirk and launched into the explanation that Dominic had given me for the door and Clarissa. When I was finished, Madeline looked at me with incredulous eyes.

"Clarissa came back," she said, "of her own free will. We can't get her to go home, but if they find her now…"

"What about Roger?" I asked.

"He's going out of his mind with worry," Rose said, "it's like when he lost us all over again. Madeline is watching him carefully. We don't want him to sink into depression before we can get back to him."

Rose's silence became very clear to me now. She wasn't enjoying the sibling rivalry going on earlier. I would be surprised if she heard much of what happened. Rose was terrified of what this was doing to Roger emotionally. She must have been asking Madeline to focus on him again and again. He hasn't been back to work nor has he left the house since this happened, according to her.

"Rose, this is over in a week. I don't know that I would have let Clarissa stay either," trying to ease her tension, "but take comfort in the fact that she can come and go as she pleases. Maybe we can influence her to go back to Roger and then come when it's time."

"She won't go; she already told us that she's not going back without us. She's having dreams again and her dreams are telling her that you're not going to keep your promise, so she's decided to stay here no matter how this turns out; no matter what it's doing to Roger. She says that I'll be back with Roger eventually and he'll be fine once I'm there."

"How can she believe both of those things, Rose? If I betray everyone, then you'd never see Roger again," I reasoned.

"I know that, but she's a child. It doesn't have to make perfect sense to her. She is just scared and wants to be near us."

"Let me talk to her," I said, "She's listened to me before, maybe I can get her to go back when Dominic returns."

"That might not be the best idea," said Thomas, "just because he says he's not bringing you and the rest of us back right away doesn't mean he's not. It's not like he has any problem lying."

"I don't think so," I said, "I know he's a great liar, but I know he really wants Clarissa. He mentioned it would be at great cost to his pride if we go without her. Pride is something he holds very dear. I don't think he'll shorten the time span he's given Rosalyn. We have to do this for your father, for Roger, I don't even have to see him to know he's suffering. We can stop that, at least for now."

"I'll go get her," Madeline said and quickly left the room.

"You've roped yourself an intelligent young man," my father said from the shadows, "you should listen to him a little more."

This is what we've been waiting for, "Dad? Are you alone?"

"No, not alone," he said with a sigh, "I happened to pick up this small, charming young lady and her frantic mother on my way back in."

Relief washed through me as I realized he had not brought Rosalyn back with him. I feared that he'd told her too much and she'd realize just how deep this opposition went. The sudden anxiety must have been obvious on my face.

"Don't worry, sweetheart, your mother was less than kind at our meeting. You were right," he finished sadly.

"Oh Dad, I'm so sorry," I said, feeling his grief. I ran to him and hugged him tight, "Tell me what happened."

As my dad composed himself and was seated, Aaron came to sit by me and Thomas wrapped his arms around my waist. By the time Dad had collected himself and was ready to tell his story, Theresa and many others had joined us, all listening for something different.

"Well," he started with a sigh, "when I made it to her place, she was shocked to see me. She immediately pounced, wanting to know how I got here. I didn't say anything about the locket or the note inside, Elizabeth, so don't worry about that. This was my thing; something that I wanted to try, but it didn't work. I thought that maybe my influence would bring her back..." he choked out those last words.

"Dad," Aaron started, "if it's too much you don't have to..."

"I have to, this is important, just give me a sec," he said above Aaron's objections.

"He shouldn't have to relive this," Aaron said to me.

"I know he shouldn't," I said sadly, "I never should have left that note."

"That's not what I meant."

"Okay, you two. This was my decision," said our father, "now let's get on with it. I'll be fine...as I was trying to say before, my influence is not going to be enough. Once I explained to her the story we talked about before, she could no longer doubt how and why I was here.

"I tried to convince her to come home. I told her how much I'd missed her. I told her how much her son and daughter miss her. She kind of scoffed at that one," his eyes flashed to me then, "I basically got down on my knees and begged, but nothing that I could say would break her devotion to Dominic.

"She kept telling me how she'd been a different person then and Dominic had shown her what it was to truly live. She told me that their partnership had been fulfilling in a way that our marriage hadn't because I'd never really seen her as an equal. She was happy that Aaron and Elizabeth had become successful, but that they were raised now and I had done a fine job, with Aaron anyway...those were her words, Elizabeth. She said she wished me no ill will and for that reason she'd let me go my way without collecting me for the trip below, but that she would not alter her course. She said she will not alter course and that even though he's not following through on all of his promises, she still has a more prominent place through following him. Is he actually planning on taking you both now?"

The disgust was apparent on my face and I had to take a moment to collect myself before I could answer.

"That's what he's letting her believe for the time being, yes," I said, then getting defensive, "if I play along and act the part, we get the time we need to make our escape. Especially since he's now thinking of going without Clarissa. If I were to oppose him he could decide to go back right now without any warning and then all hope would truly be lost."

"This truly has been excruciatingly hard on Elizabeth," Thomas came to my defense, "and me too, but it's been what's working so far, though I hate every minute of it."

"Well then," my Dad said, ready to change the subject, "what's our strategy? If we only have a week, what are we going to do?"

"I'm not going back," said Clarissa, reading my mind.

"Honey, let's think about this reasonably for a minute, okay? Will you at least talk to me about it?" I asked.

"Okaaaaay," drawing out the word to indicate her hesitancy, "but I'm still not going back."

"You love your grandpa, right?" I asked her.

"Yes, but he'll be fine. Grandma is going to go back to him. The dreams have told me," she said.

"Tell me about your dreams; the ones you've had recently."

"They change sometimes," I caught on to the word 'sometimes.'

"But sometimes they're the same?"

"Sometimes. One shows grandma coming home and me staying here with Mom and you guys. In that one you go away with Dominic and the rest of us go to the red place....it's not nice there..."she continued, trying to explain, "there are fires, but you never have to go in like the rest of us...and your eyes are red."

She covered her face when she finished that explanation as if she were living the dream at that moment. She was obviously scared of me despite all of my assurances.

"The other dream is just a large window with all of us walking through. That one never scares me like the red place, but I always wake up when we go through."

"Are those the only two you remember?" I asked.

"One more," she said hesitating, "in this one...sometimes I wake up screaming."

"You don't have to tell us, it's okay."

"I…will tell it…it's important that you know," she sounded beyond her years. Madeline scooped her up and put her on her lap.

"There is a shorter man, one that looks different, scary. He has red eyes too," she explained. My mind immediately went to Sanje, "he was standing next to Rosalyn in her house, he was looking at all of us standing together. He said something about levels and getting clean. Then we were taken to the red place, and had to jump into the fire. I always wake up screaming when I jump."

Madeline hugged her tight and we all took turns thanking her for sharing her dreams. I was worried about Sanje being in her dreams. Dominic I think we have a good hold on, but Sanje would add a whole other level to this equation and I wasn't sure we could get around him. I figured it was best to share with the group what I knew.

"This other that she's referring to, the short man in her dreams, his name is Sanje and he's Dominic's brother. I met him when Dominic took me below. I know he's leery of us coming down there, or at least of me coming down as Dominic's queen, but I didn't say anything that would give us away. Dominic told me that he doesn't trust anyone; that he had a distrustful nature to begin with. He's not nice at all," I shivered as I remembered the scowl on his face.

"What if the scariest one comes true?" Clarissa asked in a small voice.

"We can't allow ourselves to believe that it will," responded Thomas.

"Death can't even save us now," said Rose sadly, "it will only bring us right into Dominic's hands."

"Let's try to keep some optimism in the room, shall we," Aaron threw up his hands in frustration, "Thomas is right, the worst case scenario has to be pushed aside if we have any hope of coming out of this. There could be many reasons that Clarissa is seeing Sanje in her dreams. Elizabeth told Madeline about her trip there and meeting him, right? Maybe some of those thoughts translated to Clarissa and now are appearing in her dreams. It's possible. We've said it and now we realize what will happen if the worst case plays out. Let's now focus on what will happen when the best case scenario is the one that comes to be. Clarissa, you said that you saw a window that everyone walked through? A window, not a door?"

"It was this way," she said as she stretched her arms on either side of her, "real long; a rectangle."

"That makes sense," I chimed in, "Dominic admitted as much. He said that it's more than a door, but that's just what everyone sees."

"Interesting, so if we're going to take Clarissa's dreams as more than just dreams, then this wide opening is enough to accommodate a group. This is a good thing. If we go through together and lock hands, there's no way that they'd be able to force all of us back through. There's no more than fifteen of us left, right? When we make it to the other side we go to the other shore. Once there, we're beyond their reach, and we can go back to our lives. I know that I'm ready for that, how about the rest of you?" Aaron said with an enthusiasm that was catching.

Suddenly everyone was throwing in ideas for the great escape. I didn't want to put a damper on things, but I wasn't sure it would be as easy as all of that. I'm not entirely sure they couldn't come after us in one form or another, but this was our best bet and certainly brought in some badly needed positivity so I kept my thoughts to myself for the time being.

"Yes," Thomas said, "If it can be more than a door, we have to figure out how to make that happen. Once we know that, it's just a matter of waiting for Dominic to leave and come back again. We'll all be able to go, together," he said, nodding at me.

"You'll have to do that, Elizabeth," my father chimed in, "when Dominic comes back you'll have to find out how that door can change from a door to an opening."

"I know, I can do that. He's like putty in my hands," I said, laughing with everyone else.

"Maybe my first dream will come true," said Clarissa with a smile, "the one that makes me happiest."

I envied her confidence. I wanted to feel like this could all be okay. I wanted to believe that I'd be able to look back on this some day for the nightmare that it is. But nothing is as easy as we'd like it to be. That's perhaps why I was not surprised at the new visitor that was coming to the entrance just as my father was getting ready to throw in his own hopes.

He opened his mouth to speak, caught her face from the corner of his eye, and froze. He didn't know what to think and Rosalyn continued her approach; her face unreadable.

"So, this is where you've all been hiding? And Theresa, didn't we just finish a treatment session dear? Has my effectiveness really drained that much? I suppose it has, seeing all that are here. Madeline, Rose, I knew that you were planning something. I had no idea how many you'd gotten in on your little charade. And Aaron, my son, I should have known you wouldn't go anywhere your father had not. The only two that seem to be missing from our little reunion party are Roger and Clarissa. Don't tell me that they're not here, too," she said patronizingly.

The color that had drained from my face on her arrival started to make its way back as I realized she hadn't heard Clarissa. We all stayed very still wondering what was the right next move.

"Well, you know what they say," she continued, smiling at my father, "if you can't beat 'em and all that. I needed some time to be on my own and think, but now I am ready to join this little band of miscreants."

"Oh Rosalyn, you came," my father said, surprised, "I was hoping you'd change your mind."

I was appalled he was so ready to believe her and take her back in, "Oh no, you can't just accept her arrival just like that. She's every bit as deceitful as Dominic; she's learned a lot from him. Dad, I know you still love her, but are you ready to sacrifice all of us?"

"Oh stop it, Elizabeth," the gulf of years stood between us, "I am here for you just as much as I'm here for everyone else. Do you really think I want to see you go below with Dominic and provide him offspring in that horrid place? Have I really become that evil in your eyes?"

"Are you seriously asking me these questions? A few hours ago you were telling me that you were willing to go down there with me. Why should I believe you now?"

She looked at me for a moment before answering, and I found that I could not doubt the sadness and sincerity in her eyes.

"I have been incredibly mean and unfair to you. Dominic did have a large part in that and that is the truth; he didn't like the way that I was softening when I saw you, so he acted through me. Your father put a lot of things into perspective for me," she smiled at him and reached her hand toward his which he took.

"I thought you said you didn't get through to her," I said rounding on him with fire in my eyes, "I thought it was too late to change her."

"I told you she wouldn't take this easily," said Rosalyn from behind me.

"Give her time, Rosie, it's a lot to take in all at once," said the calm voice of my father using his pet name for my mother. He looked up at her, "you really have been harsh."

"Yes, I suppose I have, and I won't try to make excuses. I can just say that I'm sorry you got involved in any of this, Lil," Rosalyn said.

I understood that my parents had come to some sort of agreement and didn't want to tell me right away. They were worried about how I would react. I could even understand why they did it, but my emotions made no sense. I wanted to laugh and cry.

"Elizabeth, now listen to me," my Dad's voice took on the commanding tone that I remember from my rebellious teenage years, "she is putting us in no more danger than any of the rest of us. There is more of this than you know. She has been fighting to come back home almost as long as she's been gone. Now she has a chance. We are all in this together."

"What do you mean *almost*?" I asked suspiciously.

She got distracted by Dominic, but she's come back to her senses now and she's part of the escape," he looked at me with fierce eyes.

My jaw dropped and I could not even think of words to express my anger, resentment, and general shock at what I'd just heard. I simply stopped. I couldn't move, I couldn't think. I looked at the others and saw them eyeing me with concern, but none of them looked as shocked as I did. None of them seemed surprised at the idea that Rosalyn was suddenly one of us.

Aaron spoke softly, "Lily, sis, she's our mother. Nothing will change that and you know the powerful influence that Dominic has," he said nodding his head in Thomas's direction, "she does love you. Give her a chance to earn back the trust that you once had in her."

I heard Aaron's words, but I wasn't ready to digest them. I had forgotten to breathe and suddenly the ground started to spin. I wasn't going to be able to hold myself up much longer. Thomas must have recognized this as he was at my side in a second, supporting my weight.

It seemed to happen very slowly. I turned to look at Thomas; an action that should have taken a second seemed to take several. It was like I was under, watching everything happen around me. Voices came to me, but they sounded wrong, like I was in a fishbowl and they were talking to me through the glass and water.

"Elizabeth, Elizabeth, are you okay?" Thomas was panicking now.

"Elizabeth, it's me, Madeline, talk to me," I didn't know why she was shouting.

I heard in the distance, "don't go over there. I don't think she's ready for comfort from you."

Aaron then came into view, "it was hard for me to believe at first too Lil, but it's her. She's back and she's going to help us defeat Dominic."

"Huh," was all I could get out before the room went dark.

I was out for not even a minute, but it was enough to boil over all of the various tensions in the room. Fingers were being pointed.

"It was too much," Thomas said roughly, "she shouldn't have been brought in yet."

Wow, everyone knew about this in some capacity except for me. What else are they keeping from me? These were thoughts I'd keep to myself for the moment, but they certainly gave me pause when it came to where they were placing their trust in me.

Rosalyn threw in, "We can't delay this. Dominic is bound to be back in the next day and we have to have the first group prepared by then. Elizabeth and I have to have our stories straight. We have to make sure that she can still do this."

That was enough to bring me around. I would not have her doubting me. I narrowed my eyes as I looked directly at her, "Of course I can do this."

She looked relieved, "Elizabeth, honey, I'm so sorry about all of this. I know what I've said and done. I'm not going to pretend that I wasn't unforgivable in the beginning, but I'm not that person. That was the Rosalyn that Dominic had under his power. I'm not there anymore and I promise, I am here to help," she said and I wanted to not doubt her sincerity, but I had to be sure. I knew who would confirm, at least for now, the truth of Rosalyn's words.

"Where is Theresa? I want to talk to her. Is she still here with us?" I asked.

"Right here, Elizabeth, and I understand why you want to ask me," she said, "As much as I hate to lend any kindness in her direction, she is telling you the truth. I told you from the beginning, he's a gifted manipulator. But she has come back with intentions of going home to her family," Theresa said and narrowed her eyes at Rosalyn.

"Okay, Theresa. If you believe, I guess I'll have to go with it," I turned to look at Rosalyn, "but don't think I've come anywhere near forgiving you."

"I don't expect you to, any of you. I know what I've done," Rosalyn said and dropped her eyes. She held up her hand to silence my father who had opened his mouth to defend her, "It's okay, Ben. She has every right to her anger. What you don't know, Lily, is the absolute truth of this. If you'll let me, I'll explain exactly what happened the day that everyone thought I'd died. It won't excuse who I've become or what I've done, but it may help you understand."

"I'm listening," I said, careful not to show too much softening.

"The part you've heard already was the truth. When it was apparent to me that I wasn't going to survive the car accident and you were, I was angry. I was not angry at you, dear, that's not something you've heard anyone say. I was angry at the world, at fate, at whatever you want to call it. And yes, there was a side to me that was upset that I was going to die and you were going to live a full life without me," she said with

shame in her eyes and followed up quickly, "please understand, I didn't
see my loss as suffering to you. I wasn't thinking clearly.

"That's the best way that I can explain it. Dominic came and offered
me what I had no hope of, he offered me life. His words were, 'do you
want to live?' Of course, I said yes; not having the first idea of what that
would mean. He took me in his arms and led me directly to this island.
I was the first through that door and discovered quickly that I couldn't
come back out of it of my own free will. He told me that this would all
be mine; that I would rule this land and be treated like a queen. I asked
him about my family and he said in time you'd come and seek me out,
then we'd all be together again. He made me believe that he was extending my life when otherwise I would have been dead."

The world entirely turned on its axis at this point, but this time I
managed to maintain my balance. In all of my anger and despair, it had
never once occurred to me that my mother was a prisoner on this island
as well. It was my turn to feel shame for not coming to that realization
myself.

I reached out to grab her hand, "Jesus Mom, I never even realized that
you were a prisoner here. I'm so sorry. But how do you know that this
is still not his plan? How do you know that he isn't watching all of this
right now?"

"I don't," she said simply, "but if he had any idea of what was going
on here, I couldn't imagine why we'd all still be here."

I guessed she was right about that. He'd simply take us all away and
this would be over. That made me think of Sanje and Clarissa's dream. I
shuddered silently not wanting to disturb this moment.

"He created this grand plan and I did everything I could to talk him
out of it. There was no way I could. He was determined that it be you,
and probably later, Clarissa. He already calls her his little queen-in-wait-
ing. So he went around keeping an eye on you and as soon as he saw
the chance to get you out here and to cross paths with Clarissa, he did.
It was no accident that your moped stopped working where it did. What
he wasn't counting on was your feelings for Roger or Thomas or your
ability to find information.

"Once that happened, he knew he'd have to play games to get you
here. I went along with it because I had to. If he discovered me he'd dis-
cover you," she said, "honey, you're my daughter. No matter how much
we disagree, I love you and will always protect you. I have stood from
the sidelines as I watched both my children become successes in their
own right and I was never more proud than when Dominic would come
back to report on your lives."

"I never really thought you actually hated me," I conceded, "until I came here, but having to do the things that I've done and hurt people I cared about too," I looked at Thomas as I said this, "I can understand why. I will try not to cringe when I see you, but I can't promise that the bitterness will go away quickly."

"I completely understand and I will do what I can to make that cringe go away quickly. I am so sorry I couldn't keep you away from this," she walked over and put her arms around me.

The tears were streaming freely from both of our eyes as we hugged away the anguish of the intervening years. I could truly feel how miserable she's been and how she was finally able to let at least some of it go. This was the woman that I remembered; the one I lost all those years ago.

"You don't have to be sorry," I said when I could finally manage words, "I'm not sure you could have found a way around him. It does seem to be better to make Dominic believe he's getting his way; it makes him less suspicious."

"At least we can compare notes now," Rosalyn said quietly, "it sure beats trying to work against each other."

"Yes, it does," I said trying to take the hurt out of my voice.

My father looked up at Madeline and told her to bring Clarissa out now. She returned with her quickly and we all sat down and discussed how we would move forward.

Clarissa would bring some others over when Dominic returned. Once he is back, it will be up to me to find out how to extend that doorway into something more like a window. Rosalyn also offered to try to find out, but we decided that if we tried too hard, he may become suspicious. We also decided that we needed to try to find a way to block him and his brothers from returning. We didn't want anyone else to go through what we have.

We came to a consensus that Rosalyn would draw out the search for Clarissa a few days in order to force two more trips out of Dominic. In that way, we'd have two opportunities to bring the rest of the others through.

I sat sleepily and wondered what tomorrow would bring. Would Dominic come? There was a shadow of the feeling I had earlier that wanted to see him again, but mostly I just wanted to get this over with.

I was extremely nervous about our chances for success, but figured everyone must feel the same as I did.

"Should we get back to the compound?" Rosalyn asked me, noticing how my eyes were drooping.

"I suppose we have to keep up appearances just in case Dominic decides to surprise us," I said quietly, smiling.

"That we do, come on," she said and extended her hand. I took it and let her raise me up.

I said goodnight to everyone, kissed Thomas, and went out into the forest with the one person that could have deceived us all. We had just let her in on every secret we had for a safe return, yet I felt calm. I could feel no lie in her presence, only great, powerful relief for having had an opportunity to reconcile her family. We walked quietly side by side enjoying the cool night air. As we neared the compound she spoke softly.

"I'm so sorry, I know that doesn't even begin to cover my behavior since you've been here…," she drifted off trying to find the right words.

I looked up and saw that tears had been streaming down her cheeks for a while.

"I'm sorry too," I said, knowing I had hurt her too, "I lost faith in you. You do want this just as much as we do."

"Yes, I do. I can't explain the anger I felt for you when I thought I was dying. I wish I could blame Dominic for that too, but I can't and I'm extremely ashamed of that. I just wanted to live. I didn't want you not to live, but I wanted to live too. The stuff about you becoming the kind of person I wanted did not come until Dominic started feeding it to me," she said, then added, "I'm not trying to make excuses, if you never forgive me I will have to live with that; I just wanted you to know that I love you very much."

"I love you too, Mom," and I knew it was true. All of the hurt feelings and the negative thoughts had suddenly vanished.

The next day was pretty uneventful. I spent as much time as I could in Thomas's arms. We decided, since we'd pretty well worked out the details of our plan already, that we'd all just spend a day on the beach. We did our best to relax and enjoy one another's company.

As day started to fade toward evening the mood turned to a more somber one as the clouds began to gather on the horizon. Dominic would be back among us tonight or at latest tomorrow morning. We came together one more time to make a final pass through our plan until we could safely meet again. Rosalyn and I would have to guard our thoughts more than ever to make sure that Dominic didn't get a hint of what had transpired since he'd been gone. Clarissa was already preparing the group that she would bring through the door when Dominic arrived, reminding them that they'd have to be quick. We all tried to talk her into staying on the other side until we needed her again. She refused just as strongly as before. She was afraid that if she went back now Roger wouldn't let her out of his sight; he'd probably camp in her bedroom with her. She was probably right.

I would have to talk to Dominic tonight. I'd have to try to learn the secret to the door. Flirting was a given. My sexuality was my strongest ally right now and I'd have to use it.

Chapter 17

When we got back to the compound I went to my room to watch the storm as it arrived. It didn't take long for the clouds to move in closely. Dominic was in a hurry. Before he could get too close I wished Clarissa and her band a silent "good luck," and tried to focus my mind on what he would expect me to be thinking. I thought it might be better to wait for him outside, so I left my room and went quietly into the cooling evening air.

At first I stayed in the cover of the trees not wanting to let the rainwater soak me, then suddenly, before I even realized I was doing it, I rushed out. I felt invigorated and intensely excited to see Dominic again.

"This is his doing, remember Thomas and the rest of us," Madeline hissed in my mind at great risk to all of us.

I felt the excitement ebb, but I couldn't go back now. He knew I was waiting for him. I stayed where I was, but my mind was my own again.

"Elizabeth, darling," Dominic said as he settled at my side, "I've missed you."

As he said that another being settled just across from us and I recognized Sanje immediately. He still wore the same untrusting scowl that he'd had the last time I'd been in his presence.

"You remember Sanje," he said to me lightheartedly.

"Of course, how are you?" I asked him, trying to mirror Dominic's polite exterior.

"'Bout the same as I was, nothing's changed here," he said and I could tell he was talking less about his mood and more about his distrust for me.

"What made you come on this little journey?" I asked.

"What's it to you?" he snapped.

"Well, I wasn't expecting company and I only brought out wine glasses for two," I said, glad that I had thought to bring out a celebratory drink for his arrival.

"Don't want any anyway," Sanje snarled.

"Sanje is here to help me make some decisions…such as what to do with Rosalyn when we go below. She obviously can't go with us now and I can't exactly let her go. I was thinking it was time that Sanje got a new queen. Sanje is too old for procreation and so is she and she's not bad looking. I thought as surly as he is and as pissed off as he is, they might get along just right," Dominic said with a bright smile.

"You brought Sanje here for my…Rosalyn?" I almost slipped, I've never referred to her as my mother in front of Dominic. In fact, I'd always let him know how much I detested our familial bond.

"Yes, doesn't that make you happy. Now she will have a place along with the rest of us and she'll be out of the cleansing too. It's a win win," he smiled at his own genius, "but he has to agree to this too. If he wants her though, it would work very well."

"He may not want her?" I said, incredulous.

"It's ultimately up to him. He could have any one of a thousand queens," said Dominic.

"Oh, that's pretty good, then," I said trying to sound happy, but not quite making it.

"I thought you'd be ecstatic; now she can fulfill her duty and there will be not further problems for you and I," he said, surprised.

"I am happy about that, I just didn't realize you were still going to make her a queen," I was trying to sound jealous.

"That's up to me," Sanje snapped again. It must be his default mode. Dominic noticed also, but dismissed it quickly.

"Well, well, we do have a little more anger than I thought. Oh well, it's out of our hands now," said Dominic matter-of-factly, "On to more important things; how was your time away from me?"

"Difficult," it wasn't even a lie. It had been difficult, but I wanted to reassure him. His smile returned and he kissed me softly.

"Me too, I wasn't going to come back until tomorrow, but I just had to see you again," he said, sounding like a man in love.

"Hmph," Sanje said in the background.

"Sanje, why don't we introduce you to Rosalyn. Then you can go bother her with your bad attitude," Dominic said smoothly.

"I can take him…Rosalyn and I have reached an understanding while you were away," I added when Dominic looked at me questioningly.

"Why don't we all go?" Dominic said with finality.

We walked into the compound and came to Rosalyn's rooms where she had fallen asleep. I walked in toward her and started softly.

"Mom, you'll never guess who's here," I said.

"What, Elizabeth, what's going on? How long was I out?" she asked, confusion clouding her eyes for a moment.

"Since when do you call her mom?" Dominic asked.

"Since we decided to get along," I answered.

"Who's here? Dominic, is that you?" She sat up and looked around, taking in the second set of devilish eyes in the room, "Who's this?"

"This is my brother, Sanje. I told him of our little dilemma here and he agreed to come and meet you."

"Oh, hello Sanje, how are you?" she asked nervously.

"Not nearly as trusting or smooth as my brother so you'll forgive me, but I'm also here to watch over him." he said.

"I understand, would you like to have a tour?" she asked him.

"Yes, I think that would be good; it would give us a chance to talk privately," he said and a smile lit up his cruel face.

Rosalyn got up from her bed and ran her fingers through her long chocolate brown hair. She smiled at Dominic and Sanje, and then led the way with Sanje at her heels.

"I think that went well," said Dominic, "what do you think?"

"I think it did too; hopefully they'll get along, but I don't really want to talk about her now. How are you? Did you get everything done that you needed to?" I asked with interest.

As we talked, Dominic led me to my own rooms.

"Just about, I'm probably going to need to make one more trip and time is running out so the next one will be quick, just a jaunt over for a few hours to clear out room that is going to be much needed soon. My brothers will be returning too so I'll have more help," he said.

"Were they gone again?" I asked.

"They had come and gone a few times. When my father's there it slows them down. He can't be out for very long; but we have more restraint and can stay away for longer periods of time," he explained.

"Restraint from what; I'm confused," I admitted.

"It's actually hard for us to come up here and be among the living souls. It can become quite painful if we stay up here too long. One might say they could entirely wipe us out if we couldn't return below for more than say three or four days. The sunshine and the warmth are too much for those of us that live among the darkness. It's pretty gross actually. I once had the opportunity to observe it and will not take that offer again. That's why we travel in the cover of the clouds," Dominic said.

"I had no idea. I thought you said it caused atmospheric interruptions, not the other way around. Isn't that what you told me?" I asked.

"That's the story that we tell people, yes. It makes sense to them without having to go into long explanations."

"What about when you take off? I didn't see the rain and lightning form when you left to go below."

"Remember, we didn't have it when I took you below either. We only really need the cover when we return. On the way up we're exposed for such a short time that it doesn't even affect us after a while. I don't ever feel anything now when I am on my way out," he said with a proud smile.

"And what in the world could hold you here? Couldn't you just take off whenever you like and return below?" I asked.

"Not if we can't get through the barrier between worlds. When someone passes back through, back to your world, the divide between universes becomes blurred allowing no one back in or out until the boundaries have had a chance to reset themselves. That's why those that try to turn around and go back through can't go anywhere and by the time the boundaries are reset, they can no longer see the door. Effectively, they are stuck. They wouldn't know to concentrate anyway so the divide wouldn't really be there for them, but they would also feel like they were up against a brick wall even though they wouldn't see one," he explained.

"Just out of curiosity, why do you come down? Aren't there enough people that have died a natural death or otherwise to keep you busy?" I know you said tensions can be high between you and your siblings, but you also said there are miles and miles of rooms to separate you."

"To keep us busy, yes. There is certainly plenty to do and miles to keep feuding siblings in check, but there certainly isn't enough going on up there to keep us entertained or offer us a continuation of our bloodline. Once a person has passed their natural life cycle, they obviously cannot bear children, so we need living humans to be our queens. The rest that are coming in this group, well, I'm distracting my father. I've already explained that. You didn't forget, did you?" Suddenly he looked at me as if I needed medical attention.

"No, I didn't forget. I was just curious. But now I'm curious about something else," I said.

"Ever the curious one," he rolled his eyes and smiled, "go on."

"When I'm no longer of use to you and you find a new queen, what will happen to me?" I asked, remembering Thomas asking the same things.

"Elizabeth, my darling, I told you nothing bad would come to you there; once you are replaced you will be sent into the light. Your soul will have to be cleansed too, of course. We're not allowed to send on any unclean souls, but your cleansing will be of the less intense variety since you will have spent so much time at my side," Dominic's voice was as smooth as silk.

He was now revealing that he'd openly lied to me in the past. In past conversations, Dominic had told me that I'd be spared the cleansing at all as his queen, but now the story has changed. I brought my hand up and traced the lines of the heart that was again hidden under my clothing; very lightly and distractedly, as though I was simply musing over what he had told me.

"Do I get to see it ever or will you always just paw at it under that shirt of yours?" Dominic asked and caught me off guard.

"Of course you can see it," I said as I began to pull the chain out of my shirt. As I touched the heart on the chain, the one in my chest began to beat harder. As soon as the necklace was in view Dominic reached for it and held it in his hand lightly. He studied the intricate design weaved into the solid silver heart.

"It's almost as beautiful and rare a find as you are," he looked at me and smiled, he released the necklace and let it fall back to my chest, "I wonder why you hide it?"

"I don't hide it," I lied, "It's just very important to me so I like to keep it close," I said truthfully, "It's as important as she was."

"I thought necklaces were designed to adorn those wearing them?" he argued, "Isn't that the purpose, to accentuate your beauty? You wouldn't hide something that would make you more beautiful, at least I wouldn't."

I was starting to get nervous. He clearly didn't like my flimsy explanations.

"I am afraid that something will happen to it. It could get caught on something and the delicate chain would break. If that happened the heart may fall off of it and end up somewhere that I couldn't retrieve it."

"Okay, okay, I guess I've just been listening to Sanje too much. Put it back if it makes you feel better," he still wasn't happy.

"I'll leave it out if that's what you'd like," I said, trying to soothe the sudden tension.

"It is beautiful," he repeated after a minute.

"Then I'll keep it where you can see it," I said feeling doubly relieved that I could concentrate on it freely and that our little argument was over. I was trying to work my way back to the line of questioning I had started on; it had been going so well.

"I'm curious again," I said with a smile.

"What about this time?" his indulgent tone was back so I knew we were back on solid ground.

"Why does the door only open when you come here? Why doesn't it open again when you leave?"

"The door, as you know, is not really a door. It doesn't appear when I'm leaving because my mind is on wherever I'm going, but on the return trip, I have to concentrate hard enough on finding it. We talked about how it always exists, but you really have to concentrate to find it so that's what I do. I'm just me, so it appears to be a door that opens with enough room to allow me to pass. It lingers for a few minutes, as I've explained, in order to reset the blurred universal lines that the opening causes, and then it's gone again until it is needed," he said smiling seductively, "you know, you really are incredibly irresistible when you get all curious."

He kissed me then and I could see that my stalling tactics were at their end. When his lips touched mine my entire body responded in desire. The fire was now a blazing inferno. Every single cell in my body cried out for his touch. I had felt intense passion for him before, but nothing like what I was feeling now. I couldn't not respond to his touch. Before I even realized what I was doing, I was kissing him back passionately. Our lips and tongues moved and explored together and when they'd gotten the full picture of the inside of our mouths, they moved on to new territory. That opposite direction feeling of his forked tongue felt so different, so intense as it worked its way down my neck and to my chest.

My hands worked quickly as I undid the buttons on his shirt. In my excitement and haste, I worked too quickly for the button that held his chest behind his shirt and it popped free from the thread that held it in place. We both laughed briefly at that before our lips could find each other again. As soon as I had his shirt off I explored his muscular chest with my lips, trying to kiss every bit of him that I could.

My mind caught up with my actions slowly and I did what I could to push away my thoughts of Thomas. With every bit of personal will power that I had, I stopped my hands from their southward journey and pulled away from him.

"What's wrong?" he asked at once.

"I thought we weren't going to do this until the day that I'd return with you?" I asked while catching my breath.

"How can you stand that?" he asked instantly frustrated, "How can you not act on the passion that is flowing between us?"

"It's not easy," I admitted, "but I was under the impression that that day would be special."

"It's already special," he said smiling, but obviously not giving in, "you're going to come home that day. What's more special than that?"

He wrapped the word 'home' with emotion that I finally recognized, he was feeling vulnerable and this was not something that he was used to. He truly wanted to make a home with me and that scared me more than I could even think about.

"Isn't beginning the act of procreation on the day that I come home special enough to wait for?"

It was a weak attempt, even I was only persuading halfheartedly. I knew it wasn't going to change anything and I was beginning to feel like I didn't want it to. I no longer wanted to fight against the raging fire within when I looked at him. I could almost even imagine it, a life with Dominic, protected from the fires, living at his side, and it almost made me smile. Weakly, I tried to bring Thomas's heart into my mind's eye, but Dominic would not have it.

"That thought has no business here right now," Dominic said with a devilish smile, "your grandmother would not want to know what you are doing."

An image flashed, the heart had broken into two pieces and Dominic and I lay between them. I knew that what I was about to do would break the heart of the man I truly loved. I couldn't think about it anymore, any kind of focus was impossible. The heart was gone and so was any of my good sense. Passion was all-consuming as we fell together on the cot and were nothing but a tangled mass of limbs pulsing in rhythm time and again until the fire that burned between us ran stronger at first, but in the end was all but quenched.

Night had fallen and the absence of the moon was noticeable. Dominic's breathing came slow and steady now and I was surprised to find that he'd fallen asleep. He said that he didn't sleep much and I wondered if he'd slept at all since making the decision to bring everyone down in a week. I looked at him closely as he dreamed and noticed in the absence of a facade to hide behind, his features became soft just like any human man's would. He slept soundly and I found myself drifting next to him thinking about what my life would be like if he got what he wanted; I shuddered at the thought.

When I woke it was morning and Dominic was nowhere to be seen. I noticed the compound was very quiet and so I got up, got dressed, and went to find everyone. I looked everywhere and there was no one. A feeling of dread washed over me as I feared what this silence meant. I gave Dominic what he wanted, had he gone and taken everyone without me? Have we started the final exodus?

I continued to look and continued to be met with silence. I even walked around the outside of the compound and listened carefully at the entrance to our underground bunker, but was met with stillness. Rosalyn was gone and not even Sanje was responding to my increasingly panicked calls.

I ran into the trees that led from the compound to the beach and noticed that even the animals seemed to be taking the day off as well. The leaves did not seem to move in the trees, no living creature was foraging, no bird was singing. It was too quiet. Something had gone wrong.

As the trees began to thin out I began to hear the first rumblings of a conversation that was coming from the beach. My heart plummeted and my feet were frozen to the ground as I recognized the voice that was addressing the crowd. My friends and family and the few remaining strangers that hadn't gone with the group were huddled on the beach. I wondered if they knew the depth of my shame and the lengths of my betrayal.

"So where is she?" I heard Dominic ask, "Where is Clarissa?"

"She's not here," Madeline spoke up, "she left with the group."

Oh no, they know about the group? I could barely hold myself up, though Dominic could read my thoughts at any time, he wasn't focused right now. He was angry. He'd been betrayed and he'd get to the bottom of it if I didn't do something.

"She's not going to stay here," Rosalyn started, "she knows when she's in danger and she leaves. That's what I've been trying to tell you. You've made this child your personal conquest, but she can and will continue to evade you."

"I don't think so," said Dominic, "she will come around. Sooner or later she will find that there is no beating me once I've determined to do something."

"And that deceitful bitch that you shared your bed with last night, what about her?" Sanje threw in and I silently cringed at Thomas's reaction to his hurtful words.

It was all over. I might as well allow myself to feel the misery that was hanging just over my head.

I was entirely shocked out of my morbidity when I heard Dominic's response, "Don't you ever call her that. She's not in league with them. She's been deceived too. They were planning on leaving her here," I chanced a peek through the trees and saw that Dominic had grabbed Sanje by the throat and was squeezing, hard. His eyes had turned again from the emerald green to the gleaming red he reserved for the most intense of emotions. Sanje looked scared, but stayed still in Dominic's outstretched grip."

"Clarissa was bringing them back a few at a time," Dominic continued oblivious of his hand still on Sanje's throat, "you guys messed up. Upon intensely questioning Madeline, she finally admitted that Clarissa has been here and taken several of you to the other side and was planning on coming back for more. If anyone should have a broken heart, it's Elizabeth to know that these," I saw him gesture toward the group with his free hand, "these supposed friends and family would be so unkind to her. If they really thought she was in mortal danger like the rest of them, shouldn't they be including her in their plans? There was no thought of that in Madeline or any of the rest of them. They were going to leave her."

For just a moment, I found myself impressed with Dominic. He was angry on my behalf and I did wonder, ever so briefly, if there could possibly be truth in what he was saying. Is it possible that they'd given up on me and decided to simply make their escape? There really was nothing stopping them now. I had all but told them more than once that I would willingly give myself up to make their escape possible. Maybe they were taking me up on the offer.

I shook off that depressing thought. I knew that I'd have to play along. Three things that I had feared had not happened. Number one, we were not entirely sunk yet. They had not included me in their thoughts at all, even under torture. They were still protecting me. Number two, Dominic still didn't know it was Thomas that had my heart so he's safe from any inhumane treatment. And number three, Dominic knew nothing of my father and brother being here. If we were going to be able to extend this much longer, I'd have to brave Sanje's anger and mistrust and come out there at Dominic's side supporting everything he'd just said.

I came through the thin layer of trees and took in the scene. Dominic and Sanje were still standing aggressively, though Dominic had finally released his throat. The look on Sanje's face was more grave and angry than I'd ever seen it. Rosalyn, Madeline, Rose, and Theresa were standing about twenty feet from them. They were each staring right at Dominic with both stubborn resistance and fear in their eyes.

"What is this?" I asked as I cleared the trees and made my way onto the beach to join them.

"This, my dear, is your friends turning against you," Dominic said as he looked at me.

"How? Why? What's going on here?" I asked again, deliberately sounding hurt and confused.

"Oh, honey," said Dominic, attempting sympathy, "this is what it feels like to find out that those you thought cared about you work to save themselves at your cost. This is why there is no devotion. You think I'm incredibly selfish, but look at what these people have done to you. This is why you will have a much better home with me among my family than you can ever hope to have here."

"My, my, Dominic, are we becoming a humanitarian?" I asked playfully, "You look like your sympathizing with me. I thought you didn't do that?"

"I guess you're rubbing off on me," he said with a smile and kissed me softly, "So, what should we do with them?"

"You're asking me?" I asked, surprised.

"Well, yes, you are going to have to be answering that question when we go home. So, what do we do with them? We can't just stand by and let this go unpunished. That would show weakness where we need to be showing strength," he added quietly only for me.

I was being tested. He wanted me to dole out the punishment to see how far I'd go.

"Well, my mother is mine. I thought we'd just come to an understanding, but now I'd like her to know just how cruel I can be. I'll ensure that she shares where the little miscreant has gotten off to. As for the rest of them, they will go to the compound and they will work. There are few enough of them left now that they will all fit there. No one needs to have an individual house anymore. That will allow us to better monitor their movements as well. They will help prepare everything for our impending departure. They will be under my constant supervision," I tried and failed to infuse wrath into my voice.

"I told you she was one of them," sneered Sanje from where he still stood, inches from Dominic, "Being babysat is no punishment."

"Dominic," I started to defend myself, "you know I can't hurt them, not even Rosalyn. These are people and I just don't hurt people."

"Maybe you don't, now, dear, but you will," he growled at me as his patience was finally breaking under Sanje's constant barrage of insults, "This is your new life...a life that you'd have me believe that you've chosen. Why don't you do this for me...why don't you take each and every one of those ungrateful traitors and give them a real punishment? I know, those little underground tunnels you've held so dear in recent weeks, how about you have them go and fill those in. There are enough shovels here for each of them to have their own. When they're done, or when the daylight fades, or when they drop of exhaustion, then they can return to the compound to be babysat. How does that suit you? Hmm...

unless you'd like to join them, that is."

"Sanje will oversee their work and make sure that their progress is satisfactory. If someone gets out of line or Sanje feels they need to be taught, you will administer their punishment. He has his whip and you will use it. Rosalyn will focus all of her efforts on getting Clarissa to come here and you will help her when you have the time. Sanje will keep his eye on you for me. I would take you with me, but I cannot afford the loss should my father get greedy. I will be back in two days. When I come, I will be bringing all of you home with me. Elizabeth will sit beside me as my queen, bear my children, and release souls into the light. The rest of you will be assigned by my father to your personal level of cleansing and remain there for as long as necessary. You will not see one another again."

Sanje overseeing everyone working was the real punishment. Me having to dole out punishment was designed specifically for me for quailing in the moment and trying to go easy on them. I was not able to prove to Dominic, beyond a doubt, that I didn't care for them anymore and I would pay for that.

Sanje smiled smugly and looked at Rosalyn, "she's too old anyway brother, don't worry about me."

"Good of you to not be upset, Sanje," said Dominic cooly, "I hope you don't mind staying behind and babysitting."

"Not at all, nothing would give me more pleasure than to put these traitors in their place," he said.

"I wouldn't push Sanje, people," Dominic spoke, addressing the group again, "he hasn't been in a good mood for about a thousand years. I wouldn't expect that to change any time soon."

Dominic turned to look at me and put his finger gently under my chin. He kissed me softly once, then again with as much passion as before, "don't disappoint me, darling. I would hate to find out that that pretty necklace was an heirloom from someone more important to you than me…I don't think he'd be long for this world either and I'd make sure that his suffering was worse than any of the others."

The threat rolled off of his tongue as sweetly as if it was a lollipop. His eyes were severe. He couldn't prove my love for Thomas but he certainly suspected it. That's why he made such a show in front of him, just as he'd done with Rosalyn when he wanted to make her suffer.

Chapter 18

Sanje was every bit the tyrant that Dominic had promised he would be. Dominic had not been gone for thirty minutes and already all of those left, Thomas, Madeline, Rose, and Theresa were each given shovels and told to start turning the dirt where they'd dug their tunnels. There was no extra dirt to fill in as the dirt that had been removed had been carefully deposited around the island.

While they worked, Rosalyn and I "searched" all along the island.

"Rosalyn…Mom… did you always know about the underground tunnels? That isn't something that I ever shared with Dominic and we were all under the impression that those had been created without your knowledge."

"Yes, I knew about them. They couldn't very well hide the equipment that they'd used to make them. Also, there were periods where they were just so tired. I told Dominic of my concerns and he blew it off. He said it was important that the subordinates feel that they had control over something so as far as I was concerned, there was nothing more to be said about it. Today was the first time he's brought them up since.

"To be honest, and honey, I'm not blaming you, but I think he got so angry because he could sense the connection between you and Thomas. He was certainly vocal about that necklace and I saw Thomas cringe when he brought it up. When you didn't want to dole out punishment, he used it as an excuse to take back control. Or to at least feel like he has some control."

"Yeah well, I don't know that he'll have anything to get upset about anymore anyway. After Sanje so outwardly discussed Dominic and I, I'll be surprised if Thomas ever wants to talk to me again. I know we discussed the possibility that it may happen, but I was doing such a great job holding my own, until I wasn't."

"Don't be so hard on yourself. I can't tell you what's going to happen with that, but I have seen how much Thomas loves you in the time that you've been here. I won't give up hope just yet."

"We have barely been together longer than we've been on this island. Do you really think that he'd hold out for me after what I've done? If we pull this off, he can go back to his life in Boston with his family intact and forget all of this ever happened."

"If we pull this off," she stopped and looked at me, brushing my hair back from my shoulder, "you will be in the same boat. Your family will be whole again and both you and Thomas will need some serious healing time. Don't be so quick to jump to the negative. It will all work out, you'll see. You, my dear, are a good person with a huge heart and Thomas knows that. Have faith."

I was amazed that our relationship could have taken such a giant step forward in such a short time, but suddenly I realized that my mom was truly back in my life and I smiled at her.

"Are you okay?" she asked.

"Better than I have been in a long time. I missed you mom," I hugged her for what seemed to be ages while I felt a lifetime's worth of anguish release itself. I felt ten pounds lighter when we finally separated and decided that we'd better get on with our sham of a search. As the sun began to make its way back toward the horizon, we found ourselves nearing everyone else and feeling superiorly guilty that we weren't there helping them.

They had worked all through the day. It was clear that they were nearing exhaustion as they struggled to lift the shovel fulls and move them. Sanje saw us arrive and took much pleasure in calling me over. He had a glint in his eye that I did not like.

"Elizabeth," he started, "Dominic said he'd like you to administer punishments and though I take great personal pride in doing that job, I think it's time you learn. Thomas here has not been doing his job to my satisfaction. I think it's time he felt that whip again."

As I turned to look at them, unmasked sympathy resided in all of their faces. Sanje was elated. This is what he'd been waiting for. He wanted to prove that I still cared for Thomas.

"*Just do it, it'll be easier for you and Thomas,*" Madeline sent her thoughts out.

"I don't think I can do that," I said quietly expecting his response, "Dominic knows what a humanitarian I am and he wouldn't make me hurt any of them like that."

"Dominic is not here, and his instructions were clear," Sanje snarled, "now take the whip and do your duty."

"No," I said stubbornly.

"If you don't do what I've asked you to do, you will feel that whip yourself," he threatened.

"Fine, go ahead, see how Dominic will react to that," I threatened.

"Elizabeth, just do it," Thomas said.

Sanje's grin grew deadly, "don't want to see your girlfriend suffer, huh?"

"Sanje, you just don't get it, do you? We all care about one another and no one wants to watch another suffer."

"Now you can each suffer, Thomas and Elizabeth, get up against those trees," Sanje growled.

I could feel Thomas's anguished eyes on me as we both turned to follow his command. I could take this. Thomas was next to me and I watched him cringe as the whip found his back. I knew it was coming. I braced myself, but it didn't come. The whip landed and Thomas flinched and whimpered quietly. I now understood what Sanje was doing. He'd make me watch as Thomas stood there in pain. The whip came down three more times and I watched Thomas try to absorb it bravely. Finally, Sanje spoke again.

"Next time you refuse me, there won't be any blood left."

I glared at him and asked, "can I go now? I have a job to do."

"Be my guest," he replied.

They took a break for lunch, then another one for dinner later. At nightfall, when they couldn't see the ground anymore, they were allowed to stop and given places to sleep. There were rooms enough for each of them. They were utterly exhausted and filthy. I went to Sanje and asked him if they'd be allowed to bathe in the stream that was nearby. Though he grumbled about me still caring for them, he agreed.

"Go and tell them they have one hour to bathe, then they must be back in their rooms and you will be back here within five minutes," he said.

I got to Madeline and Rose's room first and relayed Sanje's message. They were grateful to be able to wash the dirt off of themselves.

"I'm so sorry," I said as they started to gather their things for their baths, "I never wanted any of this to happen."

"We know," Madeline said speaking for both of them, "we're not angry with you, don't worry about that. We just don't know where Clarissa is and it's driving us out of our minds. Please say you'll try to find her."

"You know I will Madeline, Rose," I said, "but it's going to be hard, I'm not sure that she trusts me right now."

"She doesn't, but she will. I'll be in touch with her. Thank you," Madeline said, her gratitude reaching all the way to her tired eyes, "I'll tell the others about the bath. Thomas is next door, go talk to him."

At the mention of his name I felt the guilt rise up and try to escape from my insides. I growled to myself in frustration and self-loathing.

"He understands," Madeline tried futilely to comfort me, "he knows how hard this is for you too."

"Thanks Madeline," I said and turned to face Thomas.

As I entered the room I immediately took in his feelings and I was more disgusted with myself if that were possible. He was sitting on the bed, head in both of his hands. His back was riddled with red stripes and it was obvious that the most severe punishment had been reserved for him. He had been replaying Dominic's and Sanje's words this afternoon. I could feel his anger but he wanted to talk so I went into his room quietly, pushed myself all the way up against the wall opposite where he was sitting, and looked at him for a full minute.

"I wish I knew what to say to make this right; I look at your back and I want to scream, then go subject Sanje to the same kind of treatment," I whispered, "I want to tell you that I love you, that I'm in love with you, but I don't want it to sound like a lie."

He was choosing his words very carefully now, "I'm not upset with you. I love you. I'm just a little scared. Dominic seems content to drag you off to be with him and you did what you had to to convince him. I'm not upset or hurt. But Sanje scares me and I'm afraid that if you continue to stand up to him the way that you did today…I…I…I don't know what he'll do. If you'd just done what he asked today…"

I cut him off, "and hurt you further? It's bad enough that I have to pretend all the time with Dominic, but I will not physically hurt you too. I know how this is affecting you. I wouldn't blame you if you never want to see me again, but I won't do what he's asking."

"And if he asks you tomorrow?" Thomas asked and I knew the direction his thoughts were taking. Was I really willing to let him suffer for my stubbornness?

"I don't know," I admitted and let my eyes drop to the ground, "I'm going to do everything I can to be busy with Rosalyn all day."

He put his finger under my chin and lifted my face so he could look directly in my eyes, "I'm not going anywhere. No matter what you have to do to convince Dominic. To think of you feeling that whip on your back, to think of you being cut like that, it's too much. If you just do as he says, it will be over."

"I have to get back, Sanje only gave me a few moments to be gone and I've used them up. He'll come looking soon. I love you. This will be over soon," I tried to smile as I walked out of the room.

I made it around the doorway and halfway down the hall before the grief took me and I was not able to move another step. I was losing Thomas by inches; I felt it despite his words. If I decided to go, told Sanje the truth, told Dominic that no matter what his father did I wouldn't leave his side, would that be enough for them to let the others go?

I gathered myself up to move forward and saw Thomas peer around out of his room. He gestured for me to come to him. I didn't hesitate. Thomas ducked back into the room as I approached his doorway. I took a quick glance behind as I entered, saw no one and ran headlong into his strong, waiting arms.

"I love you," he said quietly while holding me tight, "I'm not letting you go. I get the feeling you think I'm mad at you or worse. I said it before and I'll say it a thousand times if I have to. I'm not leaving you."

I knew he was steeling himself for what was to come. He'd made a decision; he would fight. He would do what it takes to keep me with him even if that meant both of us leaving this life; we'd do it together.

He bent his head down to kiss me then, "now go tell Sanje that you've told us of the bathing times and get on his good side. It's him you're going to have to convince more than Dominic."

I left feeling much happier than before. Thomas's fate would be the same as mine and that was enough to get me through whatever was to come. I rounded the final corner and entered my room. Sanje was there waiting for me as I knew he would be.

"That was more than five minutes," he said.

"Sorry, I did stop to talk to Madeline and Rose a little. I felt bad for them having to work so hard," I admitted proudly.

"Are you going to feel sorry for all of those creatures below that are being cleansed too? Madeline, Rose, and the others are going to have it rough. It's not going to feel good to them. What are you going to do when friends and family of yours are suffering?" he asked, enjoying the growing disgust on my face.

"I will feel just as sorry for them as I do now, but at least Dominic won't make me hang around and watch them suffer or worse, participate in it," I said honestly.

"No, no, I'm sure he'll spare you all of the gory details. It doesn't mean that you won't know they're there suffering while you're enjoying life pain free," he was cruel, but also telling the truth. They would be down there suffering their own fate and whether I was in the room with them to witness it or not, I'd know that I was not among them.

"I'm tired now Sanje, isn't it time you go?"

"I suppose it is, sleep tight Elizabeth. Day after tomorrow Dominic will be back and we can all go home," he said. I heard anxiety creep into his voice and remembered what Dominic had said about it being hard for them to be away from their home. Then I realized that Sanje was home when he took me there before, yet all of his brothers and his father were out. He may already be feeling some pain and extending his stay here would only cause him more. Maybe he was even frailer than Dominic realized. I jumped at the thought before Sanje could elude me completely.

"How old are you, Sanje?"

"Centuries older than Domnic, why?"

"I was just curious about how age worked with you guys," I said.

"It takes many centuries for us to go through a lifespan. I would be the equivalent of a great grandfather where Dominic would be a father in his prime, if that helps," he said scowling when he realized he told me more than I asked.

"Goodnight Sanje."

"Yeah, goodnight, I guess I need some rest too," Sanje said, trying and failing to regain his former bad mood.

"Rest? Dominic said you guys hardly ever sleep."

"He hardly ever sleeps, he's still young, that changes as centuries slip by."

I smiled softly after he walked out of the room. That was all I needed to hear. I struggled to keep myself awake. The day's exertions were weighing on me heavily. It had been a stressful day and my body longed to shut down and relax for a few hours. I couldn't let that happen. I had to wait until it was late enough, then I had to go and wake the others.

Long into the night I heard the sound of snores coming from Sanje's room and I knew this was the time to chance it. I left my room and quietly went to wake up Madeline. Apparently the mind reading thing even worked in her sleep as she was sitting up expecting me when I arrived.

"Do you know why I'm here?" I asked her.

"No, but Rose should be up too, right?"

"Yes, we need to get everyone up and meet outside, just before the treeline becomes the beach should be far enough," I said excitedly.

"Okay, I'm on it. You get Thomas and we'll get Theresa, your Dad, and Aaron. We'll meet you there," she said.

I went into Thomas's room next and when he saw me, though not quite awake yet, he smiled and said a soft "hi." He pulled me next to him and for the next few minutes, our lips were occupied. It took me a minute to remember why I was there and that we didn't have time. I sat up, pulled him up to a sitting position and told him about the impromptu meeting.

Within minutes we were all there ready to talk. They all looked at me as I entered with Thomas.

"I have some important information and I wasn't sure when I'd be able to share it," I said and tore right through what I'd learned, "Sanje sleeps just like any human, so we have tonight and tomorrow night to wrap things up. Sanje said Dominic would be back the day after tomorrow, but we have no way of knowing what time. But none of that is what I really want you to know.

"Sanje," I started to get excited, "is an old man. And he's weak. He talks a good game, but Dominic told me that it was difficult for them to be away from their home; that it causes physical pain. From what Sanje was telling me tonight, I think he's already feeling that pain. I'm thinking if there's some way to keep them here, grounded, we may be able to eliminate the problem altogether."

"What about the door?" asked an exhausted Aaron, "With them gone, how will we get through?"

"This is even better," I said, "he is not necessary for the door, and neither is Clarissa, though she'll make it easier. In fact, it's not even a door, it's an opening between parallel universes and it spans the length of the island. Dominic said if he concentrates hard enough he can will it into existence. Clarissa has always believed so completely that she didn't have to concentrate, it was easy for her to see, though she didn't realize it was always here."

I told them what I thought we could make happen. I went into detail about what Dominic had told me that they could only survive here for so long. The pain that Sanje was already feeling would lead to his death. Dominic would take longer because he was younger, but it would be inevitable if he can't get through that door. If we could get the barrier to open and all go through at the same time, we could hold Sanje and Dominic on the other side by remaining within the doorway. It wouldn't be able to reset itself, and therefore it would stay closed as long as we needed it to. Sanje and Dominic would be stuck here. If we took turns not allowing the barrier to open, we'd be rid of them and this would finally be over.

My excitement started catching on as the others began to see this as a real possibility. For the first time in this long, hard day, I could see hope springing up in the eyes of those around me. I echoed that hope with my own eyes, but then grew somber for a moment realizing that we still had a day in between. Sanje would be no better tomorrow, and being that he'd be in more pain, he was likely to be worse. Rosalyn and I were still supposed to be out searching for Clarissa, so I knew everyone else would take the brunt of his punishment.

Thomas read my mind, "then tomorrow, you and Rosalyn go out and look for Clarissa. We have no time left. You have to find her. The rest of us will do our jobs without complaint. We don't know what time Dominic will come back the day after, but we will have the warning of the clouds forming in the distance. Chances are he will not take his time as he's done here and there so we have to assume that when we see the clouds, he'll be here very soon. Knowing that, once we see the clouds, we will meet on the beach. No matter what you are doing. When Dominic is coming, we all meet together. We won't go through until we see him touch the ground. In the meantime we'll all be focused on seeing that divide open for us. When it does, we go through; I'll take the first watch holding them behind the divide," he said and looked around at many doubtful faces, especially those of my father and brother.

"If it doesn't work, we all know where we'll be going anyway so we might as well do this. It's just as well that we go together…and I don't want anyone trying to stop me so I may as well tell you my plan if things don't go well."

Thomas was the only one that seemed to have any idea of what I was getting at and he looked at me with a pained expression.

"If things don't go well," I continued, "I am prepared to do what's necessary so that my fate is no different from yours. You don't understand just how much it's hurt me to see you all suffering today. I know that I should be among you and I will not rank myself out of that fate."

"You're talking about ending your life?" my father asked.

"Only if it's absolutely clear that we are not going to win," I said trying to reassure him, "it's a last resort. I will not be used for Dominic's every desire. If I go, I will go the same as the rest of you and it will be on my terms, not his."

"How will you do it before he stops you?" Thomas asked sadly.

"There are many sharp objects lying around all over the place; I know exactly where my heart is. If it's a quick movement when he's least expecting it, he won't have any clue."

"If you do that," Rose started, "and you come to him, don't you think you'll get a longer cleansing than if you just follow his lead? Please understand," she turned to Thomas, "this is not what I want to happen, but you shouldn't have to take on more punishment."

"I appreciate that, Rose, and I know that your heart is in the right place, but Sanje pointed it out to me today and I spent some time thinking about it. It would be just as painful for me to stand by and watch while your fleshy bodies are removed a little at a time so that your souls can be free. I wouldn't be sparing myself anything if I decided to go the less physically painful route," I said honestly.

"Then I suppose we should all get our rest. Tomorrow's bound to be another long day," said Madeline, looking at her brother with the same amount of horror that I had earlier.

"Thomas," I said quietly as we departed back to our beds, "were you the only recipient of the whip today?"

"Yes, I think Sanje's very smart and he knows exactly what's happening though he can't prove it. Be very careful around him. He has murderous eyes," he said.

"Maybe I can try to distract Sanje with something tomorrow, at least give you a little rest."

"Do not do anything like that," he said, placing a caring, warm hand on my cheek.

"I will do my job and you do yours. If this all works out the way we planned, we will get our revenge. Let that be enough for now," he pleaded.

Sanje had no trust for us whatsoever; any variation from what we were told to do would surely bring more punishment down on us and after the display today, I knew tomorrow would only be worse. I decided to listen to Thomas and do as I was told; at least for the next twenty-four hours.

I went to bed and all too soon was woken by Sanje's rough voice, "come on deary. Your time is drawing short and Dominic requires that little girl. Go get Rosalyn and get out there to find her. She couldn't have gone far; the island's not that big."

My eyes were much heavier than I was expecting, but I was grateful that he wanted me to go to Rosalyn. We were down to the wire and we needed everything to work perfectly. I found myself wondering where Clarissa would have gone. She must be terrified and I started envisioning her somewhere within the trees huddled close into herself. I came into the main room hearing that Rosalyn was already up and having a conversation with Sanje.

"...she couldn't have gotten far. I have been dealing with this little girl for a few years now and I'm telling you she's incredibly stubborn. Once she gets something in her mind, she sticks with it. The thing in her mind when the group went through was her grandfather. She didn't want to worry him. I'm telling you she's back on the main island with him; out of your reach," she said strongly.

"She's not out of our reach," he countered, "she hasn't left the island.

You can't protect her; just give her up so this can all be over. It's time to go back."

I was glad to hear a pleading tone in his voice. He was trying to get Rosalyn to give up the search so that we could go back immediately, but she was not being cooperative. He was getting more and more bothered by being here. I didn't want it to get too bad for everyone digging today though so I thought I'd break up the party.

"Sanje, why don't you let Rosalyn and I get out there and do our job today. We'll let you know anything we find out about Clarissa. The two of you can pick up your argument from there if you'd like when we return," I said.

He scowled at me, but didn't seem ready to contradict me either. He was ready to take on something he felt in complete control over. He left to get the others out of bed and ready to shovel for another day. I wished that they had an easier job to do as it was very hot outside on top of the hard work that they'd be doing.

"Oh Sanje, please make sure that the subordinates have water today. It's awfully hot out there and I don't think Dominic would be happy if he was missing anyone else, do you?" I asked quietly enjoying the fact that he was severely irritated with me.

"Yes, Elizabeth, I will make sure they stay hydrated in the heat," Sanje started eerily sounding like he was reading my mind, "especially since some of them insist on losing blood, too."

He left then and Rosalyn and I were alone. We'd go wander the island and search every nook and cranny for Clarissa. It was imperative that we find her today as this would all be over, one way or the other, in twenty-four hours. What would happen in these next few hours would determine the course of the rest of our lives; Dominic and Sanje included.

I decided to take a chance and lead Rosalyn back to the area that Thomas had led me to when we needed to talk. I saw exactly what I was hoping for. The blanket was still laid out across the ground in the middle of the fall-like leaves that were scattered everywhere. In the middle of that blanket sat a very quiet and very still Clarissa. She looked up as she heard our approach and stared. It was obvious immediately that she was terrified. She didn't know what had happened since Sanje had called everyone out and she wasn't sure if she could trust us. She immediately got up and started backing away. She kept turning her eyes toward the trees planning which escape route could get her away from us the fastest. Then I remembered Madeline had said she'd talk to her. I figured it was safest to start from there.

"Clarissa, honey, everything is okay," I said, "hasn't your mom talked to you yet?"

"Yes, but she said only you would be coming, not her," she said pointing toward Rosalyn.

"Mom, could you leave us alone for a few minutes?" I asked and added in a hushed whisper, "don't go far."

"Of course, Elizabeth, I'll just be over there," she said, pointing toward the path from which we'd come.

I turned back to Clarissa and saw that she was still very uneasy with us being here.

"Why didn't my Mom come?" she asked.

"Your mom is doing some work right now, but she's okay, she asked me to come and talk to you," I added, trying to calm her.

"That's what she told me too. She said that I should trust you even though it looked like I shouldn't," she admitted.

"We're all on the same team; all except Dominic and Sanje. We're all working to get back home. I am going to keep my promise to you. I will get all of us back home and your family will be back together. You know what? It looks like my family is going to be reunited as well," I threw in making her smile.

"You're part of my family now, too," she said, "Uncle Thomas loves you."

"I love him too," I smiled at her and sat on the blanket next to her. Her eyes told me she wasn't scared anymore.

"So, how did you do it? How did you get away from them so fast?"

"I...," she hesitated, then seemed to make a decision, "I stayed with the group until they made it through, but when I was coming back I saw Sanje and he saw me," she said nervously, "I stayed in the opening, but walked down very far; further than they know about, and then I came back through and hid here."

"What do you mean, further than they know? They know that it spans the island," I explained.

"They know that it spans this island, they don't know that it goes across. If they did, they would have taken me a long time ago. I've come here before to see my mom and even she didn't know that I was here," she looked up to see my reaction, "I came here and stayed waiting for them to leave again."

My eyes must have grown to their fullest size because suddenly Clarissa looked scared again. This time though, she didn't look scared of me, she looked scared for me.

"Elizabeth, Auntie Elizabeth, are you okay?" She asked; the 'auntie' threw me out of my stupor.

"Auntie Elizabeth?" I smiled at her.

"Uncle Thomas said it was okay. It is, isn't it?" she asked.

"Of course it is sweetheart; you can call me Auntie Elizabeth. I'd like that," I said honestly and smiled again, "so you walked along the opening and continued across the water? How did you make it? Did you swim?"

"Not the whole way," she said, "just a little when I got closer to the other shore."

"I didn't know there was anywhere shallow enough that went across."

"When they searched the lake for you, they made the high sand," she said matter-of-factly, "I heard them talking about it. Something about being able to get back without boats."

"How do you know that?" I asked, not realizing just how long she's been coming and going.

"I saw the search. My mom showed me because I was afraid of the dreams that I was having. I just meandered back over when she didn't know and I overheard them talking about it."

"I am terribly sorry about the dreams. I hope you're going to be able to sleep better real soon. I am very sorry that I worried you, but we have a plan and I'm going to let anything knock me off course. We need you to be a part of that plan. Can you do that for us?" I asked.

"You're not going to change your mind and leave with that man?" Or worse, lead him to me?" She was still scared.

"Oh honey, no way! Your Auntie Elizabeth wouldn't do anything to hurt you. Never, never!" I said, horrified at the thought.

"I'm afraid of the dreams, except my favorite one," she said with a smile.

"I like your favorite one too. That's the one where we all walk out together, right?"

"That was...but..." she was blushing.

"There's a new one?" I guessed.

"Yes, a new one...you're in it...and so is Uncle Thomas...," she trailed off, smiling again.

"You don't have to tell me, honey," I said, sensing her embarrassment.

"No, I want to tell. I like you Auntie Elizabeth, I want you to stay."

"Okay then, I'm listening," I said smoothly.

"I get to have a new cousin," she said quickly, her face turning beet red.

"Really?" I asked, wondering just how powerful her insights could be, "A boy cousin or a girl cousin?"

"A boy cousin…his name is Mitch. He has funny green eyes," she said and my stomach dropped.

"Green eyes? What makes them funny?" I asked.

"They're real sparkly, but they look different," she said happily.

"Oh, well that sounds like a great dream," I smiled back at her trying to share in her excitement, worried about what it could mean. I was ready to change the subject, "Are you ready to talk to Rosalyn now and everyone else?"

"Yes, I think I can do that now. I want to help," she said.

"Wait here; let's talk to Rosalyn a bit, okay? We can tell you what needs to happen."

I turned and went down the path to where Rosalyn was waiting patiently. I told her that Clarissa was feeling more comfortable now and that she could come back. I did not tell her about Clarissa's dreams. For the moment, I didn't even want to think about them. I could see myself staying with Thomas. I could see myself as part of this patched up family, but the rest of the dream? I do want kids, but the way that he described the baby made me shudder. We returned to Clarissa to talk about what would happen now.

"Clarissa, honey, you're going to have to stay here for a while. You've been so brave through all of this and we need you to keep it up for just a bit longer. We can't risk Sanje finding you here.

"When it's time, when Dominic is close by and the fabric of the parallel planes becomes visible, I want you to focus with all of your energy on seeing it open up. The length from here all the way into the water. Once it's visible, we will come to you in a group and we will step through, all of us. Your uncle has volunteered to keep the first watch on Sanje and Dominic. One of us will have to stay on the threshold until the exposure to the outside world finishes them. For Sanje, it won't be long, but Dominic is younger and stronger, it will be a while. You don't have to be concerned with that, you will not have a turn on the threshold."

She looked at me with a slight glare in her eyes. She didn't want to be discounted as part of the group in any way. Finally, she seemed to relax as she finally started catching on to what was going to be happening to them.

"They'll…go to vacation in the sky? They'll be dead?" She asked.

"Yes, that's what they've told me. They cannot exist among the living for long; but they also cannot get home without a doorway," I explained, trying to be as gentle as possible.

"Will it hurt?" she asked.

"It might; I don't really know," I said honestly.

"There's no other way?" her voice raised into a question.

"Not unless you want to take the chance of them coming after us once they're through the door. They'll take us away and we won't come back," I wanted her to realize how serious this was.

Fear crept back into her eyes and Rosalyn looked at me with shock.

"Elizabeth, is that really necessary?" Shades of my disapproving mother were being held at bay.

"Yes, I think it is. She needs to realize that any amount of sympathy we may have for them may end up making us vulnerable," I said.

"Okay, but she's already scared enough, and she's not the only one that they were trying to deceive."

That stung a bit, but I couldn't disagree.

"I guess you're right, she won't be standing guard, but the rest of us do need to know that. They will try anything they can and they can be very persuasive as you well know, or at least Dominic can. Once they know that they are trapped, and assuming we make it that far, they will try anything including turning on the charm," I said.

"Fine, let's finish telling her the plan," Rosalyn said.

"Well, that's about it. The adults will take turns holding the barrier closed until we are sure that Dominic and Sanje are gone; then I suppose we can go back to our lives as normal, or as normal as they will ever be again," I tried to smile.

"Aren't we going to check?" Rosalyn asked nervously, "make sure they're really gone."

"We'll have to check to be sure, but I'm not really sure what will happen to them. If they're not exactly human, what will they be like after…" I couldn't bring myself to say the word again in front of Clarissa who was already dealing with too much.

"If they remain, one of us will have to go to check," she said decidedly, "It might as well be me; I got you all into this mess."

"Maybe it won't be necessary," I said, but I didn't contradict her.

"If this even works," Clarissa added.

"We can't admit defeat, the game is just getting ready to start," I said, trying to cheer the mood.

"Clarissa, stay here until you hear your mother call for you…it will be one of her silent calls. When she does, come running as fast as you can, okay?" I asked.

"Okay," she said, looking slightly cheered.

With that Rosalyn and I departed. I knew Sanje would not be pleased, but he wouldn't do anything too severe. Dominic had already shown him how protective of me he was. I didn't think he'd hurt Rosalyn. We walked slowly back to the compound discussing all of the different places we would say that we've been today.

Sanje was pacing in front of the compound looking sweaty and very nervous. As he walked, he was wringing his hands and talking to himself. I couldn't tell if it was the fading light of the day or if his skin really was beginning to look sallow and pale. I wondered again just how much he was already suffering and a new thought occurred to me. I found myself wondering if Dominic had done this on purpose. If Sanje really was that old, perhaps his usefulness had played itself out too and Sanje was never meant to go back. Suddenly, I knew I was right.

Just how angry will Dominic be when he finds out that we've stuck him here too? Just how convincing will he try to be to get someone to allow him to go home? I felt vaguely sick at the thought that he could get one of us to believe in his words so much so that we'd open ourselves up to this again.

"It's about time you two made it back," Sanje started as soon as we were in view, "let me guess, you found nothing."

"You'd be guessing correctly," I said evenly, "what about the tunnels? Have they finished turning over the ground or are they still working?"

"That's not really your concern; we're not working in a partnership here. They'll be done when I say they're done. They better get used to being uncomfortable; going below while still alive will be a whole other kind of torture. Tomorrow…yes, tomorrow," he finished wistfully while twitching his neck back and forth.

"You're not okay, are you?" I asked, trying to sound concerned, "Is there anything I can get you?"

"I'm fine, I don't want anything from you," he said angrily, "go to the others, tell them to quit. Tell them they have an hour to bathe, eat, and get to their rooms. Dominic should be arriving early and they should all be ready to go when he comes."

He said that last more of an aside, but I picked up on it and from the looks of it, so did Rosalyn. We decided it would be best to simply do as we were told for now. We left the opening and went back into the trees to find the others. We were not at all prepared for what we found when we got there.

Thomas was curled up in the fetal position on the ground, his back was entirely open. There was not much skin that remained untouched. Sanje had been brutal with the whip today. Thomas was breathing, but was not lucid. As I approached him, he stiffened again not knowing that

Sanje had gone.

"Please," he begged while his eyes were trying to discern where the movement was coming from, "please spare them. I can take it."

This was obviously something he had said several times today and his half-conscious mind was repeating it. I looked at the others and saw the same horrified looks on their faces. Rose came to me and put her arm around my waist; apparently, I was going to fall. I'd become so numb I didn't even notice.

"He wouldn't let any of us feel the pain of that thing. He jumped in front of whoever it was directed at and pleaded with Sanje each time," she said, "since he left we've been taking turns getting water to try to keep his wounds clean."

"He won't be back any more tonight," I said holding back the rage that I felt, "I will get him some water and clean his back. Sanje told us to tell you to quit working and that you have an hour to bathe, eat, and get to your rooms. Mother, please stay with him while I get some water."

"Go ahead, Elizabeth," she said echoing the hollow sounds coming from me. I felt murderous and knew that if we lost this fight, at least Sanje would never be going home again.

I scavenged through what I could see and found something that would hold water. Rose had given me the cloth that they had already been using to bathe Thomas's wounds. I soaked it so that he'd have some kind of relief. As I returned, I found Thomas sitting up and talking to my mother.

"...just couldn't let my mother or sister or Theresa, with all that they've been through, feel that sort of pain. I'd gotten it enough times yesterday to know it wasn't going to be easy, but I didn't really realize just how brutal he could be. Sanje was very angry today," Thomas finished and winced as he tried to change position.

"Thomas, Sanje suspects, that's the only explanation for his cruelty to you alone," I said from where I stood. I went to him and began to each wound as softly as I could. He winced each time I brought the cloth to his skin.

"He wasn't being cruel to just me; I just stood in everyone else's way. He just wanted someone to punish," he said as he turned his head to look at me. I saw then that Sanje had not been satisfied with the whip. There were purple and blue blotches forming around Thomas's right eye.

"Did you fight back?" I asked.

"How could I? That would just make it worse for everyone. I figured I could handle one day of this, even after yesterday," he said, then smiled warmly, "but then just as I thought I couldn't take another moment, I heard your voice and I knew it was all over."

I smiled back at him, but inside I was reeling. Every open wound caused me pain as I imagined the whip cutting into his skin over and over again.

"Why did he punch you?" I asked.

"I dared to speak to him," Thomas said.

"What did you say?" I wanted to know.

"I wanted to know what had made him so angry. Why he was in such a bad mood all the time. I guess he thought it was none of my business," Thomas said.

"I'm sorry, I'm so sorry about all of this," I said miserably, continuing to clean his wounds.

"You didn't do this," Thomas said.

"We need to meet tonight, will you tell the others?" I asked.

"Finalizing plans?"

"We found Clarissa today. She is ready and waiting. She knows exactly what to do and what to listen for," I said with a smile.

"Why didn't you tell Madeline?" he asked.

"I was going to, but I got a little distracted when I saw you," I defended myself, "besides, I think Clarissa's sent word by now. Madeline and Rose should be feeling much better about things."

"How did she react when she saw you?" Thomas asked.

"She was afraid at first. I had to reassure her that I hadn't switched sides; that I was still going to keep my promise. She eventually could tell that I was telling the truth and then we talked a bit about the plan and what her part in it would be. She mentioned her dreams and we talked a little bit about them."

I did not mention her newest dream. I figured eventually she'd be telling everyone about it and they could make out of it what they'd like. I couldn't get the image of the baby with the funny green eyes out of my mind. It was as if I was afraid of this little creature that only existed in Clarissa's imagination. I tried to shake it off and think about tomorrow.

"Come on, let's get you to your mother. Sanje will notice if I spend too much time here. Late tonight; one last meeting," I said as I led him toward the compound.

As we got close, I noticed that Sanje was outside, staring at the sky, and looking even worse than he had when he ordered us away. He knew Dominic wouldn't be back until morning, but he was too anxious now to be careful. I thought for a moment that we could all go out to the beach, call up the door, and all go through before Dominic knew any better. Sanje was too weak to effectively stop that plan, but I also knew that

Dominic wouldn't rest until he had me back.

Sanje didn't seem to pay much attention to me supporting Thomas as we walked by. I thought for sure he'd make some sort of comment about that, but at this point I really didn't care. This would finally be over tomorrow morning from the looks of it.

"Go get some rest," I said to Thomas, "I will see you in a few hours."

"Please don't go confront Sanje," Thomas said, easily reading the intent in my eyes.

"Why not?" I asked.

"He wasn't aiming for me today, not every time anyway. He was aiming wherever the mood struck him. I was the one that continually got in the way. I stepped in front of that whip as often as it was directed at me. He may be old, but he's not weak. Look at my face," he said as if I needed the reminder.

"He's getting weaker each moment he's here. I'm sure that's why he was so angry today. He's literally burning at this point and I have the sneaking suspicion that Dominic has no intention of bringing him back. I think this place was a death sentence for Sanje to begin with; maybe he finally figured that out too. He can't stay away long; he's weaker than their father…they don't like burdens. They want everyone to do their part, once they can't anymore, they are done away with," I said trying to explain Sanje's fury.

"How do you know so much about that?" Thomas asked.

"I have been extremely curious and Dominic's been more forthcoming than he should have been," I said with a sly smile.

"You are good," he said returning my smile, "he probably couldn't resist those deep brown eyes, and those incredible dimples."

"It's good to see you smiling again, you had me terrified earlier, please go rest, I won't do anything that will get me hurt," I said, avoiding his eyes.

He wasn't fooled, but he didn't try to stop me again. He kissed me softly once and went to lie on his bed. I stayed for just a minute to make sure he was as comfortable as he could be. When I heard his breathing become soft and regular I decided it was Sanje's turn to pay.

All of the good humor drained from my face as I turned from his room and went in search of Sanje. The murderous rage that I felt for him had not abated. He was still pacing the grounds and stopped when he read the anger on my face. He looked at me with a sneering smile.

"I was right. Dominic wouldn't believe that you still loved Thomas. 'No,' he was mocking Dominic now, 'she loves me. She wants to be with me.', "I knew it was all a ruse. You may be able to fool him, but not me. I'll make sure he knows what kind of person you are and he can make sure that you suffer more than the rest of them."

"Funny thing," I said, trying to remain calm, "Dominic has never believed a word you said and I don't expect that to change any time soon. I feel sorry for Thomas, you could have killed him, and you made him suffer much more than necessary. You were harsh with no reason except your own miserable existence."

I calmed myself before the anger consumed me and collected my thoughts; I wanted to get this just right. I wanted to make sure the poisonous words I used would hurt Sanje as much as the whip had hurt Thomas.

"Do you know why Dominic brought you here?" I asked.

"You know why; he thought I'd want that hag of a mother of yours," Sanje said bitterly.

"I don't think that's it and I think you know it. I've seen it in your eyes the way you're watching the skies for him to come. You thought he'd be back by now. He may have told us two days, but promised you shorter, didn't he?" Sanje's suddenly angry face confirmed my suspicions so I went on, "You've come here to die. You will never see the comforts of your home again. There will be no cleansing for you; you will simply blink out of existence. How does that feel, Sanje?"

"You're wrong," he snarled at me, but I had done it. I could see the confusion in his mind. He had already come to this conclusion, but didn't want to believe it. Me coming to him and telling him this only worked to confirm those suspicions.

I couldn't stop myself, "Are you in pain yet, Sanje? Is it intense? Get used to it, it looks like you've reached your end."

I walked away knowing that there would be no retribution. I stopped as I reached the edge of the compound and chanced a glance behind me in case I was wrong. I wasn't. Sanje was as weak as a baby. I could see the truth of what I'd told him reflected in his eyes. He could no longer doubt the truth.

He suddenly had to deal with the betrayal of his own family. I wondered how he could have existed for so long and not known that this would be the way of his demise. Didn't they have to do this to other, older siblings? I remembered that Dominic told me that this plane was new and guessed that this must be a new means of ridding themselves of dead weight. I remembered who his father was and understanding dawned on me. Sanje's anger became a little more understandable, though I was having a hard time with sympathy. Sanje had been lied to, possibly for his entire lifetime. He was so used to being the one doing the lying or watching as others had been lied to that he never saw it coming. My words had taken the fight out of him completely. This would be Sanje's final resting place.

It was like my words sped up the progress of what was now inevitable. Sanje moved only slightly from the log he'd taken a seat on in the midst of our argument to fall to the ground. He lay there quietly and as I approached, I heard him begin to hum quietly. I was frozen to the ground, fascinated to see how he would reach the end of his existence. I watched as Sanje began to writhe on the ground. He didn't scream; he wouldn't allow himself to do that, but I was sure that the pain was more than he could bear.

Within minutes he went from writhing on the ground to barely moving. His skin became translucent and suddenly I could actually see the fire burning his body from the inside out. I wanted to turn my head, but my grim fascination would not allow me to turn away. I tried not to pay attention to the intricacies like when his eyeballs popped from the heat. I tried not to smell the crisp scent of singed hair hovering on the air. I simply stood, leaning on the nearest tree, and watched as the last bits of Sanje became ash.

Suddenly I was afraid; what if he was like the mythical phoenix? What if he was reborn from the ashes? Once I was sure that the burning was over, I ran to the pile of ashes and swept them up. A little at a time I spread them around with leaves I found close by. I singed my own fingers in the process, but I wanted the ash to be gone. I took the pile and spread it into different areas of the island. I don't know if the others caught the scent of what happened or if someone else was a witness to Sanje's demise, but soon I was no longer working alone. Everyone joined in and soon all of the ashes had been spread throughout the island.

I was amazed when I saw Clarissa emerge from the forest, followed by my father and Aaron, with big smiles on their faces. It occurred to me that Madeline must have sent her a silent message. Tomorrow the real game would be on, but for the time being, we could all be together again.

Chapter 19

When we were sure that all of the ashes had been spread and the threat of Sanje was starting to drift from our minds, we took a few moments to celebrate. There were smiles on each of our faces as we realized that our formidable opponents were no more than mortal creatures, sort of. Hope crept up in all of our faces. We'd inadvertently been given a practice run of our plans to end Dominic's life. We went over our plans for his arrival tomorrow. I found myself looking forward to this final standoff. I was almost giddy at the thought of going home again.

I watched as one by one everyone drifted to their rooms to get rested for tomorrow's challenges. I stayed with Thomas and we held each other close. I was as gentle as I could be knowing how sore his back was, but he kept placing my arms around his middle despite the pain.

"This is going to work you know," he said as he brushed my bangs from my eyes, "tomorrow we're all going home. Or at least taking the first steps that are going to get us there. I know this will take more than a day. And finally, I'll be able to start looking for my new home."

"Your new home?" I asked.

"Well, unless you have some objection to me being in Boston, now that my family is reunited, I plan on heading back there. That was my plan all along, remember? I already have a job there and they've been more than patient with me…." he began to look worried.

"I have no objection at all," I smiled, "and I also have a large apartment with a lot of unused space."

"Really?" he asked.

"Right in the heart of Boston too; isn't that convenient?"

"Extremely," he said and stopped whatever comment that was going to come from me with a passionate kiss.

"I think I could get used to this," I said when we took a moment to breathe.

"Yes, living together will certainly have all kinds of benefits," Thomas chuckled and kissed me again.

He pulled at my shirt indicating I should raise my hands so he could remove it, but I worried, "Thomas, what about your back? Doesn't all this movement hurt?"

"I don't feel a thing," he breathed his response and that was all I needed to hear.

When we lay in one another's arms, breathing returning to normal, I found myself dozing. I startled awake once and sat up quickly. I could not allow myself to fall asleep. I returned to myself quickly, panicked that I'd slept at all.

I moved from the bed, careful not to wake Thomas, so as not to fall asleep again. I was grateful that he hadn't woken up. He needed to heal. I, on the other hand, was not worked half to death during the last two days and had the energy and will power to last the night. We've planned too much and worked too hard to allow Dominic to come during the night when we weren't prepared. I left the compound and walked the grounds. There was nothing more to fear here.

The cool air cleared my head of any sleepiness. I walked to the beach and looked out over the water. I peered straight into Roger's yard and saw that he was there. I looked at him and he looked back in my direction. He looked lost. I took comfort in the fact that tomorrow, if all went well, would bring the return of more that he'd ever hoped for. I waved to Roger imagining that he could see me and spoke to him as I had my father during the search party.

"Tomorrow," I whispered.

At that moment he seemed to look directly at me, and then he turned to go into his home. Before he entered the front door he looked back one time and I would swear that he nodded his head, but he was very far and it was very dark, so I couldn't say for sure.

Shortly after Roger went inside the darkness started to fade to a deep blue and I saw clouds gathering on the horizon. Dominic wouldn't wait after all; the game was about to begin.

I rushed back to the compound to wake everyone. We had to be on that beach before Dominic got close. Once he was through and Clarissa showed us the door, we would join hands and walk through together. Though the joining of hands was no longer necessary, we decided to do it anyway as a show of solidarity. Rosalyn and I would be in the middle, flanked by Thomas and Madeline, Rose and Clarissa would be next to Madeline, and my father and Aaron would be next to Rose. As soon as he came through the door he would see us and realize what we're doing; we had to be through that opening and holding it closed from our side before he could manage to come back through…then the hardest part would begin. It was bound to take days for him to die. Sanje had been old and weak and he lasted two days. Dominic, young and nimble, will likely take several days. If he wins, he's likely to hunt us down piecemeal and make us suffer collectively. We decided we'd keep watch in groups. Our stay on this tiny island was not quite over yet.

I looked up and was amazed at how much progress the storm front had already made. I doubled my efforts to get to their rooms. The compound was closer now, but so were the clouds. Lightning flashed threateningly from the sky as it spiked into the land somewhere on the main island. As soon as I was close enough I started screaming.

"WAKE UP! WAKE UP! IT'S TIME! HE'S COMING FASTER THAN I THOUGHT!"

That was all it took. Everyone was well prepared. They hurried from their rooms to meet me and we took off running. I could hear the rain begin to pelt the umbrella of trees that we were still under. I scooped up Clarissa and ran as fast as my legs would go. The trees were beginning to thin and I saw lightning electrify the sky. A violent white streak came down and touched the water. I panicked, afraid we'd miss our chance.

"Focus Clarissa, start looking for that opening," I prodded.

"I already see it," she said with a smile, though I could see nothing.

"We all need to concentrate, really focus. I don't think she's going…" I stopped because I saw it now. It was like someone had taken the island and cut it in half. In the middle was something that could only be described as a black hole. It was no more than a foot in length from one end to the other. I could see, finally see, where we'd have to stop so Dominic would be fatally trapped."

"What is it, Elizabeth?" Thomas asked.

"Nothing, I see it straight ahead, keep running," I shouted back.

We continued running and the storm gained in intensity. The wind was whipping through the trees and their branches bent almost all the way to the ground. We were almost there, the opening was within our grasp, just a few feet ahead of us. The lightning struck again, this time it was inches from my feet. I ran with more intensity than I realized I was capable of. We had made the beach and the divide was just ahead, we continued like a long dart toward our bullseye.

I felt Thomas's grip on my hand and realized we'd made it. I put my hand out to grab onto Madeline. She wasn't there. My hand grasped again only to find empty air. I looked around and saw that Madeline had fallen behind. That was all it took. Dominic was on top of her in an instant. She fought back, but he wasn't like Sanje. He was strong with only a few centuries under his belt. He held tightly to her.

"Clarissa, keep going honey, we'll be right behind you," I shouted.

"I'm not leaving my Mom," she said, stubbornly.

"You have to…Auntie Elizabeth will not break her promise, now go."

"No, no, no," she reverted back to early childhood tantrum throwing, "I'm not going."

I told the others to get to the divide before it closed, but Clarissa stood obstinately in front. She would not go through.

"Clarissa honey, please go through. I will see you on the other side, I promise," Madeline called.

"Oh yes, dear, your mother will see you on the other side," Dominic's calm voice was frightening.

I went to Clarissa and I bent down in front of her so that I could speak only to her.

"Please, do this for your mom and Auntie Elizabeth. I promise, and your mom promises, we will be back in just a few minutes, without Dominic. Please go all the way through, your mom and the rest of us, really need you to do this. This will work, we just hit a snag, but we'll take care of it."

"But the dreams…" she started.

"They're just dreams. Remember your favorite one? This is our best chance at making it come true, but not if you don't go through."

"Okay, but I'm staying there until someone else comes too," she demanded.

"That's a good girl," I said and she walked through.

"Oh, brilliant performance," Dominic sneered, "the one girl that I really wanted betrays me and sends the other girl that should be mine away."

"What do you want, Dominic?" I asked, "You have no reason to hold Madeline. She's needed here."

"You know what I want, Elizabeth, and if I can't have you, then I suppose I can take a substitute," he said mockingly, "I will get what I want. Maybe it's too late for Clarissa, but you are coming with me."

"So you lie to your brother just as much as anyone else? And you expect me to believe that you wouldn't lie to me? If you take just me, you have no hope of keeping me from your father," I said, changing the subject.

"I had my orders. Maybe I wasn't going to keep you from him. Maybe you were for him," he said, the hurt clear in his eyes.

"But you were Sanje's best friend right up until you left him to die, right?" I asked.

"It's the best way. If they know what's coming, they resist," he said nonchalantly, "I guess that's what you were trying to do to me."

"You guessed right," I said coldly, "but now we have a problem."

As I was saying this to Dominic, I was also speaking to Madeline. I could only hope that keeping him talking would also keep him from catching on to what I was telling her.

"When I say 'now' turn quickly, knee to the groin, then run as hard and fast as you can. You'll make the line before he can get here."

I saw a slight nod and knew she'd gotten my message.

"So what now, Dominic? If I come with you, will you let the rest of them go? Is this what we're looking at right now?" I asked, feeling Thomas tighten his grip on my hand.

"I don't know that I have much of a choice," he said smoothly, "you've sent Clarissa away and the rest of you are only a step from freedom. I suppose trapping me here would be better, for all except me. But it seems I've been able to keep a little bit of leverage. Are you ready then, dear?"

I saw a chance and decided that it was worth it. I could always end my own life if it didn't. I already had my weapon.

"I am, Dominic. Give them back Madeline and I will go with you," I said, sounding defeated.

I unlaced my fingers from Thomas's and he hesitated. Without the benefit of sharing thoughts it was impossible to tell him what I had planned, I settled for looking at him and faking a goodbye.

"You have to let me go, Thomas," I said, willing him to understand what I was doing.

"No," he said with pained eyes, "I won't let you go."

"You don't have a choice," I said sharply and wriggled my fingers free.

He didn't know what to think, but he didn't try to resist me again. He let me go. I could feel his stunned eyes on my back, but couldn't let that distract me now. I had to time this just right so that Madeline would be able to break free.

I began to walk forward from the line. Everyone else kept their stance watching for the exchange to take place. As I came out of the dividing line, he loosened his grip around Madeline's waist.

Without a word out loud I screamed so she would sense the urgency, *"NOW!!!"*

Immediately she turned to face him, reached her arms around his neck as though she were going to kiss him, and she brought up her leg with all of her strength. He doubled over which allowed her to escape. She dug her feet in the ground and ran. Within seconds she was in the divide and I had returned to my place, holding on tight to Thomas's hand.

"Did you know?" he asked.

"Yes, we were conspiring that whole time. I'm sorry for your panic, it would have blown our cover had I said something or hesitated."

"I had forgotten you had that ability," he said quietly.

"Something I'm sure I'll miss when this is all over," I said.

"Me too," came Madeline's voice from down the line, "thank you, Elizabeth."

"Any time," I said and turned to face Dominic.

He hadn't yet fully recovered from the pain inflicted by Madeline's knee so we waited quietly.

"Madeline, Clarissa said she wasn't going to go far, she knows how to cross the water on her own; perhaps it's time that we tell Roger the truth. He can bring us supplies; we'll need to camp out here until this is over," I said.

"Maybe I'll go with her. Mom, let's go see Dad…I promise we'll be back before long," Madeline said and they disappeared to the other side.

Dominic started to regain himself and the snarl that ripped out of his throat was fearsome. He ran at me, but I held my ground. His eyes were no longer green at all; they were a fiery red. His usual smooth features contorted into rage. He ran straight into the barrier that separated him from us and lost consciousness as he bounced back and fell to the ground. I laughed slightly and relaxed my stance. I looked over at Thomas who also seemed to be taking some joy in Dominic's frustration and again saw his open back and purplish eye.

"Thomas, why don't you go get some real medicine on those wounds? The whole point of this was to save everyone's life. Go join your family's reunion."

"I don't want to leave you," he said urgently, "not until the threat is gone."

Dominic came to and picked that moment to make his first attempt at coercion, "Elizabeth, darling, it was horrible of me to lose my temper just now, but I know you still care about me. How could we have shared the passion that we did the other day for nothing? How can you forget how well our bodies worked together? How much pleasure we gave one another?"

Thomas seethed as Dominic shared more details about our one night together. I could see him physically restraining himself from going over and giving Dominic the same kind of purple-blue eye he currently had. He could have done it too; the door wasn't going anywhere with so many of us still holding it in place, but that was what Dominic wanted.

"Shut up, Dominic," I said, the guilt weighing very heavily as all of my family was witness to my shame.

"Oh, does it bother you? Or maybe it should bother Thomas. How many beds will you be jumping into when you return to your life?"

"Shut up, Dominic," I repeated.

"Honey, don't," Thomas said, "he's going to keep doing it. He's going to try everything he can think of to distract us. He can't hurt us now as long as we remain strong."

"Sanje really did a number on you, didn't he?" Dominic began a new target.

"Yes, he did, but we made sure that he was aware of your treachery. We made sure he was aware of how his own family betrayed him. He didn't like that too much," Thomas responded.

The conversation went back and forth like this for several hours. Sometimes it would be eerily quiet and we'd think that maybe he'd fallen asleep, but then he'd come back and throw some hurtful comment our way. Eventually Thomas and I took a break from Dominic and we stepped to the other side leaving my father and Aaron to supervise.

We were pleasantly surprised to find Roger already there with Madeline, Rose, and Clarissa. Thomas immediately went to his father and hugged him tight.

"I don't quite know what to say to you, Elizabeth," Roger started, "I have to apologize again for the way I treated you in the beginning and thank you profusely for bringing my family back to me…and I'll never doubt little miss clairvoyant Clarissa again."

As he finished he held his arms out to me awkwardly. I went to him and hugged him tight.

"I will help you anytime," I said smiling, "You know what's weird? I got my family back at the same time, and I wasn't even expecting it. I guess this was sort of a little blessing in disguise for me."

"Dad, we do need to talk to…," Thomas began though I didn't really think this was the time to talk about living arrangements. I glared at Thomas, but it wasn't necessary. Surprisingly, Roger finished for him.

"…your realtor? I know you're ready to go back to the city, and with such a pretty, kind, and thoughtful girl to go with, who can blame you?" he finished.

"You mean Clarissa," I joked, "But she's not going to Boston; I don't think so anyway."

"I think we're all going to Boston," Roger said to the general surprise of everyone around, "I made a few phone calls this morning and after talking to some friends, we've found a position for Elizabeth at the

Boston Globe…if she wants it. As soon as you get back to Boston, you'll call this man," he said and handed me a business card, "and he'll get you set up from there. I told him it may be a week or two before you get in touch. Madeline and Rose, you two never wanted to leave Boston in the first place and as for me, I've had enough of islands."

"Wow," I said, "that is incredibly generous of you. Thank you. I have always wanted to work for the Globe."

"I remember, you told me that once. It seems like it was so long ago, but really it's just been about a month."

"Really?" I asked, "We were here that long?"

"Huh," Thomas said, sounding as surprised as I was.

"Rose, will you please take Thomas and clean and bandage his back?" I asked, knowing his mother would jump at the chance, "he won't let me take him until this is over, but I can't leave until I'm sure Dominic is gone."

"Yes, of course. I wanted him to let me take him right away," she said.

"No, I don't want to leave you," he repeated.

"I'm not going anywhere," I smiled at him, "and I won't be alone. My mother, father, and brother aren't going to leave either until they know I'm okay, and neither is your family. Please, Thomas, after all of this, I would like us to all be able to heal, together. That won't happen if your back gets infected and your health is affected."

"Okay, okay, if you insist. I will go with her and let her clean them, but I will be back within a half an hour," he said sternly, talking to Rose as well as me.

"An hour," Rose overrode him, "you are going to get some decent food in your belly too."

"There's food here," Thomas complained.

"Thomas, please don't argue with your mother," I said quietly, "we've all just finally gotten here…."

He stopped me by putting a finger on my lips.

"Okay, an hour, I'll see you then," he replaced his finger with his lips and kissed me, and then he got up and went with Rose. He winced as he had to turn his back to get up, but at least he'd be able to get those angry red wounds clean and healing properly.

"I'm going to go relieve some of my family," I said to Roger, "I'll be sending my father and my brother. I'm sure they will be hungry."

"I'll get something going for them right away," Roger said with a smile. I noticed just how much he'd changed since that first meeting, "it'll be good to meet them."

I entered the perimeter again and saw Dominic sitting quietly on the beach staring at the water.

"Dad, Aaron, go get yourselves something to eat; do you mind staying a bit longer with me, Mom?" I asked.

She seemed to sense that I wanted to talk so she decided to stay.

"I think I can handle it for a little while longer," she said with a quiet smile.

"Can you 'hear' things anymore? You know, in your mind? Can you hear what he's thinking?" I asked Rosalyn.

"I'm trying not to," she admitted, "but no, I can't really hear anything anymore. I think he took that ability from me a few days ago. When he decided that he was going to take you below, I think a lot of things changed…"

She trailed off and I could see that as weird as it was, she was hurt by the way he'd cut her off.

"Mom, are we ever going to be able to make this right between us?"

"Of course we will, darling. I was just thinking about how horrible I was to you when you first came through and when Dominic first joined us. It's all starting to feel so very weird, almost like it was a horrible nightmare. I mean, being unforgivable to my own daughter, how could I have ever thought that was okay?"

"I know it's going to be difficult, but try to keep in mind that it was Dominic all along. He made his plans and when they altered or he discovered that there was something new he wanted, he went after it with no remorse for those he stepped on along the way. He didn't care who he had to deceive," I said, struggling to make her feel better.

"Thank you, darling. I know I was mean to you and to have you be so understanding about it…well…thank you."

"There was a time that I didn't think I'd be able to forgive you, but please know that it was always my intent to bring you with us once I knew you were alive. I realize now why you did what you did. He really didn't give you much of a choice, did he?"

"No, he didn't," she responded.

"So what now as far as you and Dad? Is it all a happy reunion, live happily ever after and all of that?" I asked.

"So far it has been," she said, smiling, "It was unbelievable how much I'd missed him when he came to the compound looking for me. Before that, I could hardly remember what he looked like, but when I saw him, it was weird, like I'd woken from a dream. You were pretty brave, you know. You risked everything to get that note to him, but once he saw it, he knew what he had to do."

I knew the 'waking from a dream' sensation she was talking about. Even her partnership with Dominic had been of his design. He blunted her feelings for her husband and her previous life to make her more compliant. He had tried to do the same for me, and that feeling lifted the moment that I saw Thomas again after Dominic had tried to gain my interest the first time.

"I didn't even know if it would work or if the paper would stay safe in the locket. I didn't know if he'd understand my clues, but when he told me that you'd been working to get away from Dominic for years already, my heart almost hit the floor. It actually took me a few minutes before I could speak again," I said, remembering the shock I was in.

"I really did pull the wool over your eyes, didn't I? You thought that I hated you," she said.

"Hate might be a little strong, but the day of the accident, we were arguing right before it happened and had I just kept my mouth shut and not tried to get you to see things my way, it all could have been very different," I admitted.

"Elizabeth Jane, don't ever regret. Yes, be sad that there were sixteen years of life that we missed of each other, but don't regret the life that you did live in that time. If none of this would have happened you may have grown up to be a very different person than you are," she smiled.

"You know, it's kind of nice to hear you call me by my first and middle name again. It reminds me of when you got frustrated with me the last time I said something stupid," I smiled halfway.

Out of the shadows, Dominic appeared. He must have been close by because he had heard a good portion of our conversation.

"Are you sure you've chosen the right man, Elizabeth? I know you don't believe me, I've given you no reason to, but I would make you happiest," said Dominic sadly.

"I disagree," I said curtly, "but I suppose I do owe you thanks at least. If it weren't for you I would have never met the man that I truly love."

Dominic began to pace and I noticed that some small changes had occurred. His eyes looked somewhat different. They weren't red anymore; they'd returned to their green hue, but it was a different kind of green. They did not shine, the color had become more pallid, as if his eyes had already accepted the inevitability of his death.

"I'm so glad, darling," Dominic said to me, softly as he bent at the middle into a dramatic bow, "that I could be of service to you."

"Why did you bring Sanje here?" I asked, ignoring his comments.

"To die, you know that. Isn't that what you told me a few hours ago?"

he asked.

"Yes, but why did you bring him here? You could have taken him straight to the sun or anywhere else on earth, but you brought him here. You wanted us to see this happen to him. Why?" I asked, suddenly curious.

He rolled his eyes, "because I thought my new queen should know what was in store for her new husband. You had asked me, remember, what happened when you were no longer useful to us; I was trying to answer that question."

"Was that supposed to make me feel better? I watched what the heat did to him. I saw him burn from the inside out. I heard the disgusting pop when his eyeballs could no longer take it. This was supposed to calm my nerves?" I asked, incredulous.

"No, not calm you, make you understand," he said sadly, "someday, and apparently much sooner than I had planned, this will be me. I know that now. I wanted to prepare you for what you'd someday have to witness. The queens outlast their husbands by decades."

"Didn't Sanje know it?" I was still wondering how he could not have known.

"He knew it was coming soon. He didn't know how or when so when I asked him to accompany me down here, he bought my story easily. I knew that by the time I came back he'd be gone. I didn't really intend for you to witness it, but I wasn't sorry that you had. I figured he'd be laying in his bed and that's where it would happen. Where was he when he went?" He asked, interested.

"He was outside looking up at the sky constantly awaiting your return. He had been unusually cruel during the day and he was standing around waiting to be able to enjoy the cruelty when he saw us come back. After we'd come and gone he couldn't go inside anymore; he was too shocked by the realization of what was happening to him," I mused remembering the sweaty features and the pacing.

"Oh, I was just curious," he said quietly, "well, I didn't expect that it would come so soon. I thought I'd at least have a chance at finding and keeping a queen before my demise, but I guess I betrayed and lied to you; you're very smart, you know. Not many would have been able to see my lies for what they were. Even those paying a lot of attention don't usually recognize me for what I am," he said, turning his gaze to my mother.

"Yes, well, it's a pity for them," I said, shortly.

"It is a pity, or was anyway, they're being cleansed even now. All of them except Karina who still sits at my father's side," he said bitterly.

"Is that the one that he took from you?" I asked, genuinely curious.

"Be careful," Rosalyn whispered at my side. I ignored her.

"Yes, my Karina was about your age, beautiful like you, and perfectly willing to come below with me," he said sadly.

"And why was she so willing?" I asked.

"She was so willing because she had no reason for life. Her parents were dead, she'd met no mate in her life here, and she found me charming," he said, clearly remembering the time they'd spent together.

"It's impossible not to find you charming, it's in your blood," I said with half a smile.

"Elizabeth," Rosalyn warned, her voice now at the edge of hysteria.

"Not charming enough though, I suppose," he said, starting to get a gleam in his deadened green eyes, "if it were enough, we'd be together."

"Yes, well, not sure about that," I said, coming back to myself a little bit, Rosalyn sighing in relief at my side.

I saw him smile then, a real smile the first I'd seen since he left the last time. I began to question what we were doing to him. Why would we let him die? I began to remember all of the reasons that I'd had for wanting to go with him.

His smile had me entranced and he moved in my direction. He ignored Rosalyn's looks of horror and outstretched his arms. He was inviting me in and somewhere in my mind, I remembered that I was supposed to be fighting this, but I didn't care. I would go to him; I would go with him. His eyes were sparkling again; he knew that I was his once more.

Rosalyn had gone from alarmed to an all out panic. She couldn't leave to get help because she knew I was no longer capable of holding the torn fabric between worlds closed. She began screaming at me, trying to break the hold that Dominic now had over my mind. I ignored her completely. I was now standing and was just about to make the move that would free Dominic when Thomas came into view.

"Oh, thank God," Rosalyn said.

"Elizabeth, what are you doing? Come over here!" Thomas demanded.

"I wouldn't treat you like that, darling," he was desperate now.

"Elizabeth, sweetheart," Thomas was now echoing Dominic's demeanor, "please look at me. Remember Boston"

That was all I needed to hear. Once again, I was immediately freed from Dominic's hold. The scared look on Thomas's face, the terrified look on my mother's, and the not so subtle reminder of all I had to look forward to when Dominic was no more brought me clear out of the deluded state I was in. In one quick movement I jumped into Thomas's arms and held on tight. I loosened my grip only when Thomas winced from the pain of my hands on his still raw back. I looked into his face expecting anger to be looking back at me, but I saw only relief.

"I'm so sorry," I said, "I was being deluded…again."

"That's what he excels at," Thomas said and looked at me lovingly, then shifted his eyes to look up at Dominic, "I'm not going anywhere. She wants to be here until this is over and I will not leave her side again."

"Thank goodness you came when you did," I smiled up at him.

"Fine," Dominic said, pouting and walking back to the beach.

The next two days were more of the same and Thomas did not let go of me once.

I couldn't explain why I needed to be there to see this, I just knew I did. I needed to know that he hadn't survived. Everyone, with the exception of Clarissa, took turns guarding Dominic. Thomas and I always took our turns together alternating between my father, Aaron, Rosalyn, Rose, and Madeline to come with us.

On the second day, when Madeline was not two feet from me, I decided to try an experiment. We hadn't needed to talk silently, so we hadn't and I was curious if we still had the ability.

"What are you thinking?" I asked her without saying a word.

"I'm thinking I was wondering if it still worked too," Madeline said and smiled at me with a big, toothy grin.

"I guess Clarissa isn't the only clairvoyant one then," I said.

"No, she's not," Madeline agreed silently and we both fell into peals of laughter.

"The two of you?" Dominic suddenly said in surprise; he'd turned to look at us, "you two were the silent communicators?"

"You knew we were communicating?" I asked, just as surprised.

"Yes, well, that someone was. I apparently can't listen to thoughts that are purposefully directed somewhere else; just ones that float out there with no important destination in mind."

"Huh, all that fear for nothing," I said to Madeline, "we could have done this sooner."

On the third day Dominic started looking a little worse for wear and by the fifth, I knew it wouldn't be long. His skin had become the sallow pale skin that Sanje's had been in his last few moments of life. The smooth exterior of his attitude had disappeared completely and he was now angry.

He would suddenly stand up and pelt himself into the forest. When he stayed close enough I could see that he was beating up a giant oak tree… punching it over and over until his knuckles were bloody. That wasn't enough. He started kicking it next until that became too painful.

I looked back at him and saw that the knuckles on both of his hands now were reduced to open, raw skin leaking blood down his hands. Droplets of it would fall to the ground. He looked up at me with evil eyes. They were no longer green at all; they were the murderous red that he reserved for his angriest of moments. He narrowed them in my direction and again was about to charge when he lost the fight with his balance. Suddenly his legs weren't strong enough to hold him up. He fell to the ground with a thud. My memory called up the same kind of falling in Sanje's last moments. This would all be over soon.

On the ground, Dominic started clutching at his neck. He looked over at me and made one final attempt to save his own pathetic life.

"Please," he whispered, "you were all that ever mattered."

"Go to hell, Dominic," I said, proud that Thomas heard no hesitation in my voice, though I couldn't help but feel a twinge of regret in my heart.

"Already there," were the last words he could choke out. Like Sanje before him, he started to burn from the inside out. He continued to mumble, but no discernible words were uttered. I turned my head but couldn't turn off my ears.

Again, I smelled singed hair. I heard crackling skin and the small pop when his eyes finally gave up their shape. He did not scream; he silently endured until his mind could take more. Finally, Dominic was dead.

As the final bits of bone were becoming ashes, something different happened. An extremely bright light illuminated the sky, so bright that I had to shield my eyes with my hand. It seemed that there was a central point that the light came from, like the sun, but shaped like a person. That was all I could make out before I had to look away. Next, purple-black clouds rushed in quickly and suddenly the storm was intense. There was only one flash of lightning, so bright that we all had to avert our eyes. It lasted an unnatural amount of time, but finally it hit the sand directly in the center of the ashes that were Dominic. I thought that it would save us the job of scattering them, but instead, it lifted them from the ground. The ashes rose slowly and swirled counter-clockwise through the air. They continued their upward progression until they became one with the clouds. The lightning disappeared back into the clouds. I thought briefly that it was odd that this did not occur for Sanje and wondered why that was. The storm quickly moved out and finally, at the same time, Thomas, myself, and Madeline all stepped through the divide between universes for the last time. The nightmare was over.

When we came to the other side, everyone was waiting.

"It's over," I said evenly, though I couldn't account for the feelings of regret, "Dominic is dead."

For a moment, everyone had their own little celebration from large smiles to touchdown dances, the elated group was showing their excitement. I looked around at the little campground that had sustained us since we'd gotten the advantage over Dominic and suddenly felt nauseous.

"Can we just leave it all here?" I asked.

"Now that wouldn't be good for the environment, would it?" Thomas asked with a cheerful smile.

"No, I suppose not, but I'm ready to go. I don't know if I can stand another minute of camping," I said with a loud sigh.

Everyone broke into laughter. It was a wonderful sound to hear, genuine laughter that was not laced with deceit or fear.

We each took some responsibility in cleaning up and carried out our large bundles to the boat that Roger had so generously provided. The boat that Thomas and I had come in, amazingly, was still where we'd left it too. We filled up both boats and made it to the opposite shore in no time.

Roger had been unbelievably kind and had gotten something in the way of a change of clothes for each of us knowing that we'd want to burn the clothes that we currently had on. Once everyone had showered and cleaned up we sat long into the night filling Roger in on every detail. He was positively glowing.

I called the hotel, found my room was still being held for me; unbelievably it was still paid as well. I felt a little twinge of guilt knowing that I'd soon be leaving the small publication that funded this trip. I told Thomas that I planned to go back to my room tonight as room was tight here and I figured the others could use some space.

"Would you like to come with me?" I asked him.

"I was starting to worry that you weren't going to ask," he replied.

We briefly excused ourselves and made our way back to my room. The phone on the desk was blinking and I was sure that I should call my editor and let them know that I was okay, but it was late now. It could wait until tomorrow, I decided. Tonight, all that mattered was Thomas.

Epilogue

Six weeks had passed since I'd made the return from what started out as my lonely trip to Martha's Vineyard. I'd come back with my family, my new family, a flourishing relationship, and no story. When I'd called Sue the day after we returned to the Vineyard she was patient and kind until I got to the part where I had no story to give her.

"What do you mean you have no story?" she asked, incredulous, "were you not just kidnapped and held against your will? Were your kidnappers not the same people that took your mother who you thought was dead for the last sixteen years? Were you not almost killed yourself in an attempt to save yourself and her?"

This was the best story that I could come up with to explain my mysterious month-long disappearance. I kept it vague, telling Sue just enough to satisfy her curiosity as to why I'd been gone for so long.

"There's just not. The story goes much deeper that what I've told you, but if I told you everything…well, I wouldn't enjoy the inside of a padded cell," and when mystifying her wasn't enough, I went ahead and crushed her spirit and faith in me too, "and not only is there no story for me to tell now, there will be no story for me to tell later, not for ECN anyway."

"What do you mean?" Sue was completely confused now.

"I know you spent a lot of money sending me down to the Vineyard and I'll pay you back every cent, but I was just offered my dream job with the Boston Globe and I took it. I've already handed in my resignation, but I wanted to tell you personally. I start first thing Monday morning," I told her feeling superior guilt.

"There's no need to pay us back, Elizabeth, but could you give us something? One farewell story that at least mentions your trip? After all, if that mini-island is still dangerous the people have a right to know," she said.

"There's no danger on that mini-island anymore," I said, remembering that Dominic said that people could not just stumble through the door, "it's a thing of the past."

"How do you know that?" she was prodding now.

"I just do. I will see what I can do to come up with some farewell story that at least mentions my trip, I doubt too many will read it anyway," I said knowing that would sting.

"If you can, we'd really appreciate it," she said, ignoring the jab, "you will be missed."

We shared a few more pleasantries and then said our goodbyes.

"Lily?" Thomas had picked up Aaron's nickname for me, "Lily, are you awake?"

"Yes, what's wrong?" I asked.

"What were you just thinking about?" he asked.

"My last conversation with Sue, why?"

"That was weeks ago. I couldn't tell if you were really awake or not; you were mumbling a lot last night. Are you still having dreams?"

"Most nights, and I did last night too, yes. Clarissa was there, but Dominic was too. He was telling me that I'd killed him before he really had a chance to live, but it was okay because there was still a chance at life for him, sort of. It was really confusing and scary, but so real," I explained.

"I'm sorry about that," he said and kissed me softly as he got out of bed. This morning routine was something I'd gotten used to and thoroughly enjoyed, but today we couldn't linger. Today we were all meeting at Roger and Rose's new house to help them move in. My mother, father, and brother were coming to help too. Even Aaron's wife and child were joining us. Madeline and Clarissa would, of course, be there too. It was the first time that we would all be together since we left the mini-island and our imprisonment there.

I got up too and both showered and dressed. I was ravenously hungry which was odd for morning; my appetite didn't usually kick in until afternoon. We took some time to swallow a bagel and some orange juice before we left. We got into Thomas's Jeep and headed toward their home. When we got there I noticed that it was small, but beautiful. It was another Cape Cod style home, similar to the one that Roger had had on the Vineyard. The floors inside were beautifully maintained mahogany hardwood. They ran in varnished parallels all throughout. The kitchen was large and lovely. The cabinets were lightly varnished oak with metallic pulls running the length of them. The appliances were all stainless steel, keeping up with current trends. There was plenty of room for a good sized dining room table in the eating area that was part of the kitchen rather than separate from it.

It was in the kitchen that we all gathered once we'd gotten the furniture where it should be and all the boxes in the house. We were taking a break before the unpacking would begin. Thomas kept throwing nervous glances in my direction as I sat on a stool and chatted with Rose and my mother about nothing in particular.

I couldn't tell for sure, but it seemed that Rose was trying to comfort Thomas through looks in his direction. I found myself suddenly nervous and I didn't know why. My stomach was feeling nauseated; it must be the nerves. But why was I suddenly feeling so nervous? Why did it suddenly feel like everyone was purposely making small talk around me but not really paying attention to what they were saying, like they were waiting for something.

Before I could think about it anymore, Thomas suddenly got up and walked over to me. I noticed that he was trembling. He took a deep breath as he stood right in front of me and before I could even fathom what he was doing, he got down on one knee. A small, velvet box now rested at the center of his hands and he reached it out to me.

"Okay, so I know it's only been a few months since we met and I know that this may sound crazy to you. I can think of nothing in this world that I want more than you at my side for as long as we both shall live. We've been through Hell together and I feel like if we can make it as far as we have and still want to be together, there's not much that could break us apart. So, in a nutshell, I guess what I'm saying is that I'm in love with you and would like to know if you, Elizabeth Jane Milton, will agree to be my wife?" Thomas said, looking at me and seeing only me despite the room full of our families.

Tears had escaped my eyes as he finished with the proposal and I just looked at him for a moment. All of this had been a set up; not that his parents didn't need help, but the reason that my parents were here, and my brother and his family. He wanted all of the people that were important to me to be there for this moment.

If it was possible, I loved him more now than I ever have before. I realized he fit me and my life so perfectly. I couldn't believe I had ever doubted that when Dominic was trying to seduce me away. I realized belatedly that I hadn't answered yet and noticed that the hope and joy in Thomas's eyes was starting to falter.

"Yes, of course I'll marry you," I finally croaked out and flung my arms around him.

I both heard and felt everyone exhale.

He kissed me then softly and he took the ring from the box and slid it gently on my finger. The fit was perfect. How had he been able to do all this? How did he know my ring size? I thought of my mother and the sizings we went through when shopping for my birthstone ring my parents had bought for me when I graduated college. When had he had time to shop? It wasn't important, this moment was important. I was amazed at how lucky I was; what a wonderful man I would be spending the rest of my life with.

Finally, I was able to glance around and saw all of the smiling faces.

My family and my now officially family-to-be, who were already family in so many ways, were waiting impatiently to congratulate us. I got out of my chair to greet everyone and faltered for a moment. My equilibrium seems to be off today. It only lasted a moment, but it was enough for Thomas to race over to me.

"Are you okay, honey?" he asked.

"Fine," I said, "just a little lightheaded."

We all relaxed and I began to make my rounds around the room, playfully scowling at everyone for keeping this secret from me. I jumped slightly when Roger uncorked a celebratory bottle of champagne that he must have had ready already assuming the outcome of Thomas's proposal.

When I saw Clarissa, I had to tease her a bit, "Even you knew about this and didn't tell me?"

"I wanted to, Uncle Thomas made me promise not to tell," she was worried.

"It's okay sweetie, this is the kind of secret you're supposed to keep," I reassured her.

"Oh, okay," she relaxed, "I can't wait until you're really my Auntie Elizabeth; hey, my dream will come true."

"What dream is that?" Thomas asked her.

"My favorite, I already told Auntie Elizabeth all about it," she said.

"That she did," I said trying to hide my worry, "she told me it was her favorite dream because all of her family could come home to her, including me."

"And my new cousin," she said happily.

"Your new what?" Thomas asked, worried that I'd been hiding something.

"Nothing, at least nothing yet, she also dreamed we'd be having a baby boy, that's all," I said.

"Oh, well, that would be quite alright by me," he said, smiling wistfully.

"Here's a crazy idea," I said playfully, "let's get married first."

"That sounds about right," he replied while leaning down to kiss me gently.

Keep reading for a sneak peek as the adventure continues…

Prologue

"He looks so much like you," Thomas said while adoring our son, "all except for those green eyes. I'm so glad our little Mitchell finally came to join us."

As Thomas finished his statement, he turned his eyes to glare at me which suddenly became flame red. His face quickly elongated and his features became razor sharp. He seemed to be struggling with a scream that wanted to break through his locked jaw. His agonized expression only lasted a moment, and then he broke into the sweetest, most charming smile. This was no longer my husband of six months; this was the man that tried to take me away from everyone that I loved. Dominic's eye color turned the superficial green that it had been during the time that I had known him. They were the emerald green that I could never quite get enough of; the same color of the son that he was still cradling in his arms. A terrified sound came breaking through the surface and before I knew it Thomas was in a panic.

"Lily, Lil, Elizabeth, honey, wake up. It's just a dream, you're safe, honey, you're safe with me."

Thomas's arms were around me, holding me tight, comforting me with their strength. The screams stopped and the tears began. As usual, Thomas rocked me gently, like I was a child, and waited for it to stop.

"This can't be good for the baby," he lamented while he held me, "I know it's hard to do, but honey, Dominic is dead. We watched him die, he's not coming back. You have nothing to fear."

"I wish I could believe that," I said quietly as I unwrapped myself from his arms and sat on the bed beside him.

"Honey, you've got to believe me, your fears are getting the best of you," Thomas got up as he spoke, "you're due to deliver any time now and yes, we know that Dominic fathered the child that you're carrying, but we're going to raise him. He's going to be perfect and Dominic will not be around to influence that one way or the other…he…Lily, Lil, are you okay?"

I had been staring at the floor as he was speaking and when he turned to look, he noticed the water pooling near my feet.

"I think it's time," I said as I looked up at him.

"Now? I thought the doctor said that we had to wait until the contractions came regularly?"

"I'm sitting in a puddle and as you were talking just now, I had three long…ouch…hee, hee, hee, whooo…no arguments, let's go," I said as I got up and stripped off my wet clothing.

I was changed and in the car in minutes. Our disagreement was quickly forgotten and a very awestruck Thomas was carefully, but quickly, navigating a path to the hospital. I was having contractions every two minutes. I was sure I wasn't going to make it, but then we arrived and I was carted away to the labor and delivery room. Once strapped to the monitors and poked, prodded, and examined, the nurses determined that I was already dilated eight centimeters and by the looks of the contractions, would be delivering within the next few minutes. It was far too late for an epidural. I would just have to deal with the pain. They were paging the doctor frantically. The contractions were coming right on top of each other now. Every time I thought I could breathe again, my uterus would contract. Out of nowhere, my body took the controls and I felt not just the urge, but an acute need to push. I vaguely heard the nurses telling me to stop pushing, but it was beyond my control now. Suddenly all of the force and energy I had were used to expel this child from my womb. I realized there was no one there to catch him and bellowed, "Thomas, get down there now."

Thankfully, he didn't even think; like a ball player sliding under a ball dangling in the sky, Thomas slid on his knees, eyes wide in disbelief, reached between my open legs, and safely caught our son, Dominic's son, in his open arms.

The on-call doctor came into the room a mere thirty seconds later. My doctor was vacationing with her family.

"I'm so sorry I didn't get here sooner," said Dr. Jones, "Thank God you were here."

"Yes, that was lucky," said Thomas a bit annoyed, "but who knew he'd come so quickly."

A nurse came with the doctor and they took little Mitchell James Renzen, Thomas cut the cord, and the baby was taken to be cleaned up and checked. His loud wails were enough to relieve me. My little boy was healthy. That assessment was seconded as the nurses finished their job, swaddled him like a little burrito, put his newborn cap on him, and handed him to me. I cuddled him close and waited for him to open the eyes that would be a constant reminder of the one that I wished to forget the most.